SCOOBY-DOO!™ TEAM-UP

VOLUME 6

SHOLLY FISCH Writer
DARIO BRIZUELA SCOTT JERALDS WALTER CARZON HORACIO OTTOLINI Artists
FRANCO RIESCO SILVANA BRYS Colorists **SAIDA TEMOFONTE** Letterer
DARIO BRIZUELA and **FRANCO RIESCO** Collection Cover Artists

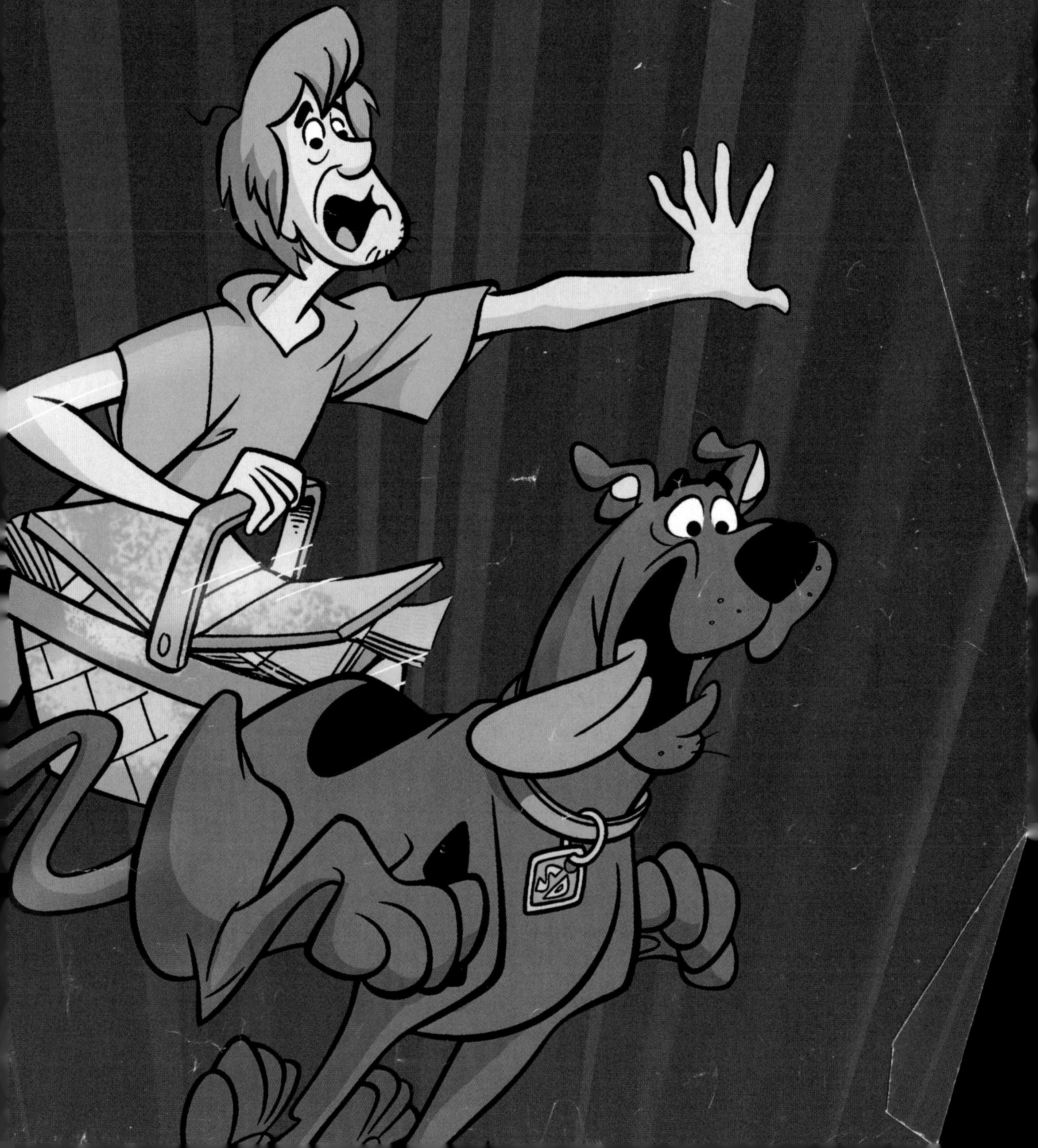

KRISTY QUINN Editor – Original Series • **ROB LEVIN** Assistant Editor – Original Series
JEB WOODARD Group Editor – Collected Editions • **ERIKA ROTHBERG** Editor – Collected Edition
STEVE COOK Design Director – Books • **SHANNON STEWART** Publication Design

BOB HARRAS Senior VP – Editor-in-Chief, DC Comics • **PAT McCALLUM** Executive Editor, DC Comics

DAN DiDIO Publisher • **JIM LEE** Publisher & Chief Creative Officer
AMIT DESAI Executive VP – Business & Marketing Strategy, Direct to Consumer & Global Franchise Management
BOBBIE CHASE VP & Executive Editor, Young Reader & Talent Development • **MARK CHIARELLO** Senior VP – Art, Design & Collected Editions
JOHN CUNNINGHAM Senior VP – Sales & Trade Marketing • **BRIAR DARDEN** VP – Business Affairs
ANNE DePIES Senior VP – Business Strategy, Finance & Administration • **DON FALLETTI** VP – Manufacturing Operations
LAWRENCE GANEM VP – Editorial Administration & Talent Relations • **ALISON GILL** Senior VP – Manufacturing & Operations
JASON GREENBERG VP – Business Strategy & Finance • **HANK KANALZ** Senior VP – Editorial Strategy & Administration
JAY KOGAN Senior VP – Legal Affairs • **NICK J. NAPOLITANO** VP – Manufacturing Administration
LISETTE OSTERLOH VP – Digital Marketing & Events • **EDDIE SCANNELL** VP – Consumer Marketing
COURTNEY SIMMONS Senior VP – Publicity & Communications • **JIM (SKI) SOKOLOWSKI** VP – Comic Book Specialty Sales & Trade Marketing
NANCY SPEARS VP – Mass, Book, Digital Sales & Trade Marketing • **MICHELE R. WELLS** VP – Content Strategy

SCOOBY-DOO TEAM-UP VOL. 6

Published by DC Comics. Compilation and all new material Copyright © 2018 Hanna-Barbera and DC Comics. All Rights Reserved.
Originally published in single magazine form in SCOOBY-DOO TEAM-UP 31-36 and online as SCOOBY-DOO TEAM-UP Digital Chapters 61-72.
Copyright © 2017, 2018 Hanna-Barbera and DC Comics. All Rights Reserved.
DC characters, their distinctive likenesses and related elements featured in this publication are trademarks of DC Comics.
The stories, characters and incidents featured in this publication are entirely fictional.
DC Comics does not read or accept unsolicited submissions of ideas, stories or artwork.

Compilation Copyright © 2018 Hanna-Barbera.
SCOOBY-DOO, ATOM ANT, YOGI BEAR and all related characters and elements © & ™ Hanna-Barbera.
WB SHIELD: ™ & © WBEI (s18)

DCCO41636

DC Comics, 2900 West Alameda Ave., Burbank, CA 91505
Printed by Times Printing, LLC, Random Lake, WI, USA. 12/14/18. First Printing.
ISBN: 978-1-4012-8576-0

Library of Congress Cataloging-in-Publication Data is available.

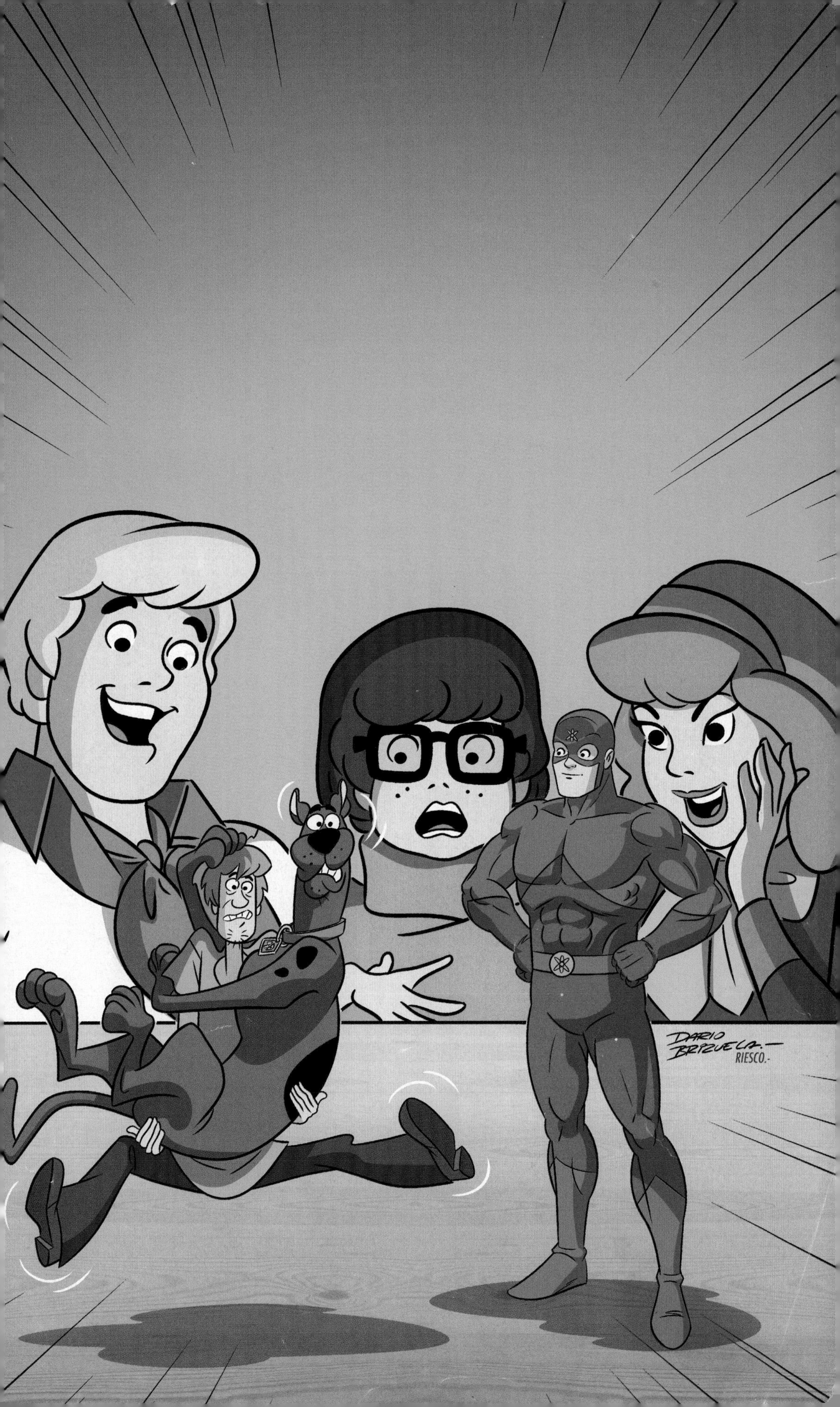
DARIO BRIZUELA
RIESCO.-

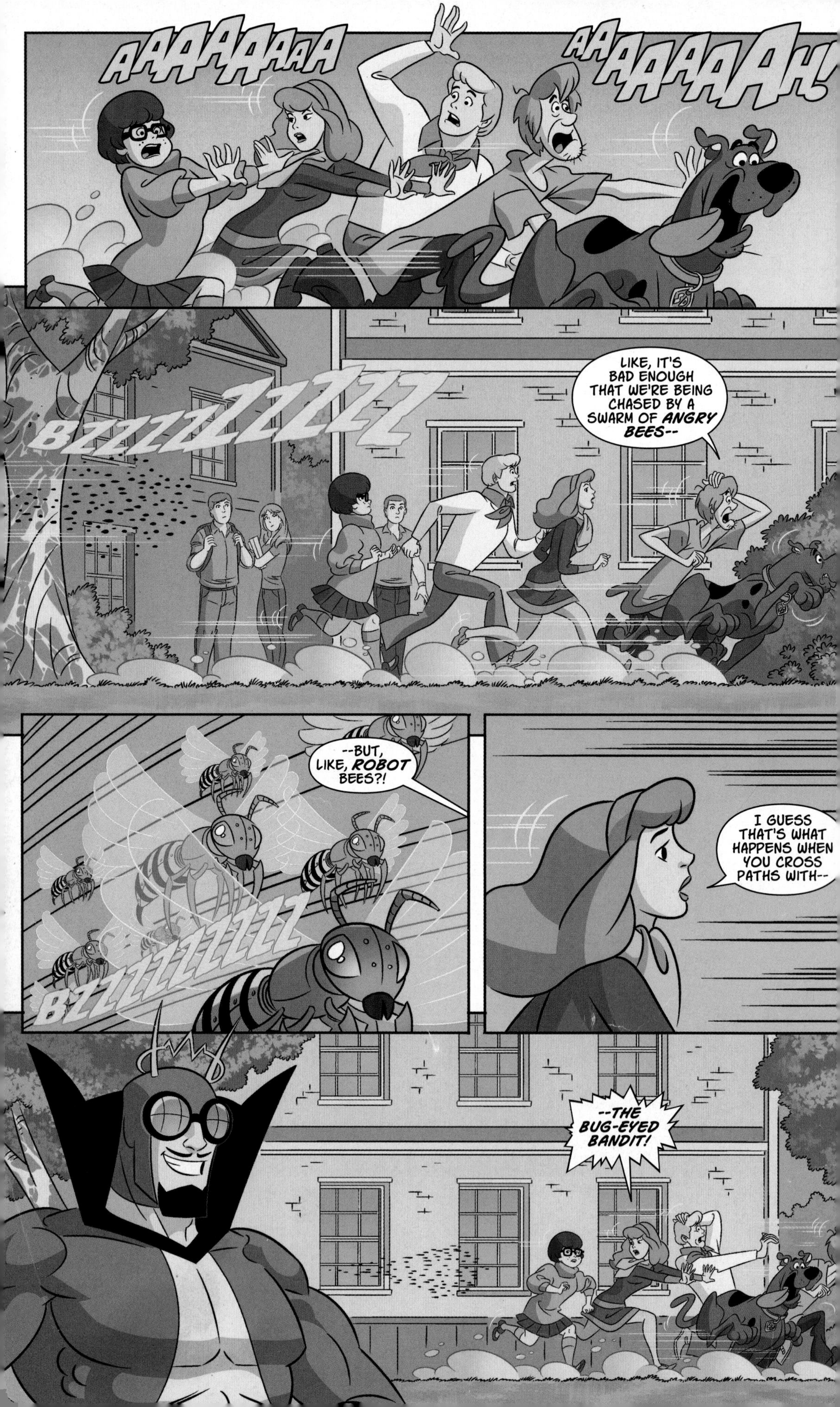

AAAAAAAA
AAAAAAAAH!
BZZZZZZZZZZ
LIKE, IT'S BAD ENOUGH THAT WE'RE BEING CHASED BY A SWARM OF ANGRY BEES--
--BUT, LIKE, ROBOT BEES?!
BZZZZZZZZZZZ
I GUESS THAT'S WHAT HAPPENS WHEN YOU CROSS PATHS WITH--
--THE BUG-EYED BANDIT!

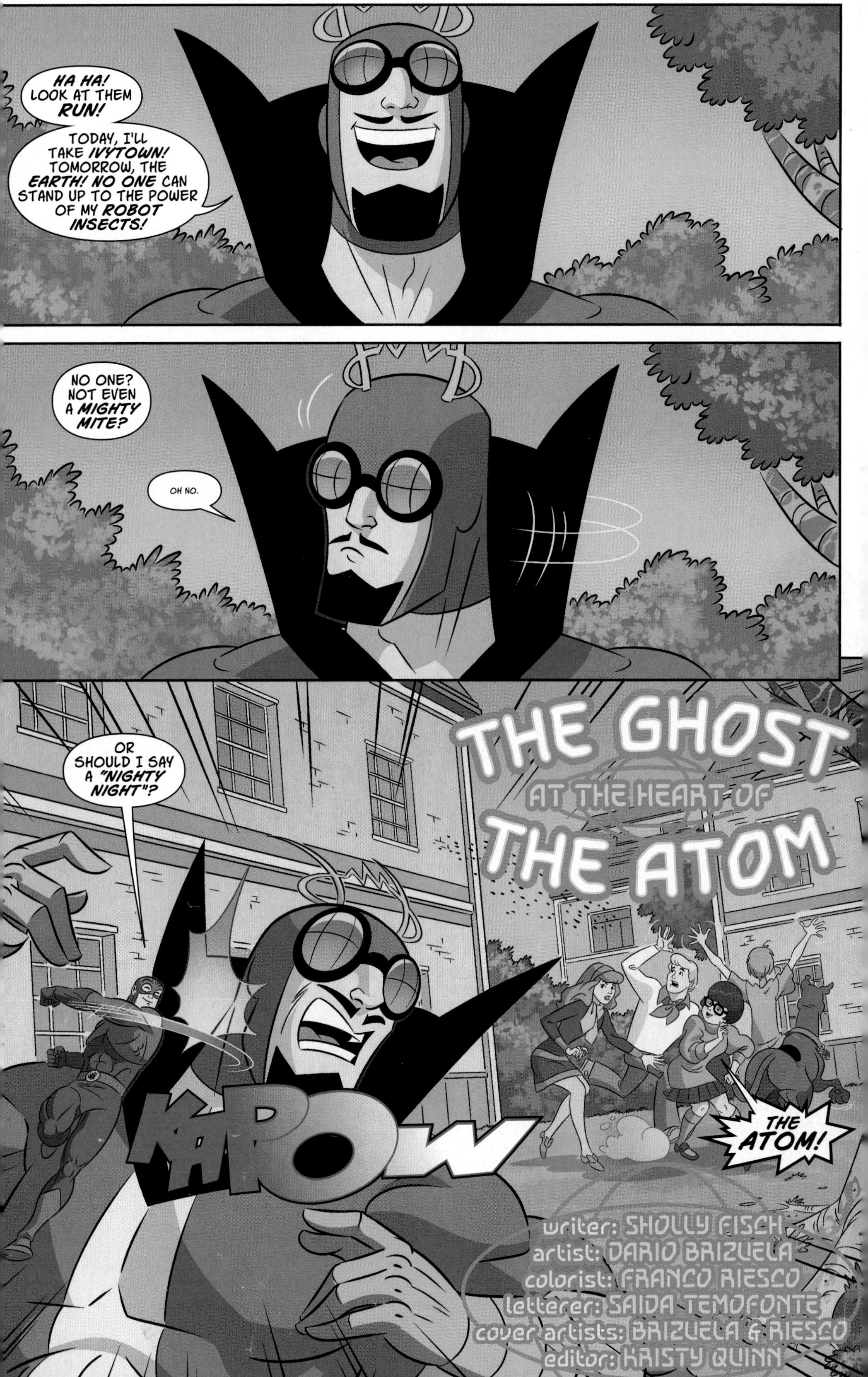

HA HA! LOOK AT THEM RUN!
TODAY, I'LL TAKE IVYTOWN! TOMORROW, THE EARTH! NO ONE CAN STAND UP TO THE POWER OF MY ROBOT INSECTS!
NO ONE? NOT EVEN A MIGHTY MITE?
OH NO.
OR SHOULD I SAY A "NIGHTY NIGHT"?
THE GHOST AT THE HEART OF THE ATOM
KAPOW
THE ATOM!
writer: SHOLLY FISCH
artist: DARIO BRIZUELA
colorist: FRANCO RIESCO
letterer: SAIDA TEMOFONTE
cover artists: BRIZUELA & RIESCO
editor: KRISTY QUINN

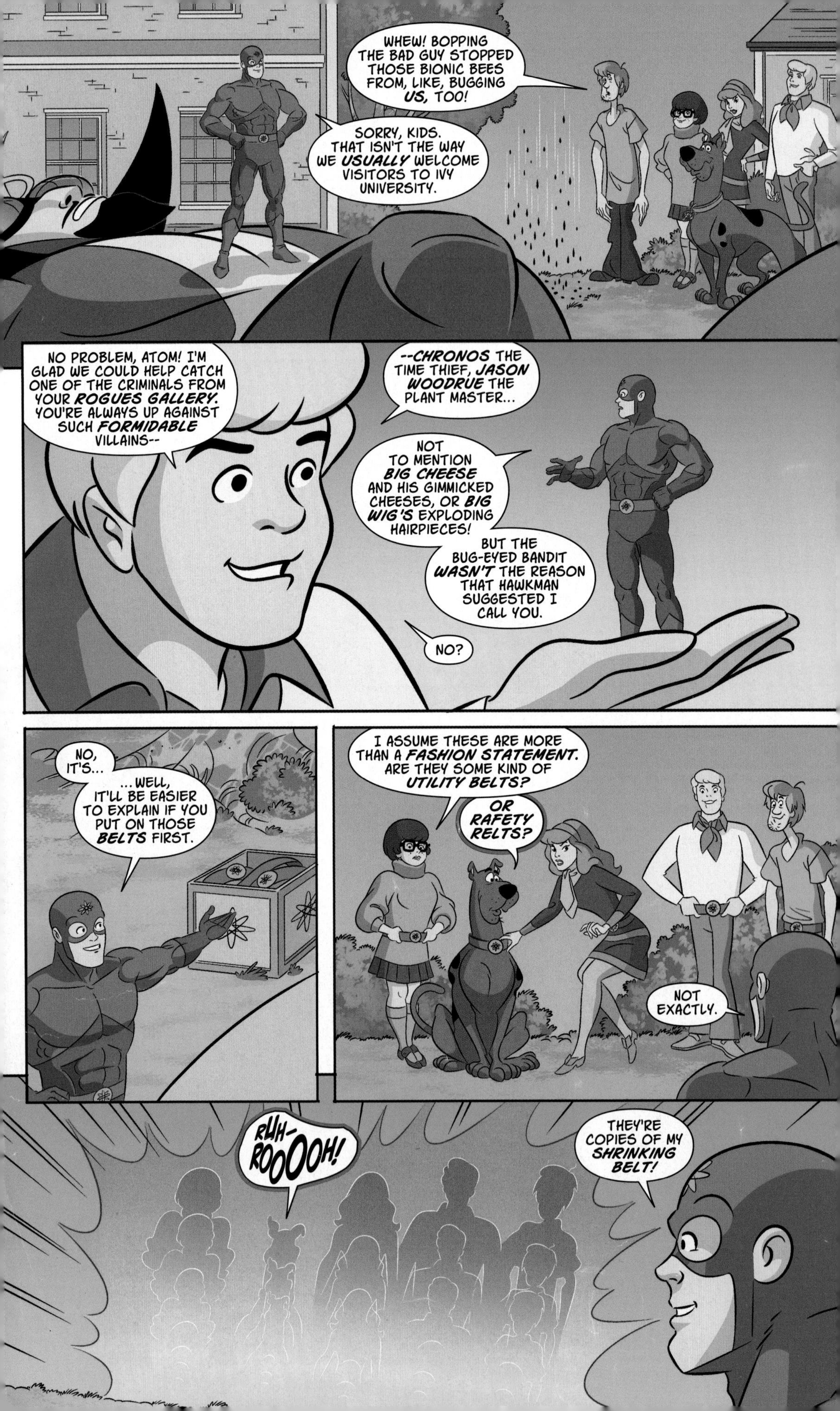
WHEW! BOPPING THE BAD GUY STOPPED THOSE BIONIC BEES FROM, LIKE, BUGGING *US,* TOO!
SORRY, KIDS. THAT ISN'T THE WAY WE *USUALLY* WELCOME VISITORS TO IVY UNIVERSITY.
NO PROBLEM, ATOM! I'M GLAD WE COULD HELP CATCH ONE OF THE CRIMINALS FROM YOUR *ROGUES GALLERY.* YOU'RE ALWAYS UP AGAINST SUCH *FORMIDABLE* VILLAINS--
--*CHRONOS* THE TIME THIEF, *JASON WOODRUE* THE PLANT MASTER...
NOT TO MENTION *BIG CHEESE* AND HIS GIMMICKED CHEESES, OR *BIG WIG'S* EXPLODING HAIRPIECES!
BUT THE BUG-EYED BANDIT *WASN'T* THE REASON THAT HAWKMAN SUGGESTED I CALL YOU.
NO?
NO, IT'S...
...WELL, IT'LL BE EASIER TO EXPLAIN IF YOU PUT ON THOSE *BELTS* FIRST.
I ASSUME THESE ARE MORE THAN A *FASHION STATEMENT.* ARE THEY SOME KIND OF *UTILITY BELTS?*
OR RAFETY RELTS?
NOT EXACTLY.
RUH-ROOOOH!
THEY'RE COPIES OF MY *SHRINKING BELT!*

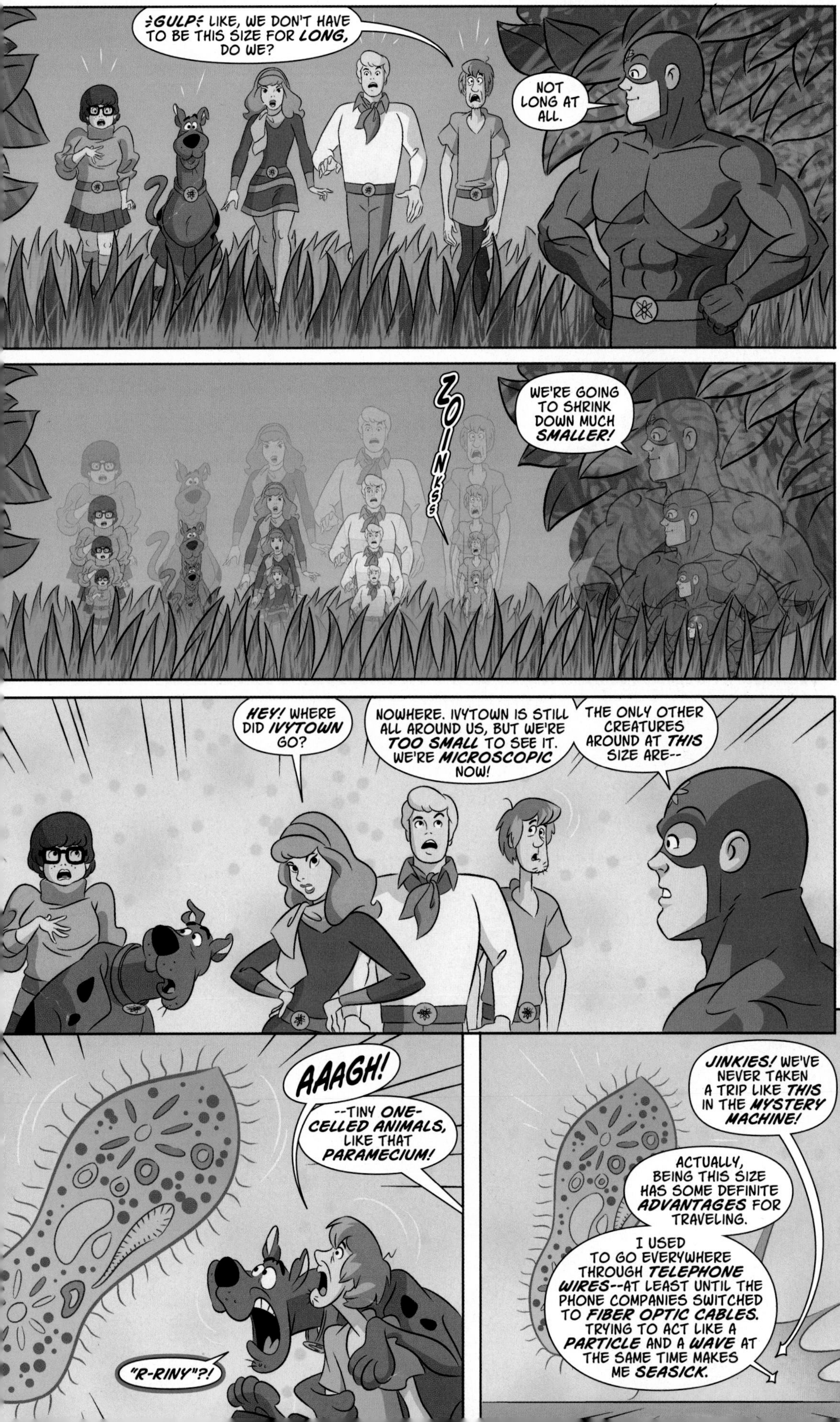

GULP LIKE, WE DON'T HAVE TO BE THIS SIZE FOR LONG, DO WE?
NOT LONG AT ALL.
WE'RE GOING TO SHRINK DOWN MUCH SMALLER!
ZOINKS
HEY! WHERE DID IVYTOWN GO?
NOWHERE. IVYTOWN IS STILL ALL AROUND US, BUT WE'RE TOO SMALL TO SEE IT. WE'RE MICROSCOPIC NOW!
THE ONLY OTHER CREATURES AROUND AT THIS SIZE ARE--
AAAGH!
--TINY ONE-CELLED ANIMALS, LIKE THAT PARAMECIUM!
"R-RINY"?!
JINKIES! WE'VE NEVER TAKEN A TRIP LIKE THIS IN THE MYSTERY MACHINE!
ACTUALLY, BEING THIS SIZE HAS SOME DEFINITE ADVANTAGES FOR TRAVELING.
I USED TO GO EVERYWHERE THROUGH TELEPHONE WIRES--AT LEAST UNTIL THE PHONE COMPANIES SWITCHED TO FIBER OPTIC CABLES. TRYING TO ACT LIKE A PARTICLE AND A WAVE AT THE SAME TIME MAKES ME SEASICK.

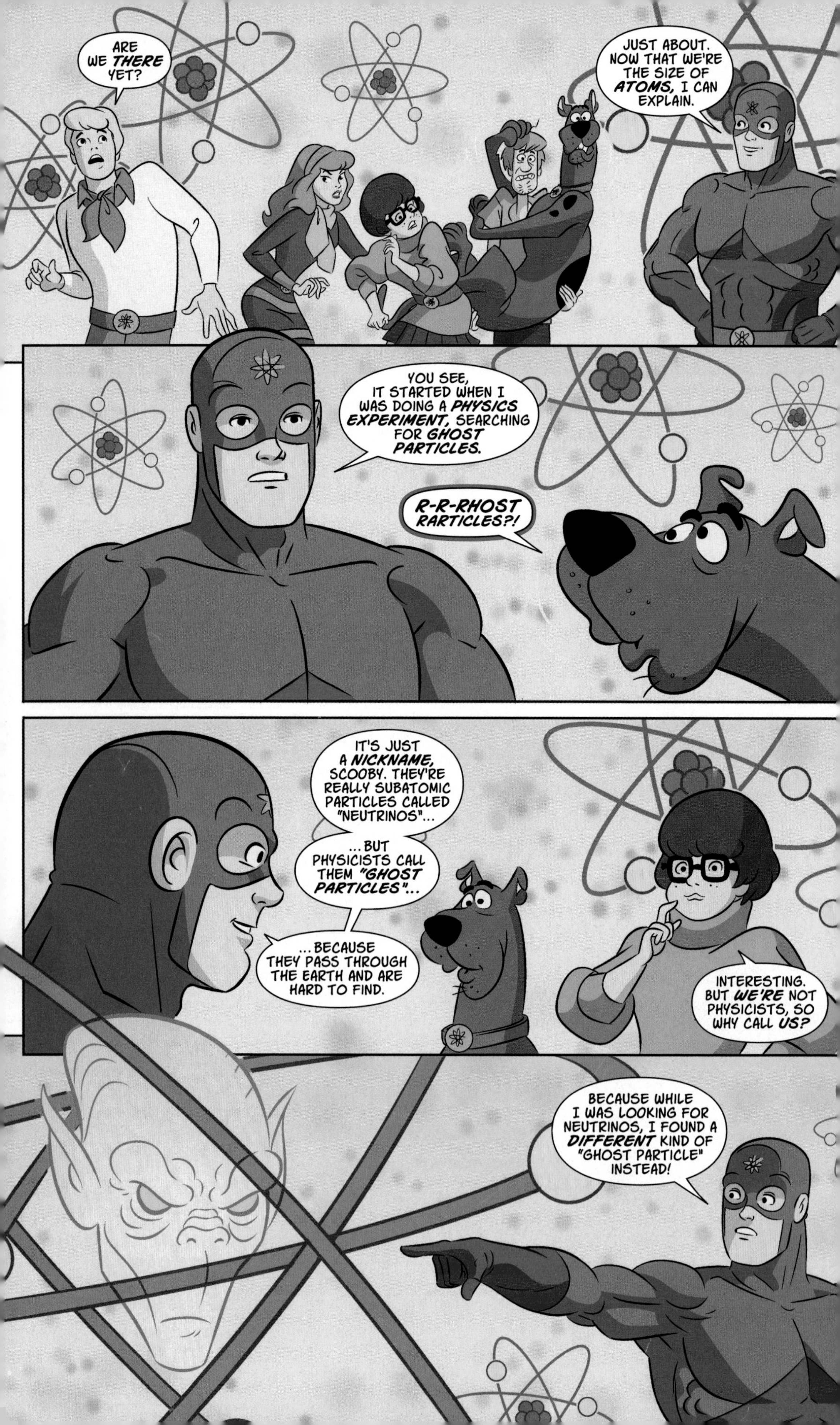
ARE WE THERE YET?
JUST ABOUT. NOW THAT WE'RE THE SIZE OF ATOMS, I CAN EXPLAIN.
YOU SEE, IT STARTED WHEN I WAS DOING A PHYSICS EXPERIMENT, SEARCHING FOR GHOST PARTICLES.
R-R-RHOST RARTICLES?!
IT'S JUST A NICKNAME, SCOOBY. THEY'RE REALLY SUBATOMIC PARTICLES CALLED "NEUTRINOS"...
...BUT PHYSICISTS CALL THEM "GHOST PARTICLES"...
...BECAUSE THEY PASS THROUGH THE EARTH AND ARE HARD TO FIND.
INTERESTING. BUT WE'RE NOT PHYSICISTS, SO WHY CALL US?
BECAUSE WHILE I WAS LOOKING FOR NEUTRINOS, I FOUND A DIFFERENT KIND OF "GHOST PARTICLE" INSTEAD!

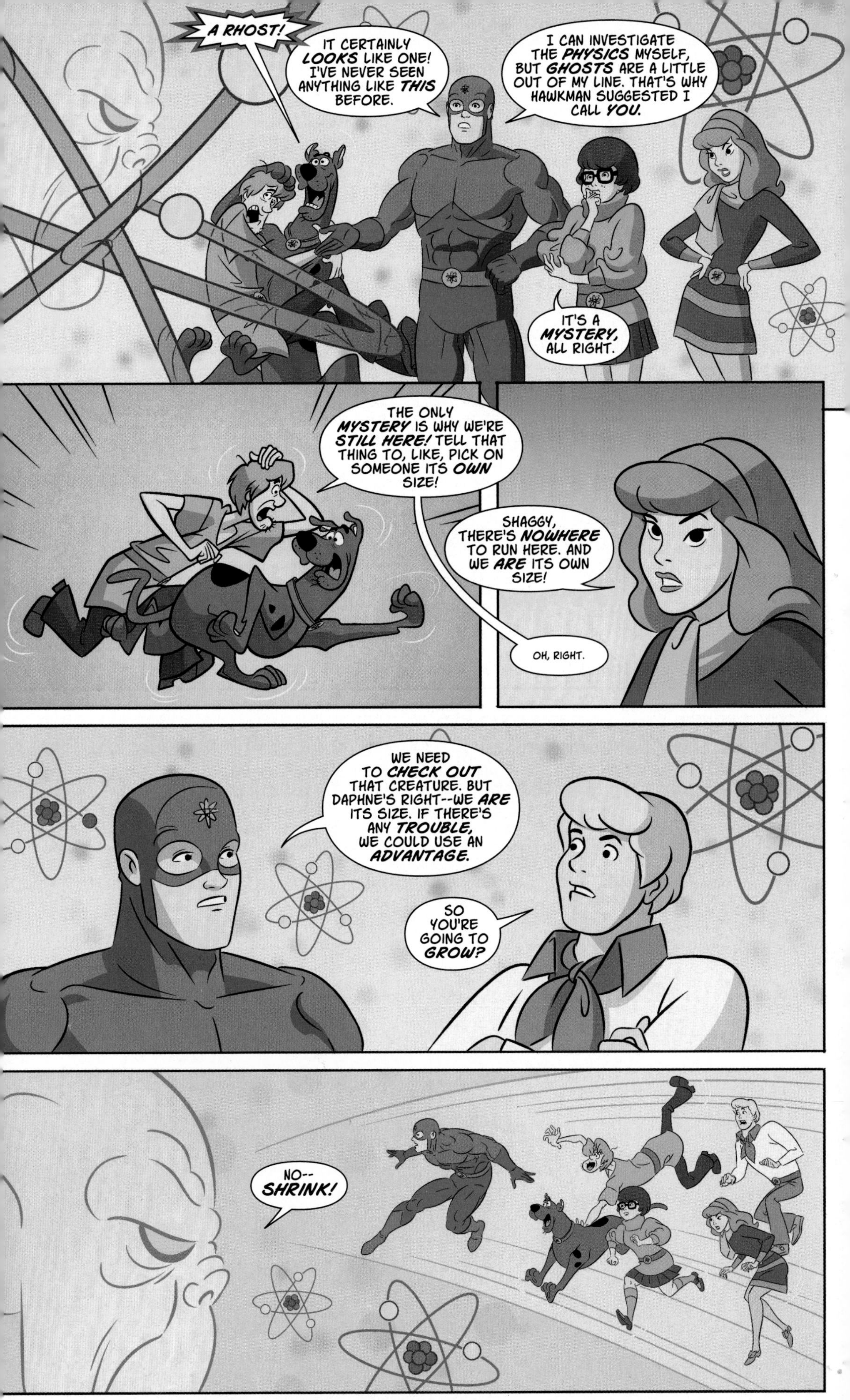
A RHOST!
IT CERTAINLY LOOKS LIKE ONE! I'VE NEVER SEEN ANYTHING LIKE THIS BEFORE.
I CAN INVESTIGATE THE PHYSICS MYSELF, BUT GHOSTS ARE A LITTLE OUT OF MY LINE. THAT'S WHY HAWKMAN SUGGESTED I CALL YOU.
IT'S A MYSTERY, ALL RIGHT.
THE ONLY MYSTERY IS WHY WE'RE STILL HERE! TELL THAT THING TO, LIKE, PICK ON SOMEONE ITS OWN SIZE!
SHAGGY, THERE'S NOWHERE TO RUN HERE. AND WE ARE ITS OWN SIZE!
OH, RIGHT.
WE NEED TO CHECK OUT THAT CREATURE. BUT DAPHNE'S RIGHT--WE ARE ITS SIZE. IF THERE'S ANY TROUBLE, WE COULD USE AN ADVANTAGE.
SO YOU'RE GOING TO GROW?
NO-- SHRINK!

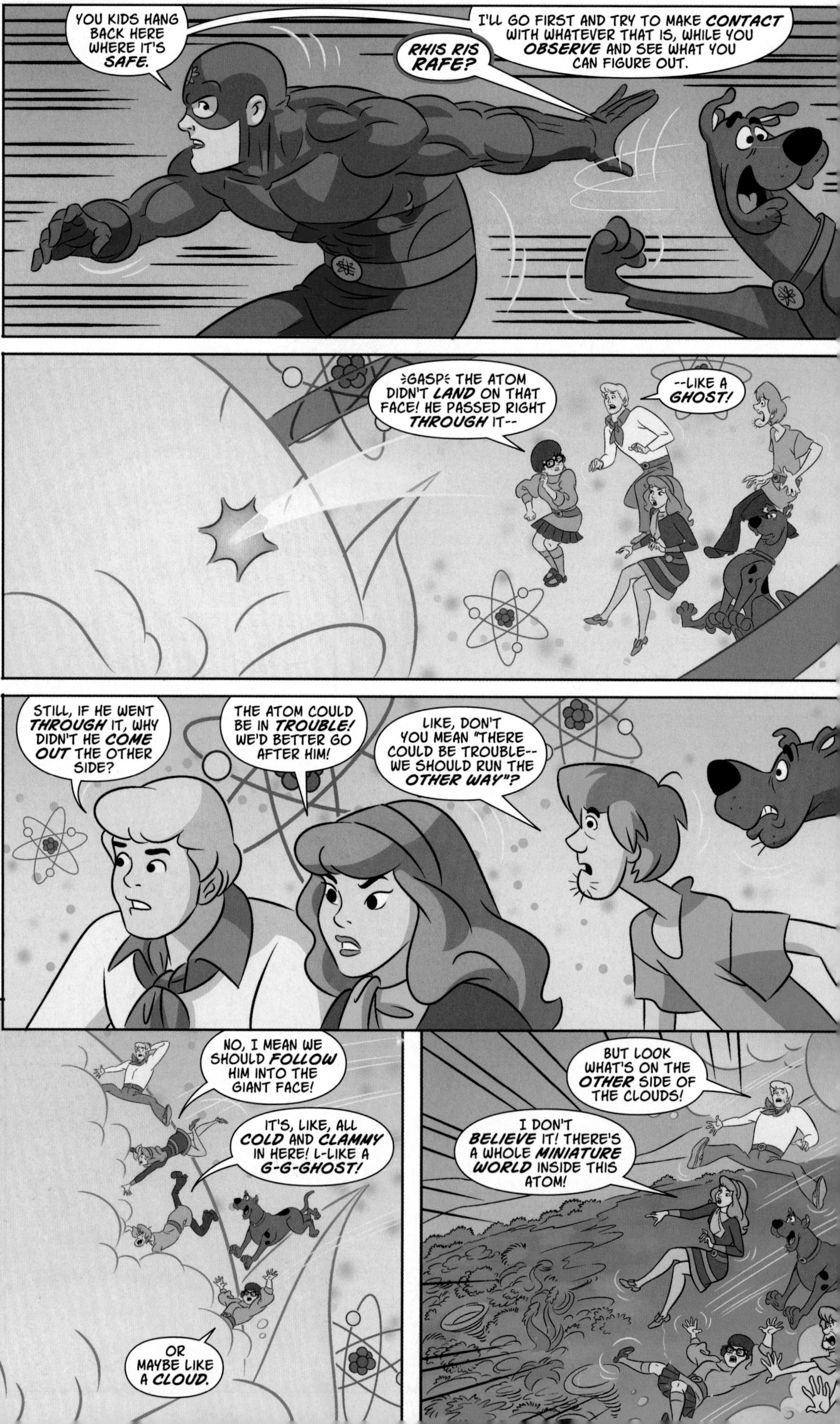
YOU KIDS HANG BACK HERE WHERE IT'S SAFE.
I'LL GO FIRST AND TRY TO MAKE CONTACT WITH WHATEVER THAT IS, WHILE YOU OBSERVE AND SEE WHAT YOU CAN FIGURE OUT.
RHIS RIS RAFE?
GASP THE ATOM DIDN'T LAND ON THAT FACE! HE PASSED RIGHT THROUGH IT--
--LIKE A GHOST!
STILL, IF HE WENT THROUGH IT, WHY DIDN'T HE COME OUT THE OTHER SIDE?
THE ATOM COULD BE IN TROUBLE! WE'D BETTER GO AFTER HIM!
LIKE, DON'T YOU MEAN "THERE COULD BE TROUBLE-- WE SHOULD RUN THE OTHER WAY"?
NO, I MEAN WE SHOULD FOLLOW HIM INTO THE GIANT FACE!
IT'S, LIKE, ALL COLD AND CLAMMY IN HERE! L-LIKE A G-G-GHOST!
OR MAYBE LIKE A CLOUD.
BUT LOOK WHAT'S ON THE OTHER SIDE OF THE CLOUDS!
I DON'T BELIEVE IT! THERE'S A WHOLE MINIATURE WORLD INSIDE THIS ATOM!

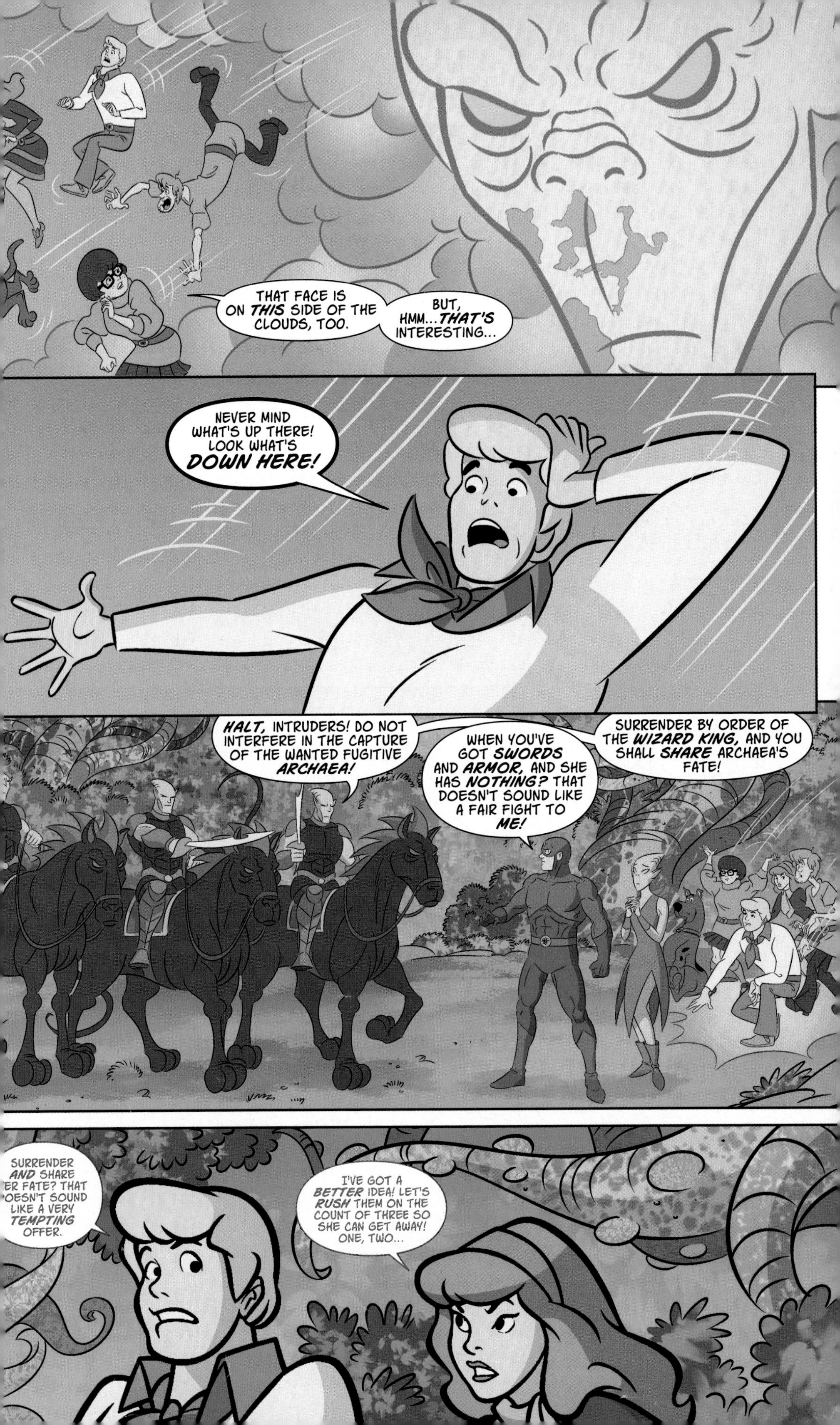
THAT FACE IS ON *THIS* SIDE OF THE CLOUDS, TOO.
BUT, HMM...*THAT'S* INTERESTING...
NEVER MIND WHAT'S UP THERE! LOOK WHAT'S *DOWN HERE!*
HALT, INTRUDERS! DO NOT INTERFERE IN THE CAPTURE OF THE WANTED FUGITIVE *ARCHAEA!*
WHEN YOU'VE GOT *SWORDS* AND *ARMOR,* AND SHE HAS *NOTHING?* THAT DOESN'T SOUND LIKE A FAIR FIGHT TO *ME!*
SURRENDER BY ORDER OF THE *WIZARD KING,* AND YOU SHALL *SHARE* ARCHAEA'S FATE!
SURRENDER *AND* SHARE ER FATE? THAT OESN'T SOUND LIKE A VERY *TEMPTING* OFFER.
I'VE GOT A *BETTER* IDEA! LET'S *RUSH* THEM ON THE COUNT OF THREE SO SHE CAN GET AWAY! ONE, TWO...

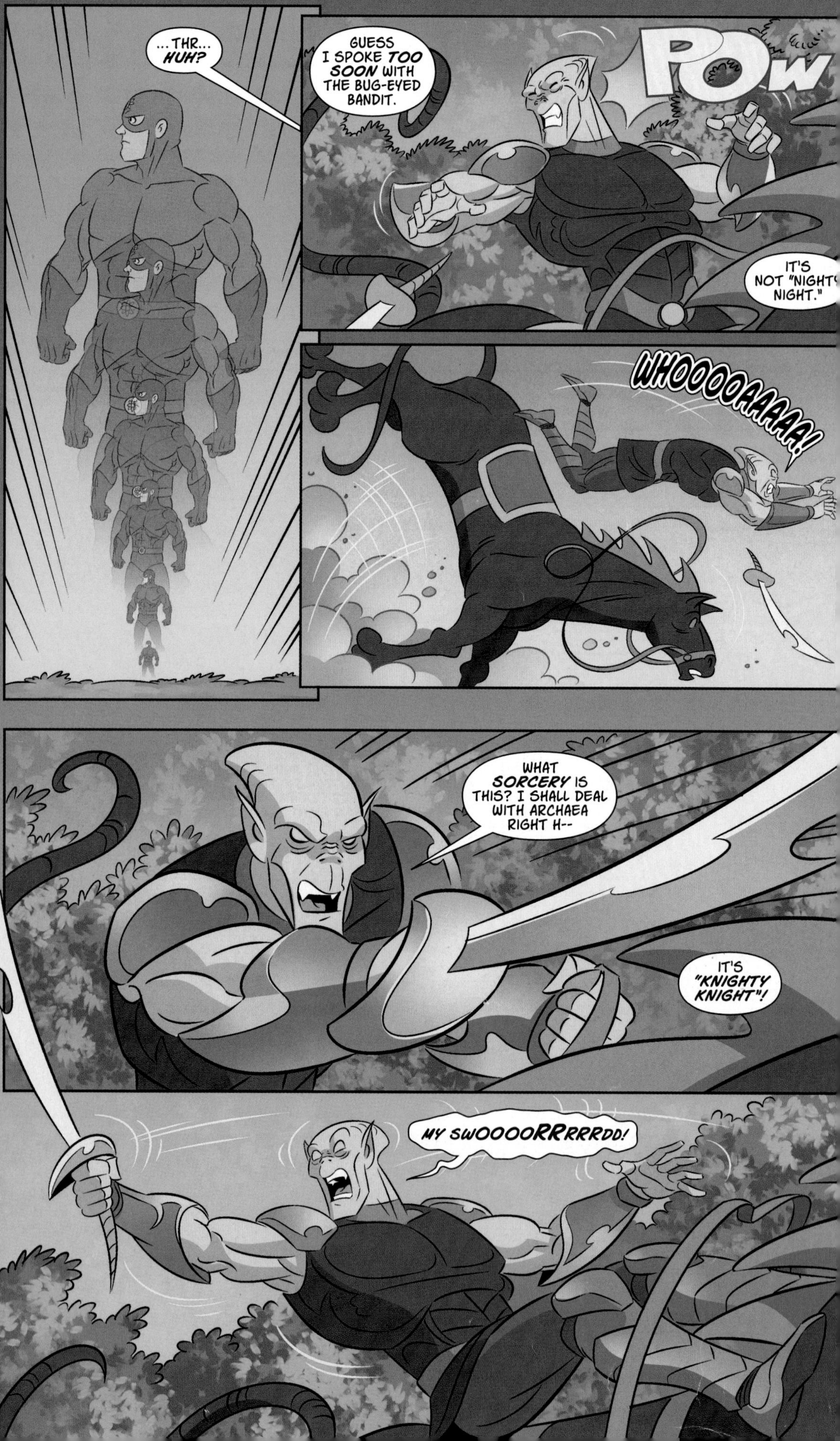
...THR... HUH?
GUESS I SPOKE TOO SOON WITH THE BUG-EYED BANDIT.
POW
IT'S NOT "NIGHTY NIGHT."
WHOOOOAAAAA!
WHAT SORCERY IS THIS? I SHALL DEAL WITH ARCHAEA RIGHT H--
IT'S "KNIGHTY KNIGHT"!
MY SWOOOORRRRRDD!

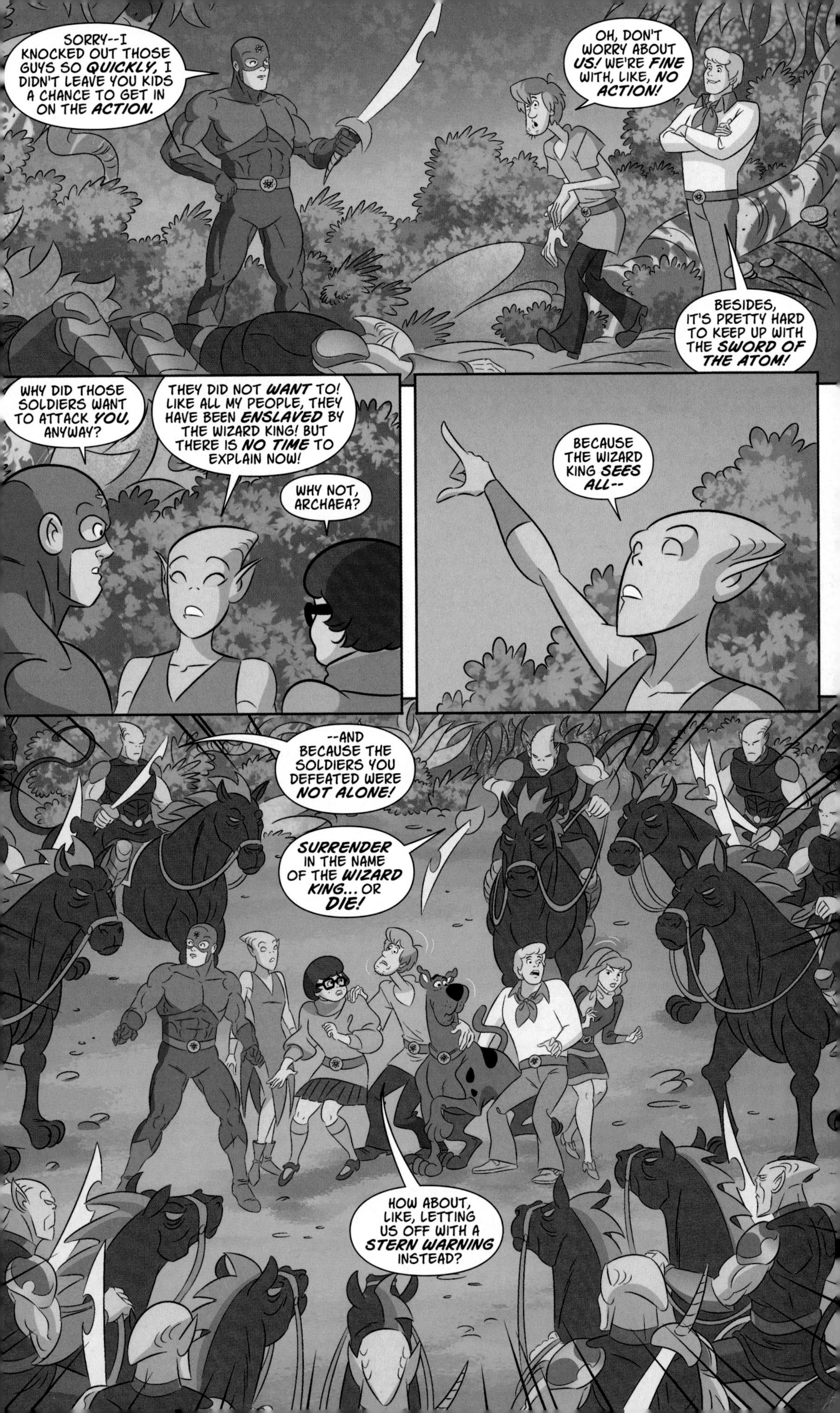
SORRY--I KNOCKED OUT THOSE GUYS SO QUICKLY, I DIDN'T LEAVE YOU KIDS A CHANCE TO GET IN ON THE ACTION.
OH, DON'T WORRY ABOUT US! WE'RE FINE WITH, LIKE, NO ACTION!
BESIDES, IT'S PRETTY HARD TO KEEP UP WITH THE SWORD OF THE ATOM!
WHY DID THOSE SOLDIERS WANT TO ATTACK YOU, ANYWAY?
THEY DID NOT WANT TO! LIKE ALL MY PEOPLE, THEY HAVE BEEN ENSLAVED BY THE WIZARD KING! BUT THERE IS NO TIME TO EXPLAIN NOW!
WHY NOT, ARCHAEA?
BECAUSE THE WIZARD KING SEES ALL--
--AND BECAUSE THE SOLDIERS YOU DEFEATED WERE NOT ALONE!
SURRENDER IN THE NAME OF THE WIZARD KING... OR DIE!
HOW ABOUT, LIKE, LETTING US OFF WITH A STERN WARNING INSTEAD?

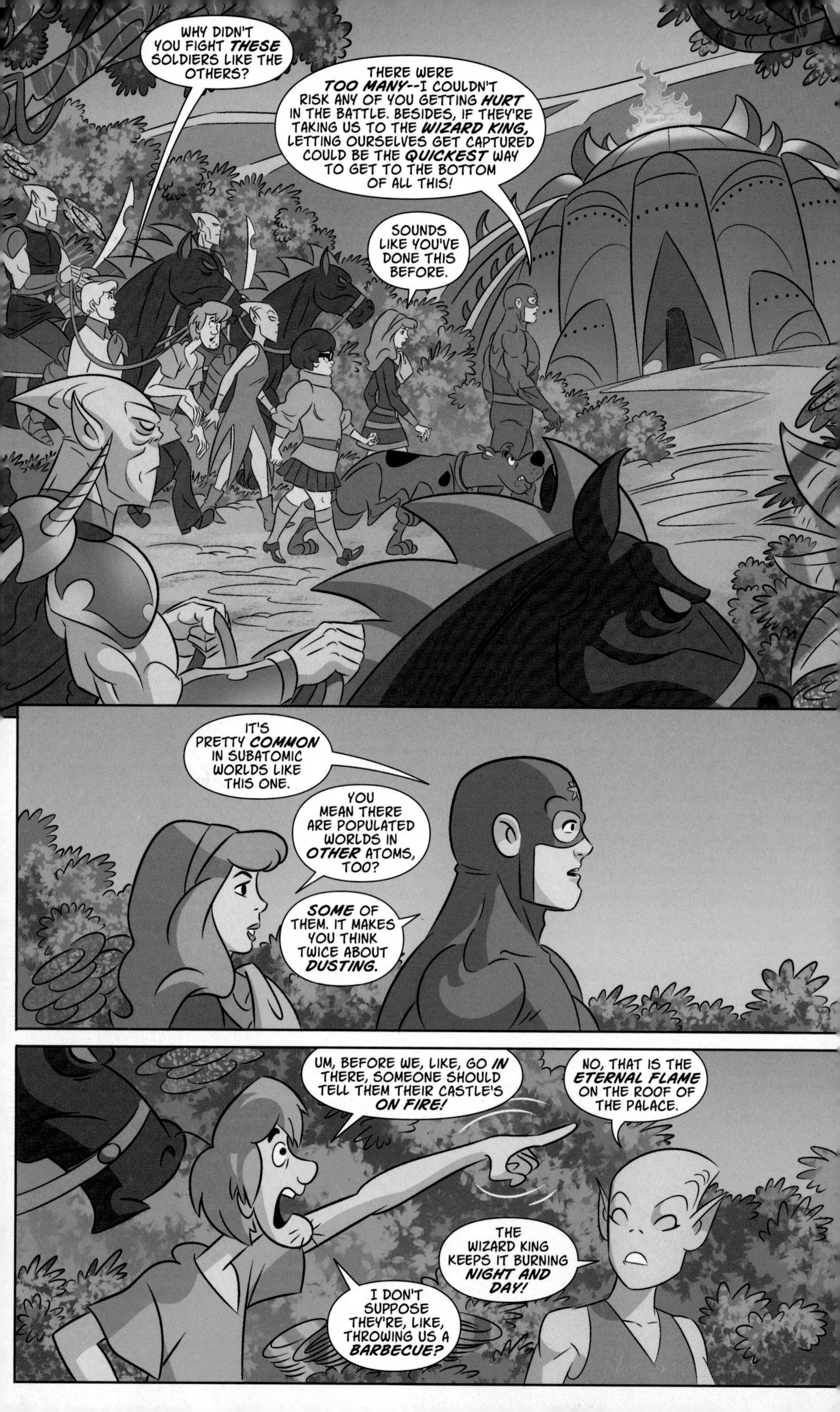
WHY DIDN'T YOU FIGHT THESE SOLDIERS LIKE THE OTHERS?
THERE WERE TOO MANY--I COULDN'T RISK ANY OF YOU GETTING HURT IN THE BATTLE. BESIDES, IF THEY'RE TAKING US TO THE WIZARD KING, LETTING OURSELVES GET CAPTURED COULD BE THE QUICKEST WAY TO GET TO THE BOTTOM OF ALL THIS!
SOUNDS LIKE YOU'VE DONE THIS BEFORE.
IT'S PRETTY COMMON IN SUBATOMIC WORLDS LIKE THIS ONE.
YOU MEAN THERE ARE POPULATED WORLDS IN OTHER ATOMS, TOO?
SOME OF THEM. IT MAKES YOU THINK TWICE ABOUT DUSTING.
UM, BEFORE WE, LIKE, GO IN THERE, SOMEONE SHOULD TELL THEM THEIR CASTLE'S ON FIRE!
NO, THAT IS THE ETERNAL FLAME ON THE ROOF OF THE PALACE.
THE WIZARD KING KEEPS IT BURNING NIGHT AND DAY!
I DON'T SUPPOSE THEY'RE, LIKE, THROWING US A BARBECUE?

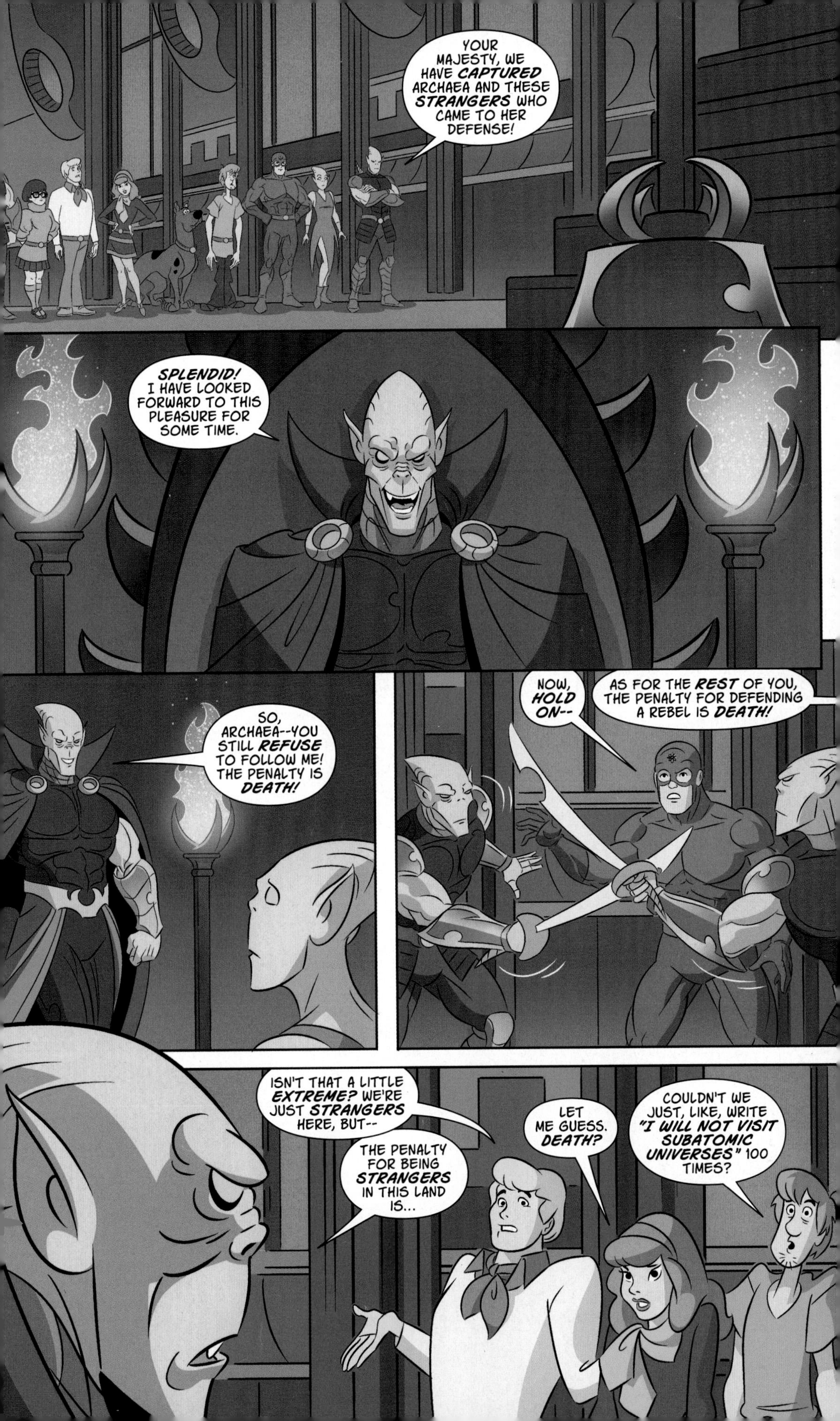
YOUR MAJESTY, WE HAVE CAPTURED ARCHAEA AND THESE STRANGERS WHO CAME TO HER DEFENSE!
SPLENDID! I HAVE LOOKED FORWARD TO THIS PLEASURE FOR SOME TIME.
SO, ARCHAEA--YOU STILL REFUSE TO FOLLOW ME! THE PENALTY IS DEATH!
AS FOR THE REST OF YOU, THE PENALTY FOR DEFENDING A REBEL IS DEATH!
NOW, HOLD ON--
ISN'T THAT A LITTLE EXTREME? WE'RE JUST STRANGERS HERE, BUT--
THE PENALTY FOR BEING STRANGERS IN THIS LAND IS...
LET ME GUESS. DEATH?
COULDN'T WE JUST, LIKE, WRITE "I WILL NOT VISIT SUBATOMIC UNIVERSES" 100 TIMES?

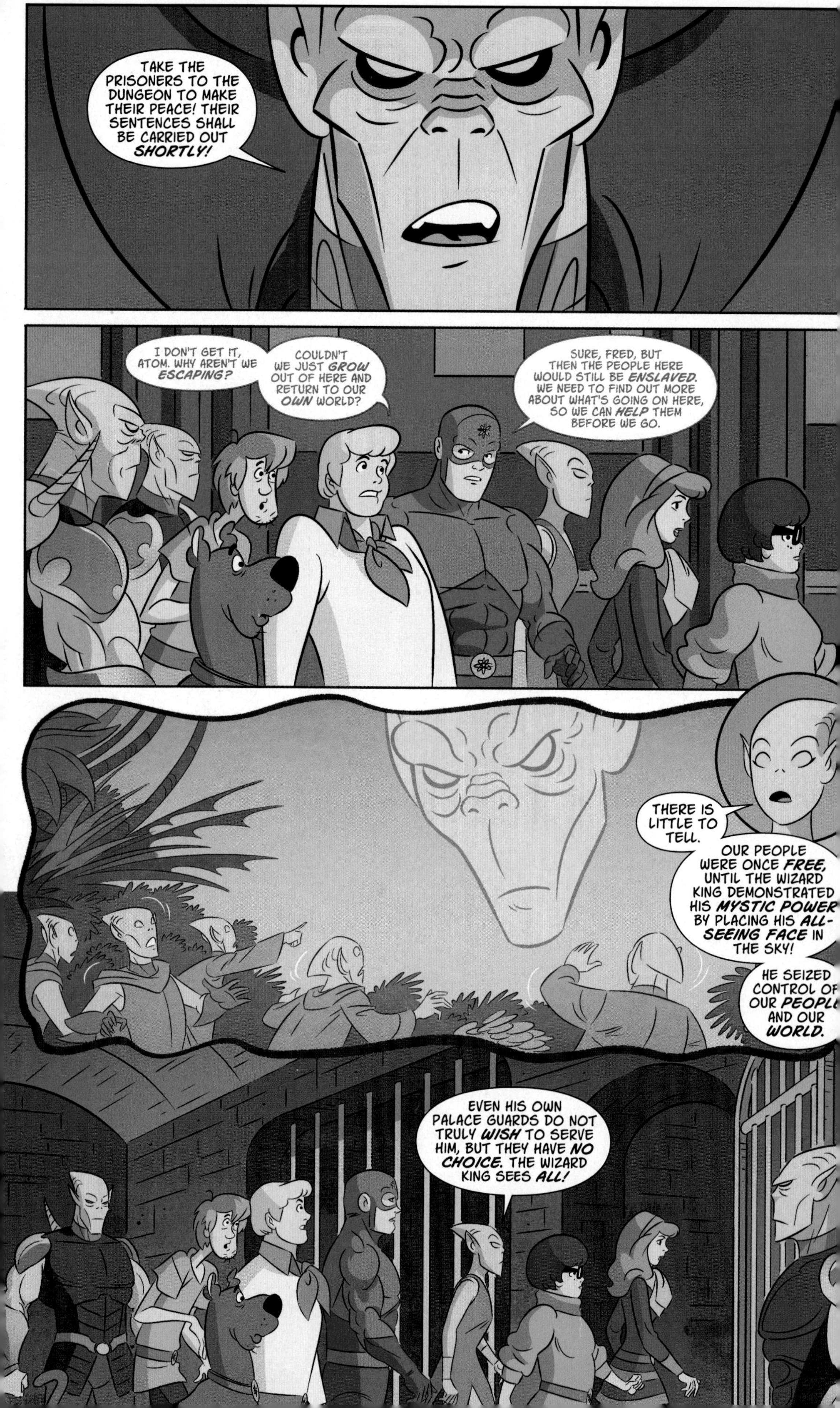
TAKE THE PRISONERS TO THE DUNGEON TO MAKE THEIR PEACE! THEIR SENTENCES SHALL BE CARRIED OUT SHORTLY!
I DON'T GET IT, ATOM. WHY AREN'T WE ESCAPING?
COULDN'T WE JUST GROW OUT OF HERE AND RETURN TO OUR OWN WORLD?
SURE, FRED, BUT THEN THE PEOPLE HERE WOULD STILL BE ENSLAVED. WE NEED TO FIND OUT MORE ABOUT WHAT'S GOING ON HERE, SO WE CAN HELP THEM BEFORE WE GO.
THERE IS LITTLE TO TELL.
OUR PEOPLE WERE ONCE FREE, UNTIL THE WIZARD KING DEMONSTRATED HIS MYSTIC POWER BY PLACING HIS ALL-SEEING FACE IN THE SKY!
HE SEIZED CONTROL OF OUR PEOPLE AND OUR WORLD.
EVEN HIS OWN PALACE GUARDS DO NOT TRULY WISH TO SERVE HIM, BUT THEY HAVE NO CHOICE. THE WIZARD KING SEES ALL!

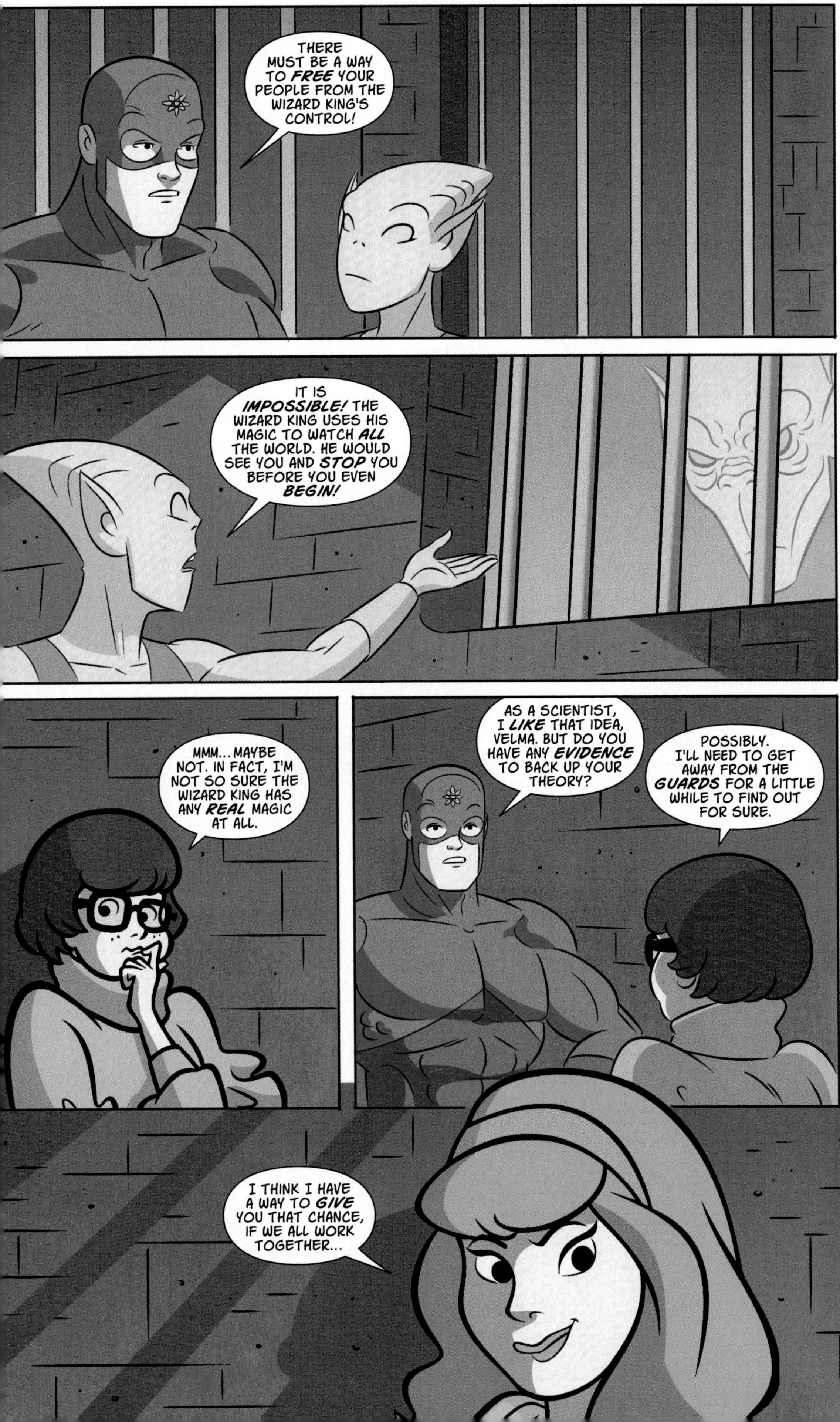
THERE MUST BE A WAY TO FREE YOUR PEOPLE FROM THE WIZARD KING'S CONTROL!
IT IS IMPOSSIBLE! THE WIZARD KING USES HIS MAGIC TO WATCH ALL THE WORLD. HE WOULD SEE YOU AND STOP YOU BEFORE YOU EVEN BEGIN!
MMM... MAYBE NOT. IN FACT, I'M NOT SO SURE THE WIZARD KING HAS ANY REAL MAGIC AT ALL.
AS A SCIENTIST, I LIKE THAT IDEA, VELMA. BUT DO YOU HAVE ANY EVIDENCE TO BACK UP YOUR THEORY?
POSSIBLY. I'LL NEED TO GET AWAY FROM THE GUARDS FOR A LITTLE WHILE TO FIND OUT FOR SURE.
I THINK I HAVE A WAY TO GIVE YOU THAT CHANCE, IF WE ALL WORK TOGETHER...

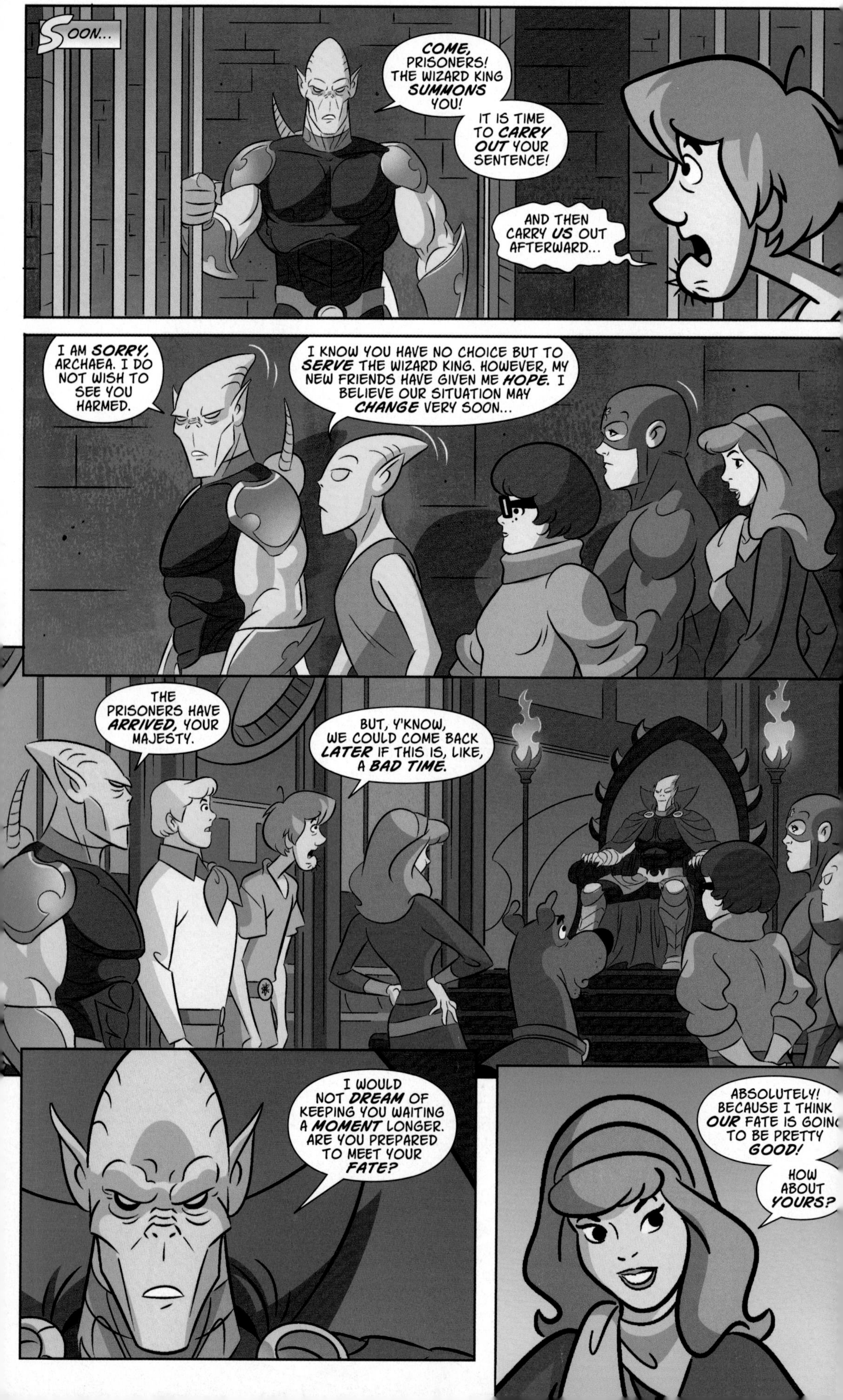
SOON...
COME, PRISONERS! THE WIZARD KING SUMMONS YOU!
IT IS TIME TO CARRY OUT YOUR SENTENCE!
AND THEN CARRY US OUT AFTERWARD...
I AM SORRY, ARCHAEA. I DO NOT WISH TO SEE YOU HARMED.
I KNOW YOU HAVE NO CHOICE BUT TO SERVE THE WIZARD KING. HOWEVER, MY NEW FRIENDS HAVE GIVEN ME HOPE. I BELIEVE OUR SITUATION MAY CHANGE VERY SOON...
THE PRISONERS HAVE ARRIVED, YOUR MAJESTY.
BUT, Y'KNOW, WE COULD COME BACK LATER IF THIS IS, LIKE, A BAD TIME.
I WOULD NOT DREAM OF KEEPING YOU WAITING A MOMENT LONGER. ARE YOU PREPARED TO MEET YOUR FATE?
ABSOLUTELY! BECAUSE I THINK OUR FATE IS GOING TO BE PRETTY GOOD!
HOW ABOUT YOURS?

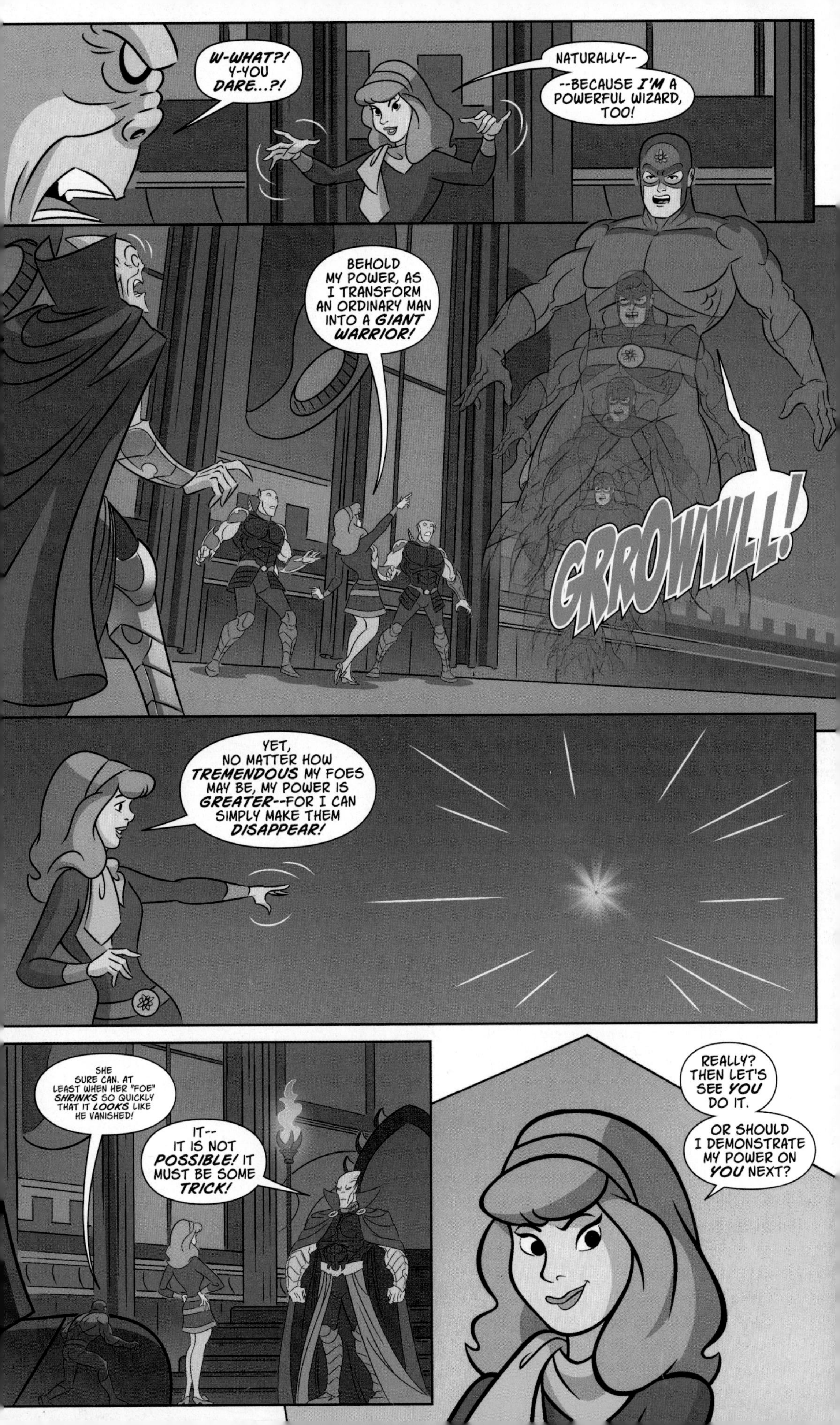

W-WHAT?! Y-YOU DARE...?!
NATURALLY--
--BECAUSE I'M A POWERFUL WIZARD, TOO!
BEHOLD MY POWER, AS I TRANSFORM AN ORDINARY MAN INTO A GIANT WARRIOR!
GRROWWLL!
YET, NO MATTER HOW TREMENDOUS MY FOES MAY BE, MY POWER IS GREATER--FOR I CAN SIMPLY MAKE THEM DISAPPEAR!
SHE SURE CAN. AT LEAST WHEN HER "FOE" SHRINKS SO QUICKLY THAT IT LOOKS LIKE HE VANISHED!
IT-- IT IS NOT POSSIBLE! IT MUST BE SOME TRICK!
REALLY? THEN LET'S SEE YOU DO IT.
OR SHOULD I DEMONSTRATE MY POWER ON YOU NEXT?

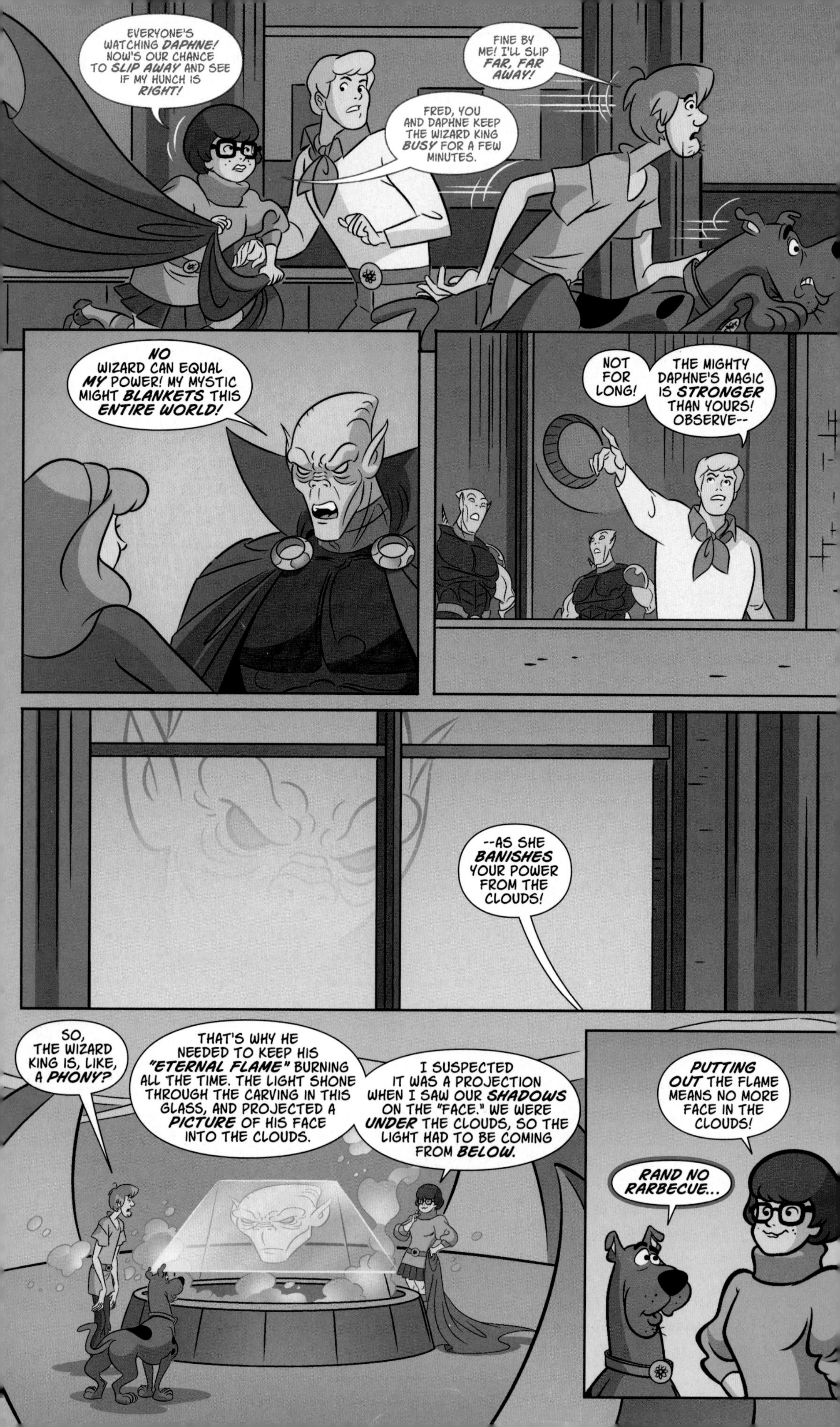

EVERYONE'S WATCHING DAPHNE! NOW'S OUR CHANCE TO SLIP AWAY AND SEE IF MY HUNCH IS RIGHT!
FRED, YOU AND DAPHNE KEEP THE WIZARD KING BUSY FOR A FEW MINUTES.
FINE BY ME! I'LL SLIP FAR, FAR AWAY!
NO WIZARD CAN EQUAL MY POWER! MY MYSTIC MIGHT BLANKETS THIS ENTIRE WORLD!
NOT FOR LONG!
THE MIGHTY DAPHNE'S MAGIC IS STRONGER THAN YOURS! OBSERVE--
--AS SHE BANISHES YOUR POWER FROM THE CLOUDS!
SO, THE WIZARD KING IS, LIKE, A PHONY?
THAT'S WHY HE NEEDED TO KEEP HIS "ETERNAL FLAME" BURNING ALL THE TIME. THE LIGHT SHONE THROUGH THE CARVING IN THIS GLASS, AND PROJECTED A PICTURE OF HIS FACE INTO THE CLOUDS.
I SUSPECTED IT WAS A PROJECTION WHEN I SAW OUR SHADOWS ON THE "FACE." WE WERE UNDER THE CLOUDS, SO THE LIGHT HAD TO BE COMING FROM BELOW.
PUTTING OUT THE FLAME MEANS NO MORE FACE IN THE CLOUDS!
RAND NO RARBECUE...

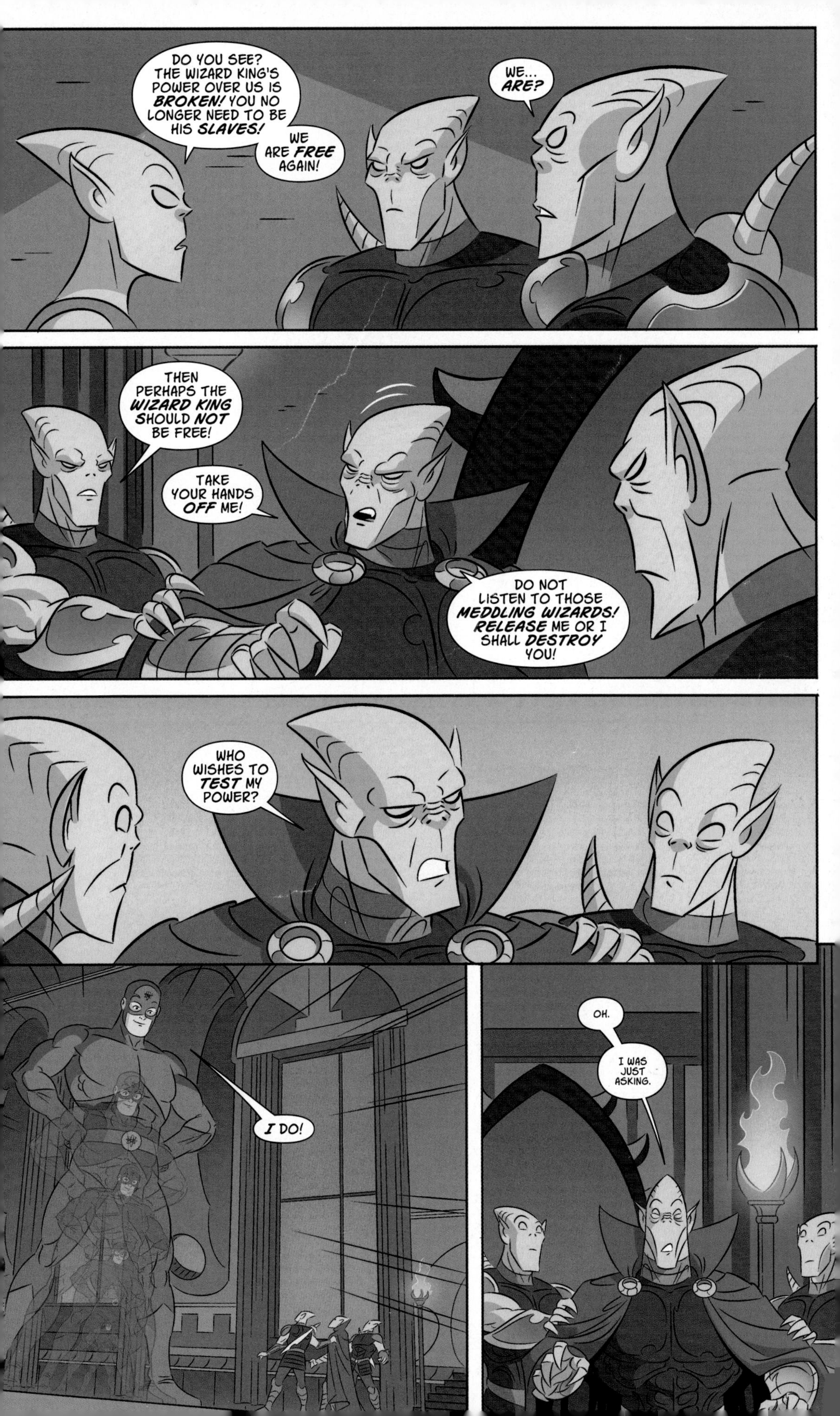
DO YOU SEE? THE WIZARD KING'S POWER OVER US IS **BROKEN!** YOU NO LONGER NEED TO BE HIS **SLAVES!**
WE ARE **FREE** AGAIN!
WE... **ARE?**
THEN PERHAPS THE **WIZARD KING** SHOULD **NOT** BE FREE!
TAKE YOUR HANDS **OFF** ME!
DO NOT LISTEN TO THOSE **MEDDLING WIZARDS! RELEASE** ME OR I SHALL **DESTROY** YOU!
WHO WISHES TO **TEST** MY POWER?
I DO!
OH.
I WAS JUST ASKING.

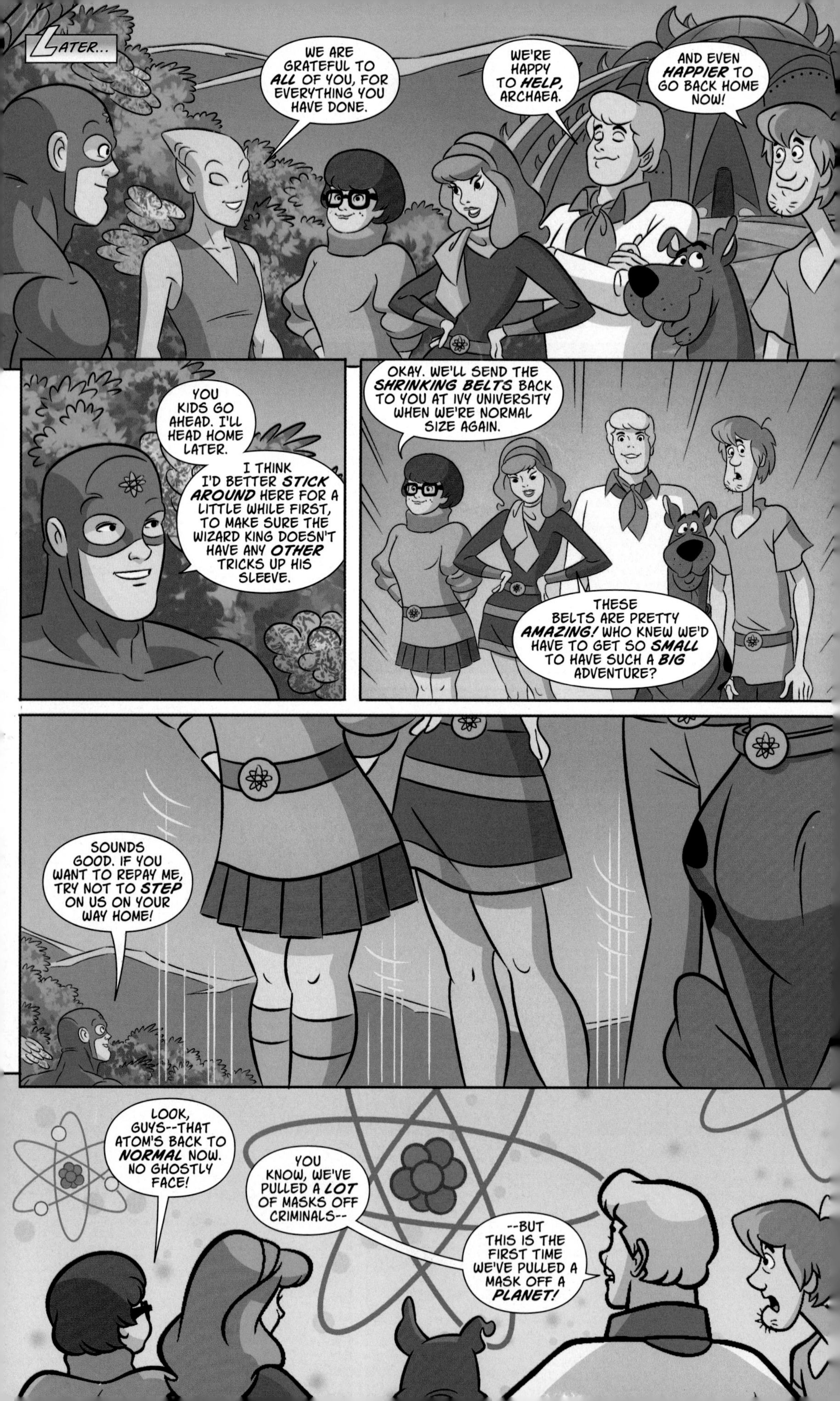
LATER...
WE ARE GRATEFUL TO ALL OF YOU, FOR EVERYTHING YOU HAVE DONE.
WE'RE HAPPY TO HELP, ARCHAEA.
AND EVEN HAPPIER TO GO BACK HOME NOW!
YOU KIDS GO AHEAD. I'LL HEAD HOME LATER.
I THINK I'D BETTER STICK AROUND HERE FOR A LITTLE WHILE FIRST, TO MAKE SURE THE WIZARD KING DOESN'T HAVE ANY OTHER TRICKS UP HIS SLEEVE.
OKAY. WE'LL SEND THE SHRINKING BELTS BACK TO YOU AT IVY UNIVERSITY WHEN WE'RE NORMAL SIZE AGAIN.
THESE BELTS ARE PRETTY AMAZING! WHO KNEW WE'D HAVE TO GET SO SMALL TO HAVE SUCH A BIG ADVENTURE?
SOUNDS GOOD. IF YOU WANT TO REPAY ME, TRY NOT TO STEP ON US ON YOUR WAY HOME!
LOOK, GUYS--THAT ATOM'S BACK TO NORMAL NOW. NO GHOSTLY FACE!
YOU KNOW, WE'VE PULLED A LOT OF MASKS OFF CRIMINALS--
--BUT THIS IS THE FIRST TIME WE'VE PULLED A MASK OFF A PLANET!

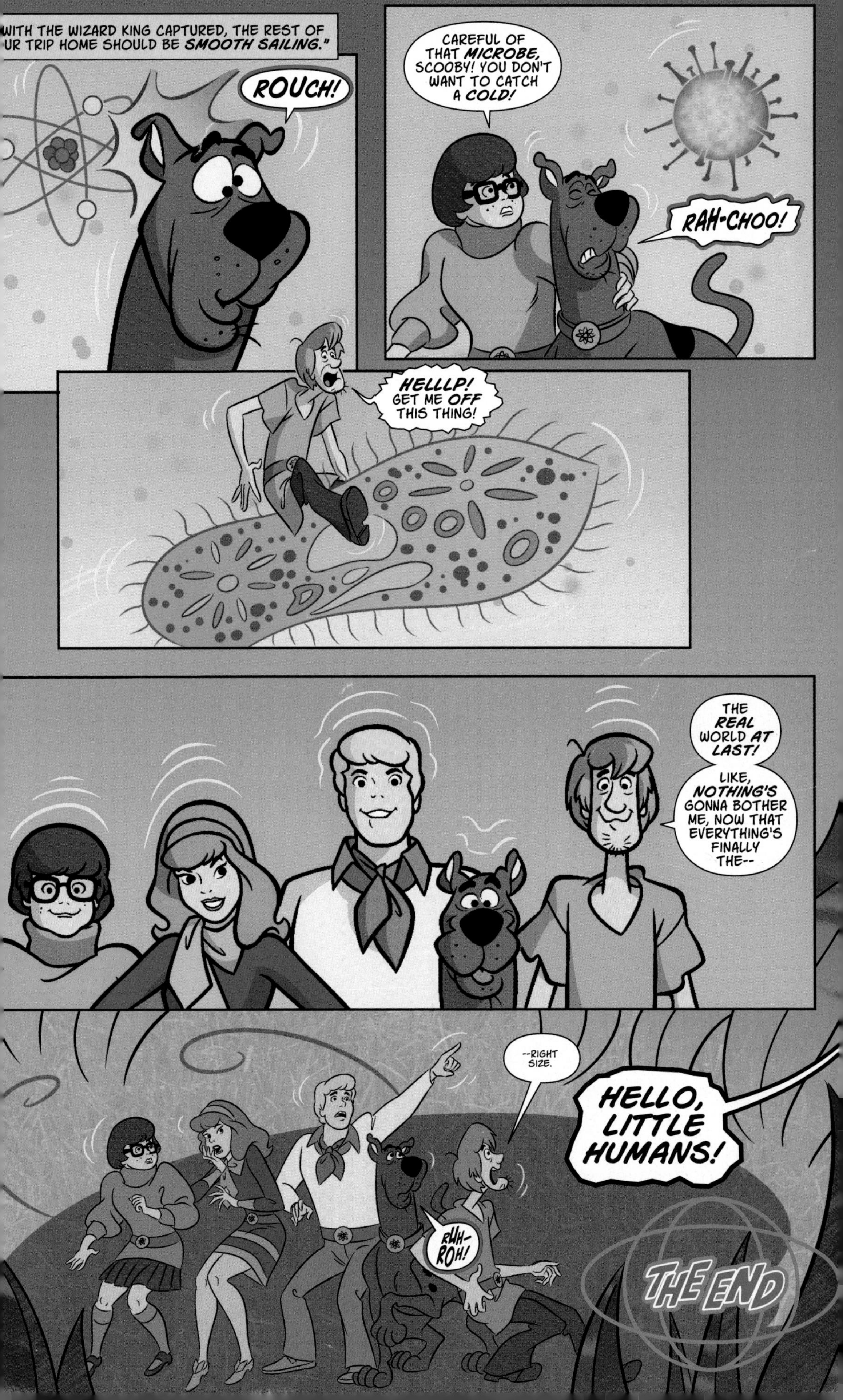

WITH THE WIZARD KING CAPTURED, THE REST OF OUR TRIP HOME SHOULD BE SMOOTH SAILING."
ROUCH!
CAREFUL OF THAT MICROBE, SCOOBY! YOU DON'T WANT TO CATCH A COLD!
RAH-CHOO!
HELLLP! GET ME OFF THIS THING!
THE REAL WORLD AT LAST!
LIKE, NOTHING'S GONNA BOTHER ME, NOW THAT EVERYTHING'S FINALLY THE--
--RIGHT SIZE.
HELLO, LITTLE HUMANS!
RUH-ROH!
THE END

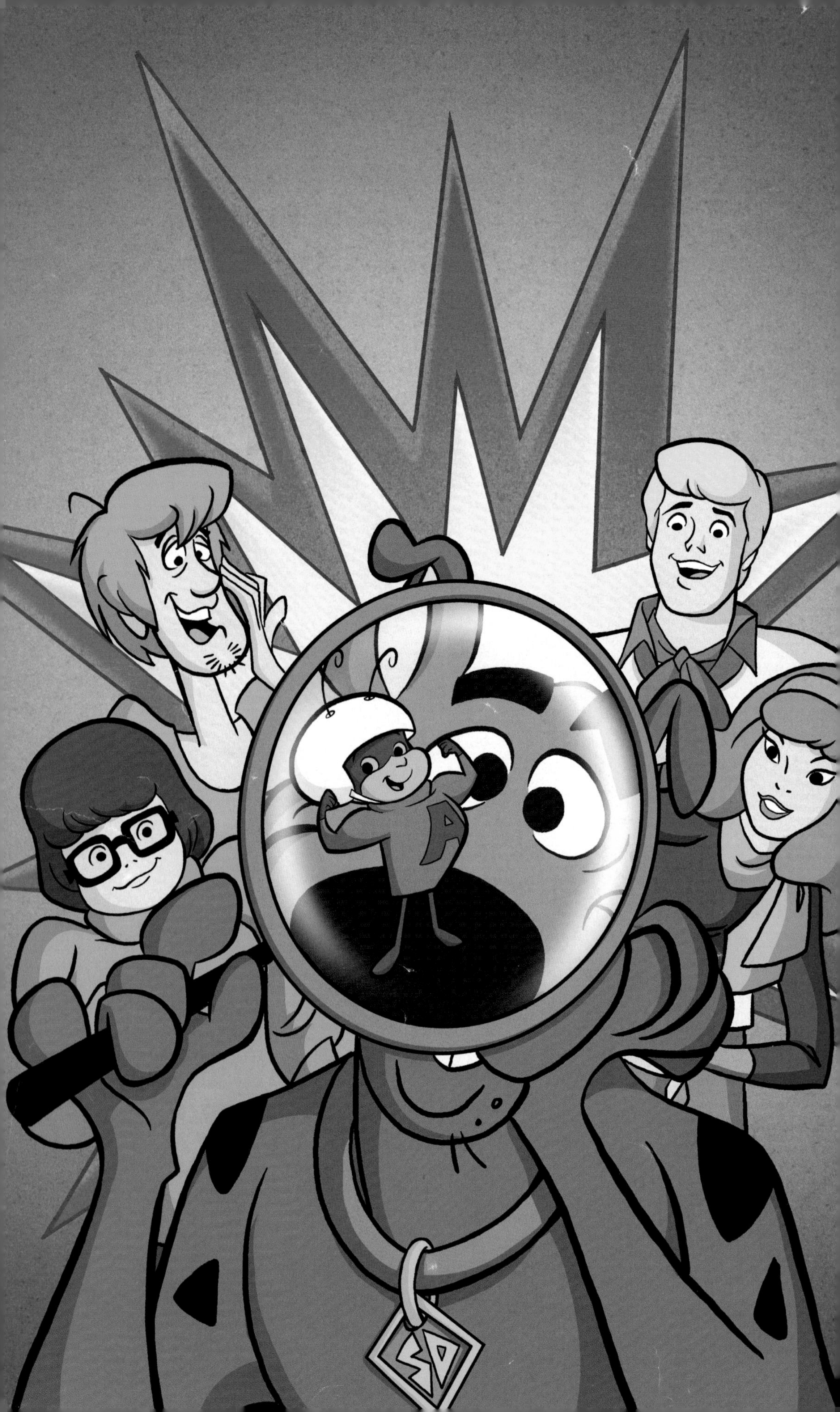

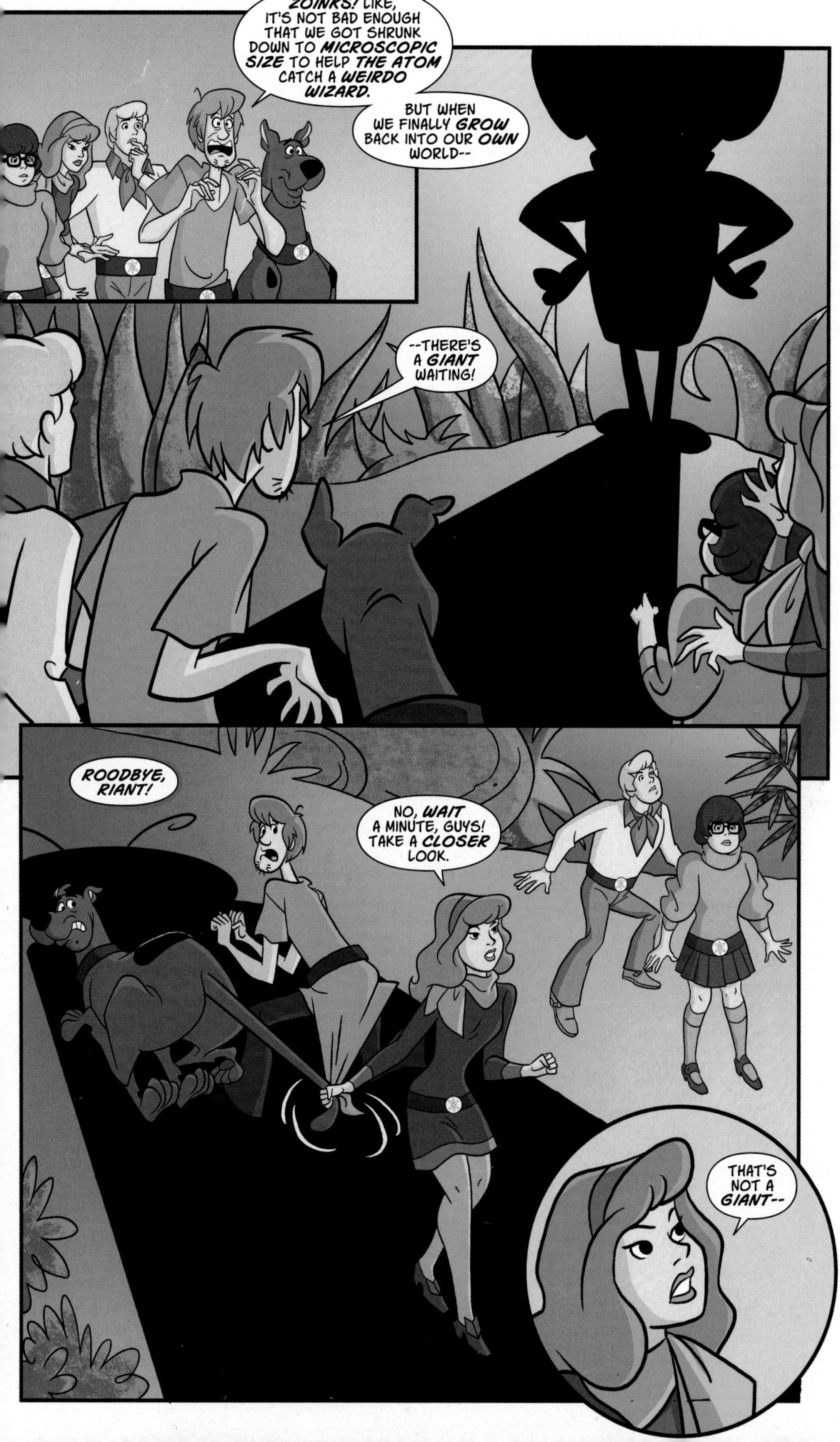
ZOINKS! LIKE, IT'S NOT BAD ENOUGH THAT WE GOT SHRUNK DOWN TO MICROSCOPIC SIZE TO HELP THE ATOM CATCH A WEIRDO WIZARD.
BUT WHEN WE FINALLY GROW BACK INTO OUR OWN WORLD--
--THERE'S A GIANT WAITING!
ROODBYE, RIANT!
NO, WAIT A MINUTE, GUYS! TAKE A CLOSER LOOK.
THAT'S NOT A GIANT--

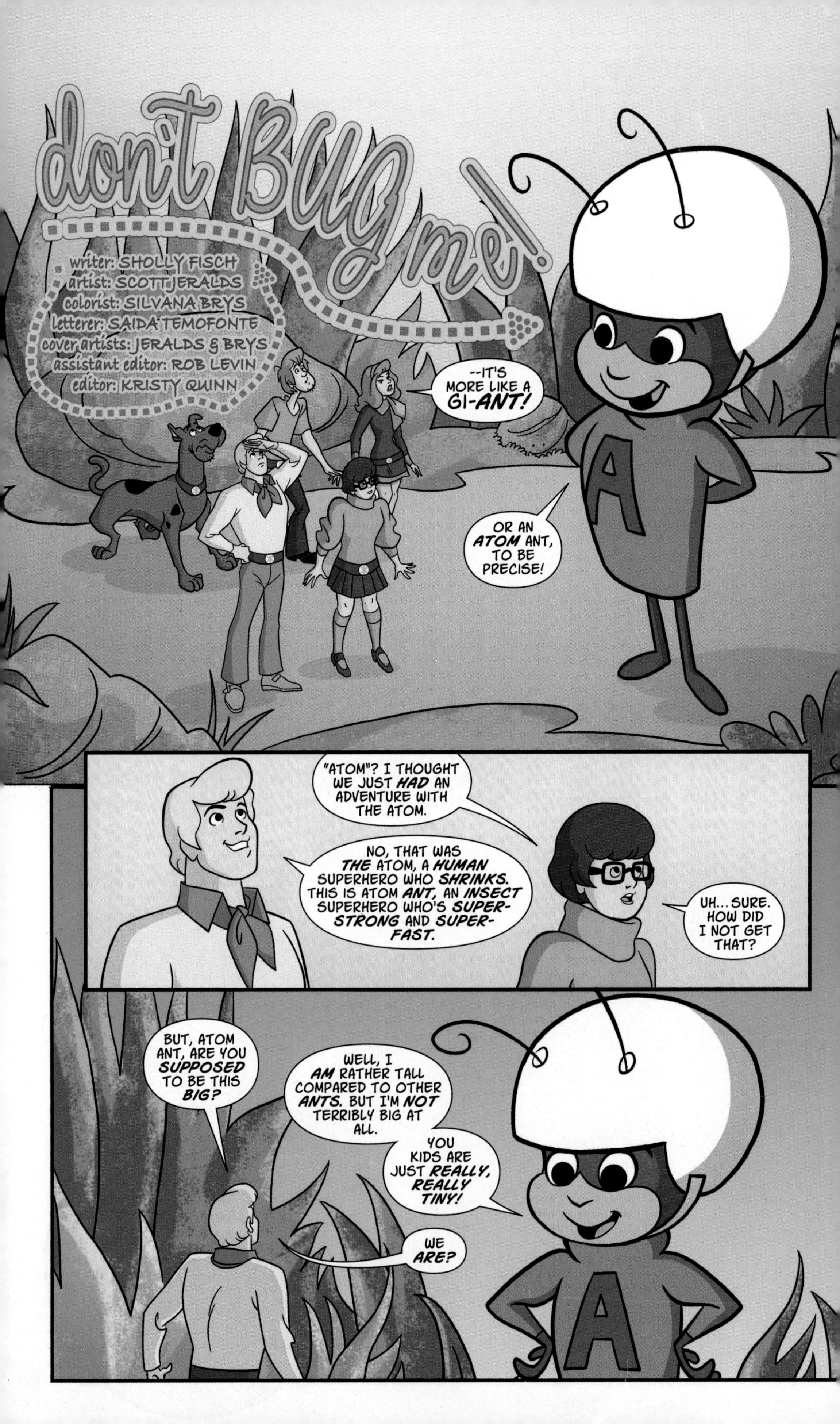
don't BUG me!
writer: SHOLLY FISCH
artist: SCOTT JERALDS
colorist: SILVANA BRYS
letterer: SAIDA TEMOFONTE
cover artists: JERALDS & BRYS
assistant editor: ROB LEVIN
editor: KRISTY QUINN
--IT'S MORE LIKE A GI-ANT!
OR AN ATOM ANT, TO BE PRECISE!
"ATOM"? I THOUGHT WE JUST HAD AN ADVENTURE WITH THE ATOM.
NO, THAT WAS THE ATOM, A HUMAN SUPERHERO WHO SHRINKS. THIS IS ATOM ANT, AN INSECT SUPERHERO WHO'S SUPER-STRONG AND SUPER-FAST.
UH... SURE. HOW DID I NOT GET THAT?
BUT, ATOM ANT, ARE YOU SUPPOSED TO BE THIS BIG?
WELL, I AM RATHER TALL COMPARED TO OTHER ANTS. BUT I'M NOT TERRIBLY BIG AT ALL.
YOU KIDS ARE JUST REALLY, REALLY TINY!
WE ARE?

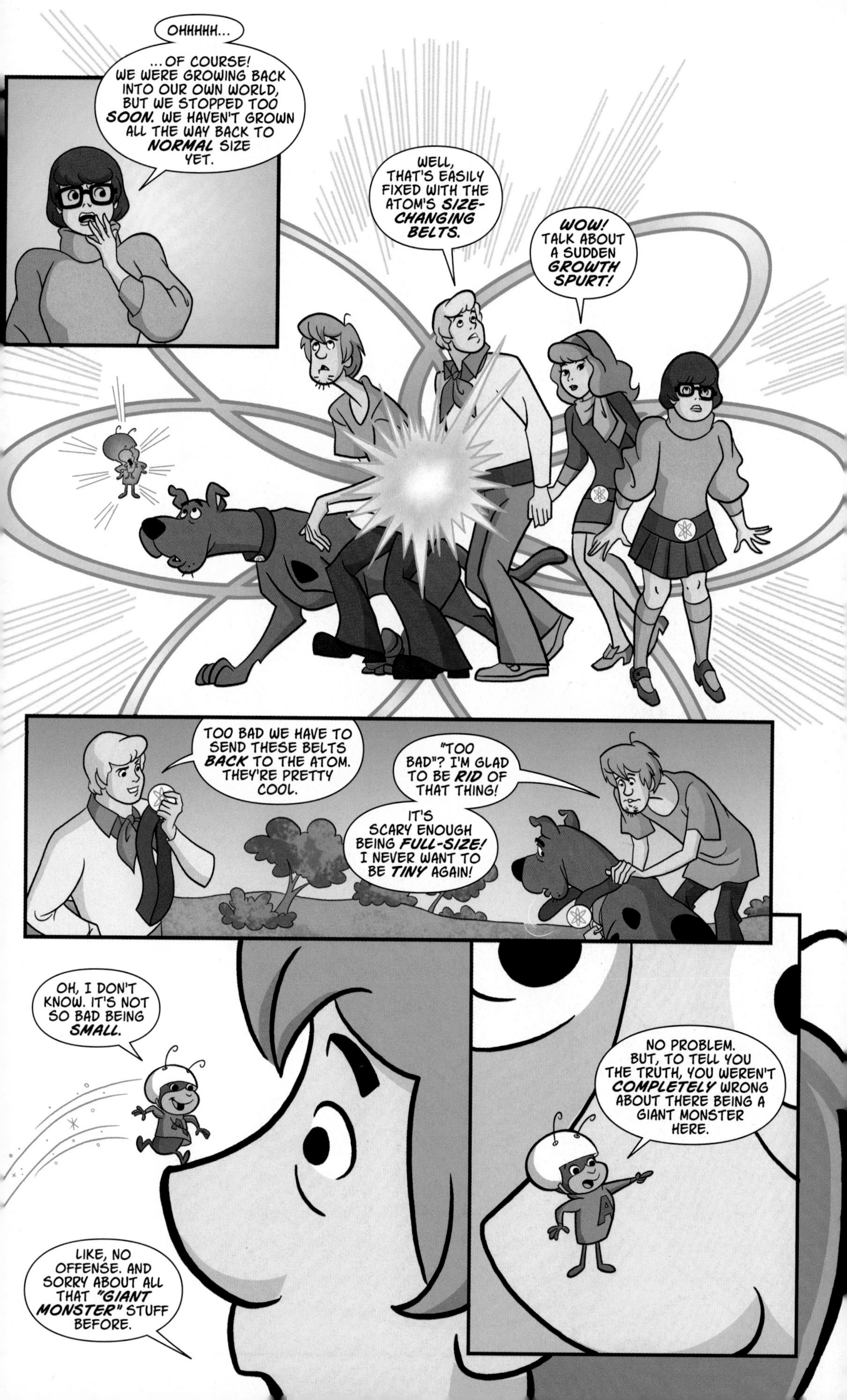
OHHHHH...
...OF COURSE! WE WERE GROWING BACK INTO OUR OWN WORLD, BUT WE STOPPED TOO SOON. WE HAVEN'T GROWN ALL THE WAY BACK TO NORMAL SIZE YET.
WELL, THAT'S EASILY FIXED WITH THE ATOM'S SIZE-CHANGING BELTS.
WOW! TALK ABOUT A SUDDEN GROWTH SPURT!
TOO BAD WE HAVE TO SEND THESE BELTS BACK TO THE ATOM. THEY'RE PRETTY COOL.
"TOO BAD"? I'M GLAD TO BE RID OF THAT THING!
IT'S SCARY ENOUGH BEING FULL-SIZE! I NEVER WANT TO BE TINY AGAIN!
OH, I DON'T KNOW. IT'S NOT SO BAD BEING SMALL.
LIKE, NO OFFENSE. AND SORRY ABOUT ALL THAT "GIANT MONSTER" STUFF BEFORE.
NO PROBLEM. BUT, TO TELL YOU THE TRUTH, YOU WEREN'T COMPLETELY WRONG ABOUT THERE BEING A GIANT MONSTER HERE.

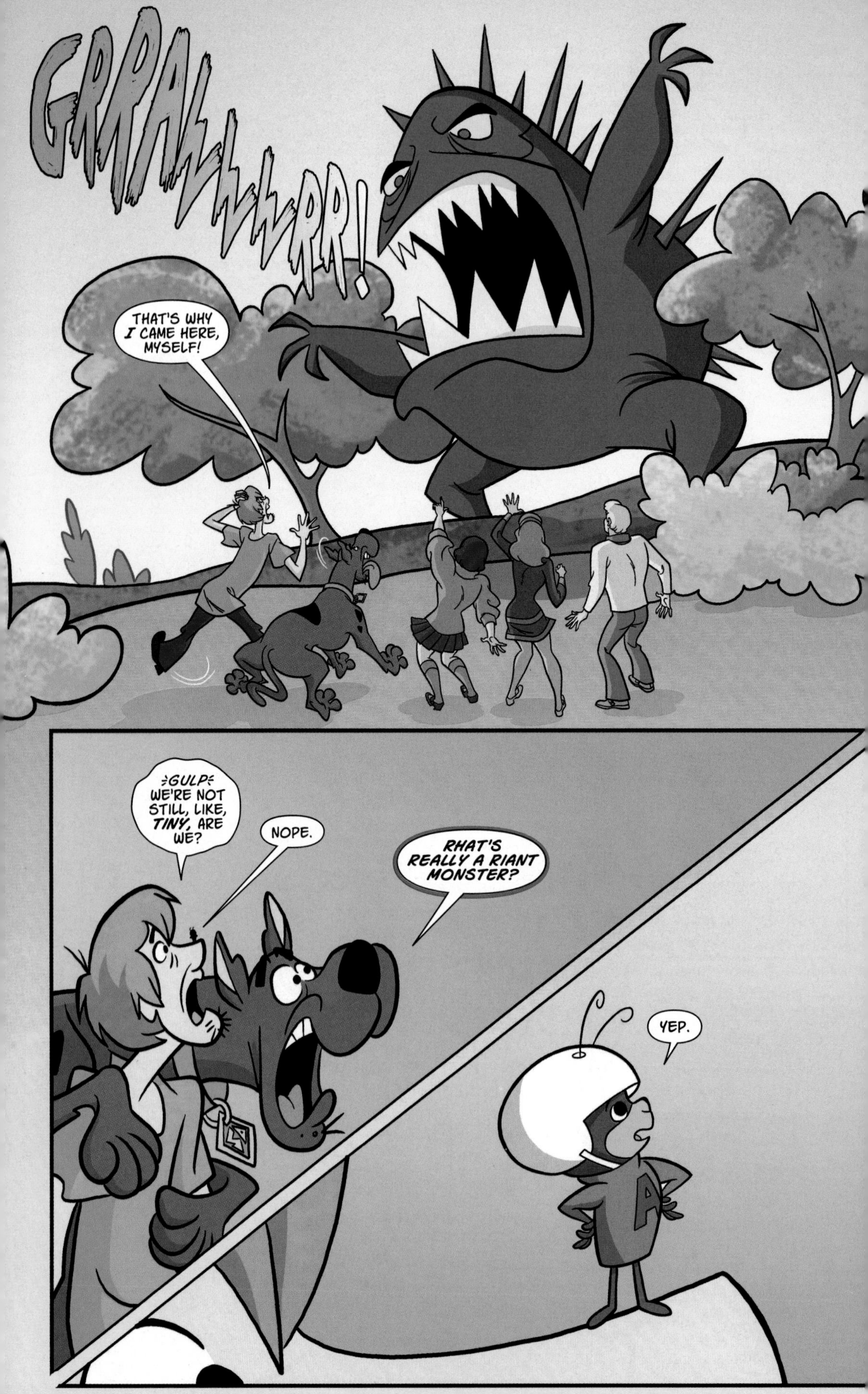
GRRAWWLRR!
THAT'S WHY I CAME HERE, MYSELF!
GULP WE'RE NOT STILL, LIKE, TINY, ARE WE?
NOPE.
RHAT'S REALLY A RIANT MONSTER?
YEP.

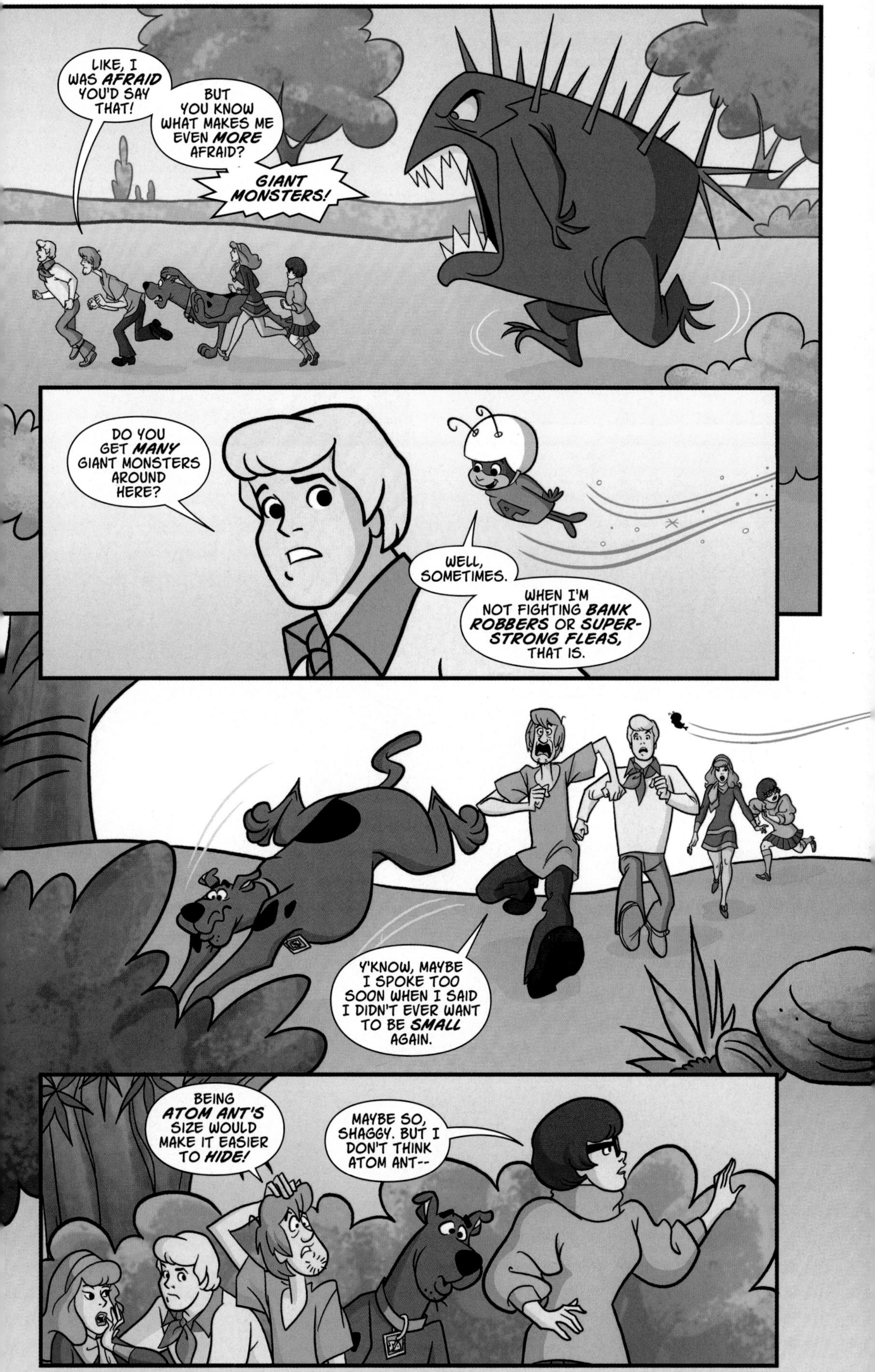

LIKE, I WAS AFRAID YOU'D SAY THAT!
BUT YOU KNOW WHAT MAKES ME EVEN MORE AFRAID?
GIANT MONSTERS!
DO YOU GET MANY GIANT MONSTERS AROUND HERE?
WELL, SOMETIMES.
WHEN I'M NOT FIGHTING BANK ROBBERS OR SUPER-STRONG FLEAS, THAT IS.
Y'KNOW, MAYBE I SPOKE TOO SOON WHEN I SAID I DIDN'T EVER WANT TO BE SMALL AGAIN.
BEING ATOM ANT'S SIZE WOULD MAKE IT EASIER TO HIDE!
MAYBE SO, SHAGGY. BUT I DON'T THINK ATOM ANT--

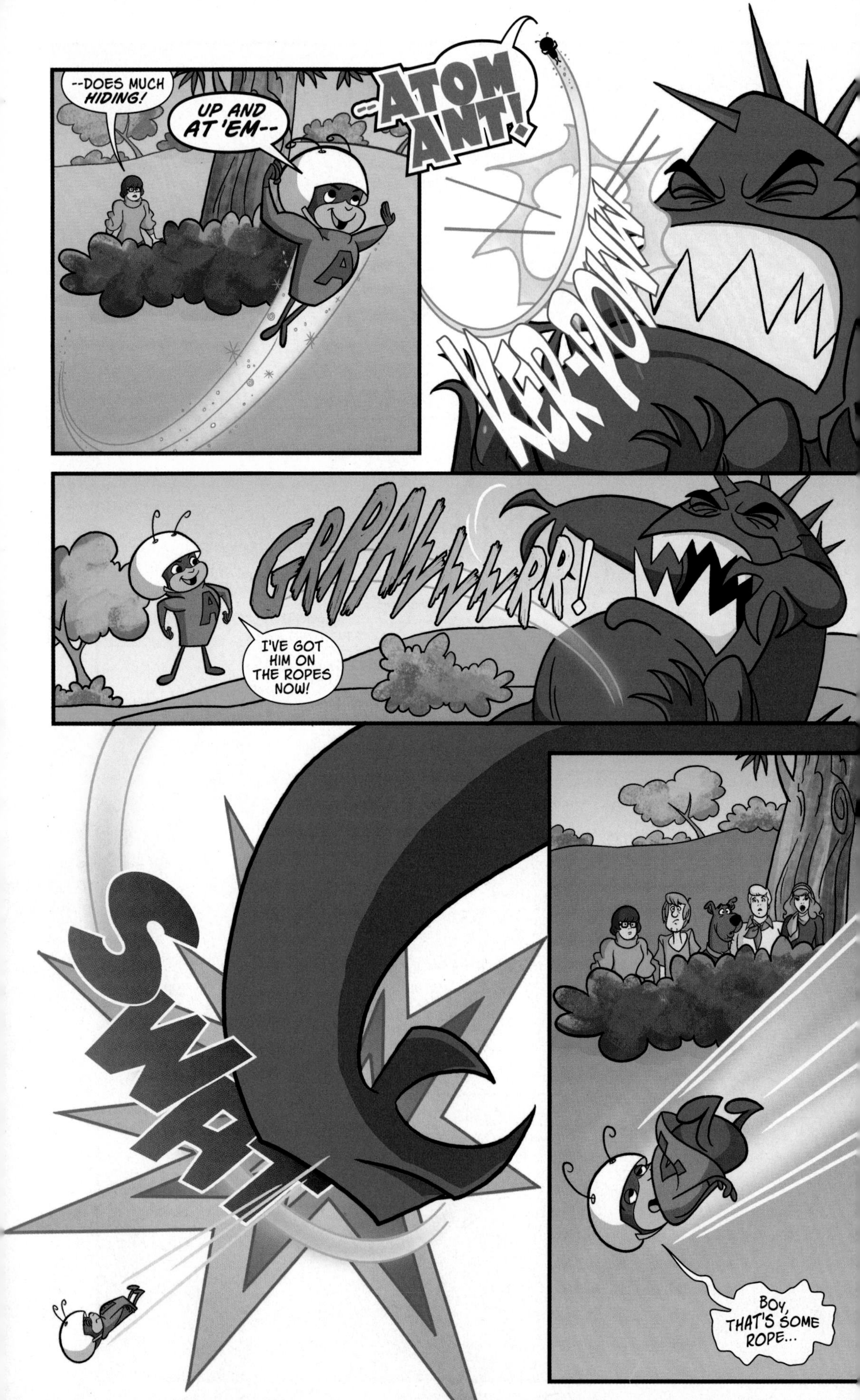
--DOES MUCH HIDING!
UP AND AT 'EM--
--ATOM ANT!
KER-POW!
GRRAWWRR!
I'VE GOT HIM ON THE ROPES NOW!
SWAK!
BOY, THAT'S SOME ROPE...

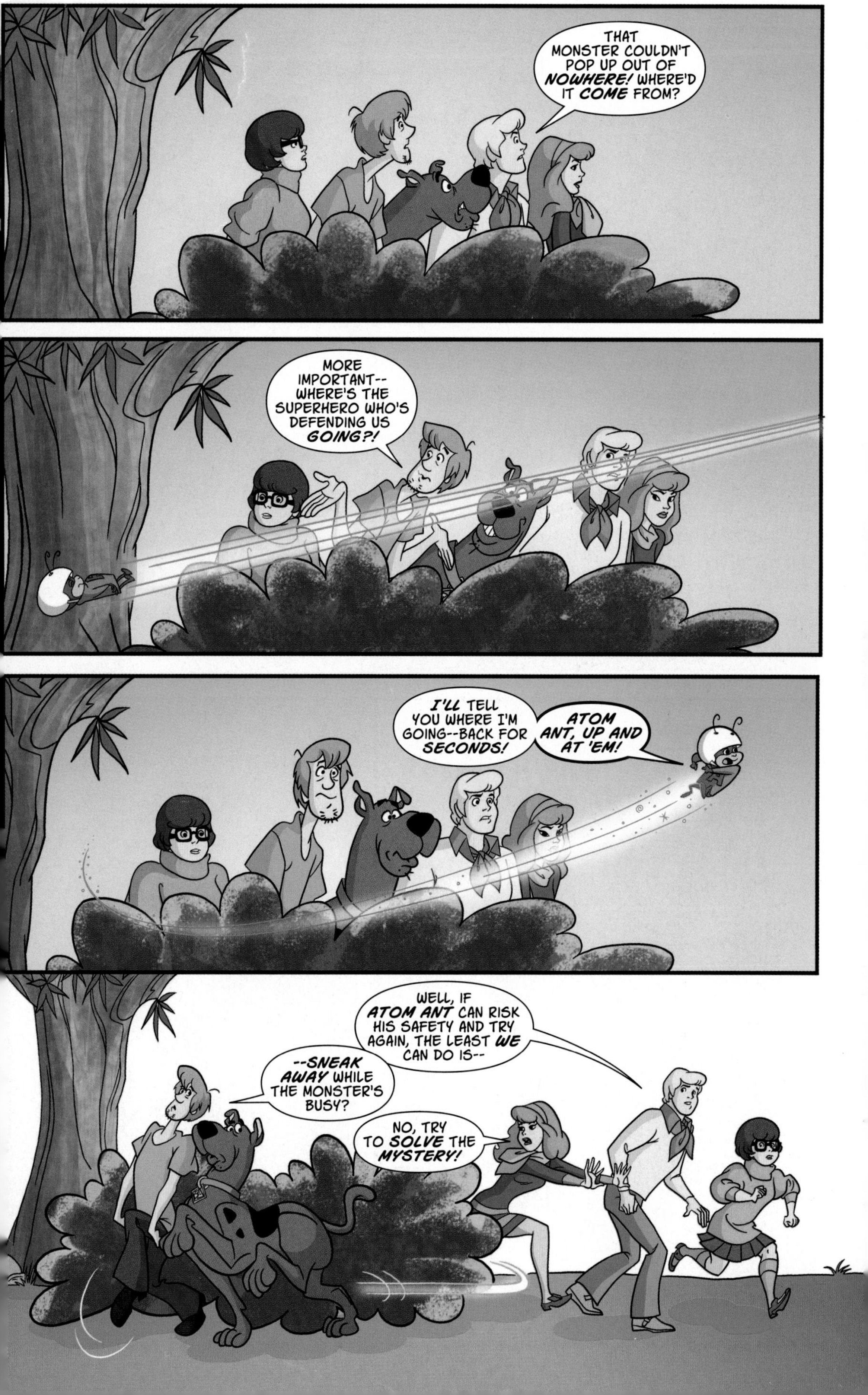
THAT MONSTER COULDN'T POP UP OUT OF NOWHERE! WHERE'D IT COME FROM?
MORE IMPORTANT--WHERE'S THE SUPERHERO WHO'S DEFENDING US GOING?!
I'LL TELL YOU WHERE I'M GOING--BACK FOR SECONDS!
ATOM ANT, UP AND AT 'EM!
WELL, IF ATOM ANT CAN RISK HIS SAFETY AND TRY AGAIN, THE LEAST WE CAN DO IS--
--SNEAK AWAY WHILE THE MONSTER'S BUSY?
NO, TRY TO SOLVE THE MYSTERY!

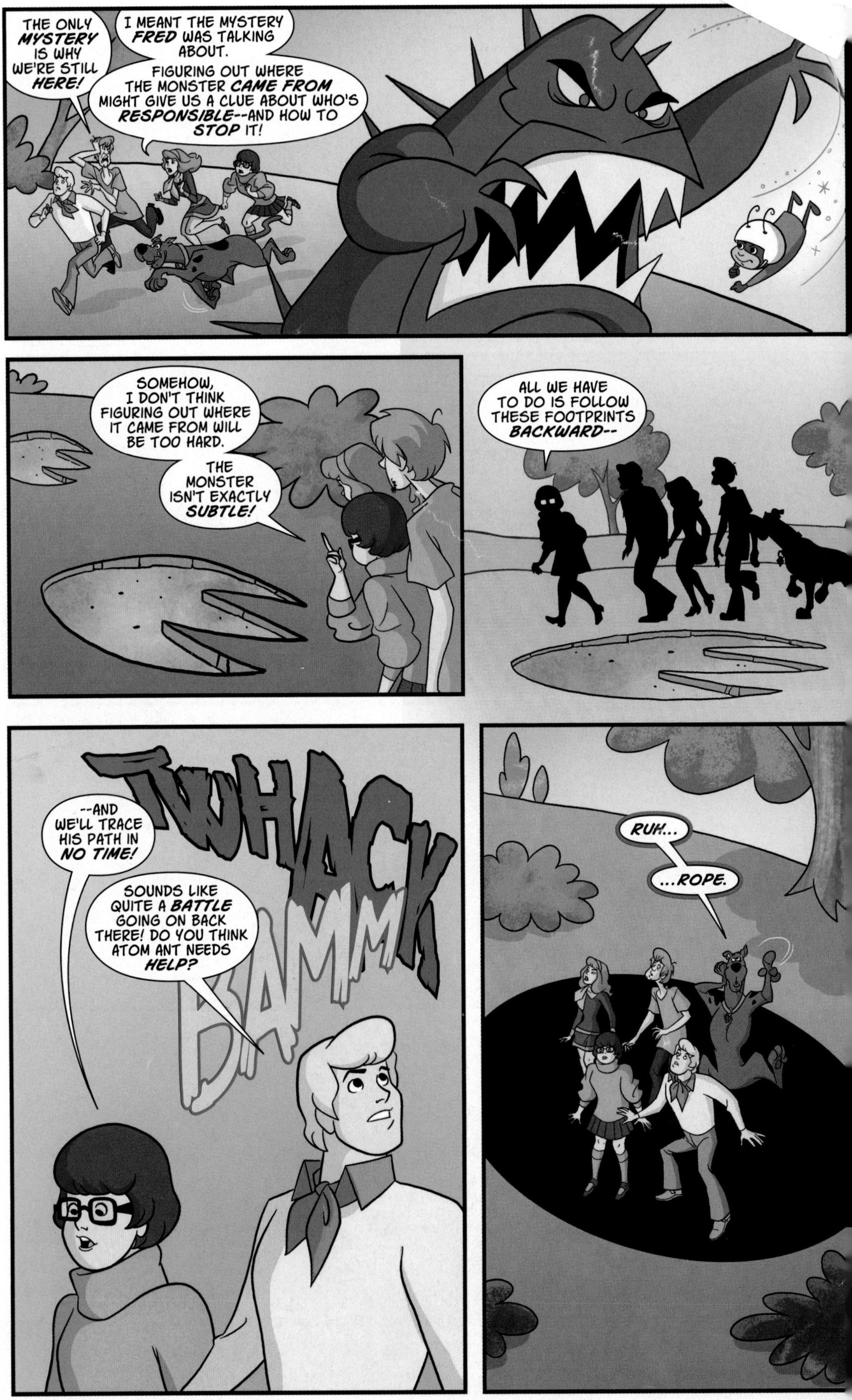

THE ONLY MYSTERY IS WHY WE'RE STILL HERE!
I MEANT THE MYSTERY FRED WAS TALKING ABOUT.
FIGURING OUT WHERE THE MONSTER CAME FROM MIGHT GIVE US A CLUE ABOUT WHO'S RESPONSIBLE--AND HOW TO STOP IT!
SOMEHOW, I DON'T THINK FIGURING OUT WHERE IT CAME FROM WILL BE TOO HARD.
THE MONSTER ISN'T EXACTLY SUBTLE!
ALL WE HAVE TO DO IS FOLLOW THESE FOOTPRINTS BACKWARD--
TWHACK
BLAMMM
--AND WE'LL TRACE HIS PATH IN NO TIME!
SOUNDS LIKE QUITE A BATTLE GOING ON BACK THERE! DO YOU THINK ATOM ANT NEEDS HELP?
RUH...
...ROPE.

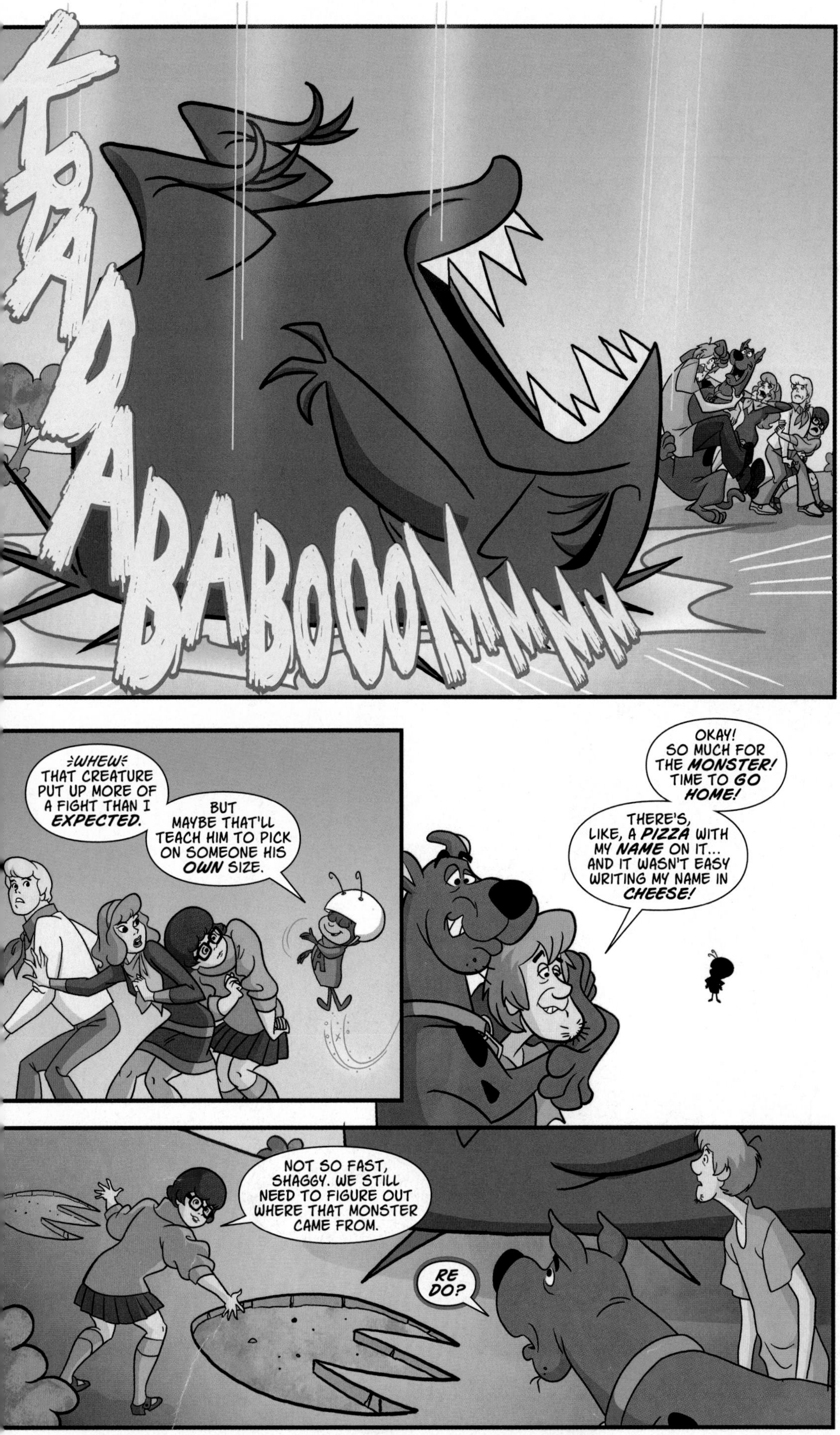
KRADABABOOOMMMM
≶WHEW≶ THAT CREATURE PUT UP MORE OF A FIGHT THAN I EXPECTED.
BUT MAYBE THAT'LL TEACH HIM TO PICK ON SOMEONE HIS OWN SIZE.
OKAY! SO MUCH FOR THE MONSTER! TIME TO GO HOME!
THERE'S, LIKE, A PIZZA WITH MY NAME ON IT... AND IT WASN'T EASY WRITING MY NAME IN CHEESE!
NOT SO FAST, SHAGGY. WE STILL NEED TO FIGURE OUT WHERE THAT MONSTER CAME FROM.
RE DO?

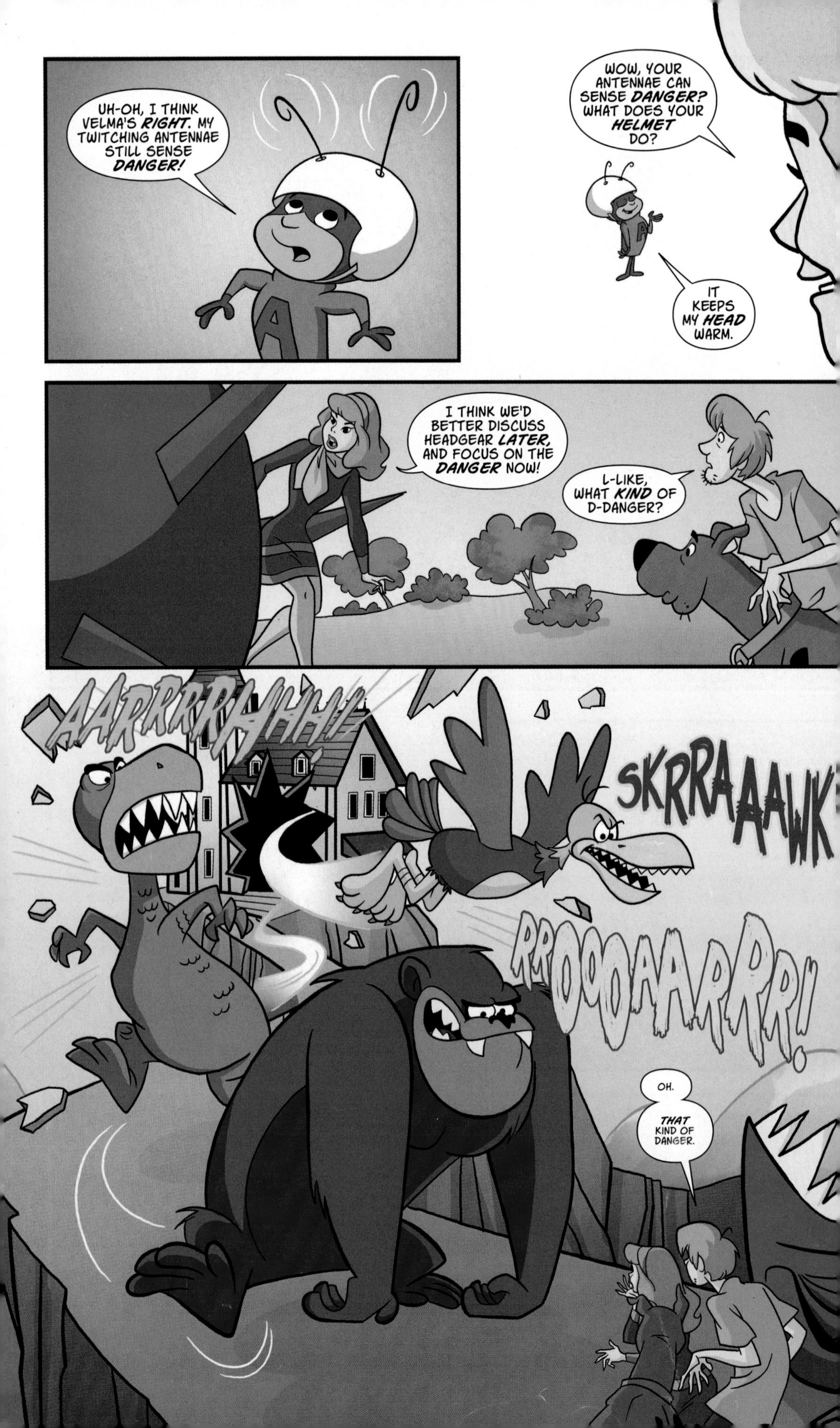
UH-OH, I THINK VELMA'S **RIGHT.** MY TWITCHING ANTENNAE STILL SENSE **DANGER!**
WOW, YOUR ANTENNAE CAN SENSE **DANGER?** WHAT DOES YOUR **HELMET** DO?
IT KEEPS MY **HEAD** WARM.
I THINK WE'D BETTER DISCUSS HEADGEAR **LATER,** AND FOCUS ON THE **DANGER** NOW!
L-LIKE, WHAT **KIND** OF D-DANGER?
AARRRRAHHH!
SKRRAAAWK
RROOOAARRR!
OH.
THAT KIND OF DANGER.

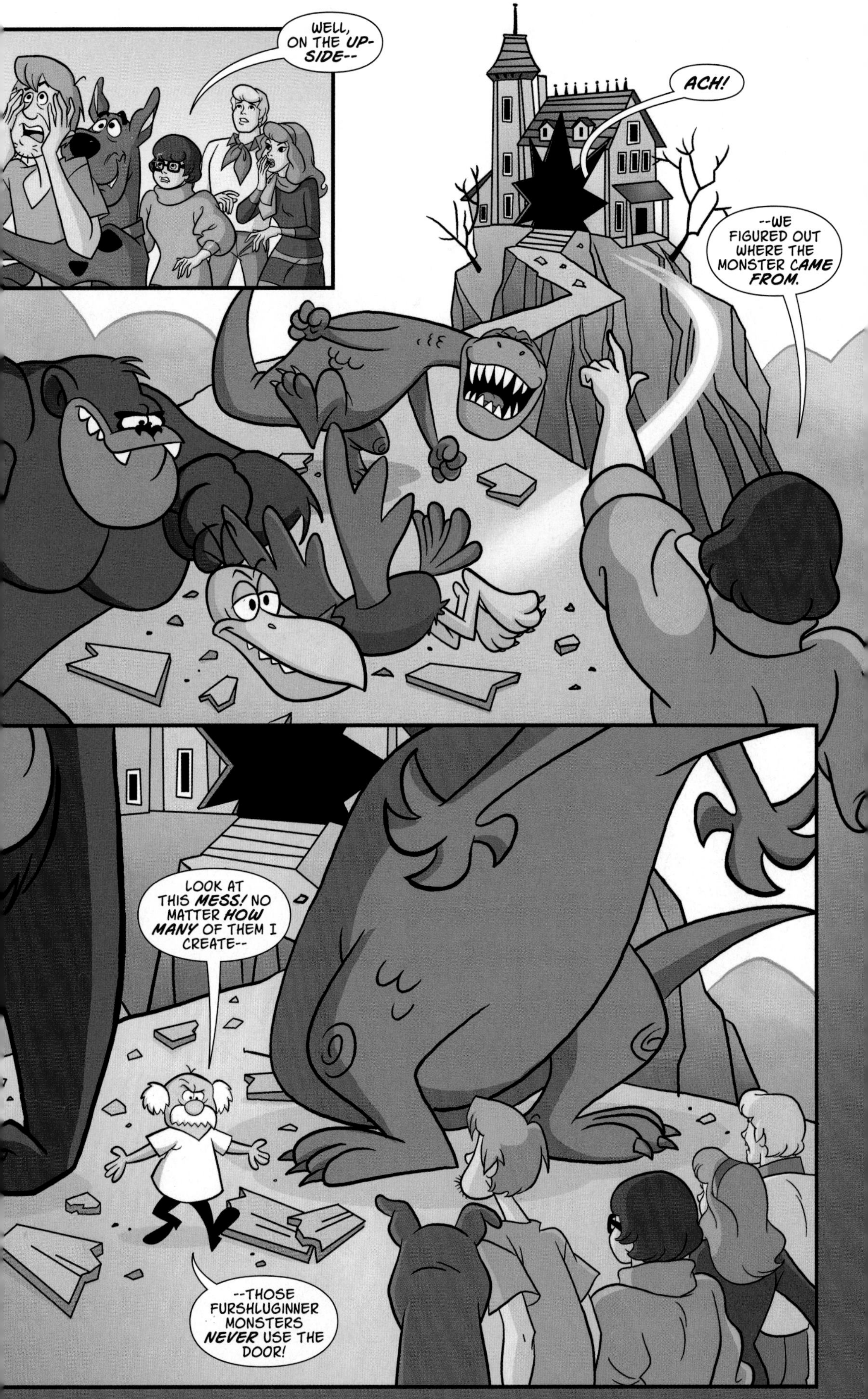

WELL, ON THE UP-SIDE--
ACH!
--WE FIGURED OUT WHERE THE MONSTER CAME FROM.
LOOK AT THIS MESS! NO MATTER HOW MANY OF THEM I CREATE--
--THOSE FURSHLUGINNER MONSTERS NEVER USE THE DOOR!

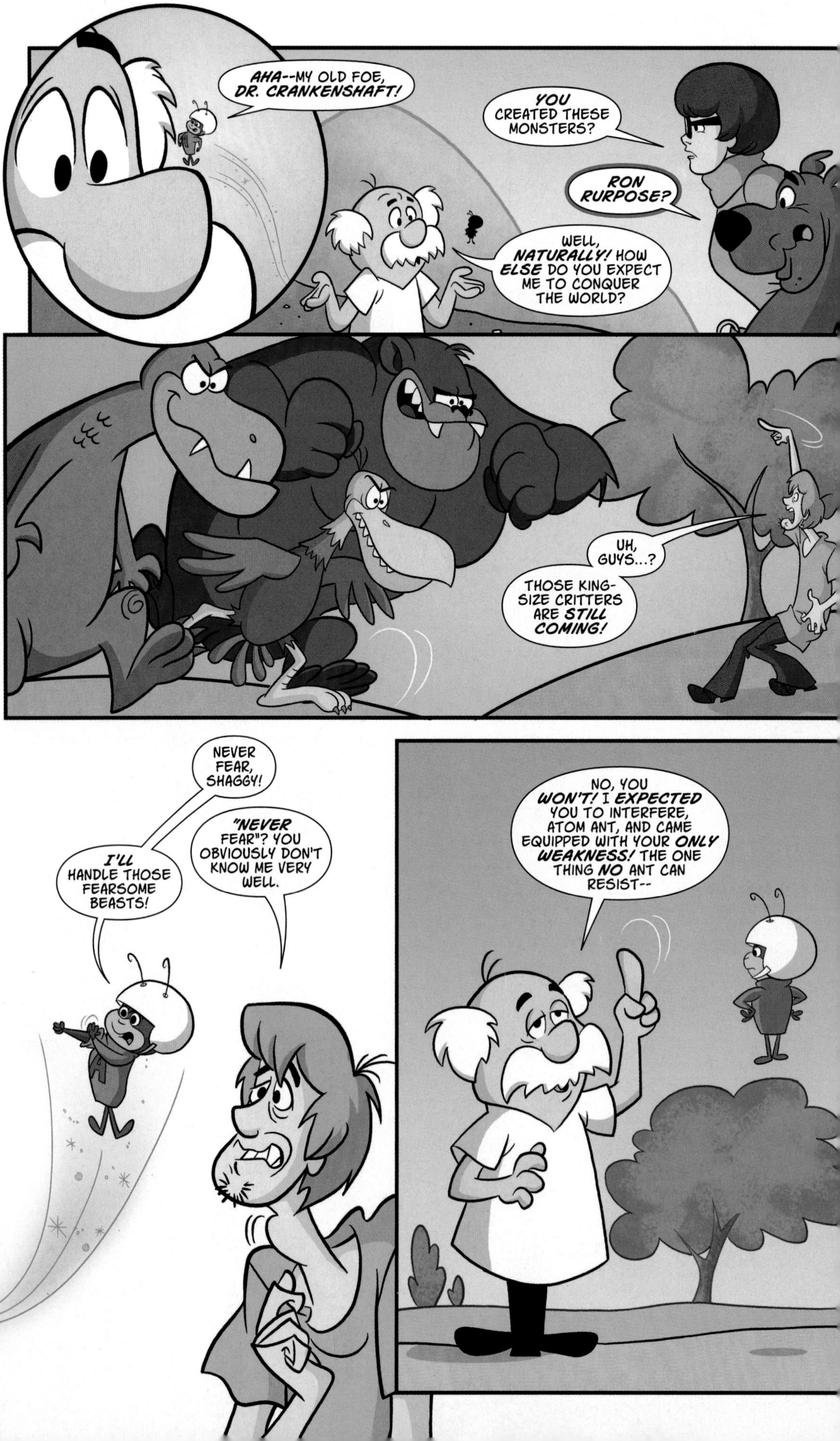
AHA--MY OLD FOE, DR. CRANKENSHAFT!
YOU CREATED THESE MONSTERS?
RON RURPOSE?
WELL, NATURALLY! HOW ELSE DO YOU EXPECT ME TO CONQUER THE WORLD?
UH, GUYS...?
THOSE KING-SIZE CRITTERS ARE STILL COMING!
NEVER FEAR, SHAGGY!
I'LL HANDLE THOSE FEARSOME BEASTS!
"NEVER FEAR"? YOU OBVIOUSLY DON'T KNOW ME VERY WELL.
NO, YOU WON'T! I EXPECTED YOU TO INTERFERE, ATOM ANT, AND CAME EQUIPPED WITH YOUR ONLY WEAKNESS! THE ONE THING NO ANT CAN RESIST--

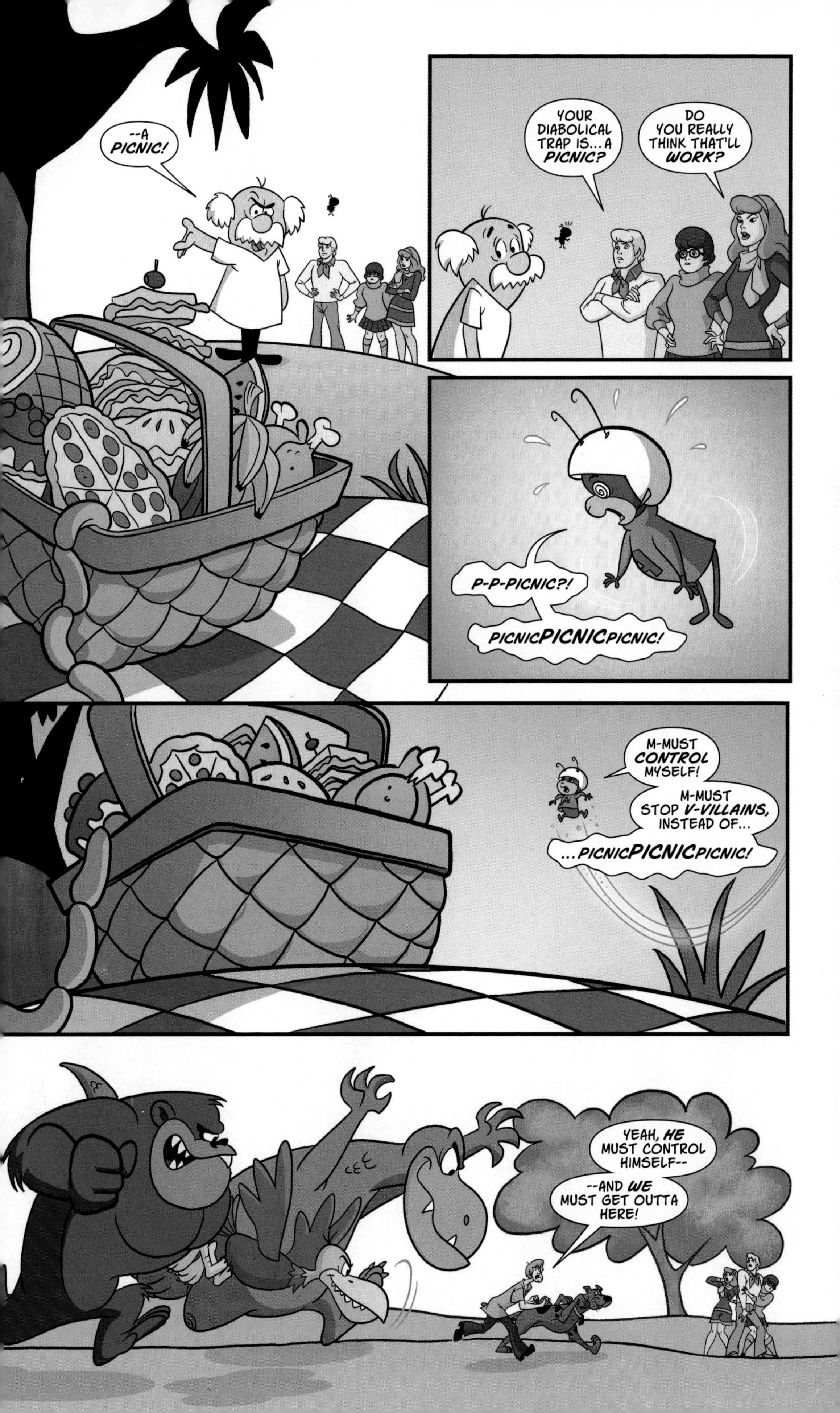
--A PICNIC!
YOUR DIABOLICAL TRAP IS... A PICNIC?
DO YOU REALLY THINK THAT'LL WORK?
P-P-PICNIC?!
PICNICPICNICPICNIC!
M-MUST CONTROL MYSELF!
M-MUST STOP V-VILLAINS, INSTEAD OF...
...PICNICPICNICPICNIC!
YEAH, HE MUST CONTROL HIMSELF--
--AND WE MUST GET OUTTA HERE!

NO RICNIC?

I'LL BE SATISFIED IF THOSE CREATURES DON'T MAKE A PICNIC OUT OF *US!*

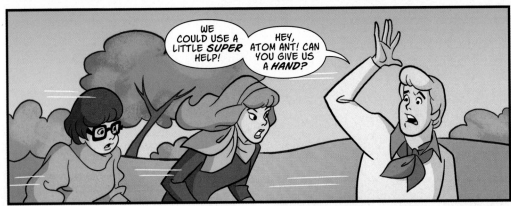

WE COULD USE A LITTLE *SUPER* HELP!

HEY, ATOM ANT! CAN YOU GIVE US A *HAND?*

picnic*PICNIC*picnic!

IT'S *NO USE!* HE'S STILL *MESMERIZED* BY THE SIGHT OF THAT *PICNIC!*

MESMERIZED BY *FOOD?* WE KNOW HOW TO FIX *THAT!* RIGHT, SCOOB?

RUH-HUH!

C'MON, BUDDY!

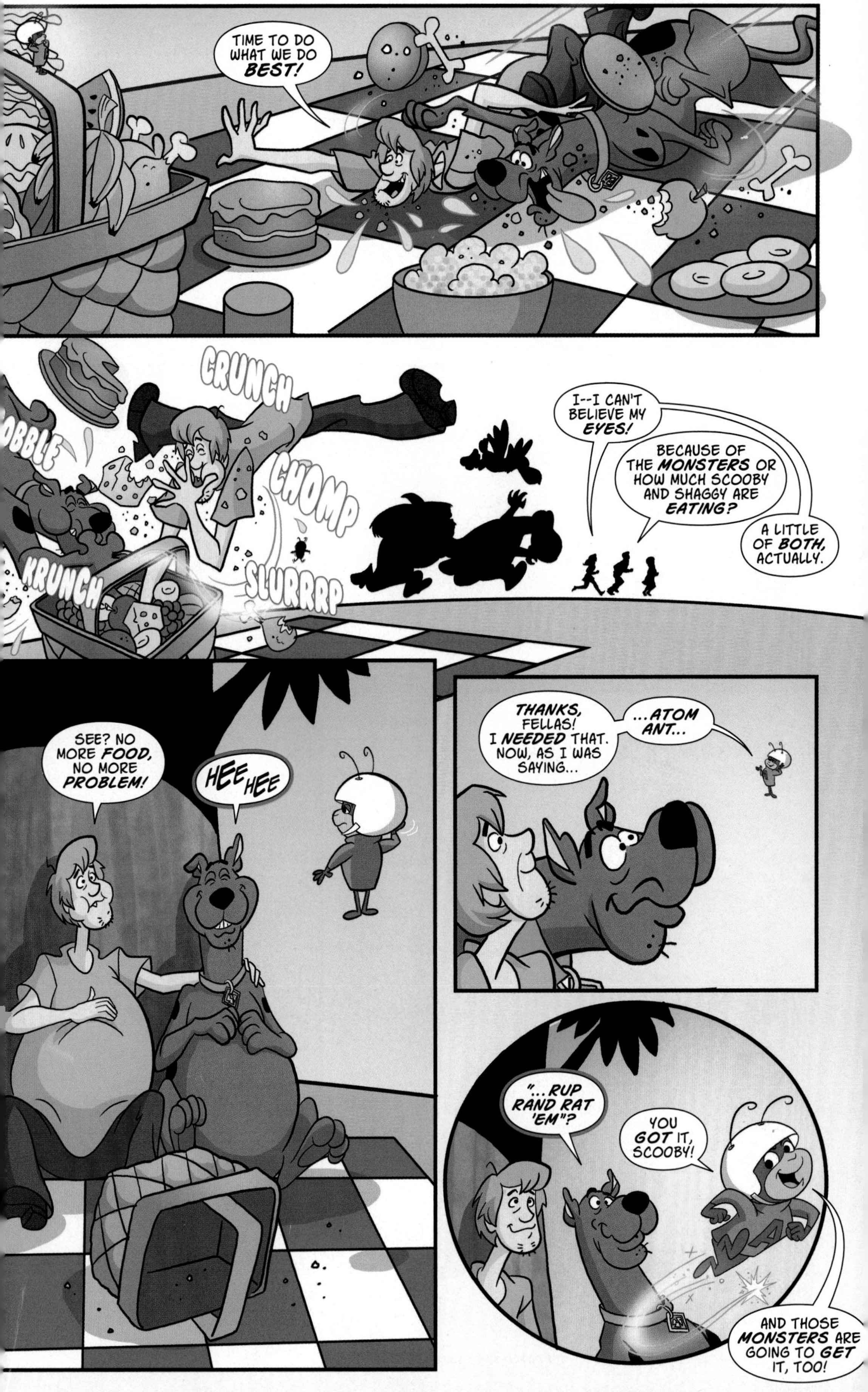
TIME TO DO WHAT WE DO BEST!
CRUNCH
GOBBLE
CHOMP
KRUNCH
SLURRRP
I--I CAN'T BELIEVE MY EYES!
BECAUSE OF THE MONSTERS OR HOW MUCH SCOOBY AND SHAGGY ARE EATING?
A LITTLE OF BOTH, ACTUALLY.
SEE? NO MORE FOOD, NO MORE PROBLEM!
HEE HEE
THANKS, FELLAS! I NEEDED THAT. NOW, AS I WAS SAYING...
...ATOM ANT...
"...RUP RAND RAT 'EM"?
YOU GOT IT, SCOOBY!
AND THOSE MONSTERS ARE GOING TO GET IT, TOO!

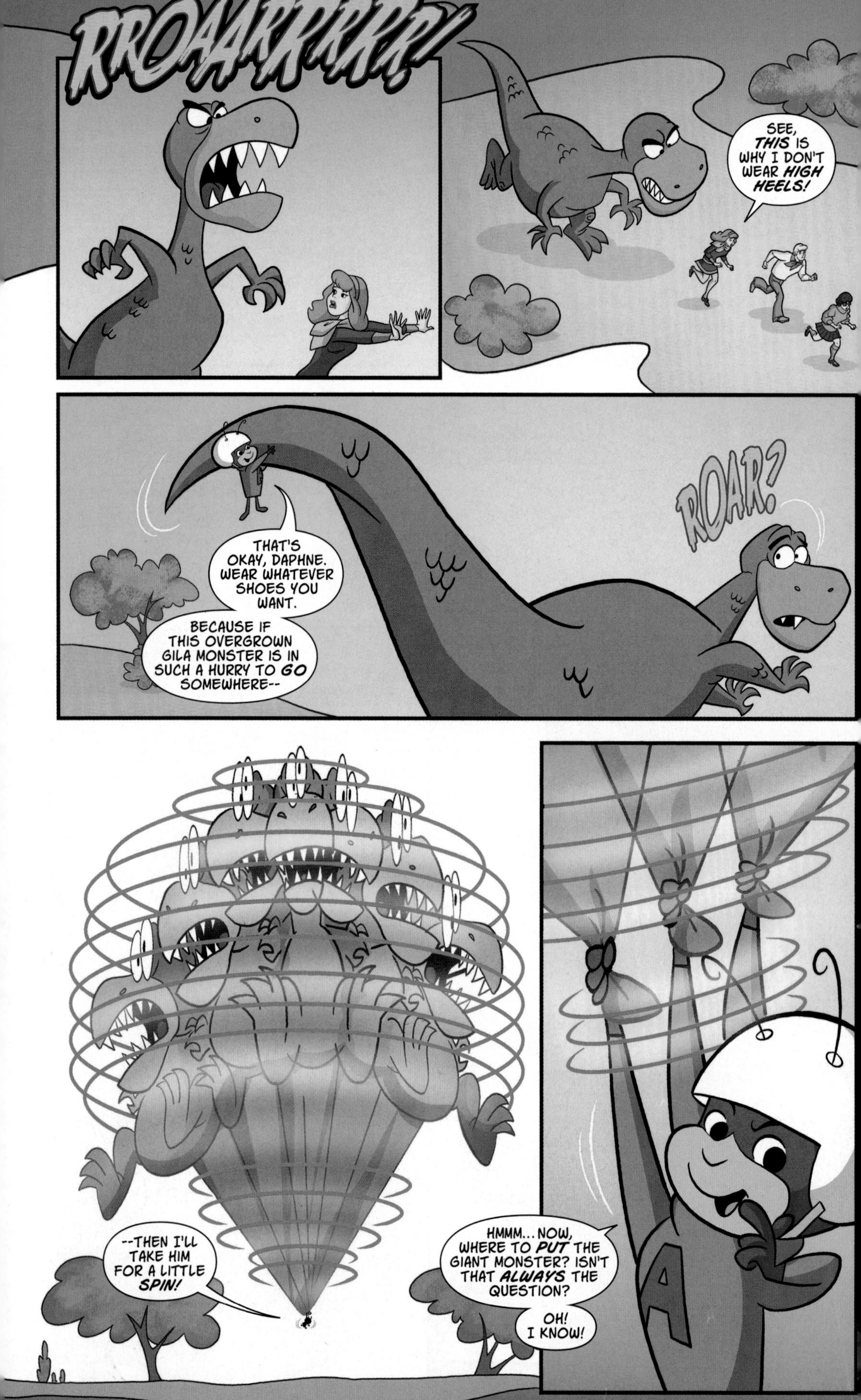
RROAARRRRR!
SEE, THIS IS WHY I DON'T WEAR HIGH HEELS!
THAT'S OKAY, DAPHNE. WEAR WHATEVER SHOES YOU WANT.
BECAUSE IF THIS OVERGROWN GILA MONSTER IS IN SUCH A HURRY TO GO SOMEWHERE--
ROAR?
--THEN I'LL TAKE HIM FOR A LITTLE SPIN!
HMMM... NOW, WHERE TO PUT THE GIANT MONSTER? ISN'T THAT ALWAYS THE QUESTION?
OH! I KNOW!
A

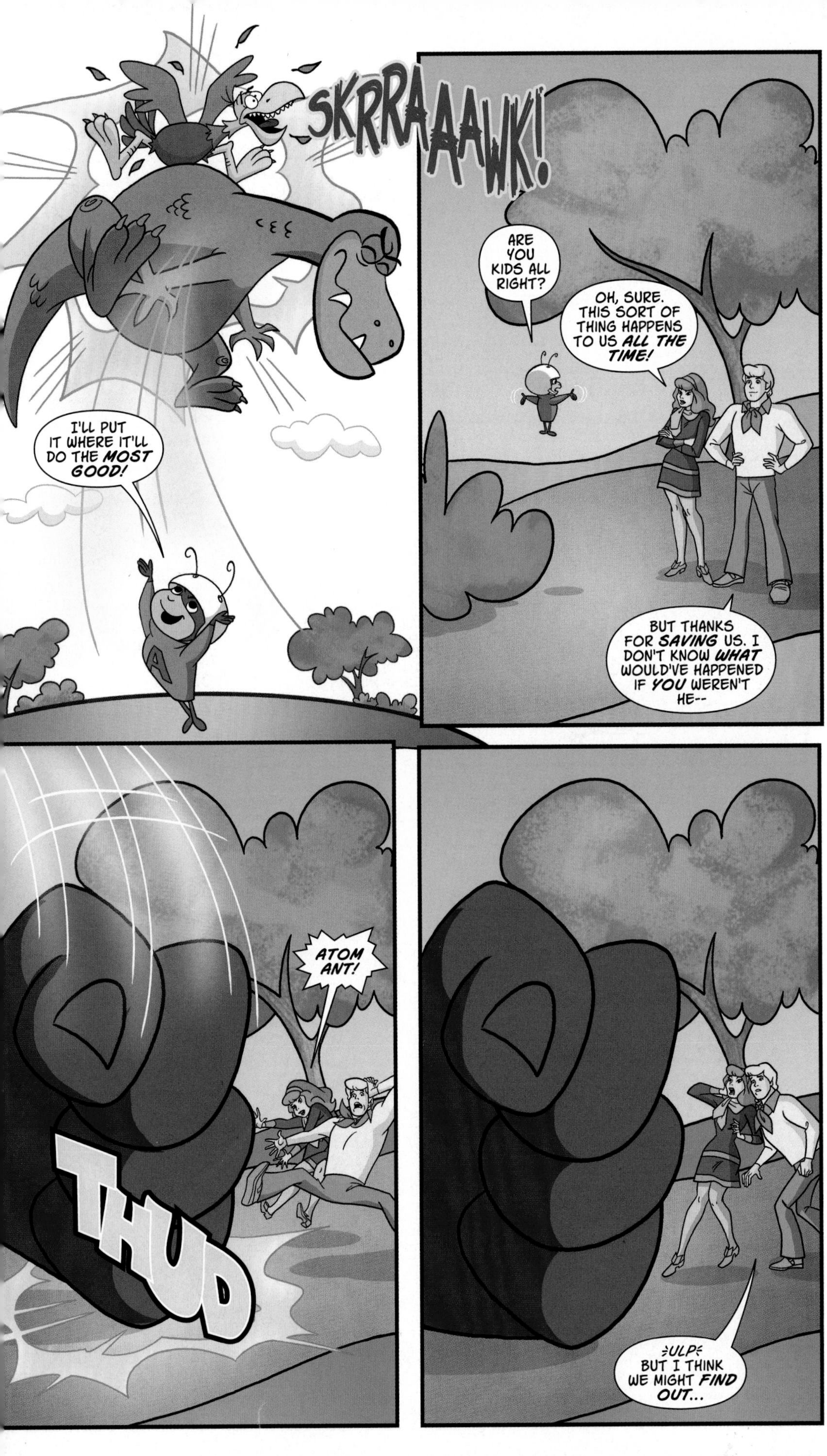
SKRRAAAWK!
I'LL PUT IT WHERE IT'LL DO THE MOST GOOD!
ARE YOU KIDS ALL RIGHT?
OH, SURE. THIS SORT OF THING HAPPENS TO US ALL THE TIME!
BUT THANKS FOR SAVING US. I DON'T KNOW WHAT WOULD'VE HAPPENED IF YOU WEREN'T HE--
ATOM ANT!
THUD
ULP
BUT I THINK WE MIGHT FIND OUT...

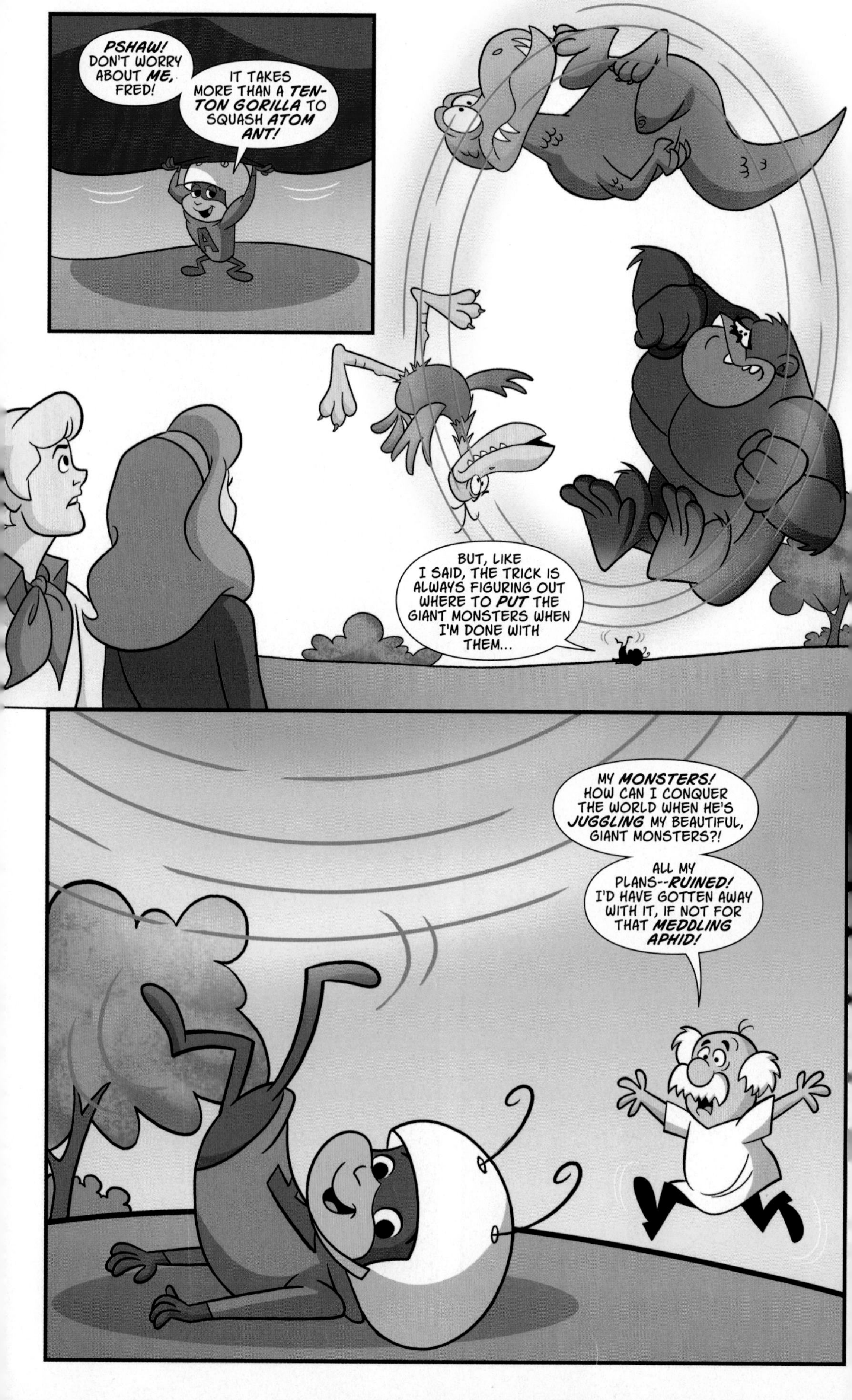
PSHAW! DON'T WORRY ABOUT ME, FRED!
IT TAKES MORE THAN A TEN-TON GORILLA TO SQUASH ATOM ANT!
BUT, LIKE I SAID, THE TRICK IS ALWAYS FIGURING OUT WHERE TO PUT THE GIANT MONSTERS WHEN I'M DONE WITH THEM...
MY MONSTERS! HOW CAN I CONQUER THE WORLD WHEN HE'S JUGGLING MY BEAUTIFUL, GIANT MONSTERS?!
ALL MY PLANS--RUINED! I'D HAVE GOTTEN AWAY WITH IT, IF NOT FOR THAT MEDDLING APHID!

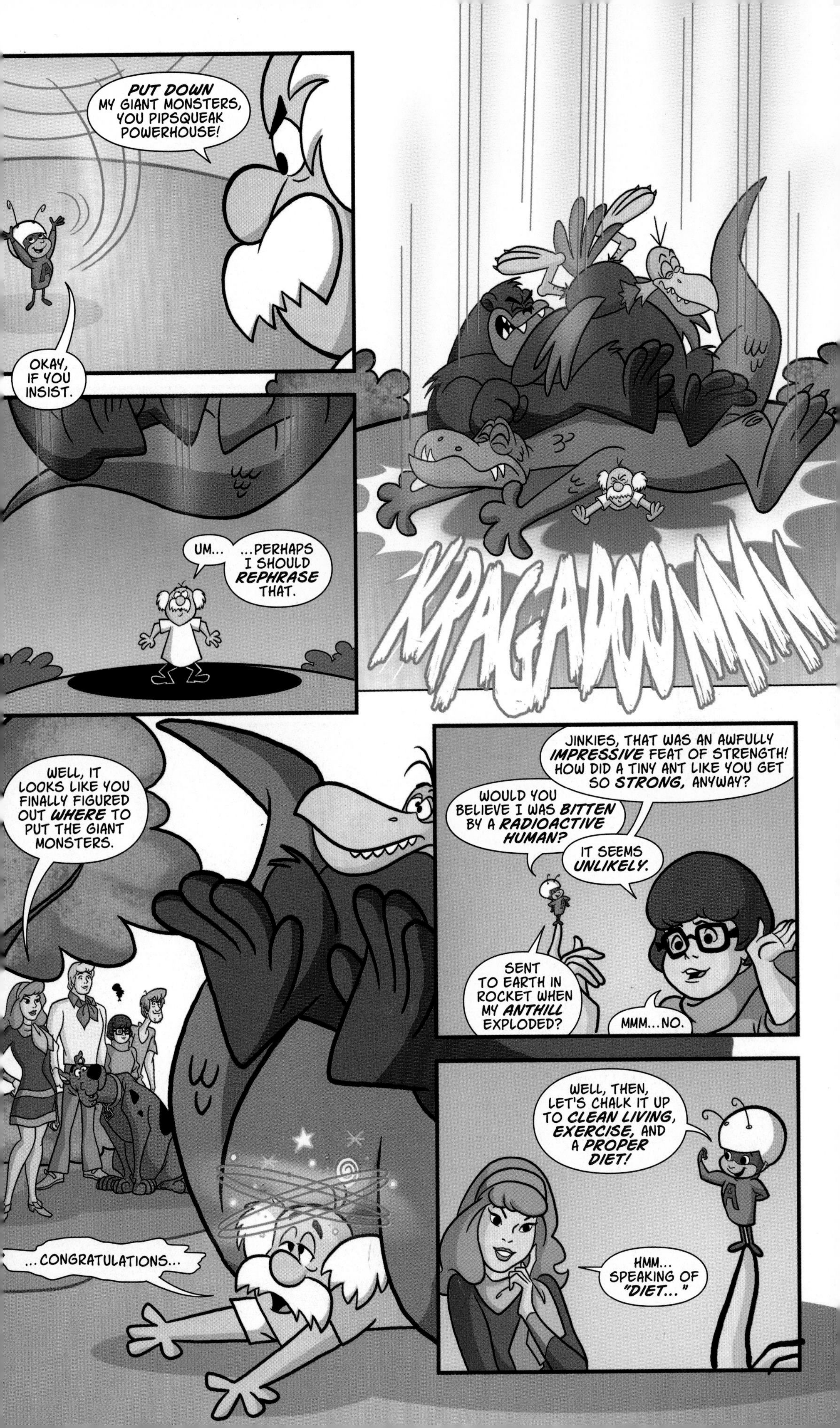
PUT DOWN MY GIANT MONSTERS, YOU PIPSQUEAK POWERHOUSE!
OKAY, IF YOU INSIST.
UM...
...PERHAPS I SHOULD REPHRASE THAT.
KPAGADOOMMM
WELL, IT LOOKS LIKE YOU FINALLY FIGURED OUT WHERE TO PUT THE GIANT MONSTERS.
...CONGRATULATIONS...
JINKIES, THAT WAS AN AWFULLY IMPRESSIVE FEAT OF STRENGTH! HOW DID A TINY ANT LIKE YOU GET SO STRONG, ANYWAY?
WOULD YOU BELIEVE I WAS BITTEN BY A RADIOACTIVE HUMAN?
IT SEEMS UNLIKELY.
SENT TO EARTH IN ROCKET WHEN MY ANTHILL EXPLODED?
MMM...NO.
WELL, THEN, LET'S CHALK IT UP TO CLEAN LIVING, EXERCISE, AND A PROPER DIET!
HMM... SPEAKING OF "DIET..."

WE WANTED TO DO A LITTLE SOMETHING TO THANK YOU FOR SAVING US. AND, SINCE YOU DIDN'T GET TO EAT ANYTHING *BEFORE*...

PICNIC*PICNIC*PICNIC!

WE EVEN, LIKE, PUT TOGETHER A SPECIAL PICNIC *MENU* WITH YOU IN MIND--

--*ANT*-IPASTO FRIED PL-*ANT*-AINS, EGGPL-*ANT* PARMESAN...

IN FACT, I DON'T MIND IF I, LIKE, HAVE A LITTLE NIBBLE MY--

GOBBLE
CRUNCH
SLURRRP
SMACK
CRUNCH
CHEW

--SELF...?

THANKS, KIDS! THAT WAS DELICIOUS!

BUT ≈URP≈ DOES ANYONE HAVE ANY *ANT*-ACID?

THE END

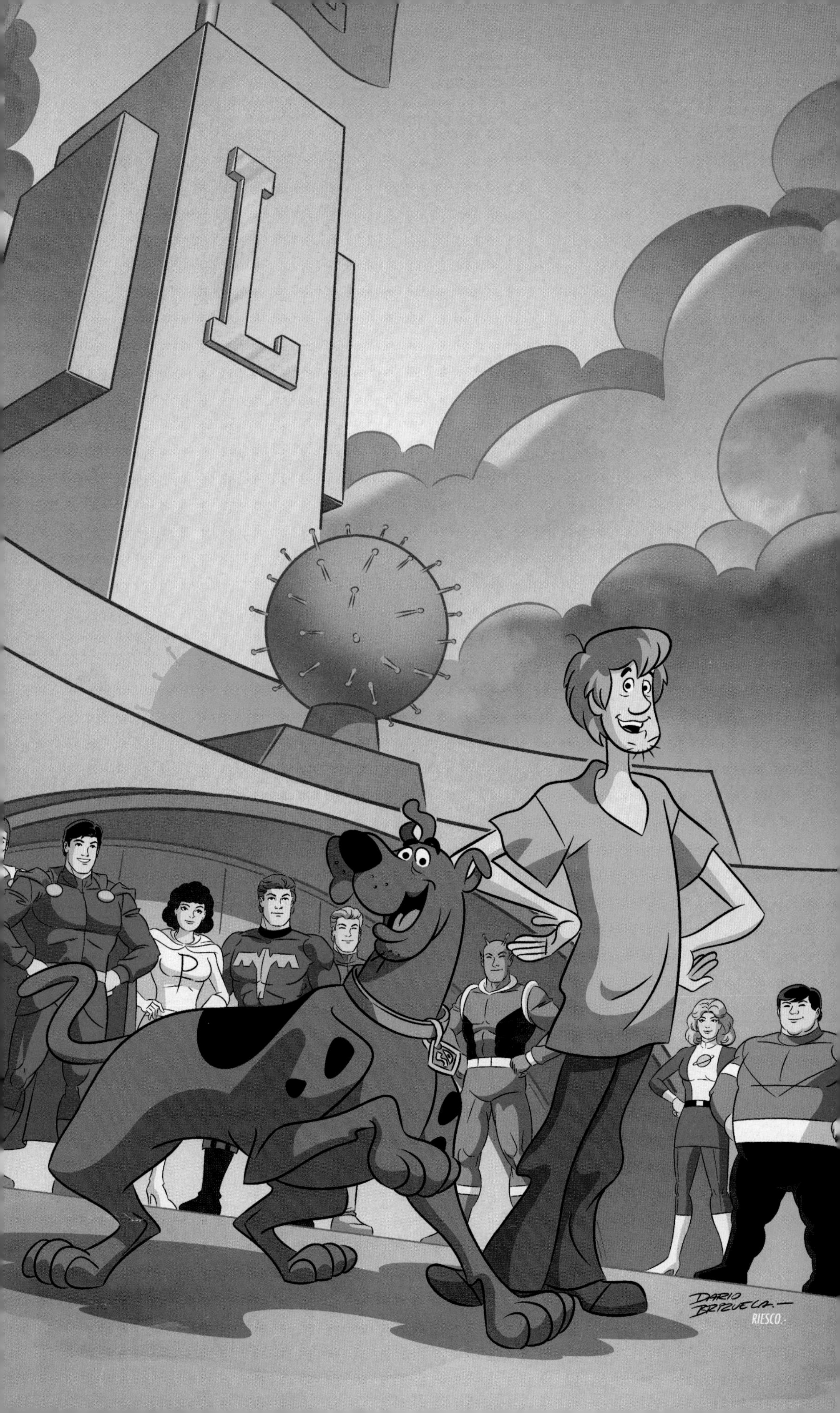
DARIO BRIZUELA
RIESCO.

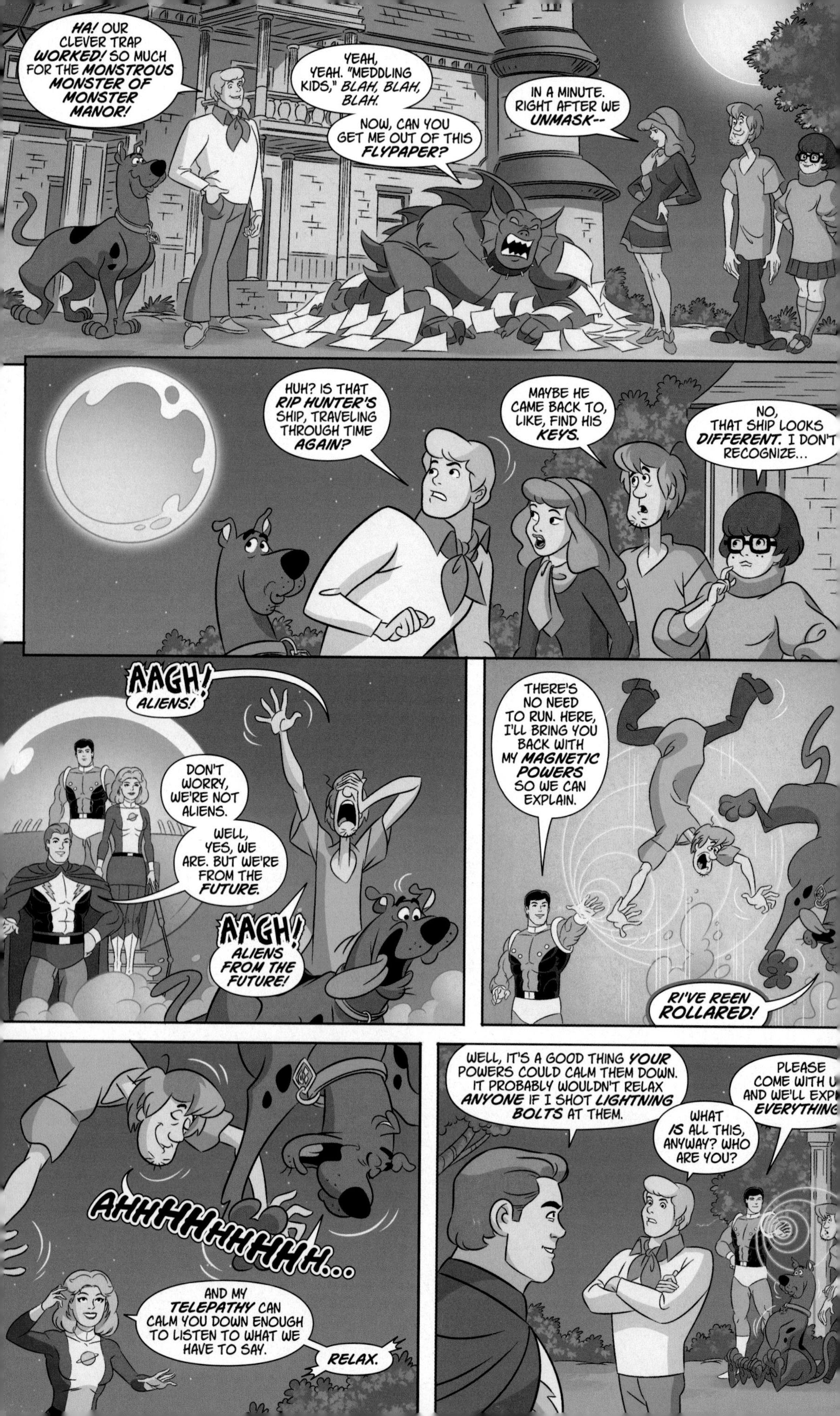
HA! OUR CLEVER TRAP WORKED! SO MUCH FOR THE MONSTROUS MONSTER OF MONSTER MANOR!
YEAH, YEAH. "MEDDLING KIDS," BLAH, BLAH, BLAH.
NOW, CAN YOU GET ME OUT OF THIS FLYPAPER?
IN A MINUTE. RIGHT AFTER WE UNMASK--
HUH? IS THAT RIP HUNTER'S SHIP, TRAVELING THROUGH TIME AGAIN?
MAYBE HE CAME BACK TO, LIKE, FIND HIS KEYS.
NO, THAT SHIP LOOKS DIFFERENT. I DON'T RECOGNIZE...
AAGH! ALIENS!
DON'T WORRY, WE'RE NOT ALIENS.
WELL, YES, WE ARE. BUT WE'RE FROM THE FUTURE.
AAGH! ALIENS FROM THE FUTURE!
THERE'S NO NEED TO RUN. HERE, I'LL BRING YOU BACK WITH MY MAGNETIC POWERS SO WE CAN EXPLAIN.
RI'VE REEN ROLLARED!
AHHHHHHHHH...
AND MY TELEPATHY CAN CALM YOU DOWN ENOUGH TO LISTEN TO WHAT WE HAVE TO SAY.
RELAX.
WELL, IT'S A GOOD THING YOUR POWERS COULD CALM THEM DOWN. IT PROBABLY WOULDN'T RELAX ANYONE IF I SHOT LIGHTNING BOLTS AT THEM.
WHAT IS ALL THIS, ANYWAY? WHO ARE YOU?
PLEASE COME WITH U AND WE'LL EXP EVERYTHING

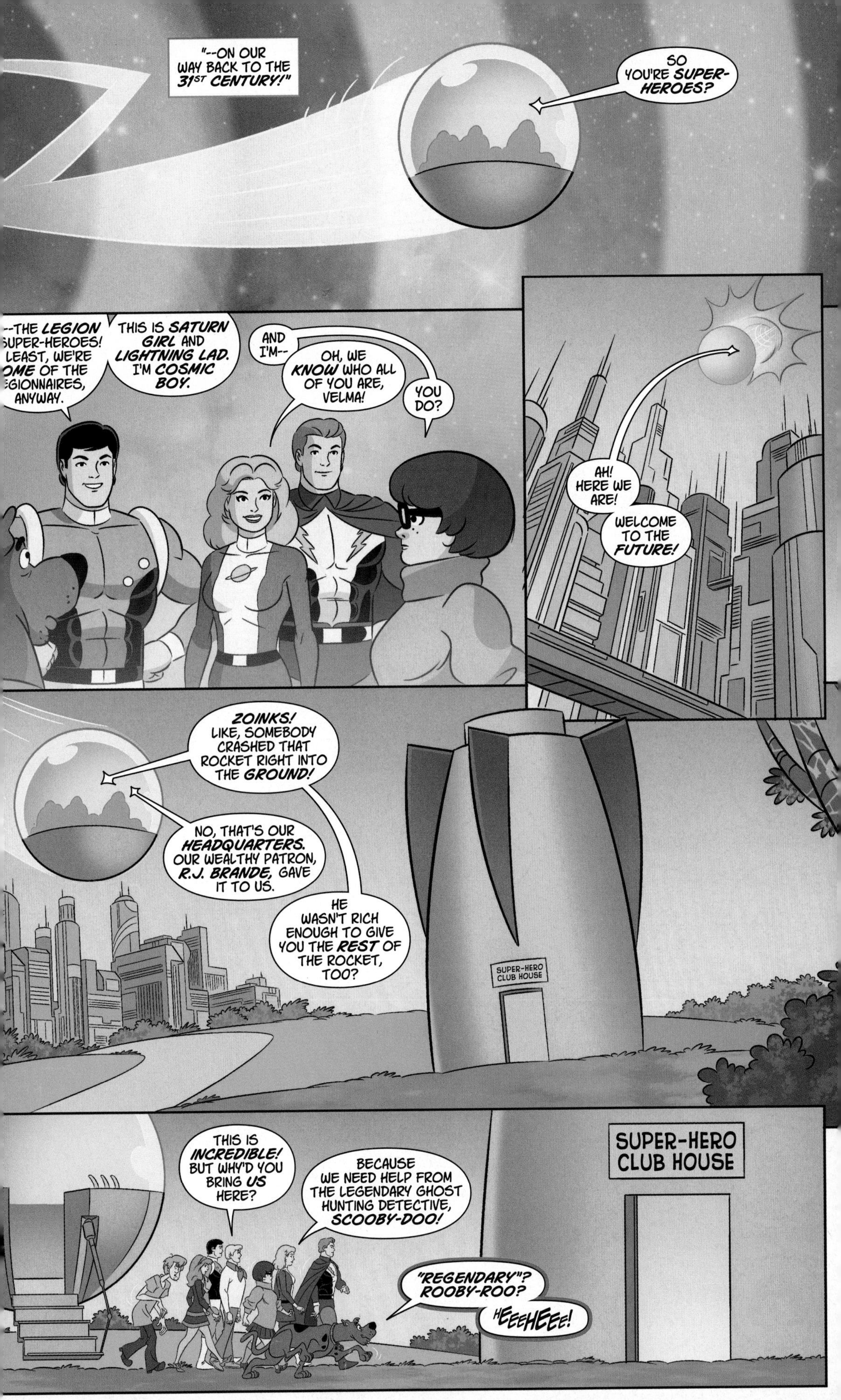
"--ON OUR WAY BACK TO THE 31ST CENTURY!"
SO YOU'RE SUPER-HEROES?
--THE LEGION SUPER-HEROES! LEAST, WE'RE OME OF THE EGIONNAIRES, ANYWAY.
THIS IS SATURN GIRL AND LIGHTNING LAD. I'M COSMIC BOY.
AND I'M--
OH, WE KNOW WHO ALL OF YOU ARE, VELMA!
YOU DO?
AH! HERE WE ARE!
WELCOME TO THE FUTURE!
ZOINKS! LIKE, SOMEBODY CRASHED THAT ROCKET RIGHT INTO THE GROUND!
NO, THAT'S OUR HEADQUARTERS. OUR WEALTHY PATRON, R.J. BRANDE, GAVE IT TO US.
HE WASN'T RICH ENOUGH TO GIVE YOU THE REST OF THE ROCKET, TOO?
SUPER-HERO CLUB HOUSE
THIS IS INCREDIBLE! BUT WHY'D YOU BRING US HERE?
BECAUSE WE NEED HELP FROM THE LEGENDARY GHOST HUNTING DETECTIVE, SCOOBY-DOO!
SUPER-HERO CLUB HOUSE
"REGENDARY"? ROOBY-ROO?
HEEEHEEE!

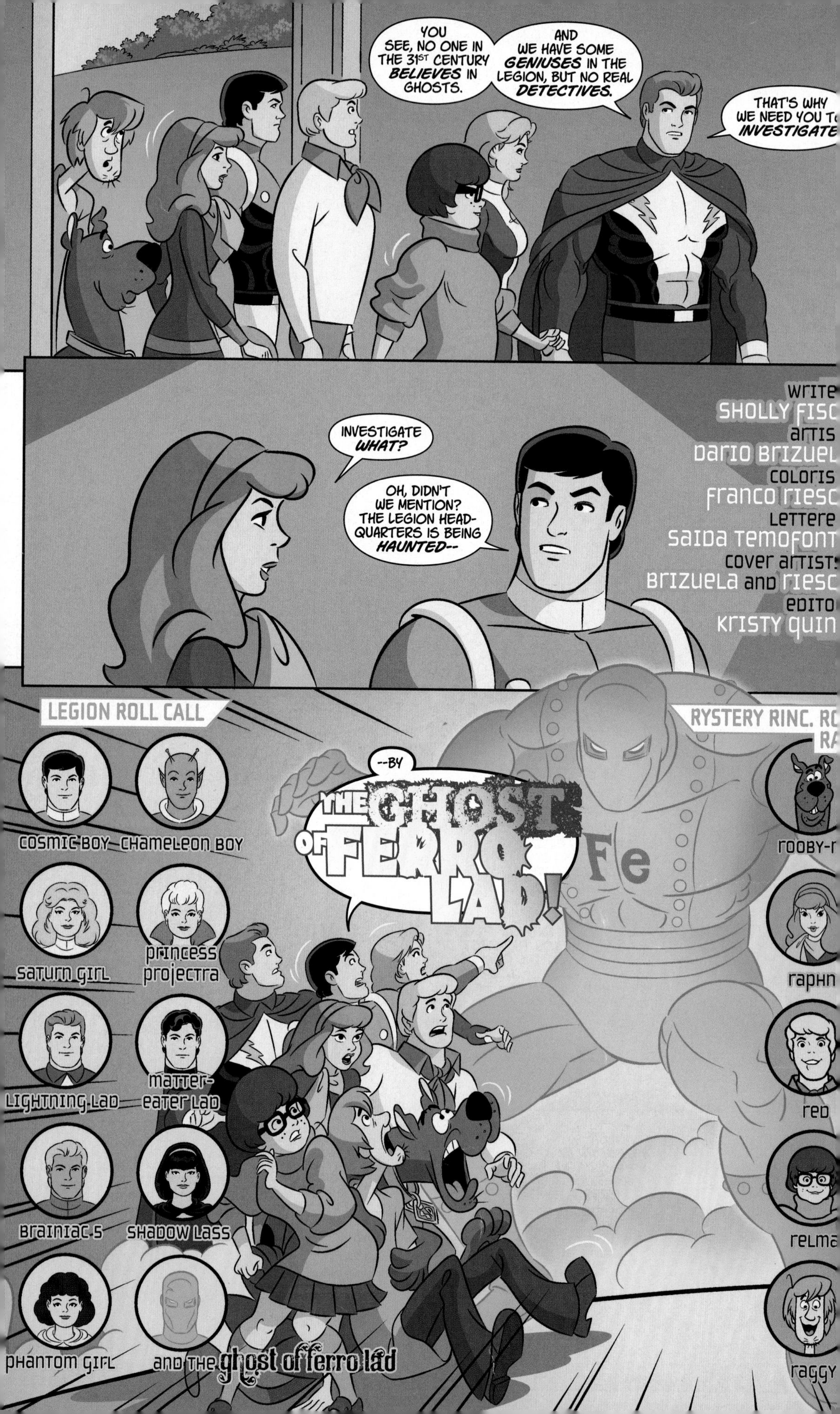

YOU SEE, NO ONE IN THE 31ST CENTURY BELIEVES IN GHOSTS.
AND WE HAVE SOME GENIUSES IN THE LEGION, BUT NO REAL DETECTIVES.
THAT'S WHY WE NEED YOU T INVESTIGATE
INVESTIGATE WHAT?
OH, DIDN'T WE MENTION? THE LEGION HEAD-QUARTERS IS BEING HAUNTED--
WRITE
SHOLLY FISC
ARTIS
DARIO BRIZUEL
COLORIS
FRANCO RIESC
LETTERE
SAIDA TEMOFONT
COVER ARTIST
BRIZUELA AND RIESC
EDITO
KRISTY QUIN
LEGION ROLL CALL
COSMIC BOY
CHAMELEON BOY
SATURN GIRL
PRINCESS PROJECTRA
LIGHTNING LAD
MATTER-EATER LAD
BRAINIAC 5
SHADOW LASS
PHANTOM GIRL
AND THE GHOST OF FERRO LAD
--BY THE GHOST OF FERRO LAD!
Fe
RYSTERY RINC. RO
RA
ROOBY-R
RAPHN
RED
RELMA
RAGGY

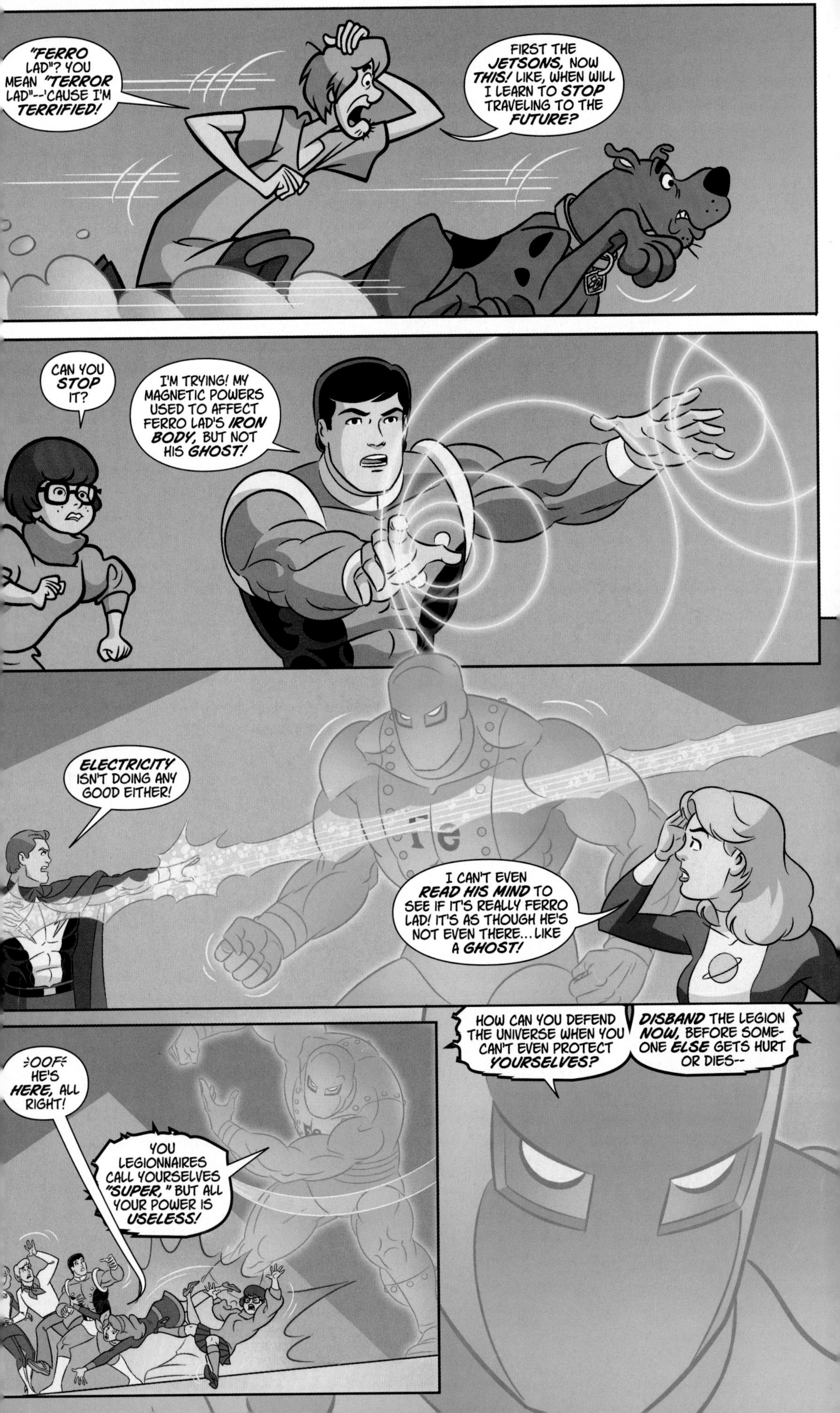
"FERRO LAD"? YOU MEAN "TERROR LAD"--'CAUSE I'M TERRIFIED!
FIRST THE JETSONS, NOW THIS! LIKE, WHEN WILL I LEARN TO STOP TRAVELING TO THE FUTURE?
CAN YOU STOP IT?
I'M TRYING! MY MAGNETIC POWERS USED TO AFFECT FERRO LAD'S IRON BODY, BUT NOT HIS GHOST!
ELECTRICITY ISN'T DOING ANY GOOD EITHER!
I CAN'T EVEN READ HIS MIND TO SEE IF IT'S REALLY FERRO LAD! IT'S AS THOUGH HE'S NOT EVEN THERE... LIKE A GHOST!
OOF HE'S HERE, ALL RIGHT!
YOU LEGIONNAIRES CALL YOURSELVES "SUPER," BUT ALL YOUR POWER IS USELESS!
HOW CAN YOU DEFEND THE UNIVERSE WHEN YOU CAN'T EVEN PROTECT YOURSELVES?
DISBAND THE LEGION NOW, BEFORE SOME-ONE ELSE GETS HURT OR DIES--

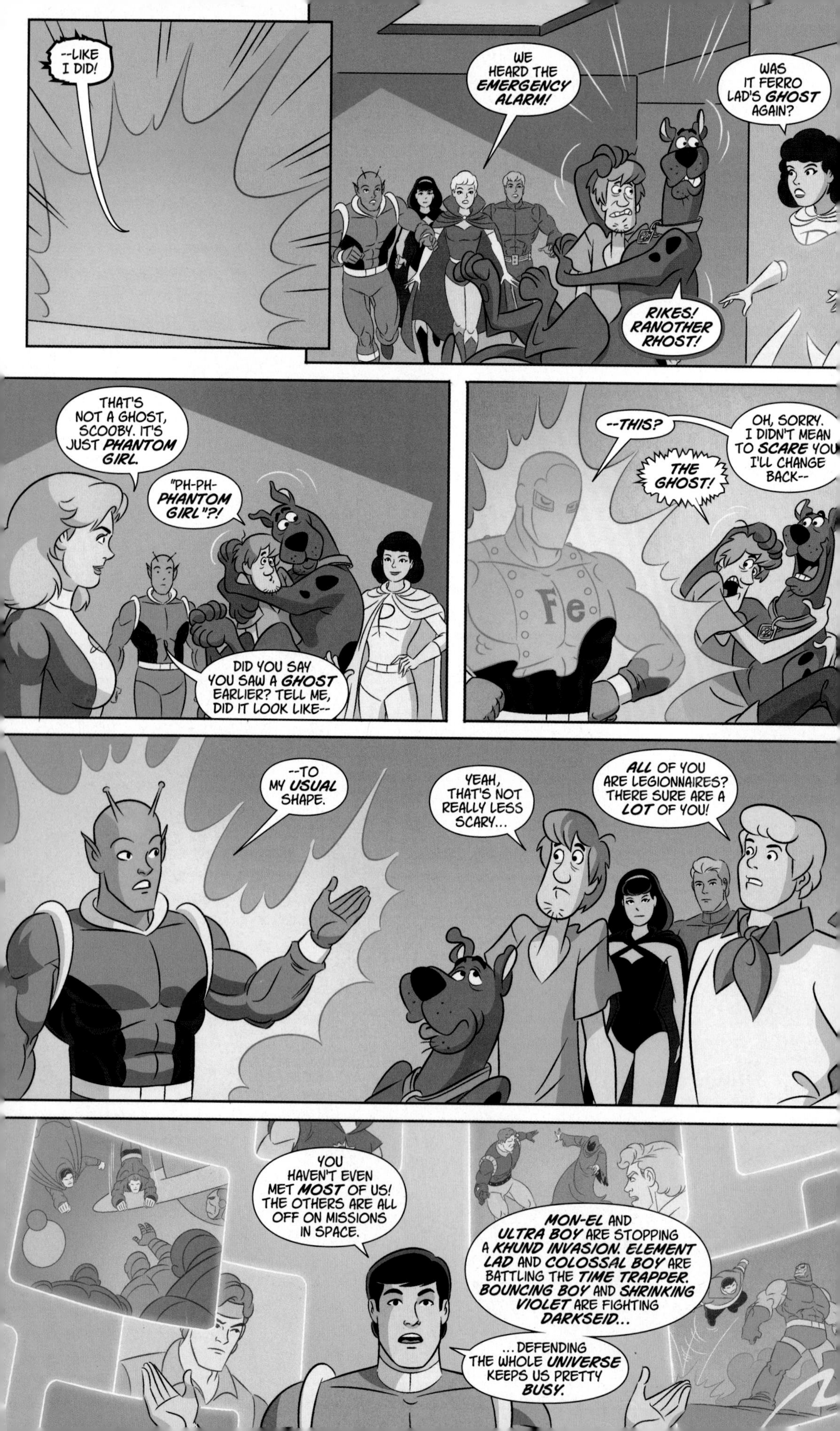
--LIKE I DID!
WE HEARD THE EMERGENCY ALARM!
WAS IT FERRO LAD'S GHOST AGAIN?
RIKES! RANOTHER RHOST!
THAT'S NOT A GHOST, SCOOBY. IT'S JUST PHANTOM GIRL.
"PH-PH-PHANTOM GIRL"?!
DID YOU SAY YOU SAW A GHOST EARLIER? TELL ME, DID IT LOOK LIKE--
--THIS?
THE GHOST!
OH, SORRY. I DIDN'T MEAN TO SCARE YOU. I'LL CHANGE BACK--
--TO MY USUAL SHAPE.
YEAH, THAT'S NOT REALLY LESS SCARY...
ALL OF YOU ARE LEGIONNAIRES? THERE SURE ARE A LOT OF YOU!
YOU HAVEN'T EVEN MET MOST OF US! THE OTHERS ARE ALL OFF ON MISSIONS IN SPACE.
MON-EL AND ULTRA BOY ARE STOPPING A KHUND INVASION. ELEMENT LAD AND COLOSSAL BOY ARE BATTLING THE TIME TRAPPER. BOUNCING BOY AND SHRINKING VIOLET ARE FIGHTING DARKSEID...
...DEFENDING THE WHOLE UNIVERSE KEEPS US PRETTY BUSY.

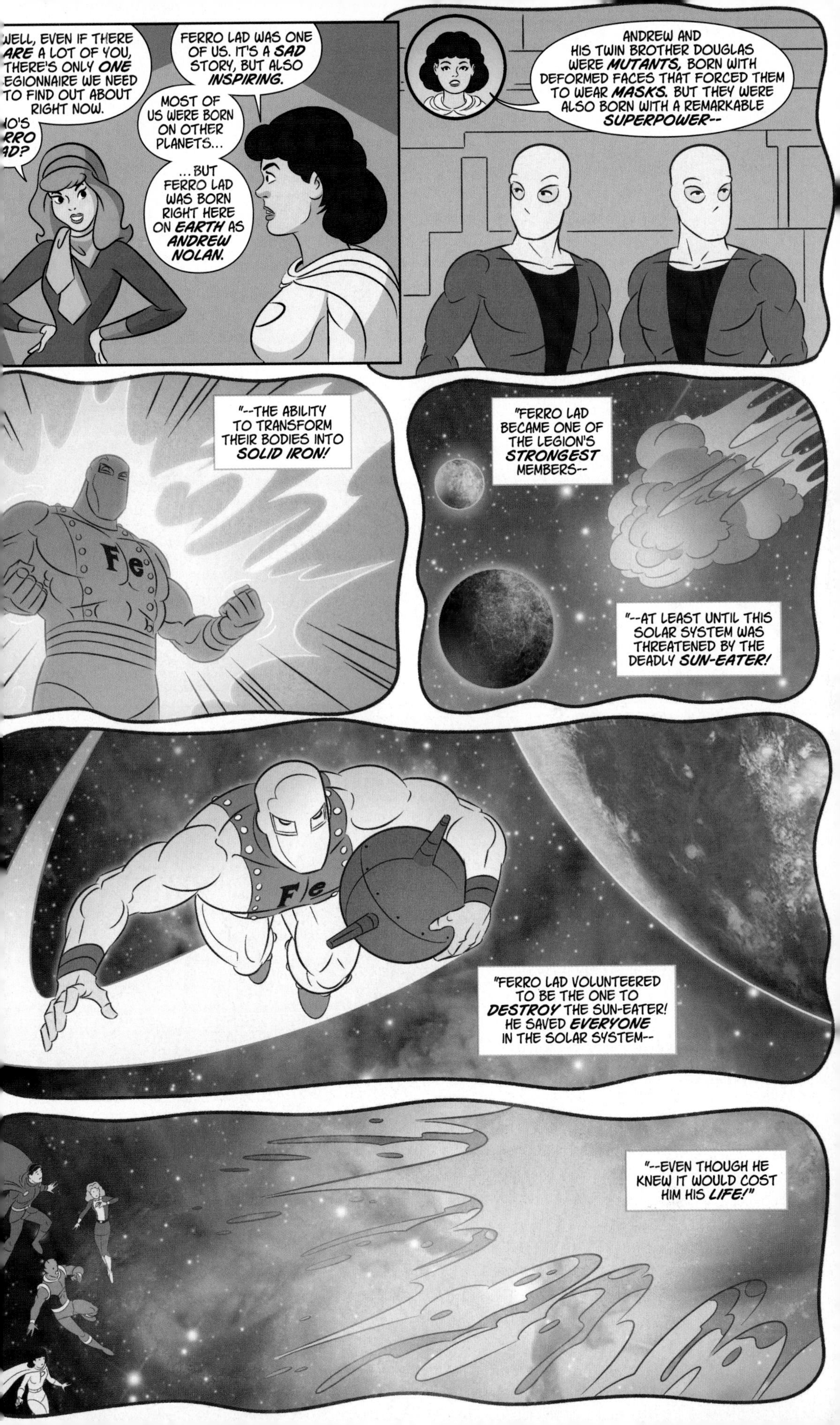
WELL, EVEN IF THERE ARE A LOT OF YOU, THERE'S ONLY ONE LEGIONNAIRE WE NEED TO FIND OUT ABOUT RIGHT NOW.
WHO'S FERRO LAD?
FERRO LAD WAS ONE OF US. IT'S A SAD STORY, BUT ALSO INSPIRING.
MOST OF US WERE BORN ON OTHER PLANETS...
...BUT FERRO LAD WAS BORN RIGHT HERE ON EARTH AS ANDREW NOLAN.
ANDREW AND HIS TWIN BROTHER DOUGLAS WERE MUTANTS, BORN WITH DEFORMED FACES THAT FORCED THEM TO WEAR MASKS. BUT THEY WERE ALSO BORN WITH A REMARKABLE SUPERPOWER--
"--THE ABILITY TO TRANSFORM THEIR BODIES INTO SOLID IRON!
Fe
"FERRO LAD BECAME ONE OF THE LEGION'S STRONGEST MEMBERS--
"--AT LEAST UNTIL THIS SOLAR SYSTEM WAS THREATENED BY THE DEADLY SUN-EATER!
Fe
"FERRO LAD VOLUNTEERED TO BE THE ONE TO DESTROY THE SUN-EATER! HE SAVED EVERYONE IN THE SOLAR SYSTEM--
"--EVEN THOUGH HE KNEW IT WOULD COST HIM HIS LIFE!"

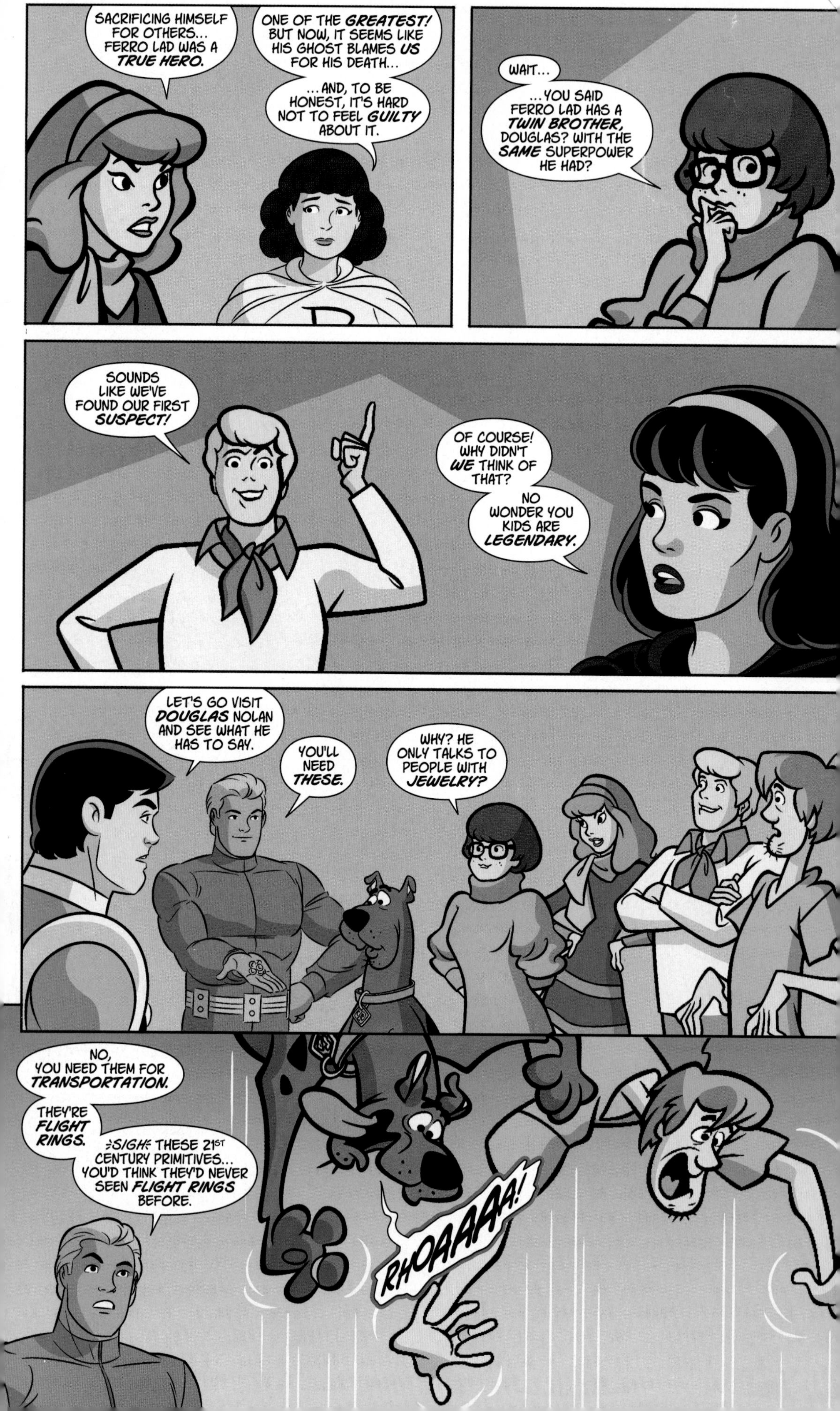
SACRIFICING HIMSELF FOR OTHERS... FERRO LAD WAS A TRUE HERO.
ONE OF THE GREATEST! BUT NOW, IT SEEMS LIKE HIS GHOST BLAMES US FOR HIS DEATH...
...AND, TO BE HONEST, IT'S HARD NOT TO FEEL GUILTY ABOUT IT.
WAIT...
...YOU SAID FERRO LAD HAS A TWIN BROTHER, DOUGLAS? WITH THE SAME SUPERPOWER HE HAD?
SOUNDS LIKE WE'VE FOUND OUR FIRST SUSPECT!
OF COURSE! WHY DIDN'T WE THINK OF THAT?
NO WONDER YOU KIDS ARE LEGENDARY.
LET'S GO VISIT DOUGLAS NOLAN AND SEE WHAT HE HAS TO SAY.
YOU'LL NEED THESE.
WHY? HE ONLY TALKS TO PEOPLE WITH JEWELRY?
NO, YOU NEED THEM FOR TRANSPORTATION.
THEY'RE FLIGHT RINGS.
SIGH THESE 21ST CENTURY PRIMITIVES... YOU'D THINK THEY'D NEVER SEEN FLIGHT RINGS BEFORE.
RHOAAAAA!

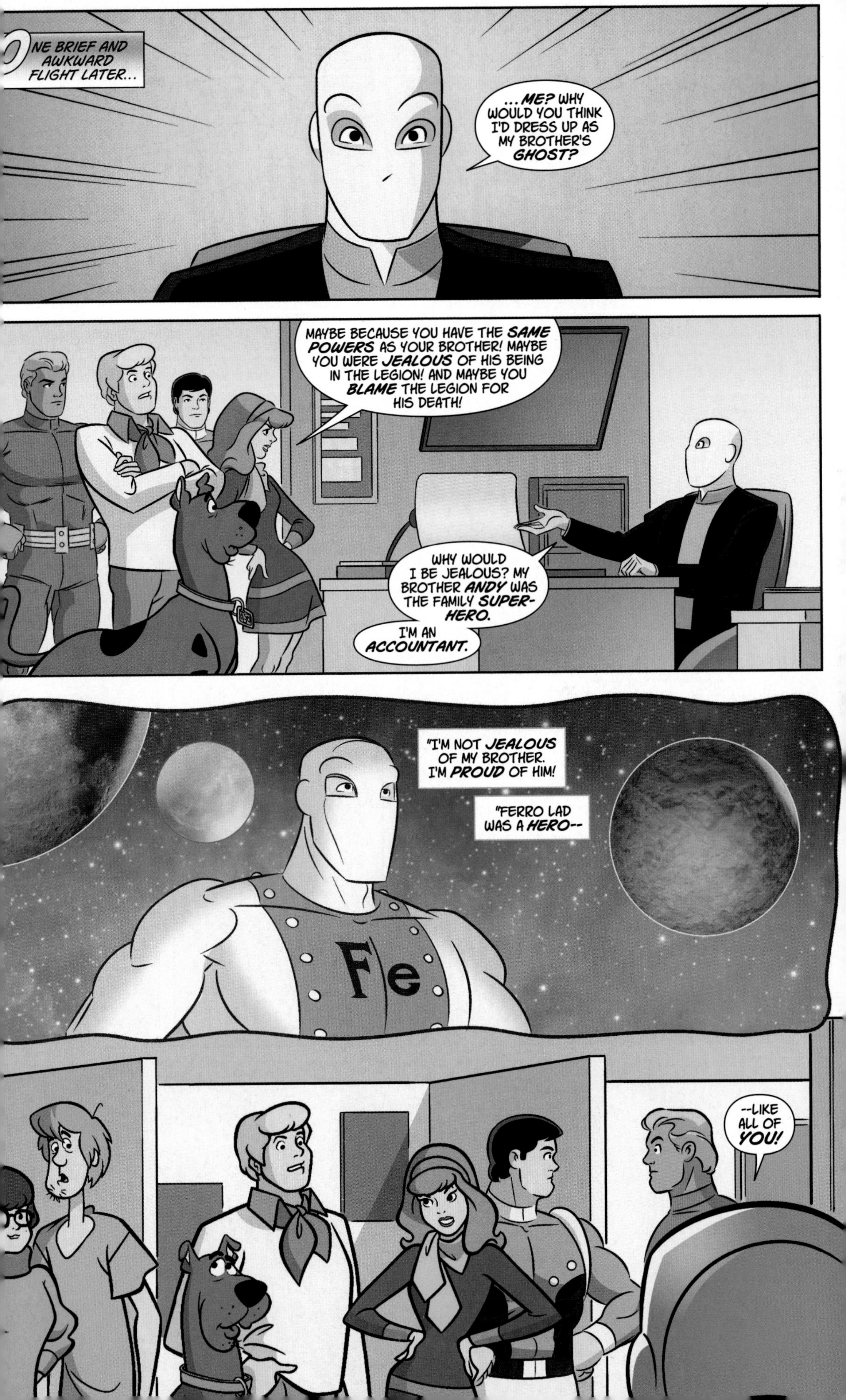
ONE BRIEF AND AWKWARD FLIGHT LATER...
...ME? WHY WOULD YOU THINK I'D DRESS UP AS MY BROTHER'S GHOST?
MAYBE BECAUSE YOU HAVE THE SAME POWERS AS YOUR BROTHER! MAYBE YOU WERE JEALOUS OF HIS BEING IN THE LEGION! AND MAYBE YOU BLAME THE LEGION FOR HIS DEATH!
WHY WOULD I BE JEALOUS? MY BROTHER ANDY WAS THE FAMILY SUPER-HERO.
I'M AN ACCOUNTANT.
"I'M NOT JEALOUS OF MY BROTHER. I'M PROUD OF HIM!
"FERRO LAD WAS A HERO--
Fe
--LIKE ALL OF YOU!

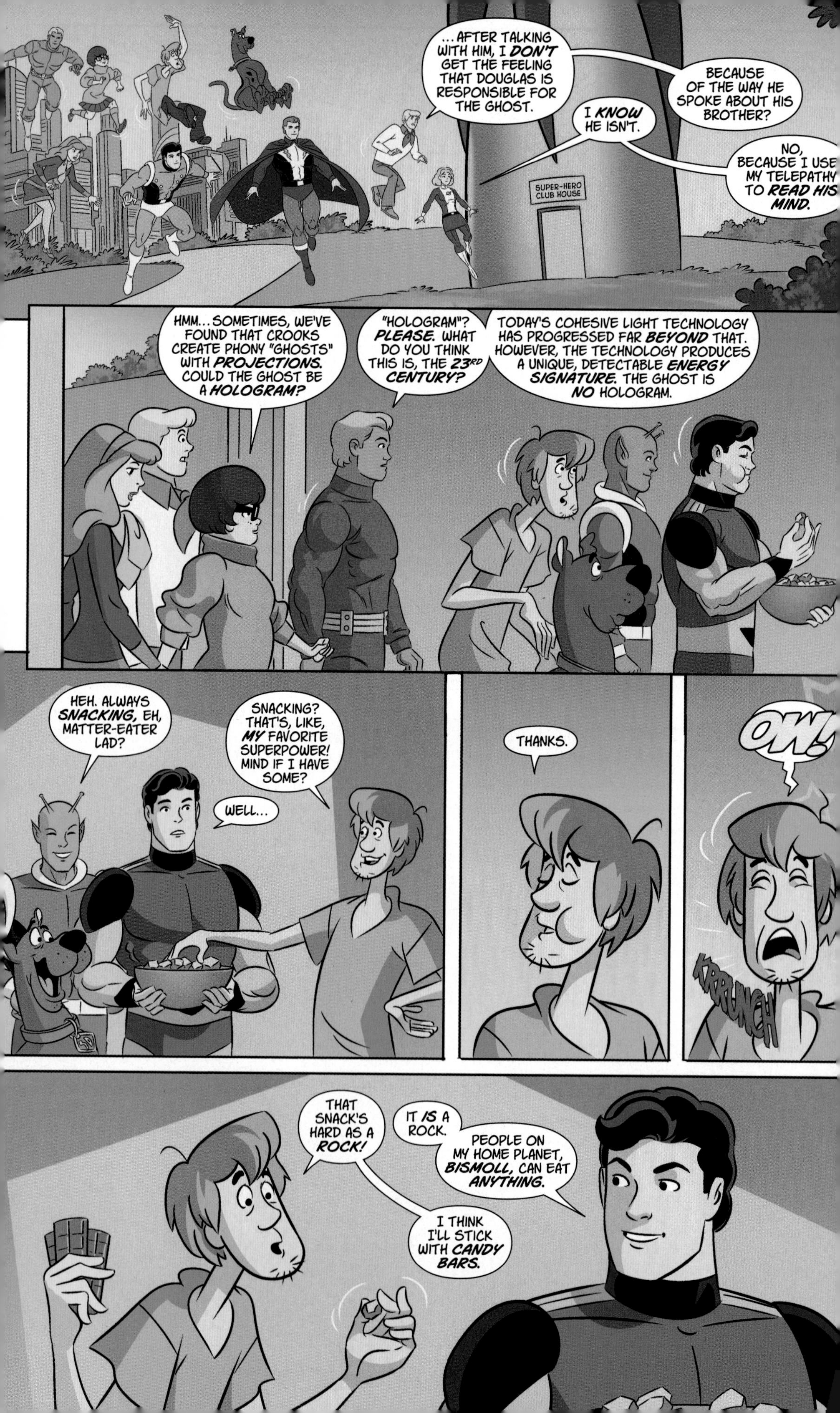
...AFTER TALKING WITH HIM, I DON'T GET THE FEELING THAT DOUGLAS IS RESPONSIBLE FOR THE GHOST.
BECAUSE OF THE WAY HE SPOKE ABOUT HIS BROTHER?
I KNOW HE ISN'T.
NO, BECAUSE I USE MY TELEPATHY TO READ HIS MIND.
SUPER-HERO CLUB HOUSE
HMM... SOMETIMES, WE'VE FOUND THAT CROOKS CREATE PHONY "GHOSTS" WITH PROJECTIONS. COULD THE GHOST BE A HOLOGRAM?
"HOLOGRAM"? PLEASE. WHAT DO YOU THINK THIS IS, THE 23RD CENTURY?
TODAY'S COHESIVE LIGHT TECHNOLOGY HAS PROGRESSED FAR BEYOND THAT. HOWEVER, THE TECHNOLOGY PRODUCES A UNIQUE, DETECTABLE ENERGY SIGNATURE. THE GHOST IS NO HOLOGRAM.
HEH. ALWAYS SNACKING, EH, MATTER-EATER LAD?
SNACKING? THAT'S, LIKE, MY FAVORITE SUPERPOWER! MIND IF I HAVE SOME?
WELL...
THANKS.
OW!
KRRUNCH
THAT SNACK'S HARD AS A ROCK!
IT IS A ROCK.
PEOPLE ON MY HOME PLANET, BISMOLL, CAN EAT ANYTHING.
I THINK I'LL STICK WITH CANDY BARS.

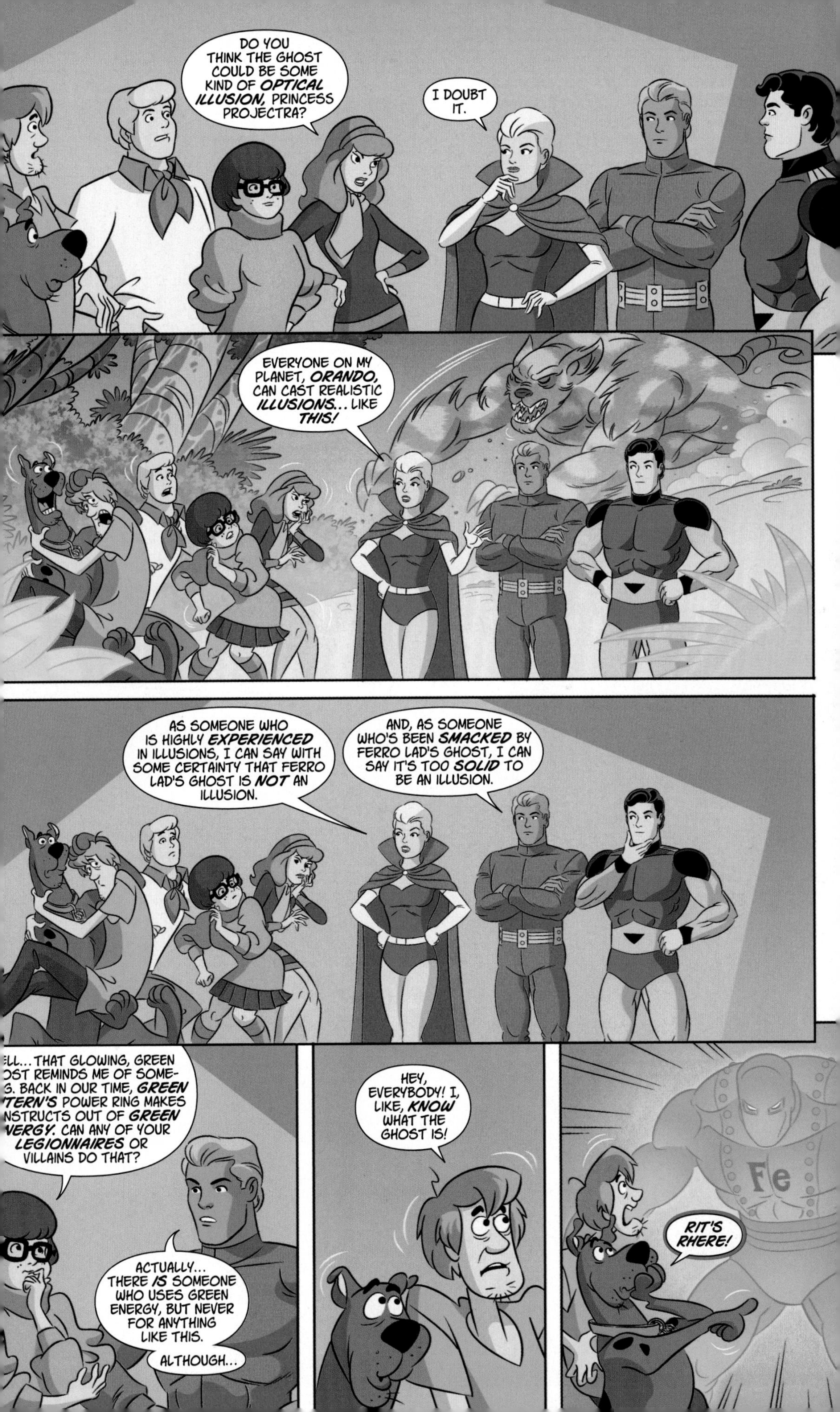
DO YOU THINK THE GHOST COULD BE SOME KIND OF OPTICAL ILLUSION, PRINCESS PROJECTRA?
I DOUBT IT.
EVERYONE ON MY PLANET, ORANDO, CAN CAST REALISTIC ILLUSIONS... LIKE THIS!
AS SOMEONE WHO IS HIGHLY EXPERIENCED IN ILLUSIONS, I CAN SAY WITH SOME CERTAINTY THAT FERRO LAD'S GHOST IS NOT AN ILLUSION.
AND, AS SOMEONE WHO'S BEEN SMACKED BY FERRO LAD'S GHOST, I CAN SAY IT'S TOO SOLID TO BE AN ILLUSION.
ELL... THAT GLOWING, GREEN OST REMINDS ME OF SOME- G. BACK IN OUR TIME, GREEN TERN'S POWER RING MAKES NSTRUCTS OUT OF GREEN ERGY. CAN ANY OF YOUR LEGIONNAIRES OR VILLAINS DO THAT?
ACTUALLY... THERE IS SOMEONE WHO USES GREEN ENERGY, BUT NEVER FOR ANYTHING LIKE THIS.
ALTHOUGH...
HEY, EVERYBODY! I, LIKE, KNOW WHAT THE GHOST IS!
RIT'S RHERE!
Fe

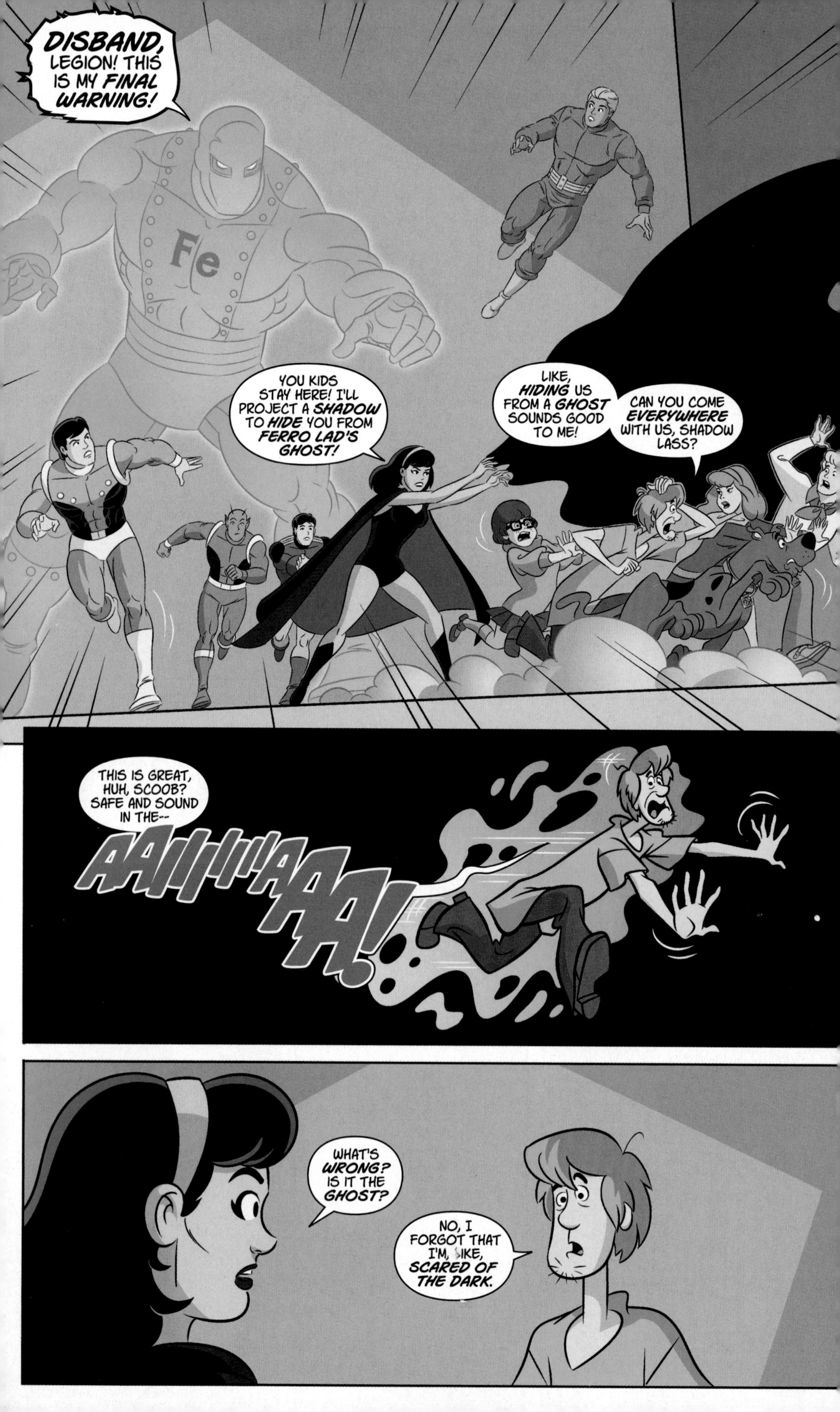

DISBAND, LEGION! THIS IS MY FINAL WARNING!
YOU KIDS STAY HERE! I'LL PROJECT A SHADOW TO HIDE YOU FROM FERRO LAD'S GHOST!
LIKE, HIDING US FROM A GHOST SOUNDS GOOD TO ME!
CAN YOU COME EVERYWHERE WITH US, SHADOW LASS?
THIS IS GREAT, HUH, SCOOB? SAFE AND SOUND IN THE--
AAIIIIIIAAA!
WHAT'S WRONG? IS IT THE GHOST?
NO, I FORGOT THAT I'M, LIKE, SCARED OF THE DARK.

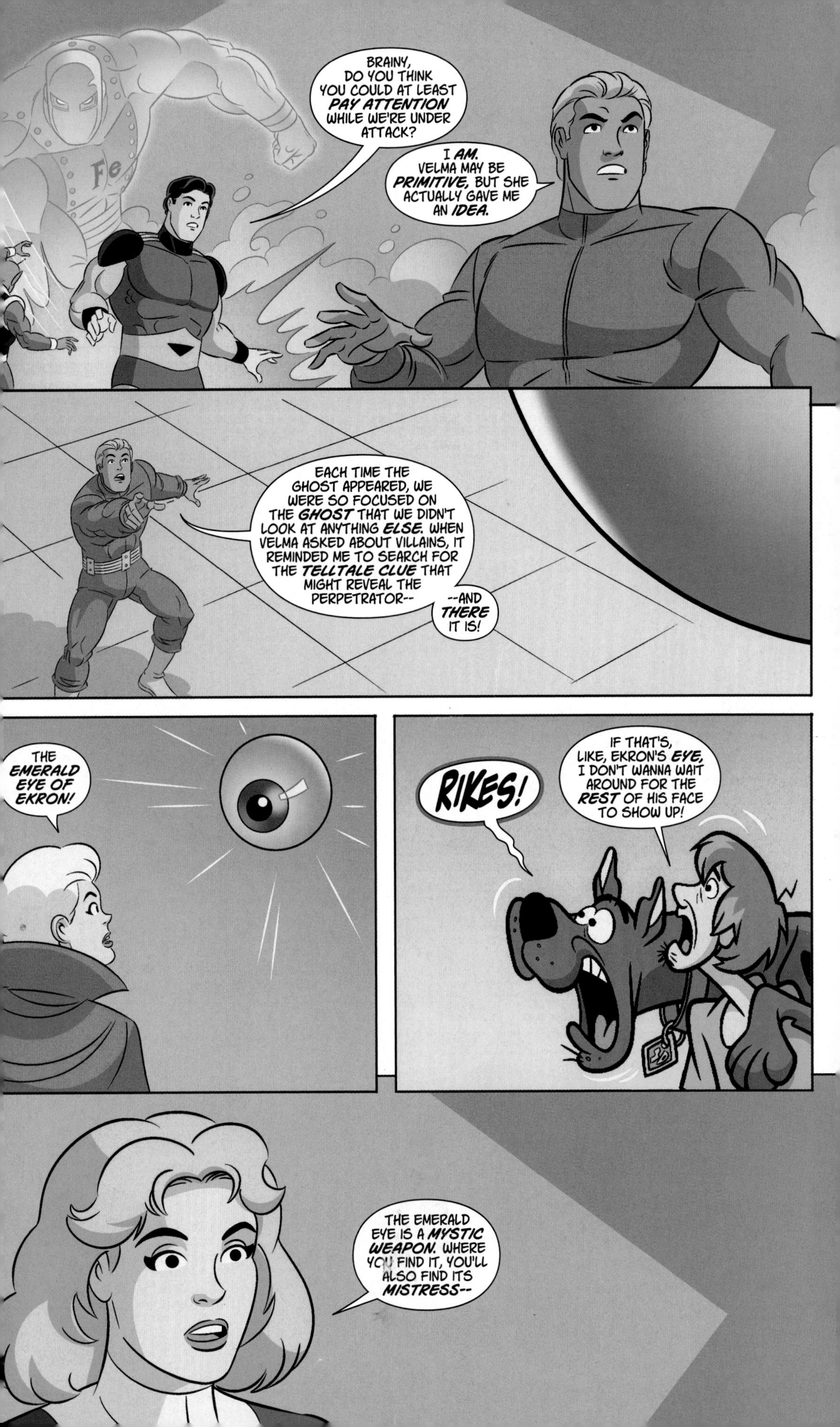
BRAINY, DO YOU THINK YOU COULD AT LEAST PAY ATTENTION WHILE WE'RE UNDER ATTACK?
Fe
I AM. VELMA MAY BE PRIMITIVE, BUT SHE ACTUALLY GAVE ME AN IDEA.
EACH TIME THE GHOST APPEARED, WE WERE SO FOCUSED ON THE GHOST THAT WE DIDN'T LOOK AT ANYTHING ELSE. WHEN VELMA ASKED ABOUT VILLAINS, IT REMINDED ME TO SEARCH FOR THE TELLTALE CLUE THAT MIGHT REVEAL THE PERPETRATOR--
--AND THERE IT IS!
THE EMERALD EYE OF EKRON!
RIKES!
IF THAT'S, LIKE, EKRON'S EYE, I DON'T WANNA WAIT AROUND FOR THE REST OF HIS FACE TO SHOW UP!
THE EMERALD EYE IS A MYSTIC WEAPON. WHERE YOU FIND IT, YOU'LL ALSO FIND ITS MISTRESS--

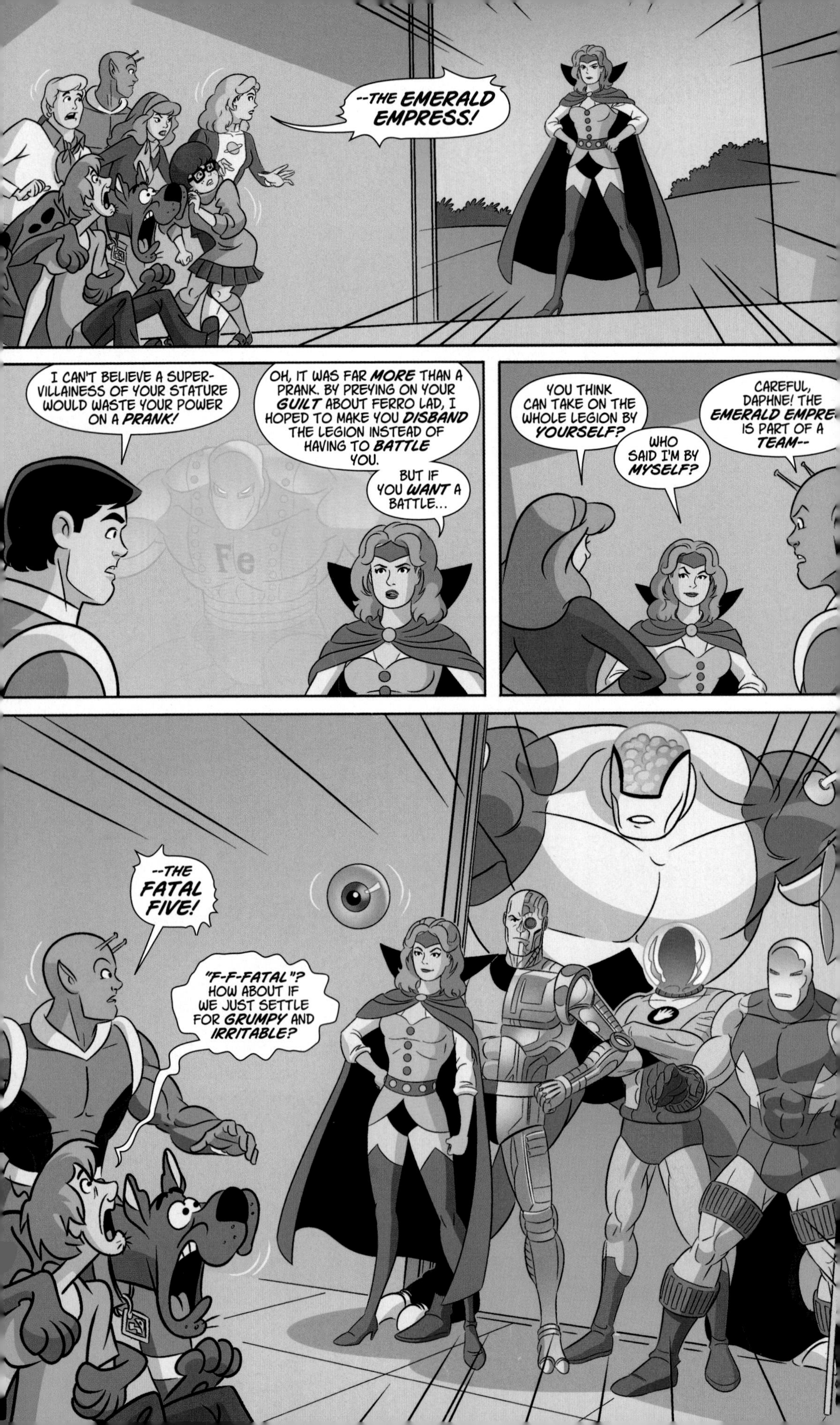
--THE EMERALD EMPRESS!
I CAN'T BELIEVE A SUPER-VILLAINESS OF YOUR STATURE WOULD WASTE YOUR POWER ON A PRANK!
OH, IT WAS FAR MORE THAN A PRANK. BY PREYING ON YOUR GUILT ABOUT FERRO LAD, I HOPED TO MAKE YOU DISBAND THE LEGION INSTEAD OF HAVING TO BATTLE YOU.
BUT IF YOU WANT A BATTLE...
Fe
YOU THINK CAN TAKE ON THE WHOLE LEGION BY YOURSELF?
WHO SAID I'M BY MYSELF?
CAREFUL, DAPHNE! THE EMERALD EMPRE IS PART OF A TEAM--
--THE FATAL FIVE!
"F-F-FATAL"? HOW ABOUT IF WE JUST SETTLE FOR GRUMPY AND IRRITABLE?

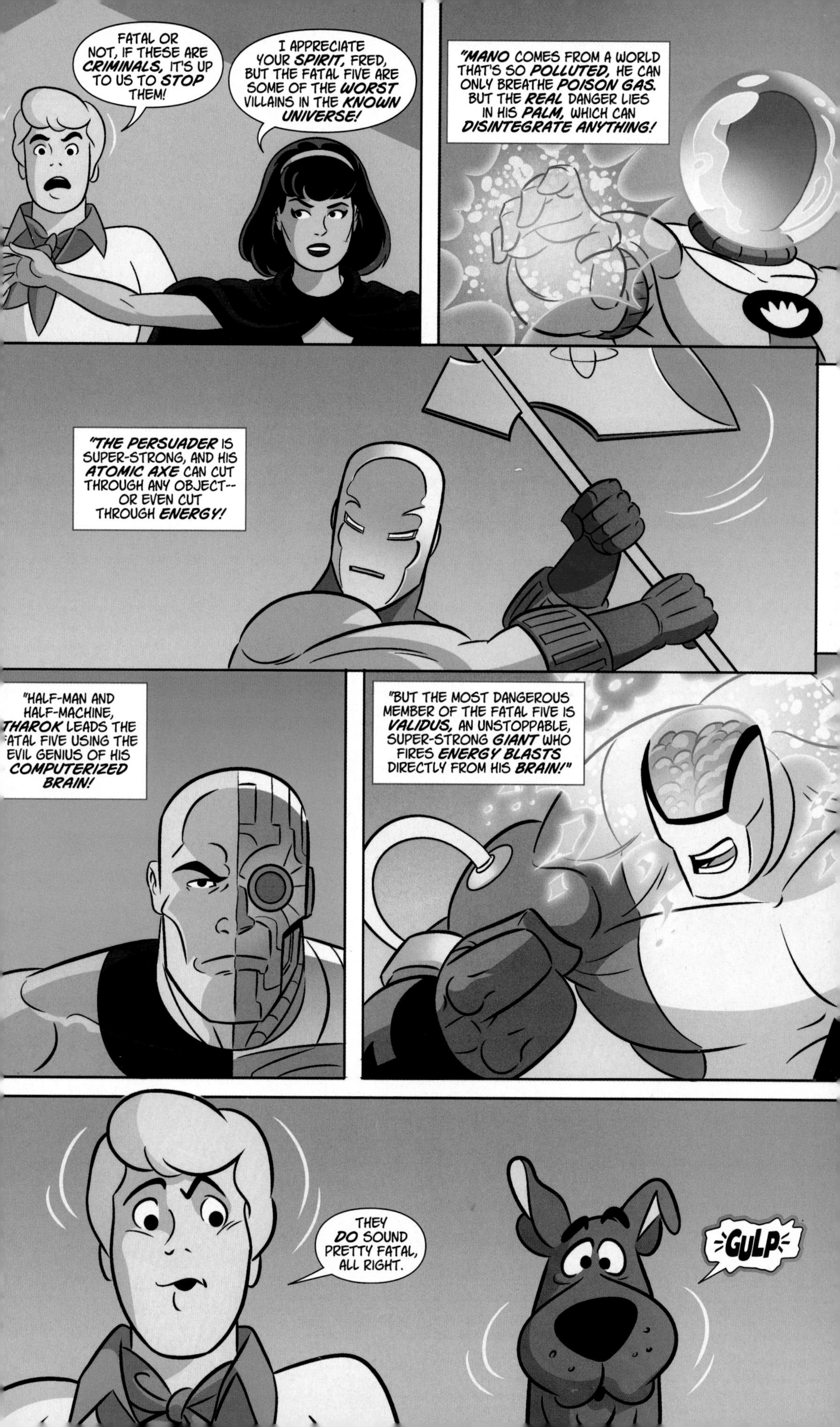
FATAL OR NOT, IF THESE ARE CRIMINALS, IT'S UP TO US TO STOP THEM!
I APPRECIATE YOUR SPIRIT, FRED, BUT THE FATAL FIVE ARE SOME OF THE WORST VILLAINS IN THE KNOWN UNIVERSE!
"MANO COMES FROM A WORLD THAT'S SO POLLUTED, HE CAN ONLY BREATHE POISON GAS. BUT THE REAL DANGER LIES IN HIS PALM, WHICH CAN DISINTEGRATE ANYTHING!
"THE PERSUADER IS SUPER-STRONG, AND HIS ATOMIC AXE CAN CUT THROUGH ANY OBJECT-- OR EVEN CUT THROUGH ENERGY!
"HALF-MAN AND HALF-MACHINE, THAROK LEADS THE FATAL FIVE USING THE EVIL GENIUS OF HIS COMPUTERIZED BRAIN!
"BUT THE MOST DANGEROUS MEMBER OF THE FATAL FIVE IS VALIDUS, AN UNSTOPPABLE, SUPER-STRONG GIANT WHO FIRES ENERGY BLASTS DIRECTLY FROM HIS BRAIN!"
THEY DO SOUND PRETTY FATAL, ALL RIGHT.
GULP

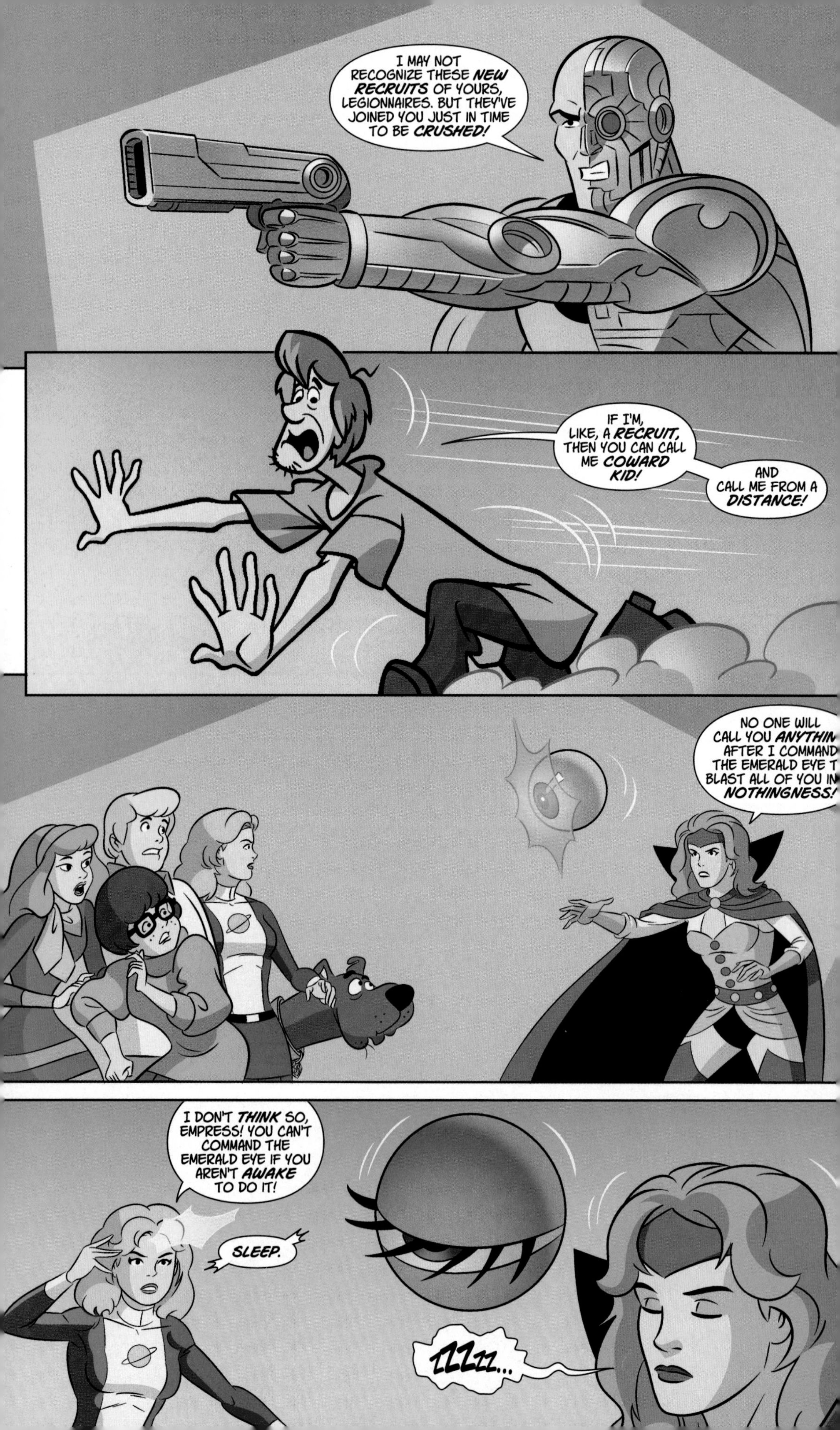
I MAY NOT RECOGNIZE THESE NEW RECRUITS OF YOURS, LEGIONNAIRES. BUT THEY'VE JOINED YOU JUST IN TIME TO BE CRUSHED!
IF I'M, LIKE, A RECRUIT, THEN YOU CAN CALL ME COWARD KID!
AND CALL ME FROM A DISTANCE!
NO ONE WILL CALL YOU ANYTHIN AFTER I COMMAND THE EMERALD EYE T BLAST ALL OF YOU IN NOTHINGNESS!
I DON'T THINK SO, EMPRESS! YOU CAN'T COMMAND THE EMERALD EYE IF YOU AREN'T AWAKE TO DO IT!
SLEEP.
ZZZzz...

CLEVER, SATURN GIRL. BUT YOU CAN'T PUT MY *ROBOT BRAIN* TO SLEEP!

NO, BUT *I* CAN SHORT-CIRCUIT THE ROBOT HALF OF YOUR BODY WITH A BOLT OF *LIGHTNING!*

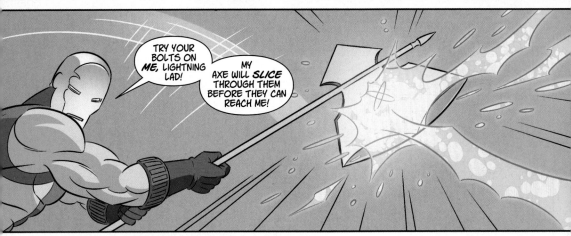

TRY YOUR BOLTS ON *ME*, LIGHTNING LAD!

MY *AXE* WILL *SLICE* THROUGH THEM BEFORE THEY CAN REACH ME!

THEN I'D BETTER *REMOVE* YOUR AXE *MAGNETICALLY!*

I DON'T NEED MY *AXE* TO CRUSH YOU WITH MY *SUPERIOR STRENGTH!*

UNLESS I USE A *MARTIAL ARTS* MOVE TO TURN YOUR OWN STRENGTH *AGAINST* YOU!

WE SHOULD INTRODUCE YOU TO *KARATE KID!*

AND WE'LL HAVE TO REMEMBER TO THANK *HONG KONG PHOOEY* FOR LENDING YOU HIS *HONG KONG BOOK OF KUNG FU!*

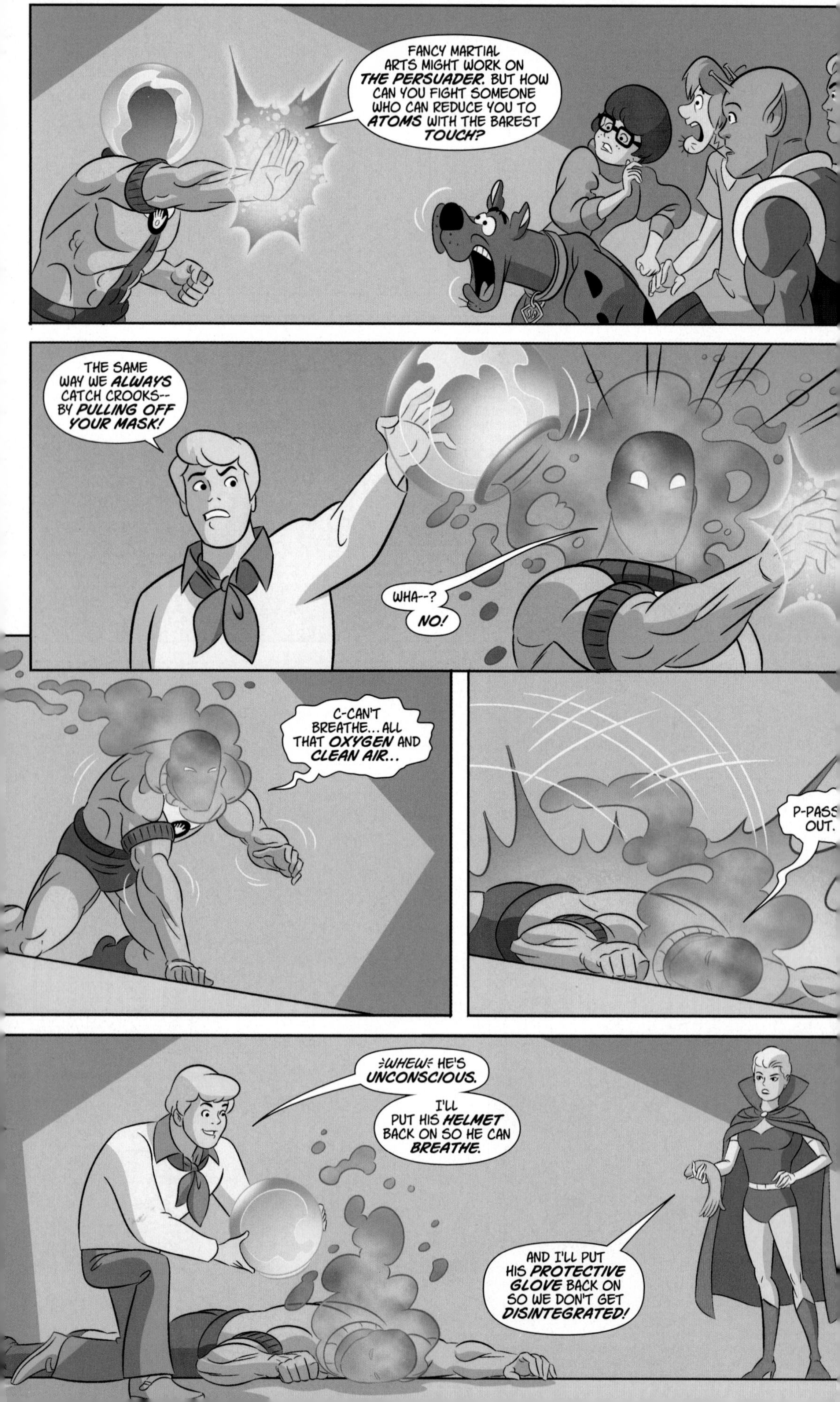
FANCY MARTIAL ARTS MIGHT WORK ON THE PERSUADER. BUT HOW CAN YOU FIGHT SOMEONE WHO CAN REDUCE YOU TO ATOMS WITH THE BAREST TOUCH?
THE SAME WAY WE ALWAYS CATCH CROOKS-- BY PULLING OFF YOUR MASK!
WHA--?
NO!
C-CAN'T BREATHE... ALL THAT OXYGEN AND CLEAN AIR...
P-PASS OUT.
WHEW HE'S UNCONSCIOUS.
I'LL PUT HIS HELMET BACK ON SO HE CAN BREATHE.
AND I'LL PUT HIS PROTECTIVE GLOVE BACK ON SO WE DON'T GET DISINTEGRATED!

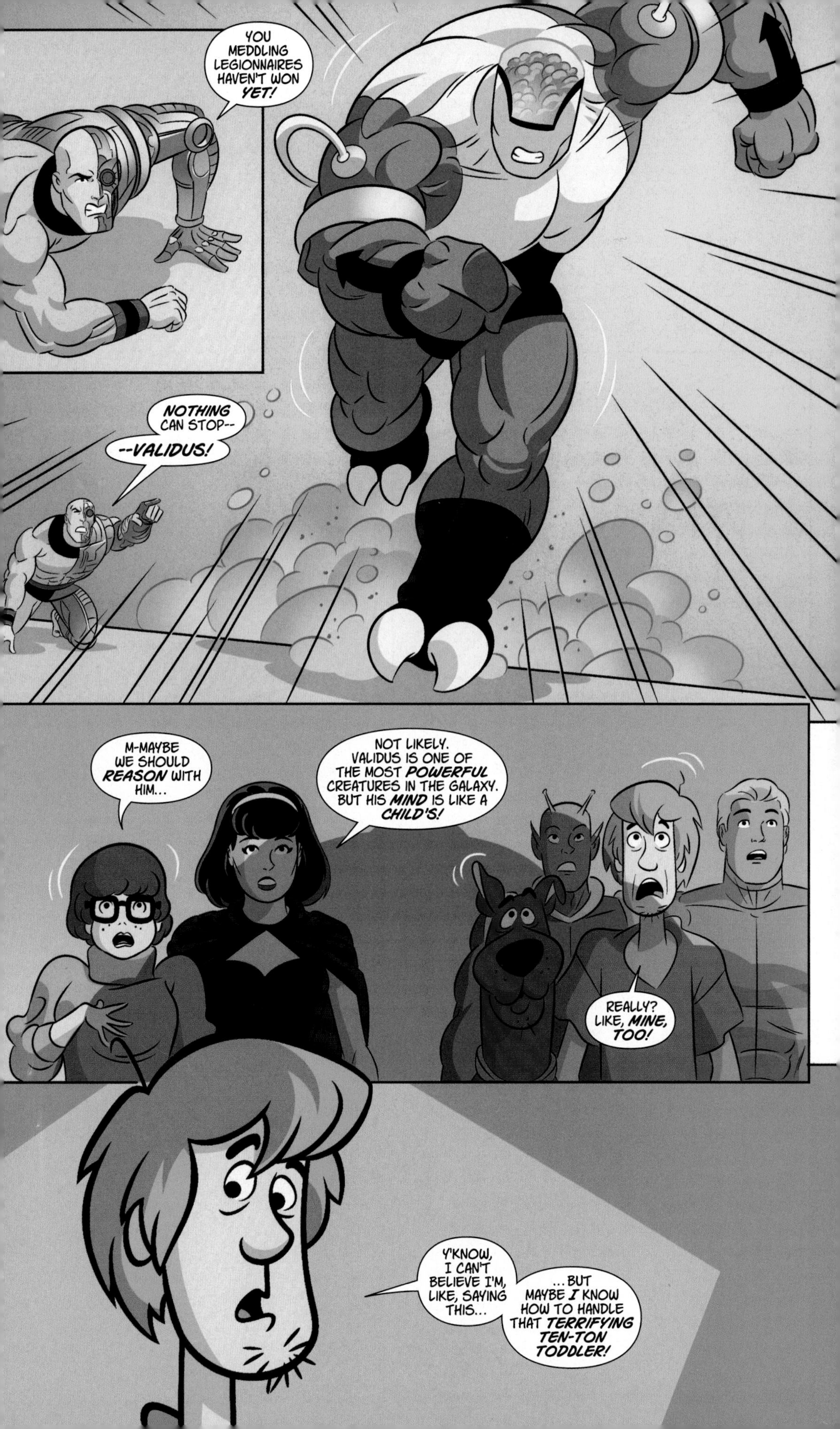

YOU MEDDLING LEGIONNAIRES HAVEN'T WON *YET!*
NOTHING CAN STOP--
--VALIDUS!
M-MAYBE WE SHOULD *REASON* WITH HIM...
NOT LIKELY. VALIDUS IS ONE OF THE MOST *POWERFUL* CREATURES IN THE GALAXY. BUT HIS *MIND* IS LIKE A *CHILD'S!*
REALLY? LIKE, *MINE, TOO!*
Y'KNOW, I CAN'T BELIEVE I'M, LIKE, SAYING THIS...
...BUT MAYBE *I* KNOW HOW TO HANDLE THAT *TERRIFYING TEN-TON TODDLER!*

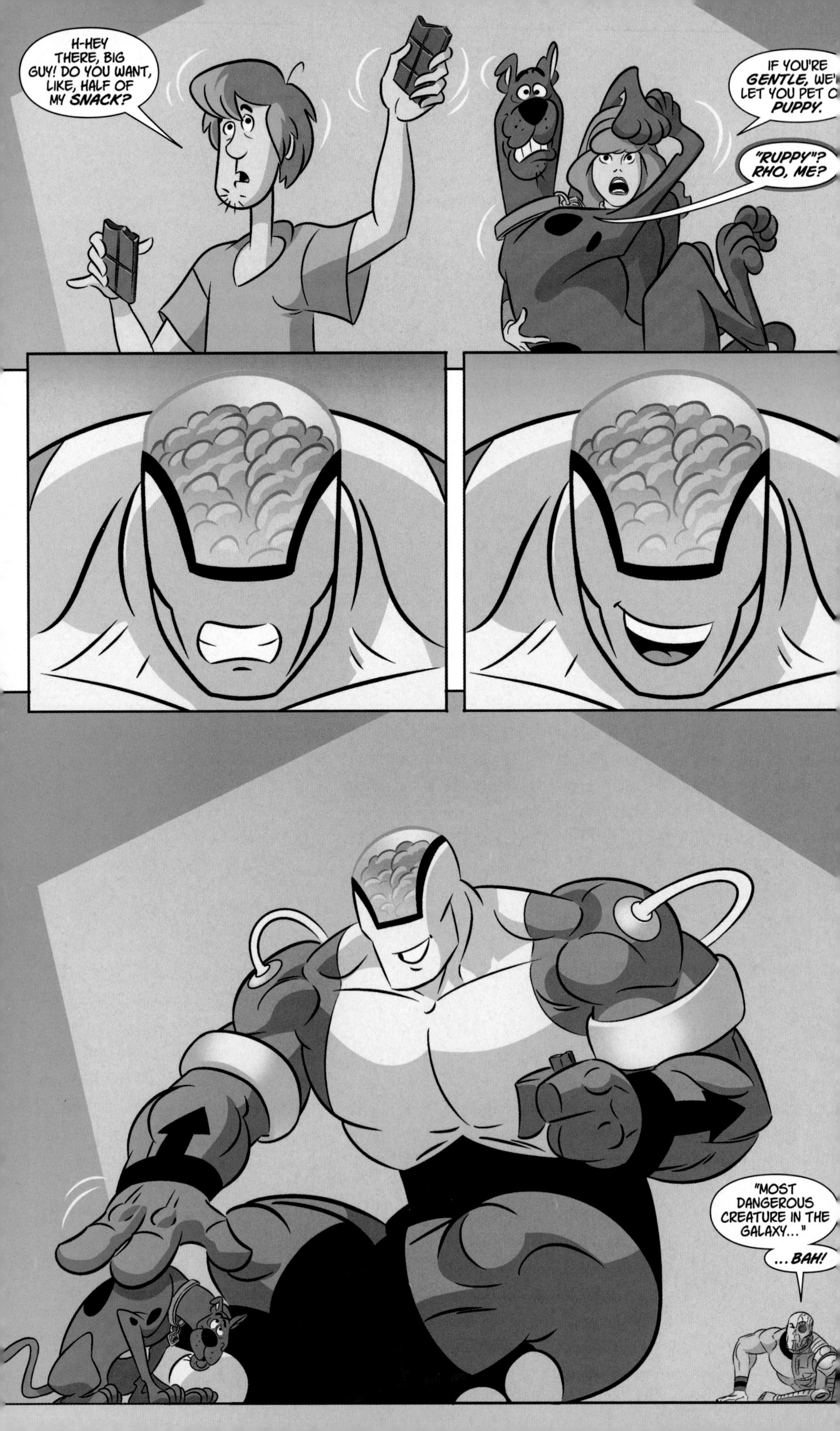
H-HEY THERE, BIG GUY! DO YOU WANT, LIKE, HALF OF MY SNACK?
IF YOU'RE GENTLE, WE'
LET YOU PET O
PUPPY.
"RUPPY"? RHO, ME?
"MOST DANGEROUS CREATURE IN THE GALAXY..."
...BAH!

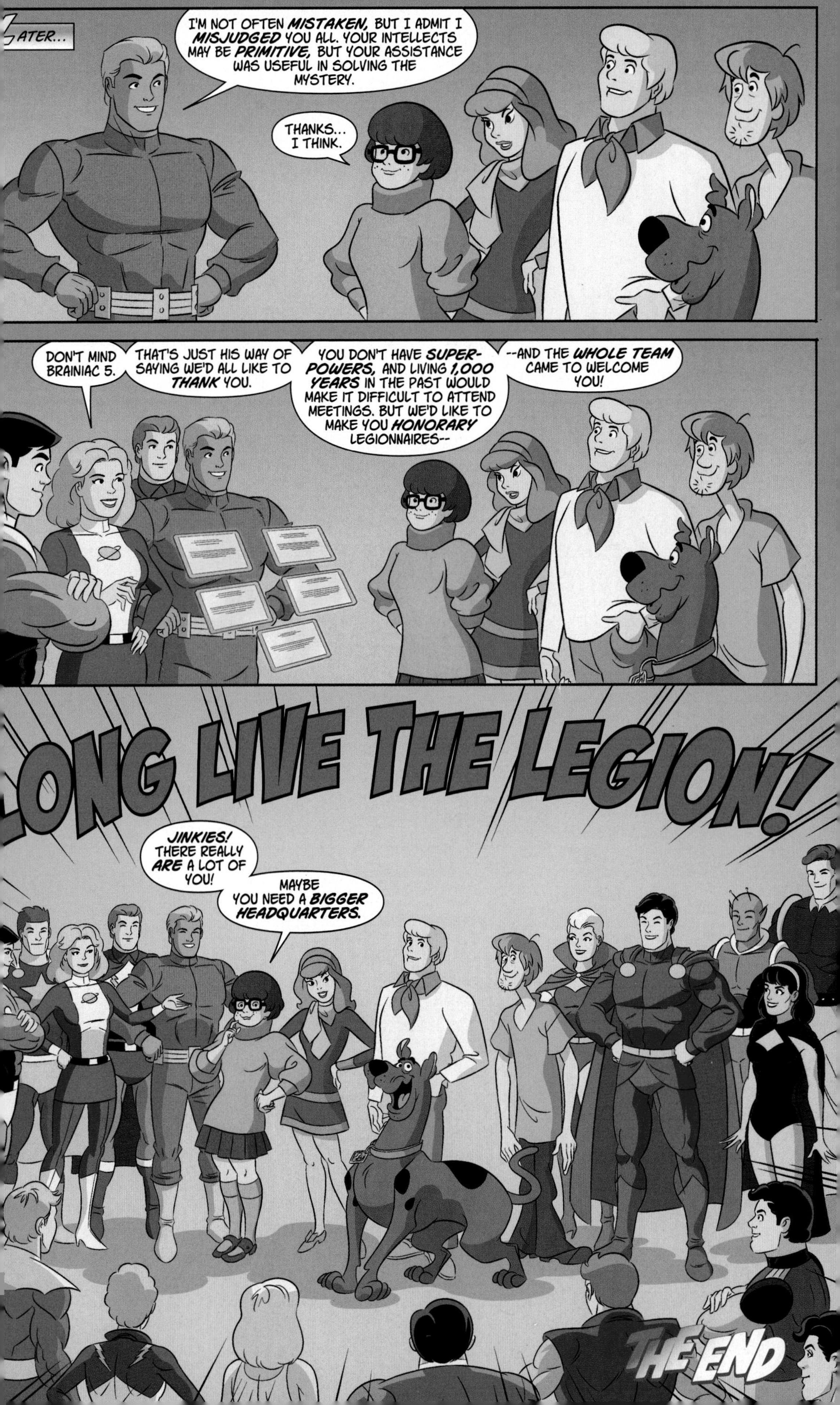
LATER...
I'M NOT OFTEN MISTAKEN, BUT I ADMIT I MISJUDGED YOU ALL. YOUR INTELLECTS MAY BE PRIMITIVE, BUT YOUR ASSISTANCE WAS USEFUL IN SOLVING THE MYSTERY.
THANKS... I THINK.
DON'T MIND BRAINIAC 5.
THAT'S JUST HIS WAY OF SAYING WE'D ALL LIKE TO THANK YOU.
YOU DON'T HAVE SUPER-POWERS, AND LIVING 1,000 YEARS IN THE PAST WOULD MAKE IT DIFFICULT TO ATTEND MEETINGS. BUT WE'D LIKE TO MAKE YOU HONORARY LEGIONNAIRES--
--AND THE WHOLE TEAM CAME TO WELCOME YOU!
LONG LIVE THE LEGION!
JINKIES! THERE REALLY ARE A LOT OF YOU!
MAYBE YOU NEED A BIGGER HEADQUARTERS.
THE END

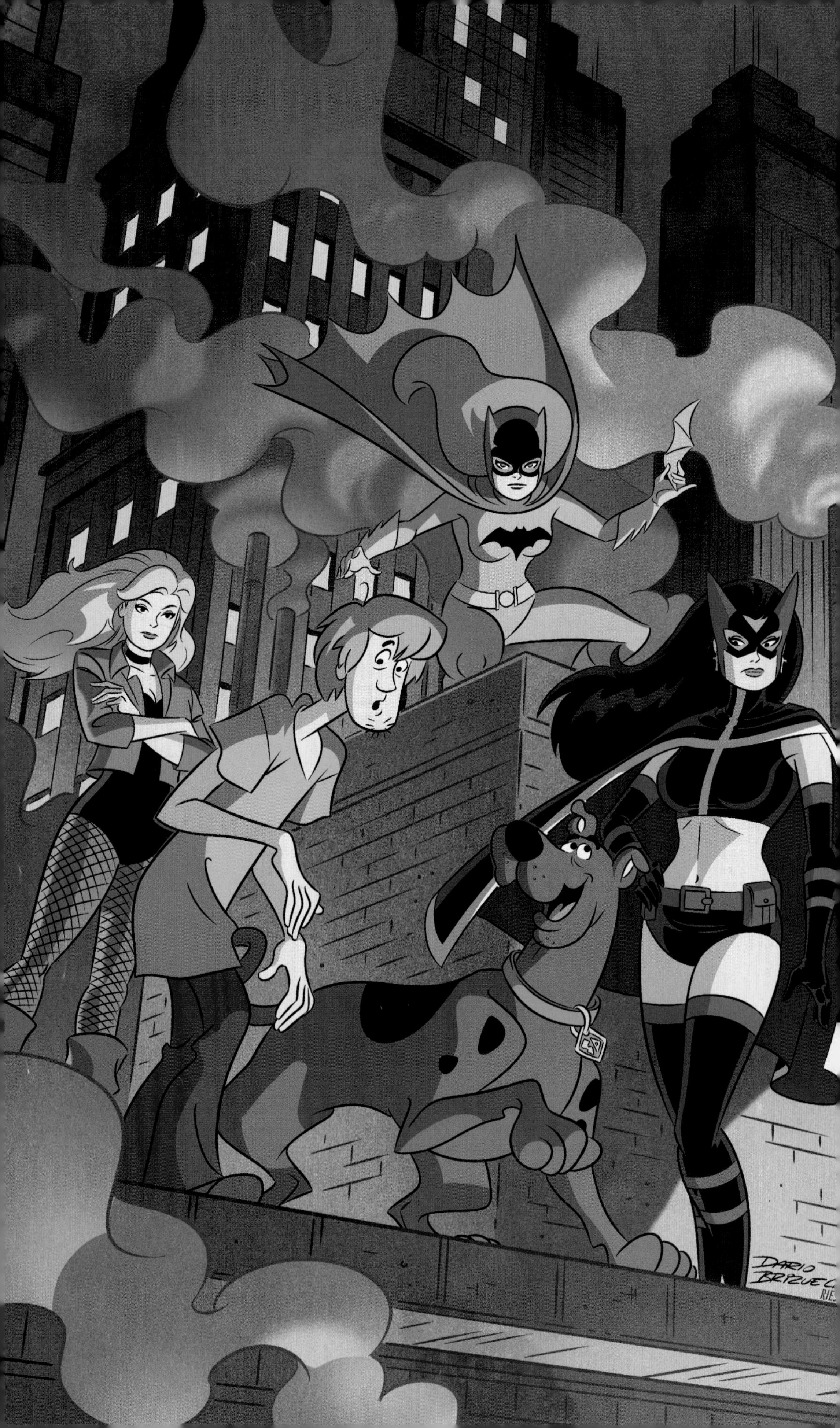
DARIO

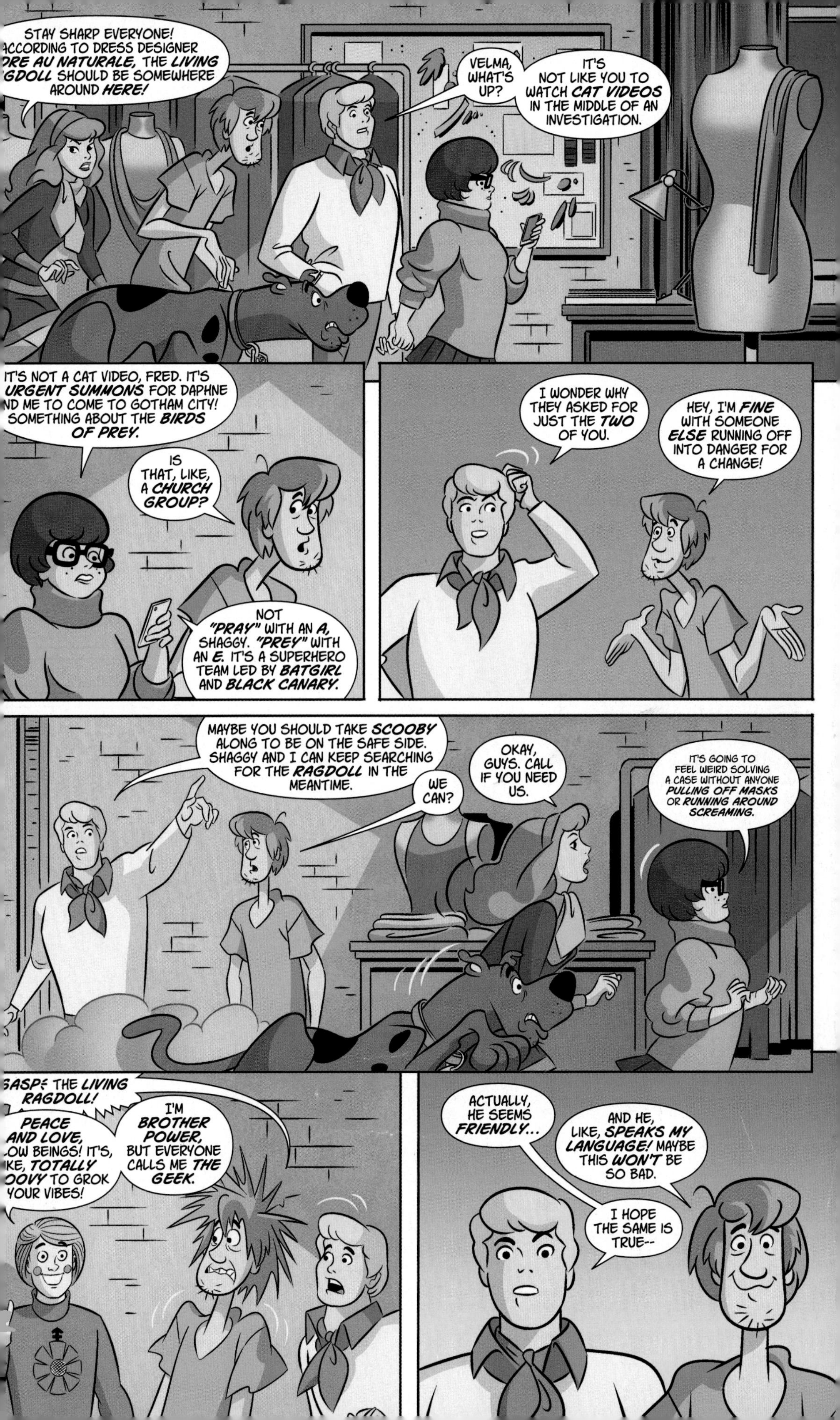
STAY SHARP EVERYONE! ACCORDING TO DRESS DESIGNER DORE AU NATURALE, THE LIVING RAGDOLL SHOULD BE SOMEWHERE AROUND HERE!
VELMA, WHAT'S UP?
IT'S NOT LIKE YOU TO WATCH CAT VIDEOS IN THE MIDDLE OF AN INVESTIGATION.
IT'S NOT A CAT VIDEO, FRED. IT'S URGENT SUMMONS FOR DAPHNE AND ME TO COME TO GOTHAM CITY! SOMETHING ABOUT THE BIRDS OF PREY.
IS THAT, LIKE, A CHURCH GROUP?
NOT "PRAY" WITH AN A, SHAGGY. "PREY" WITH AN E. IT'S A SUPERHERO TEAM LED BY BATGIRL AND BLACK CANARY.
I WONDER WHY THEY ASKED FOR JUST THE TWO OF YOU.
HEY, I'M FINE WITH SOMEONE ELSE RUNNING OFF INTO DANGER FOR A CHANGE!
MAYBE YOU SHOULD TAKE SCOOBY ALONG TO BE ON THE SAFE SIDE. SHAGGY AND I CAN KEEP SEARCHING FOR THE RAGDOLL IN THE MEANTIME.
WE CAN?
OKAY, GUYS. CALL IF YOU NEED US.
IT'S GOING TO FEEL WEIRD SOLVING A CASE WITHOUT ANYONE PULLING OFF MASKS OR RUNNING AROUND SCREAMING.
GASP! THE LIVING RAGDOLL!
PEACE AND LOVE, FELLOW BEINGS! IT'S, LIKE, TOTALLY GROOVY TO GROK YOUR VIBES!
I'M BROTHER POWER, BUT EVERYONE CALLS ME THE GEEK.
ACTUALLY, HE SEEMS FRIENDLY...
AND HE, LIKE, SPEAKS MY LANGUAGE! MAYBE THIS WON'T BE SO BAD.
I HOPE THE SAME IS TRUE--

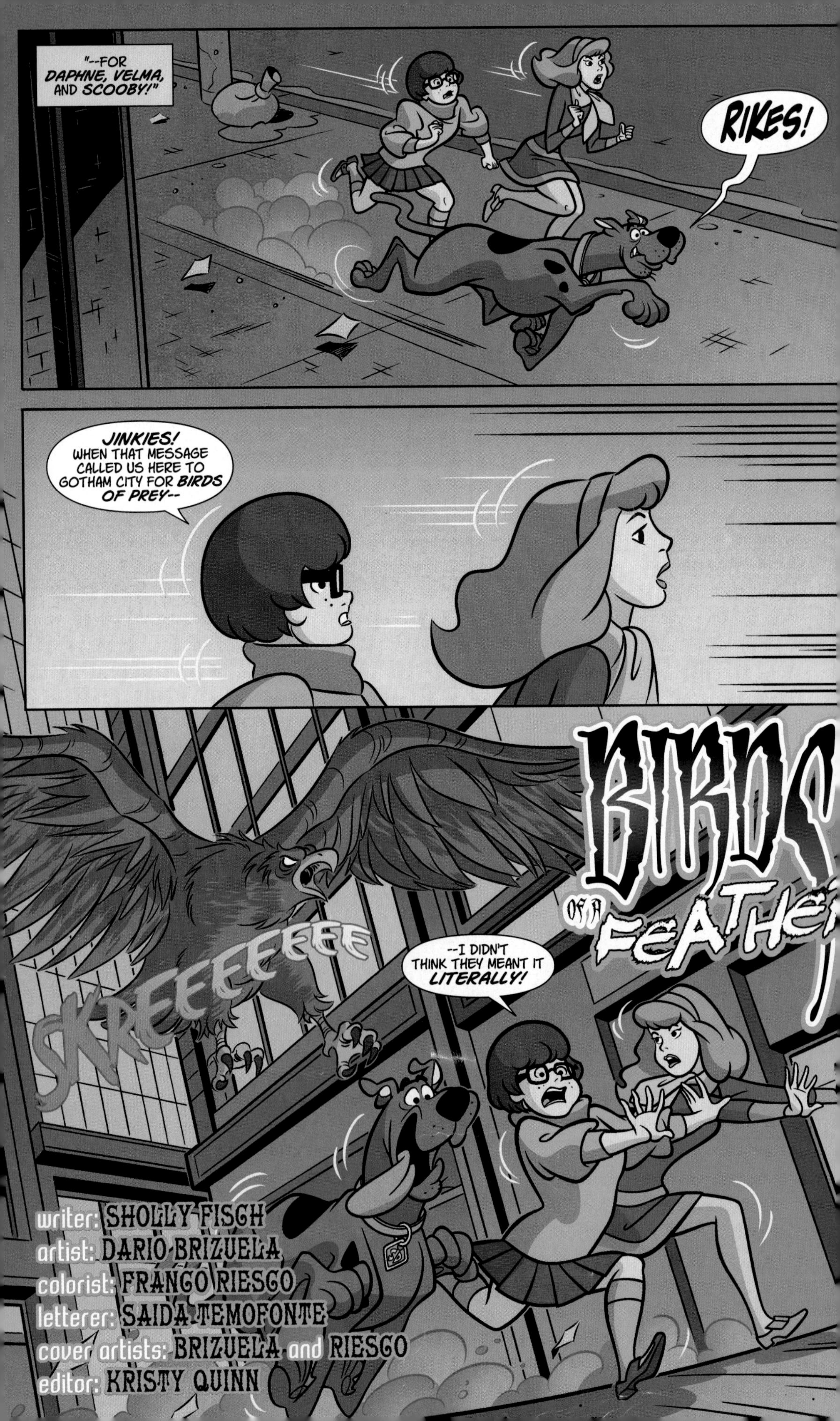

"--FOR DAPHNE, VELMA, AND SCOOBY!"
RIKES!
JINKIES! WHEN THAT MESSAGE CALLED US HERE TO GOTHAM CITY FOR BIRDS OF PREY--
BIRDS OF A FEATHER
SKREEEEEEEEE
--I DIDN'T THINK THEY MEANT IT LITERALLY!
writer: SHOLLY FISCH
artist: DARIO BRIZUELA
colorist: FRANCO RIESCO
letterer: SAIDA TEMOFONTE
cover artists: BRIZUELA and RIESCO
editor: KRISTY QUINN

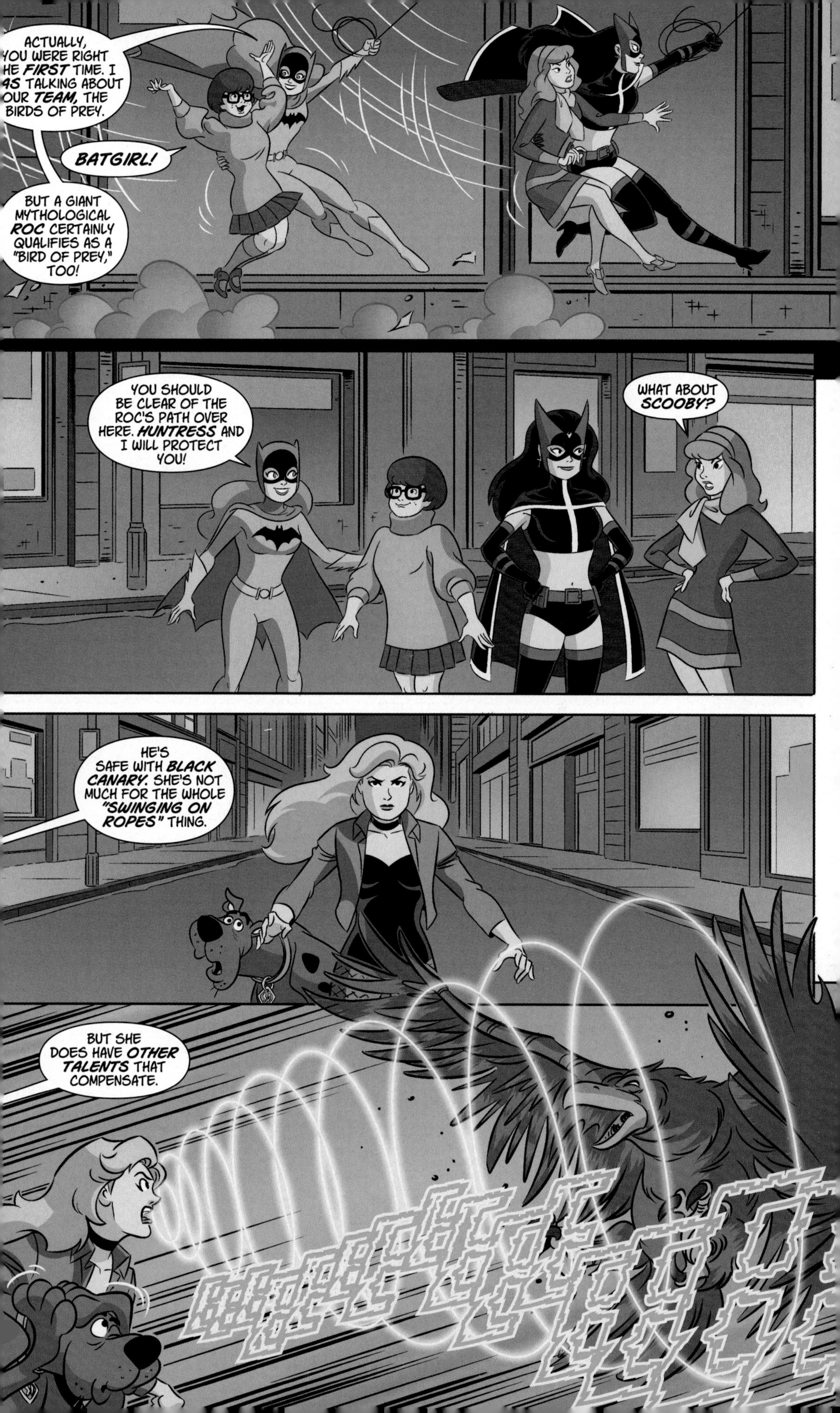

ACTUALLY, YOU WERE RIGHT HE FIRST TIME. I AS TALKING ABOUT OUR TEAM, THE BIRDS OF PREY.
BATGIRL!
BUT A GIANT MYTHOLOGICAL ROC CERTAINLY QUALIFIES AS A "BIRD OF PREY," TOO!
YOU SHOULD BE CLEAR OF THE ROC'S PATH OVER HERE. HUNTRESS AND I WILL PROTECT YOU!
WHAT ABOUT SCOOBY?
HE'S SAFE WITH BLACK CANARY. SHE'S NOT MUCH FOR THE WHOLE "SWINGING ON ROPES" THING.
BUT SHE DOES HAVE OTHER TALENTS THAT COMPENSATE.

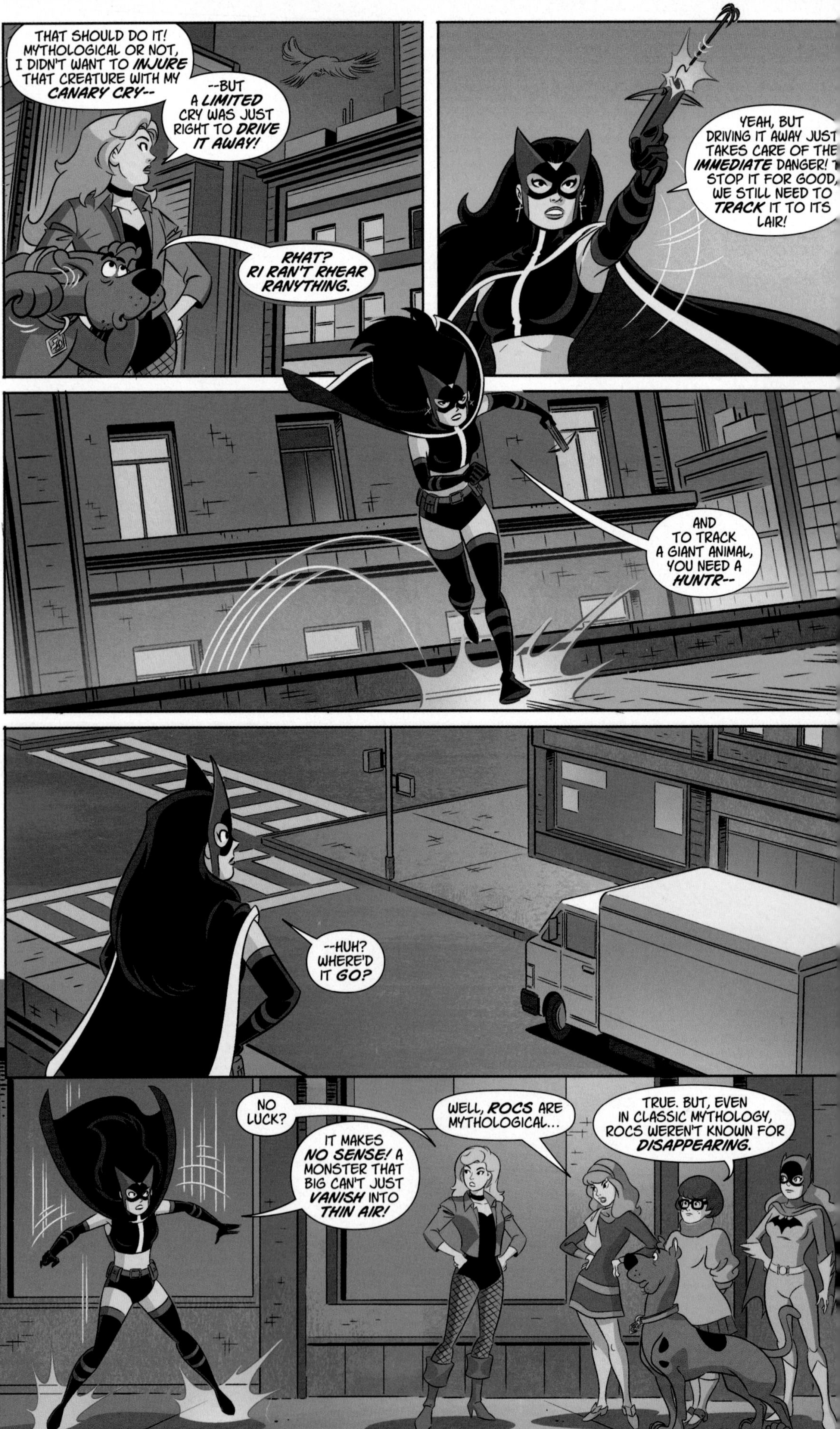
THAT SHOULD DO IT! MYTHOLOGICAL OR NOT, I DIDN'T WANT TO INJURE THAT CREATURE WITH MY CANARY CRY--
--BUT A LIMITED CRY WAS JUST RIGHT TO DRIVE IT AWAY!
RHAT? RI RAN'T RHEAR RANYTHING.
YEAH, BUT DRIVING IT AWAY JUST TAKES CARE OF THE IMMEDIATE DANGER! TO STOP IT FOR GOOD, WE STILL NEED TO TRACK IT TO ITS LAIR!
AND TO TRACK A GIANT ANIMAL, YOU NEED A HUNTR--
--HUH? WHERE'D IT GO?
NO LUCK?
IT MAKES NO SENSE! A MONSTER THAT BIG CAN'T JUST VANISH INTO THIN AIR!
WELL, ROCS ARE MYTHOLOGICAL...
TRUE. BUT, EVEN IN CLASSIC MYTHOLOGY, ROCS WEREN'T KNOWN FOR DISAPPEARING.

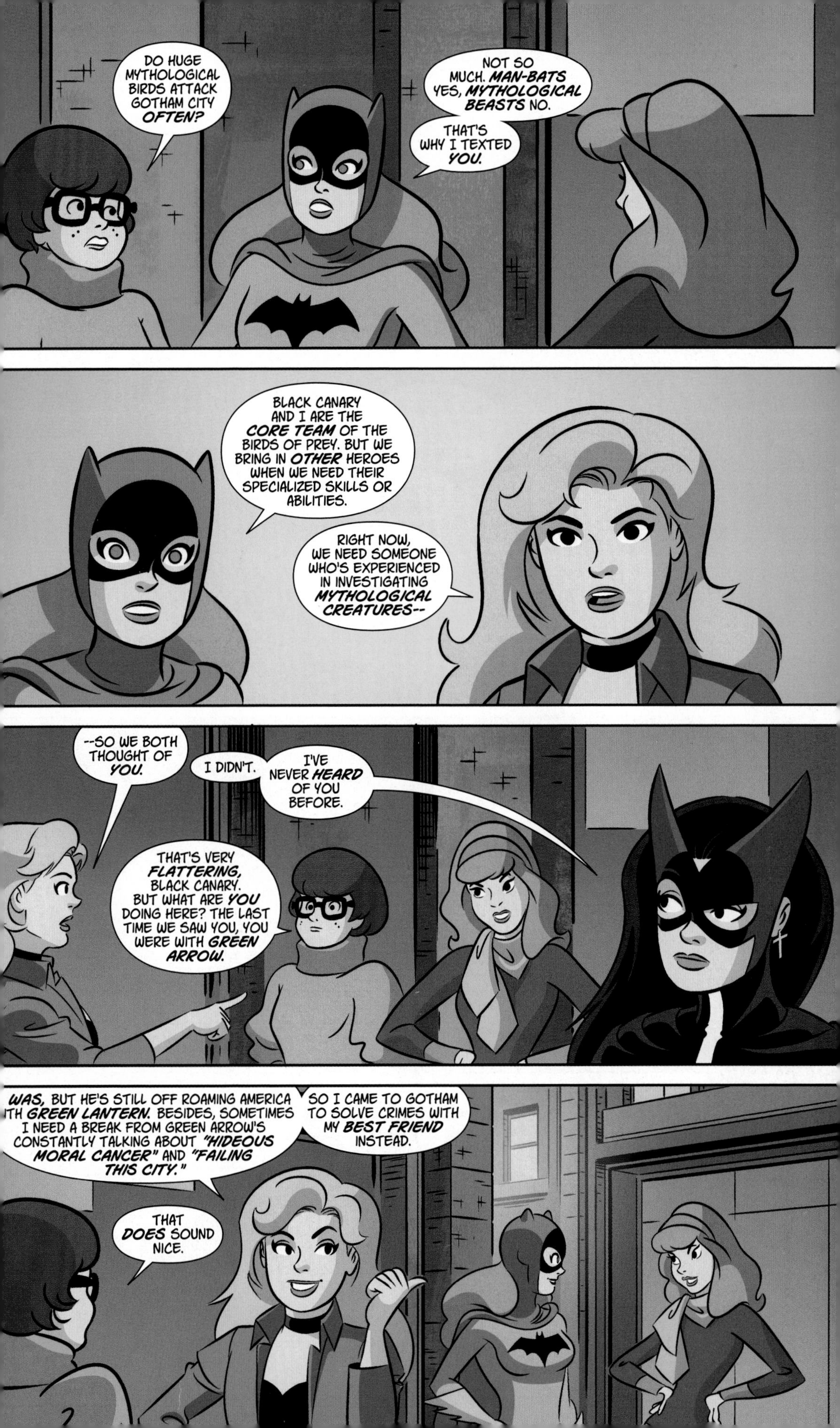
DO HUGE MYTHOLOGICAL BIRDS ATTACK GOTHAM CITY *OFTEN?*
NOT SO MUCH. *MAN-BATS* YES, *MYTHOLOGICAL BEASTS* NO.
THAT'S WHY I TEXTED *YOU.*
BLACK CANARY AND I ARE THE *CORE TEAM* OF THE BIRDS OF PREY. BUT WE BRING IN *OTHER* HEROES WHEN WE NEED THEIR SPECIALIZED SKILLS OR ABILITIES.
RIGHT NOW, WE NEED SOMEONE WHO'S EXPERIENCED IN INVESTIGATING *MYTHOLOGICAL CREATURES--*
--SO WE BOTH THOUGHT OF *YOU.*
I DIDN'T.
I'VE NEVER *HEARD* OF YOU BEFORE.
THAT'S VERY *FLATTERING,* BLACK CANARY. BUT WHAT ARE *YOU* DOING HERE? THE LAST TIME WE SAW YOU, YOU WERE WITH *GREEN ARROW.*
WAS, BUT HE'S STILL OFF ROAMING AMERICA ITH *GREEN LANTERN.* BESIDES, SOMETIMES I NEED A BREAK FROM GREEN ARROW'S CONSTANTLY TALKING ABOUT *"HIDEOUS MORAL CANCER"* AND *"FAILING THIS CITY."*
SO I CAME TO GOTHAM TO SOLVE CRIMES WITH MY *BEST FRIEND* INSTEAD.
THAT *DOES* SOUND NICE.

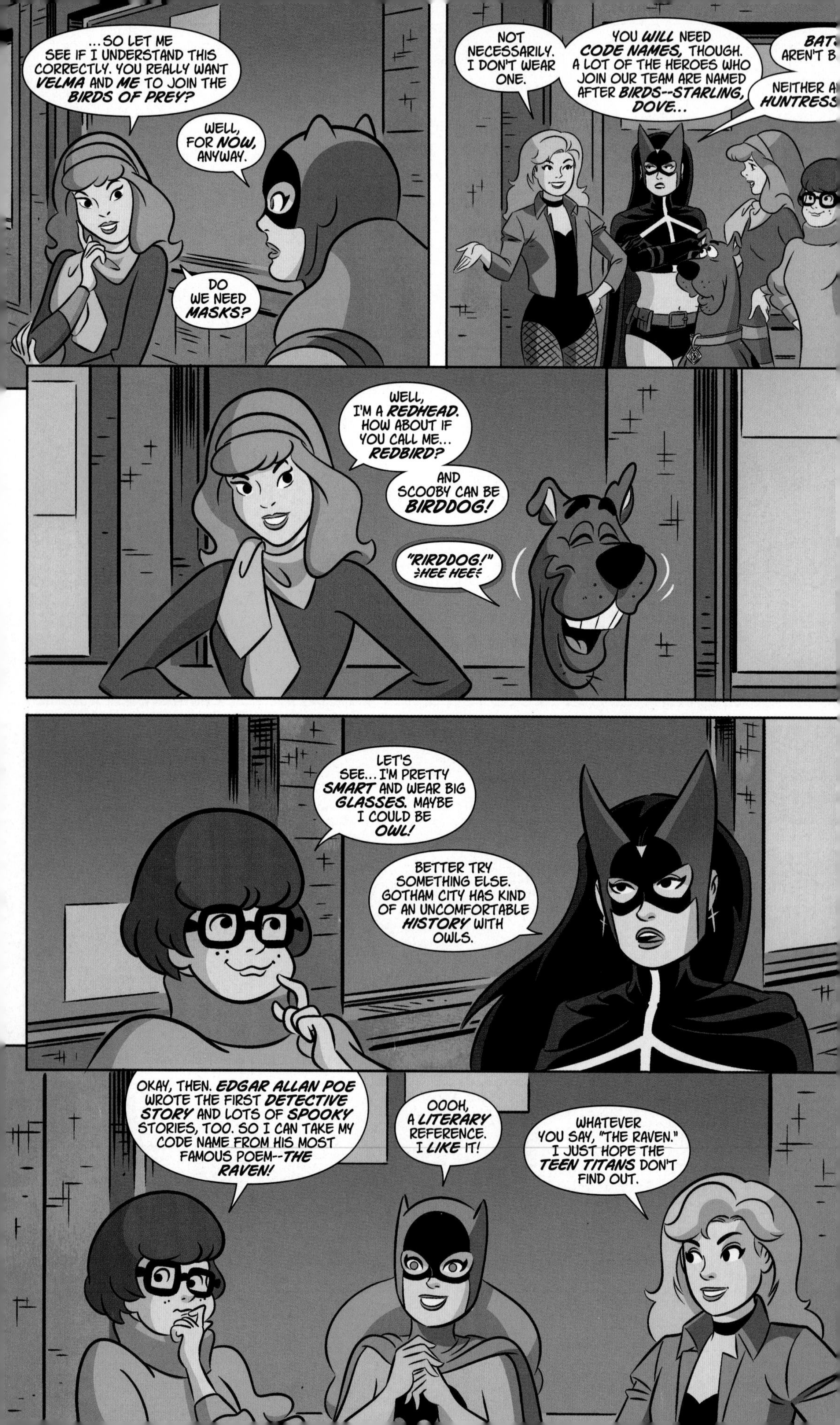
...SO LET ME SEE IF I UNDERSTAND THIS CORRECTLY. YOU REALLY WANT VELMA AND ME TO JOIN THE BIRDS OF PREY?
WELL, FOR NOW, ANYWAY.
DO WE NEED MASKS?
NOT NECESSARILY. I DON'T WEAR ONE.
YOU WILL NEED CODE NAMES, THOUGH. A LOT OF THE HEROES WHO JOIN OUR TEAM ARE NAMED AFTER BIRDS--STARLING, DOVE...
BATS AREN'T B
NEITHER A HUNTRESS
WELL, I'M A REDHEAD. HOW ABOUT IF YOU CALL ME... REDBIRD?
AND SCOOBY CAN BE BIRDDOG!
"RIRDDOG!" HEE HEE
LET'S SEE... I'M PRETTY SMART AND WEAR BIG GLASSES. MAYBE I COULD BE OWL!
BETTER TRY SOMETHING ELSE. GOTHAM CITY HAS KIND OF AN UNCOMFORTABLE HISTORY WITH OWLS.
OKAY, THEN. EDGAR ALLAN POE WROTE THE FIRST DETECTIVE STORY AND LOTS OF SPOOKY STORIES, TOO. SO I CAN TAKE MY CODE NAME FROM HIS MOST FAMOUS POEM--THE RAVEN!
OOOH, A LITERARY REFERENCE. I LIKE IT!
WHATEVER YOU SAY, "THE RAVEN." I JUST HOPE THE TEEN TITANS DON'T FIND OUT.

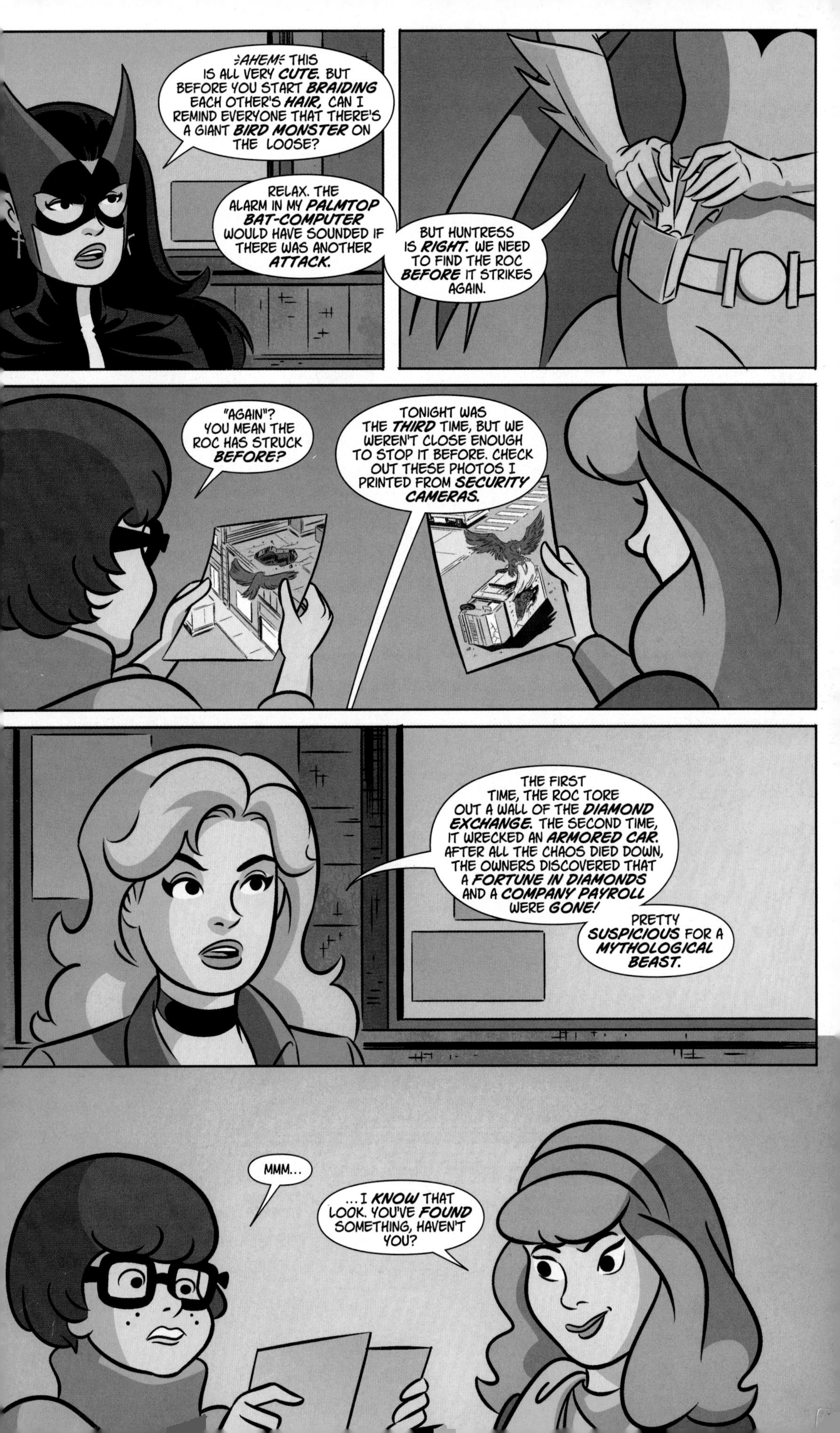

≑AHEM≑ THIS IS ALL VERY CUTE. BUT BEFORE YOU START BRAIDING EACH OTHER'S HAIR, CAN I REMIND EVERYONE THAT THERE'S A GIANT BIRD MONSTER ON THE LOOSE?
RELAX. THE ALARM IN MY PALMTOP BAT-COMPUTER WOULD HAVE SOUNDED IF THERE WAS ANOTHER ATTACK.
BUT HUNTRESS IS RIGHT. WE NEED TO FIND THE ROC BEFORE IT STRIKES AGAIN.
"AGAIN"? YOU MEAN THE ROC HAS STRUCK BEFORE?
TONIGHT WAS THE THIRD TIME, BUT WE WEREN'T CLOSE ENOUGH TO STOP IT BEFORE. CHECK OUT THESE PHOTOS I PRINTED FROM SECURITY CAMERAS.
THE FIRST TIME, THE ROC TORE OUT A WALL OF THE DIAMOND EXCHANGE. THE SECOND TIME, IT WRECKED AN ARMORED CAR. AFTER ALL THE CHAOS DIED DOWN, THE OWNERS DISCOVERED THAT A FORTUNE IN DIAMONDS AND A COMPANY PAYROLL WERE GONE!
PRETTY SUSPICIOUS FOR A MYTHOLOGICAL BEAST.
MMM...
...I KNOW THAT LOOK. YOU'VE FOUND SOMETHING, HAVEN'T YOU?

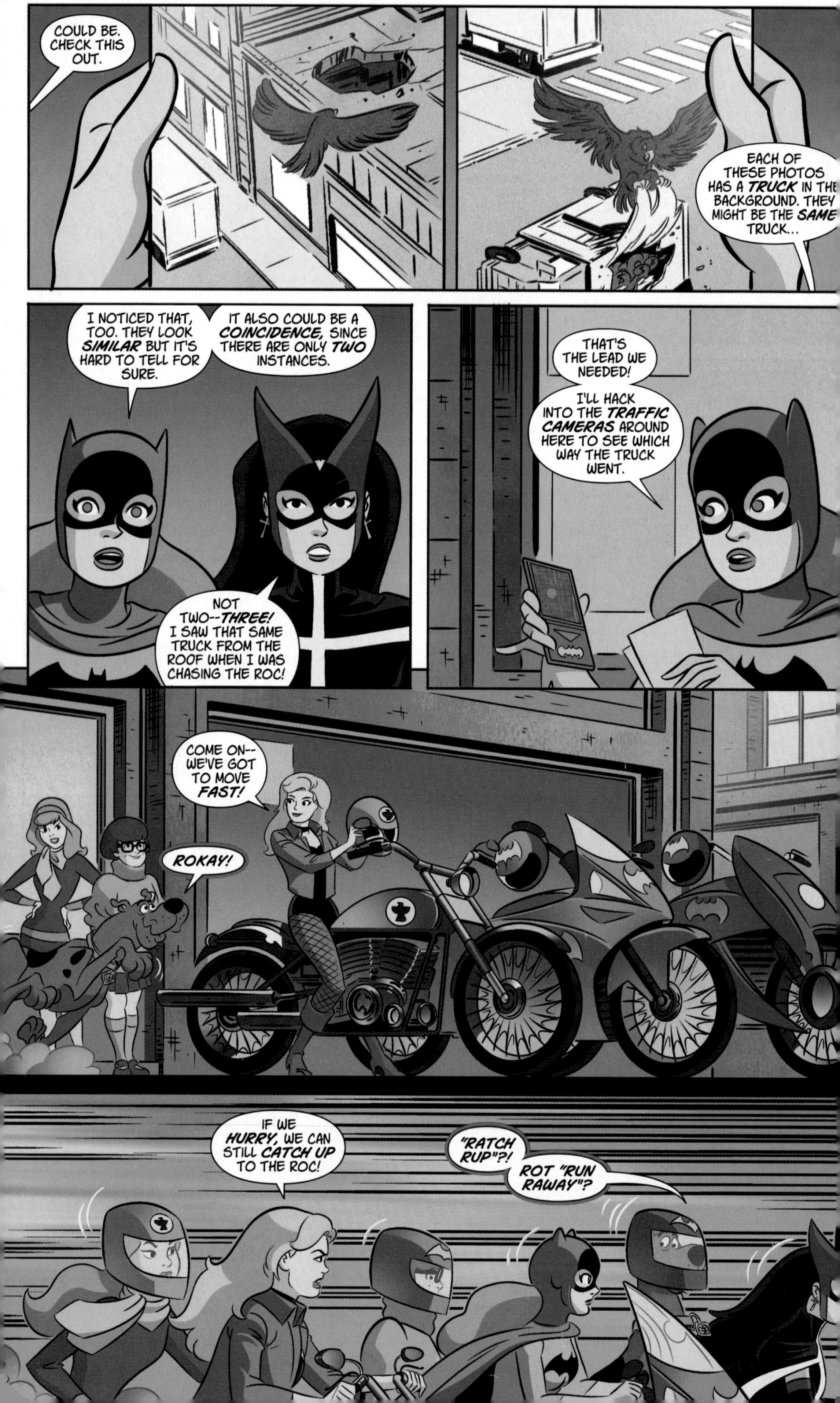

COULD BE. CHECK THIS OUT.
EACH OF THESE PHOTOS HAS A TRUCK IN THE BACKGROUND. THEY MIGHT BE THE SAME TRUCK...
I NOTICED THAT, TOO. THEY LOOK SIMILAR BUT IT'S HARD TO TELL FOR SURE.
IT ALSO COULD BE A COINCIDENCE, SINCE THERE ARE ONLY TWO INSTANCES.
NOT TWO--THREE! I SAW THAT SAME TRUCK FROM THE ROOF WHEN I WAS CHASING THE ROC!
THAT'S THE LEAD WE NEEDED!
I'LL HACK INTO THE TRAFFIC CAMERAS AROUND HERE TO SEE WHICH WAY THE TRUCK WENT.
COME ON-- WE'VE GOT TO MOVE FAST!
ROKAY!
IF WE HURRY, WE CAN STILL CATCH UP TO THE ROC!
"RATCH RUP"?!
ROT "RUN RAWAY"?

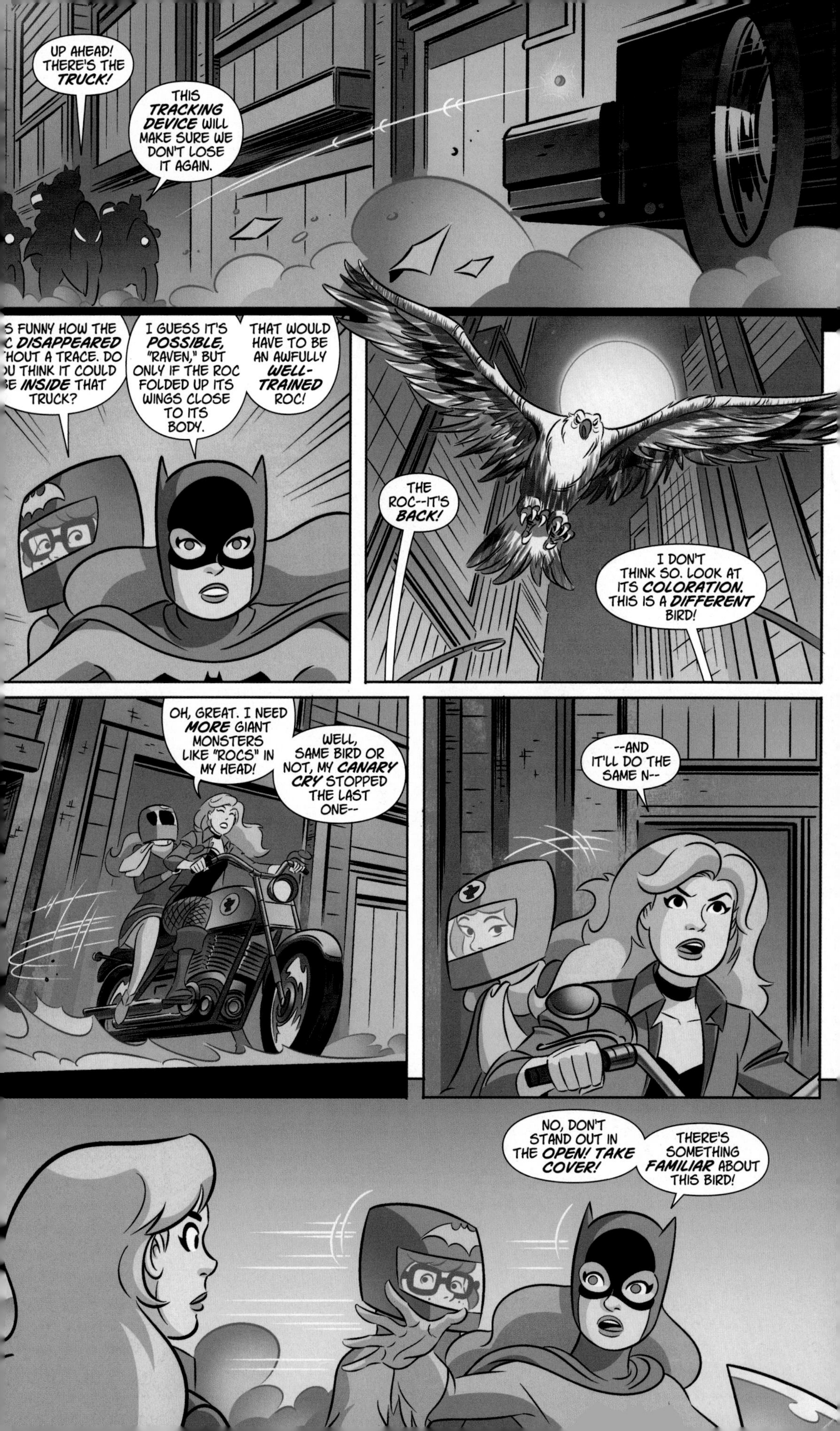
UP AHEAD! THERE'S THE TRUCK!
THIS TRACKING DEVICE WILL MAKE SURE WE DON'T LOSE IT AGAIN.
S FUNNY HOW THE C DISAPPEARED THOUT A TRACE. DO U THINK IT COULD E INSIDE THAT TRUCK?
I GUESS IT'S POSSIBLE, "RAVEN," BUT ONLY IF THE ROC FOLDED UP ITS WINGS CLOSE TO ITS BODY.
THAT WOULD HAVE TO BE AN AWFULLY WELL-TRAINED ROC!
THE ROC--IT'S BACK!
I DON'T THINK SO. LOOK AT ITS COLORATION. THIS IS A DIFFERENT BIRD!
OH, GREAT. I NEED MORE GIANT MONSTERS LIKE "ROCS" IN MY HEAD!
WELL, SAME BIRD OR NOT, MY CANARY CRY STOPPED THE LAST ONE--
--AND IT'LL DO THE SAME N--
NO, DON'T STAND OUT IN THE OPEN! TAKE COVER!
THERE'S SOMETHING FAMILIAR ABOUT THIS BIRD!

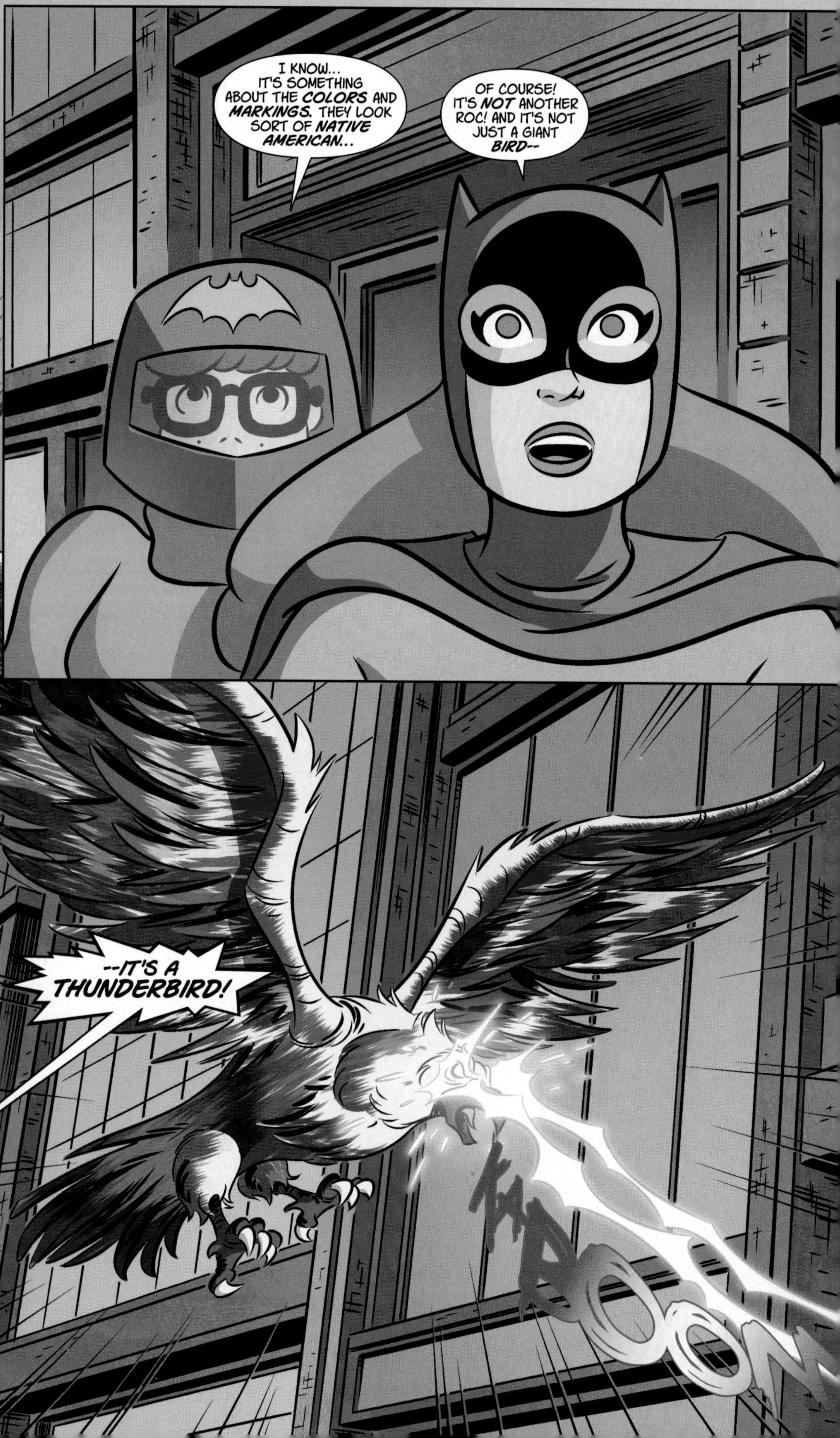
I KNOW... IT'S SOMETHING ABOUT THE COLORS AND MARKINGS. THEY LOOK SORT OF NATIVE AMERICAN...
OF COURSE! IT'S NOT ANOTHER ROC! AND IT'S NOT JUST A GIANT BIRD--
--IT'S A THUNDERBIRD!

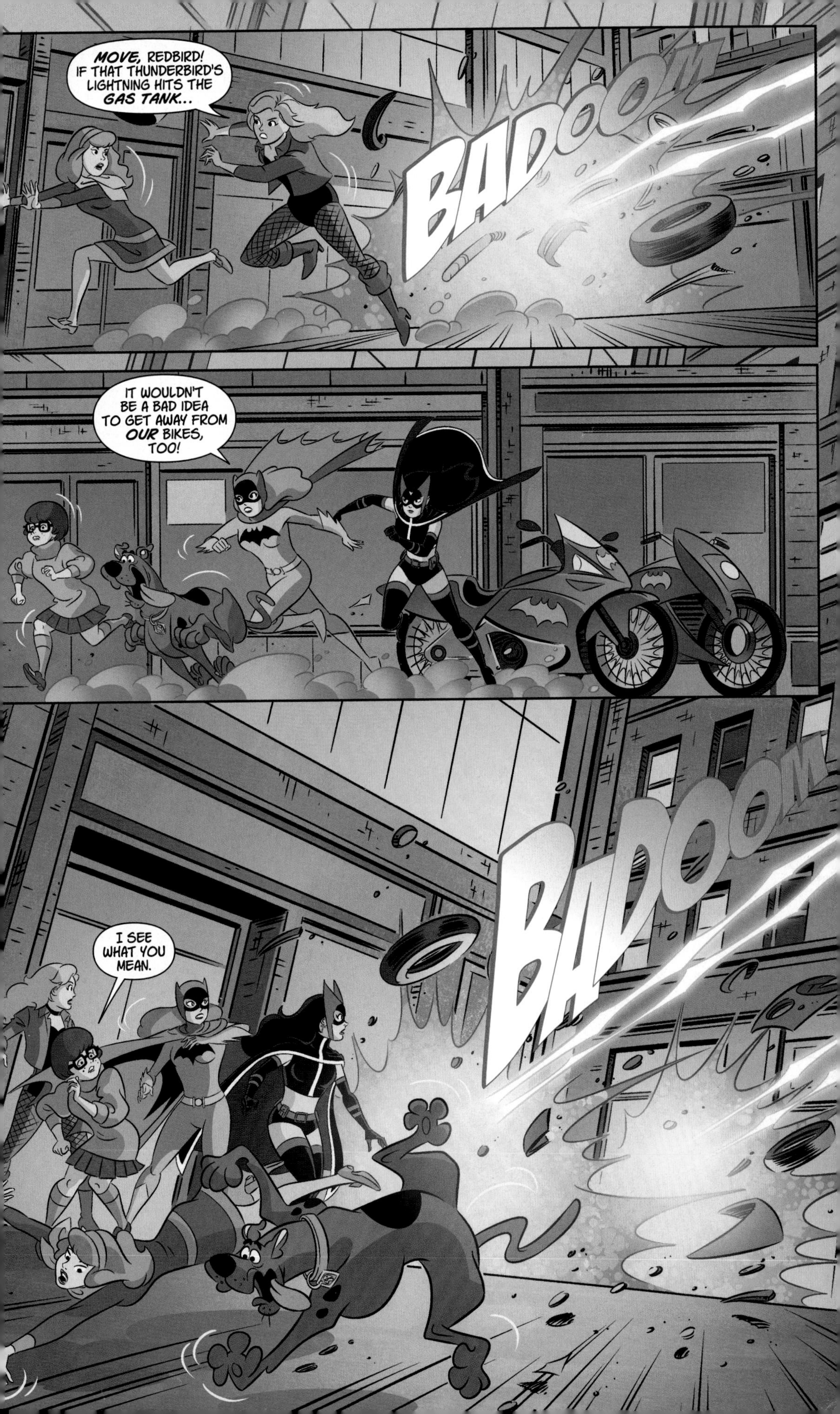
MOVE, REDBIRD! IF THAT THUNDERBIRD'S LIGHTNING HITS THE GAS TANK...
BADOOOM
IT WOULDN'T BE A BAD IDEA TO GET AWAY FROM OUR BIKES, TOO!
I SEE WHAT YOU MEAN.
BADOOOM

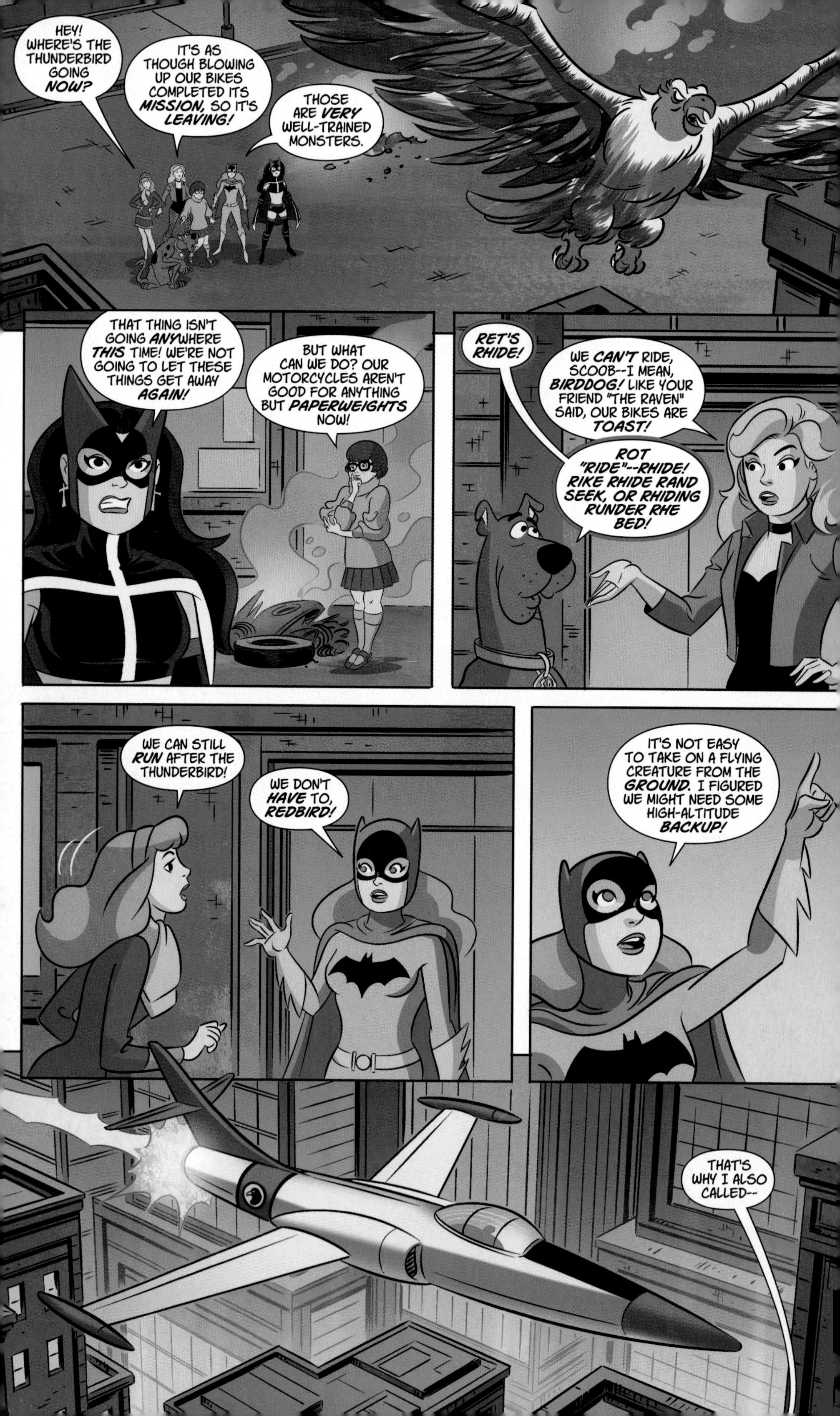
HEY! WHERE'S THE THUNDERBIRD GOING NOW?
IT'S AS THOUGH BLOWING UP OUR BIKES COMPLETED ITS MISSION, SO IT'S LEAVING!
THOSE ARE VERY WELL-TRAINED MONSTERS.
THAT THING ISN'T GOING ANYWHERE THIS TIME! WE'RE NOT GOING TO LET THESE THINGS GET AWAY AGAIN!
BUT WHAT CAN WE DO? OUR MOTORCYCLES AREN'T GOOD FOR ANYTHING BUT PAPERWEIGHTS NOW!
RET'S RHIDE!
WE CAN'T RIDE, SCOOB--I MEAN, BIRDDOG! LIKE YOUR FRIEND "THE RAVEN" SAID, OUR BIKES ARE TOAST!
ROT "RIDE"--RHIDE! RIKE RHIDE RAND SEEK, OR RHIDING RUNDER RHE BED!
WE CAN STILL RUN AFTER THE THUNDERBIRD!
WE DON'T HAVE TO, REDBIRD!
IT'S NOT EASY TO TAKE ON A FLYING CREATURE FROM THE GROUND. I FIGURED WE MIGHT NEED SOME HIGH-ALTITUDE BACKUP!
THAT'S WHY I ALSO CALLED--

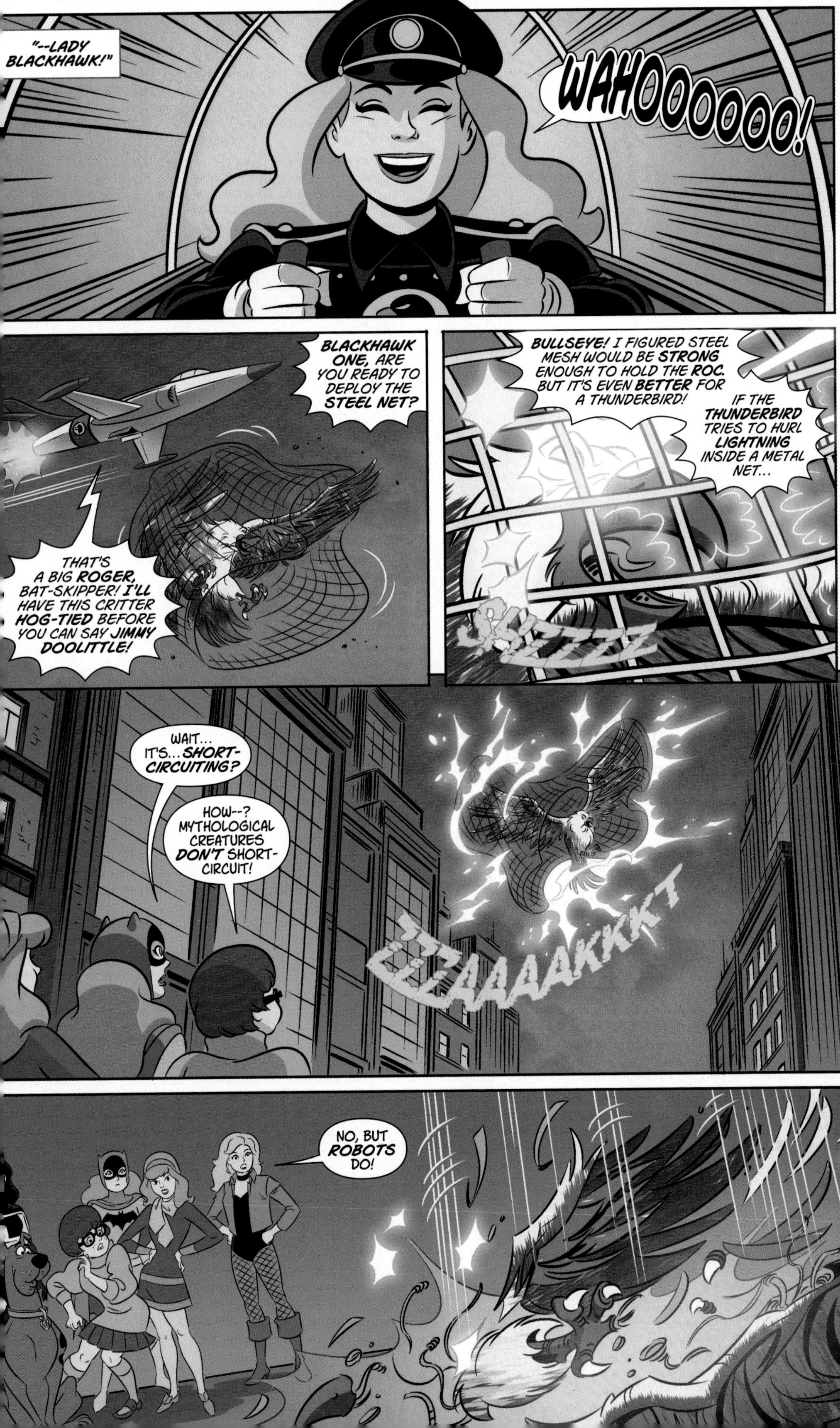
"--LADY BLACKHAWK!"
WAHOOOOOOO!
BLACKHAWK ONE, ARE YOU READY TO DEPLOY THE STEEL NET?
THAT'S A BIG ROGER, BAT-SKIPPER! I'LL HAVE THIS CRITTER HOG-TIED BEFORE YOU CAN SAY JIMMY DOOLITTLE!
BULLSEYE! I FIGURED STEEL MESH WOULD BE STRONG ENOUGH TO HOLD THE ROC. BUT IT'S EVEN BETTER FOR A THUNDERBIRD!
IF THE THUNDERBIRD TRIES TO HURL LIGHTNING INSIDE A METAL NET...
WAIT... IT'S... SHORT-CIRCUITING?
HOW--? MYTHOLOGICAL CREATURES DON'T SHORT-CIRCUIT!
NO, BUT ROBOTS DO!

THANKS FOR THE HELP, LADY B!

DE NADA, SKIPPER!

NOW, IF YOU LADIES DON'T NEED ME ANYMORE, I'M GONNA HIGHTAIL IT OUTTA HERE. I'M LATE FOR A *HOT DATE* WITH A *COOL CUSTOMER*, IF YOU GET MY DRIFT!

AFFIRMATIVE. GO HAVE FUN.

WHY WOULD SOMEONE BUILD A *ROBOT ROC* AND *THUNDERBIRD*, ANYWAY?

I DON'T KNOW. BUT, ACCORDING TO THE *TRACKING DEVICE* I PLANTED ON THE TRUCK...

...THE TRUCK-- AND THE *ANSWER*-- ARE IN THAT *WAREHOUSE!*

THAT'S ALL I NEED TO KNOW! LET'S GO!

HOLD ON! THAT'S *NOT* ALL WE NEED TO KNOW!

IT'D BE SMARTER TO KNOW WHAT'S WAITING FOR US INSIDE FIRST.

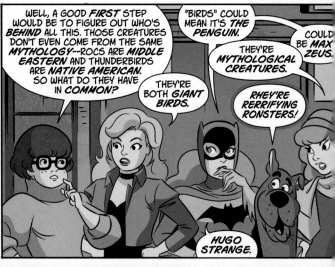

WELL, A GOOD *FIRST* STEP WOULD BE TO FIGURE OUT WHO'S *BEHIND* ALL THIS. THOSE CREATURES DON'T EVEN COME FROM THE SAME *MYTHOLOGY*--ROCS ARE *MIDDLE EASTERN* AND THUNDERBIRDS ARE *NATIVE AMERICAN*. SO WHAT DO THEY HAVE IN *COMMON*?

"BIRDS" COULD MEAN IT'S *THE PENGUIN.*

THEY'RE *MYTHOLOGICAL CREATURES.*

COULD BE *MAX ZEUS.*

THEY'RE BOTH *GIANT BIRDS.*

RHEY'RE RERRIFYING RONSTERS!

HUGO STRANGE.

WHAT DO *YOU* THINK, HUNTRESS?

I THINK WE'LL *KNOW* IN A MINUTE.

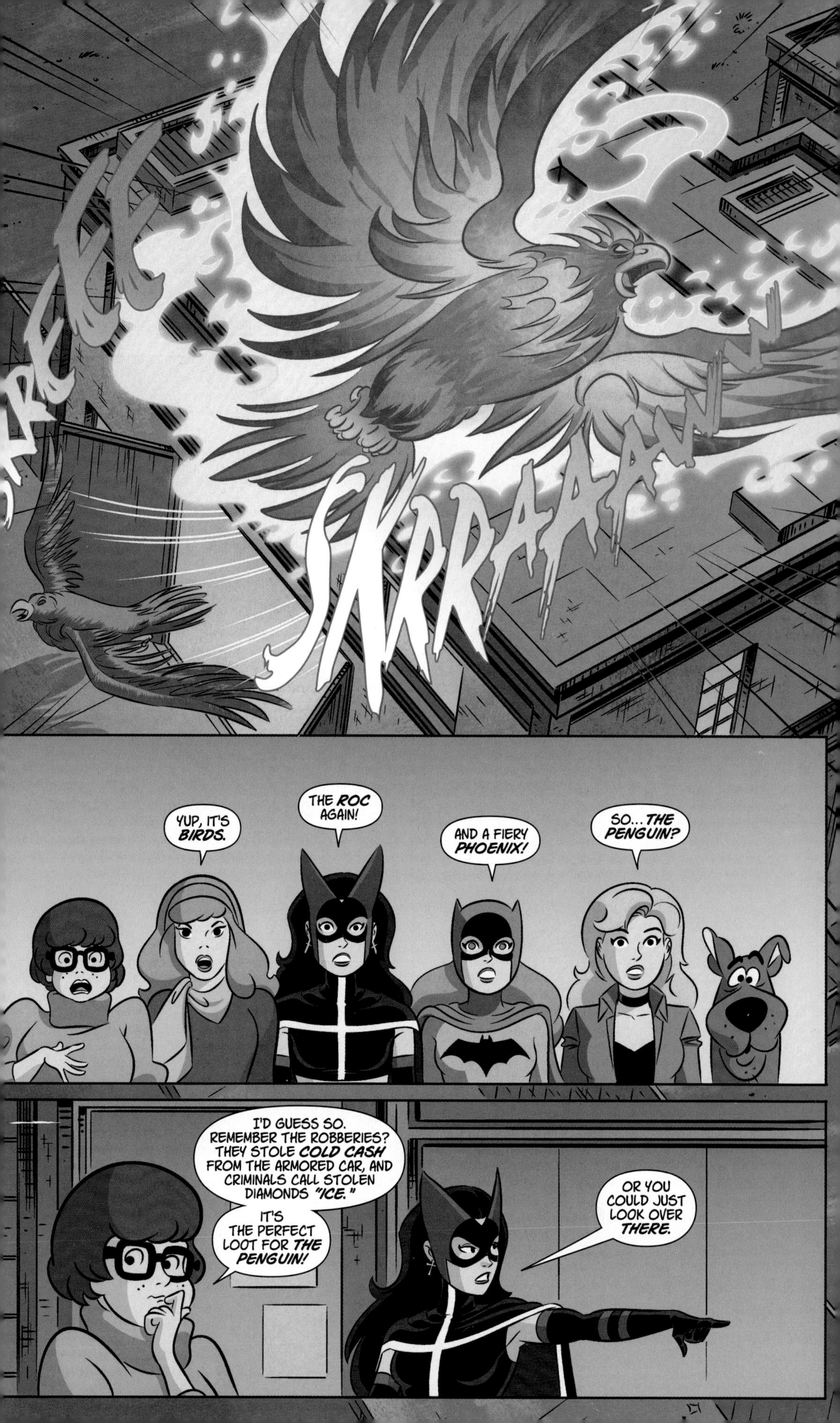
SKRAAAW
YUP, IT'S BIRDS.
THE ROC AGAIN!
AND A FIERY PHOENIX!
SO... THE PENGUIN?
I'D GUESS SO. REMEMBER THE ROBBERIES? THEY STOLE COLD CASH FROM THE ARMORED CAR, AND CRIMINALS CALL STOLEN DIAMONDS "ICE."
IT'S THE PERFECT LOOT FOR THE PENGUIN!
OR YOU COULD JUST LOOK OVER THERE.

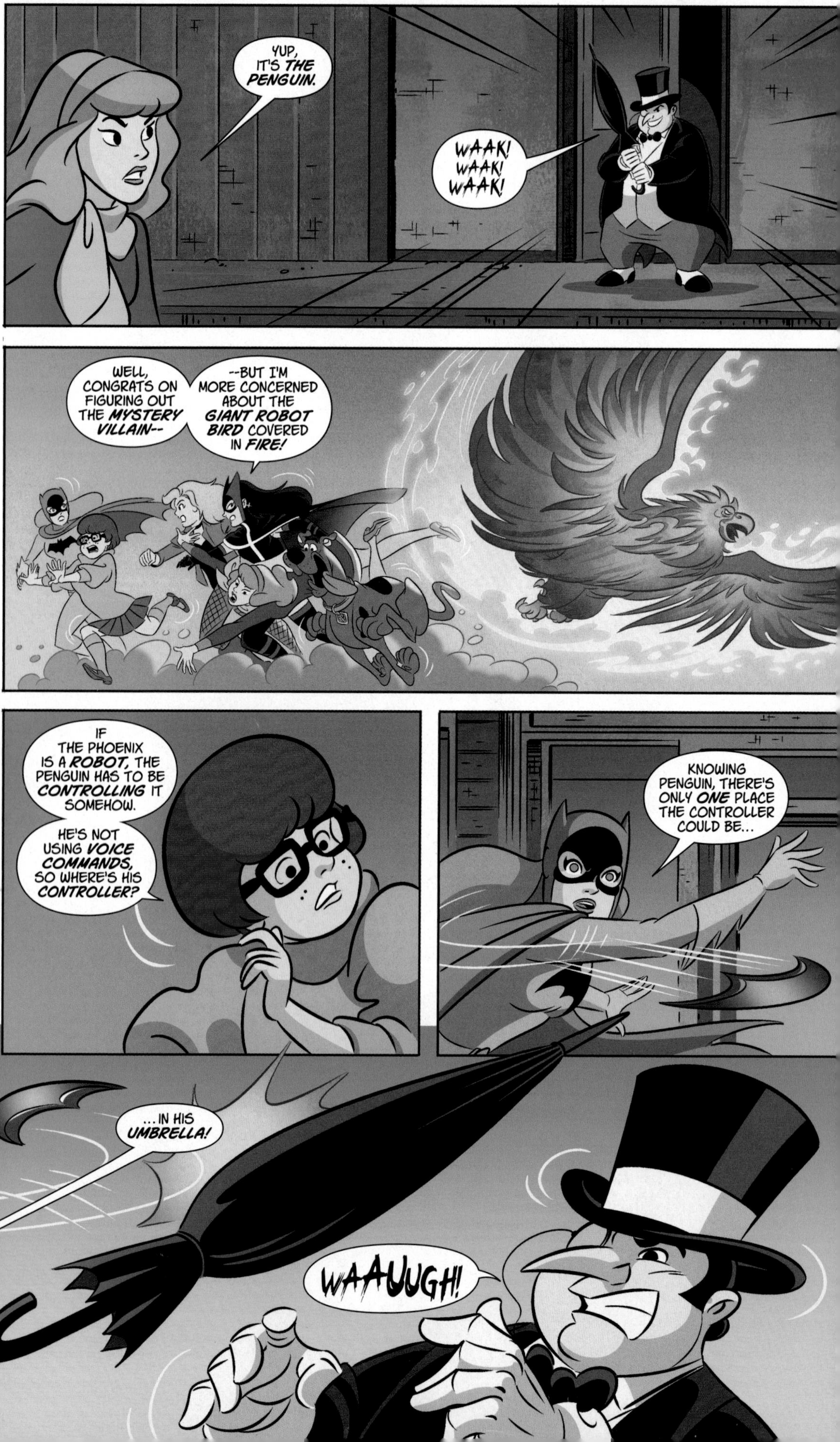
YUP, IT'S THE PENGUIN.
WAAK! WAAK! WAAK!
WELL, CONGRATS ON FIGURING OUT THE MYSTERY VILLAIN--
--BUT I'M MORE CONCERNED ABOUT THE GIANT ROBOT BIRD COVERED IN FIRE!
IF THE PHOENIX IS A ROBOT, THE PENGUIN HAS TO BE CONTROLLING IT SOMEHOW.
HE'S NOT USING VOICE COMMANDS, SO WHERE'S HIS CONTROLLER?
KNOWING PENGUIN, THERE'S ONLY ONE PLACE THE CONTROLLER COULD BE...
...IN HIS UMBRELLA!
WAAUUGH!

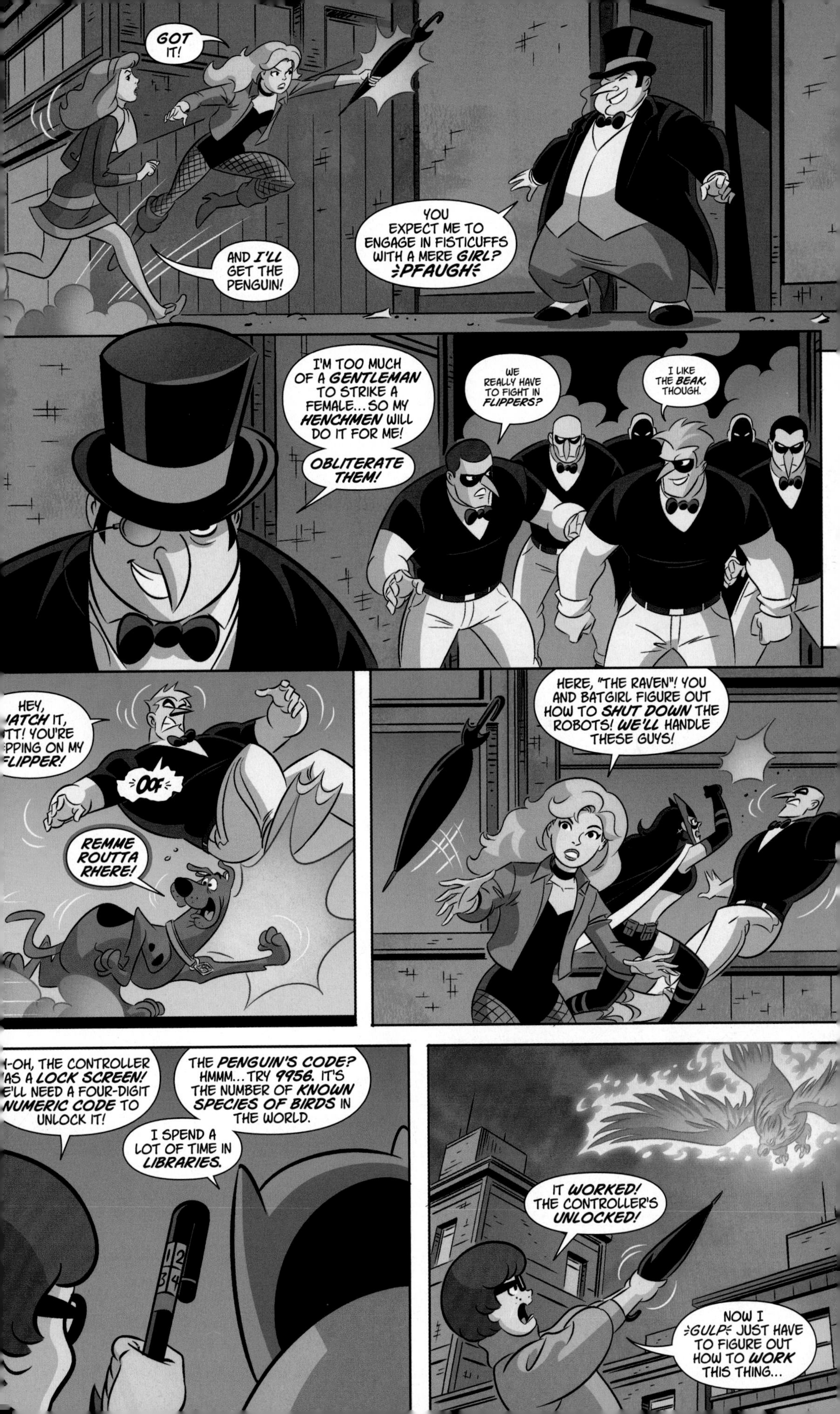

GOT IT!
AND I'LL GET THE PENGUIN!
YOU EXPECT ME TO ENGAGE IN FISTICUFFS WITH A MERE GIRL? PFAUGH
I'M TOO MUCH OF A GENTLEMAN TO STRIKE A FEMALE... SO MY HENCHMEN WILL DO IT FOR ME!
OBLITERATE THEM!
WE REALLY HAVE TO FIGHT IN FLIPPERS?
I LIKE THE BEAK, THOUGH.
HEY, ATCH IT, TT! YOU'RE PPING ON MY FLIPPER!
OOF
REMME ROUTTA RHERE!
HERE, "THE RAVEN"! YOU AND BATGIRL FIGURE OUT HOW TO SHUT DOWN THE ROBOTS! WE'LL HANDLE THESE GUYS!
-OH, THE CONTROLLER AS A LOCK SCREEN! E'LL NEED A FOUR-DIGIT NUMERIC CODE TO UNLOCK IT!
THE PENGUIN'S CODE? HMMM... TRY 9956. IT'S THE NUMBER OF KNOWN SPECIES OF BIRDS IN THE WORLD.
I SPEND A LOT OF TIME IN LIBRARIES.
IT WORKED! THE CONTROLLER'S UNLOCKED!
NOW I GULP JUST HAVE TO FIGURE OUT HOW TO WORK THIS THING...

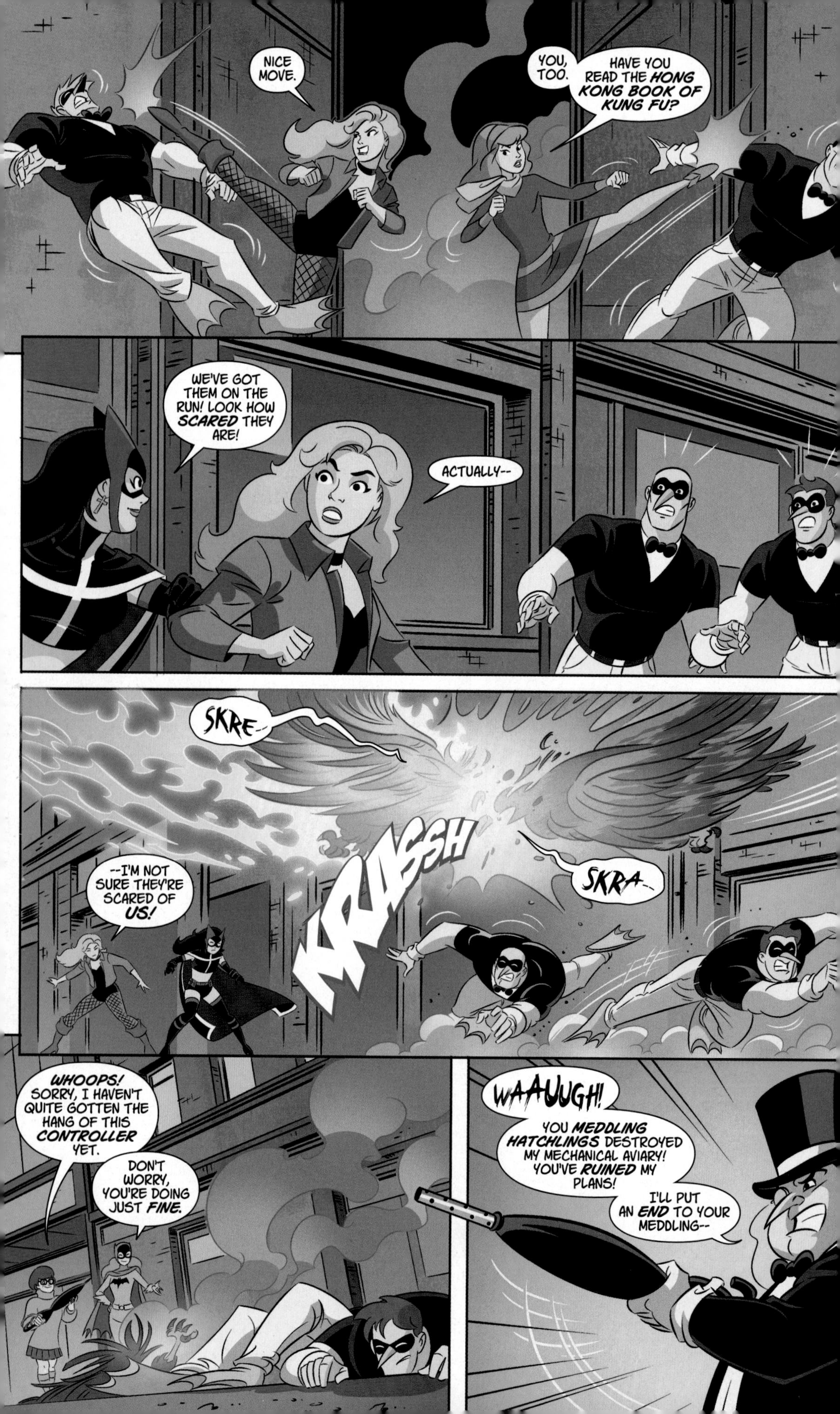
NICE MOVE.
YOU, TOO.
HAVE YOU READ THE HONG KONG BOOK OF KUNG FU?
WE'VE GOT THEM ON THE RUN! LOOK HOW SCARED THEY ARE!
ACTUALLY--
SKRE--
KRASSH
SKRA--
--I'M NOT SURE THEY'RE SCARED OF US!
WHOOPS! SORRY, I HAVEN'T QUITE GOTTEN THE HANG OF THIS CONTROLLER YET.
DON'T WORRY, YOU'RE DOING JUST FINE.
WAAUUGH!
YOU MEDDLING HATCHLINGS DESTROYED MY MECHANICAL AVIARY! YOU'VE RUINED MY PLANS!
I'LL PUT AN END TO YOUR MEDDLING--

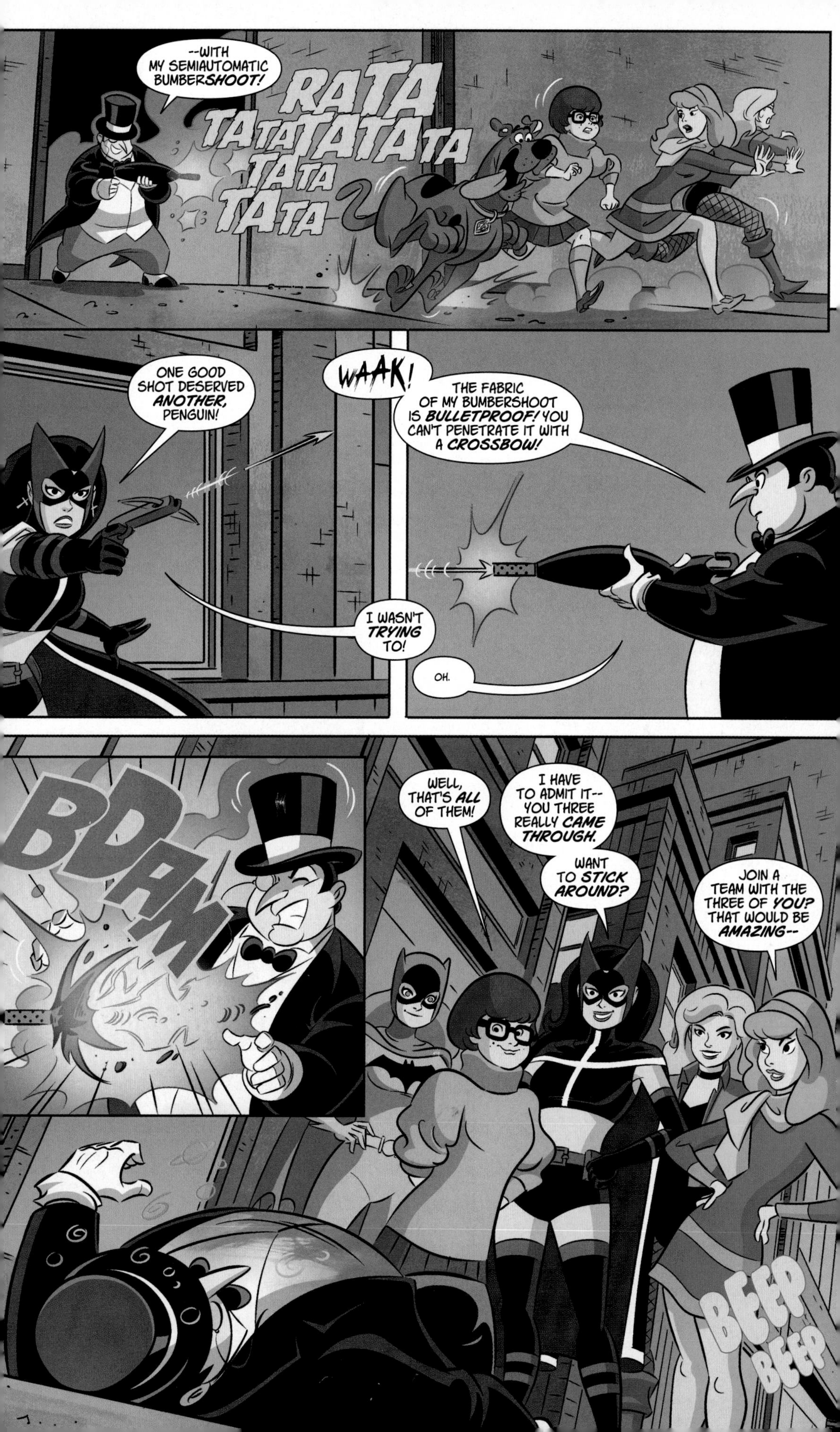
--WITH MY SEMIAUTOMATIC BUMBERSHOOT!
RATA TATATATATATA TATA TATA
ONE GOOD SHOT DESERVED ANOTHER, PENGUIN!
WAAK!
THE FABRIC OF MY BUMBERSHOOT IS BULLETPROOF! YOU CAN'T PENETRATE IT WITH A CROSSBOW!
I WASN'T TRYING TO!
OH.
BDAM
WELL, THAT'S ALL OF THEM!
I HAVE TO ADMIT IT-- YOU THREE REALLY CAME THROUGH.
WANT TO STICK AROUND?
JOIN A TEAM WITH THE THREE OF YOU? THAT WOULD BE AMAZING--
BEEP BEEP

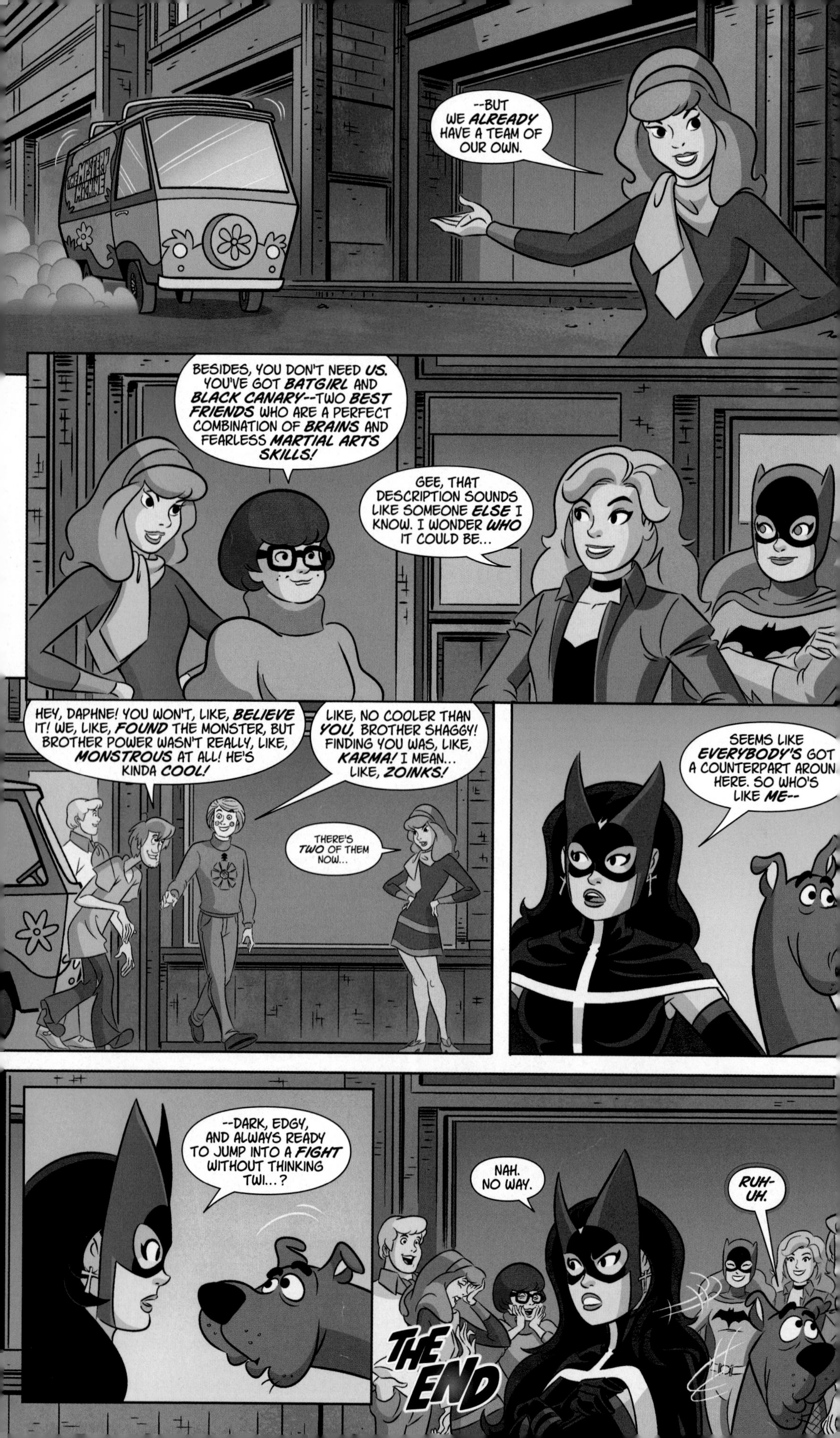
--BUT WE ALREADY HAVE A TEAM OF OUR OWN.
BESIDES, YOU DON'T NEED US. YOU'VE GOT BATGIRL AND BLACK CANARY--TWO BEST FRIENDS WHO ARE A PERFECT COMBINATION OF BRAINS AND FEARLESS MARTIAL ARTS SKILLS!
GEE, THAT DESCRIPTION SOUNDS LIKE SOMEONE ELSE I KNOW. I WONDER WHO IT COULD BE...
HEY, DAPHNE! YOU WON'T, LIKE, BELIEVE IT! WE, LIKE, FOUND THE MONSTER, BUT BROTHER POWER WASN'T REALLY, LIKE, MONSTROUS AT ALL! HE'S KINDA COOL!
LIKE, NO COOLER THAN YOU, BROTHER SHAGGY! FINDING YOU WAS, LIKE, KARMA! I MEAN... LIKE, ZOINKS!
THERE'S TWO OF THEM NOW...
SEEMS LIKE EVERYBODY'S GOT A COUNTERPART AROUN HERE. SO WHO'S LIKE ME--
--DARK, EDGY, AND ALWAYS READY TO JUMP INTO A FIGHT WITHOUT THINKING TWI...?
NAH. NO WAY.
RUH-UH.
THE END

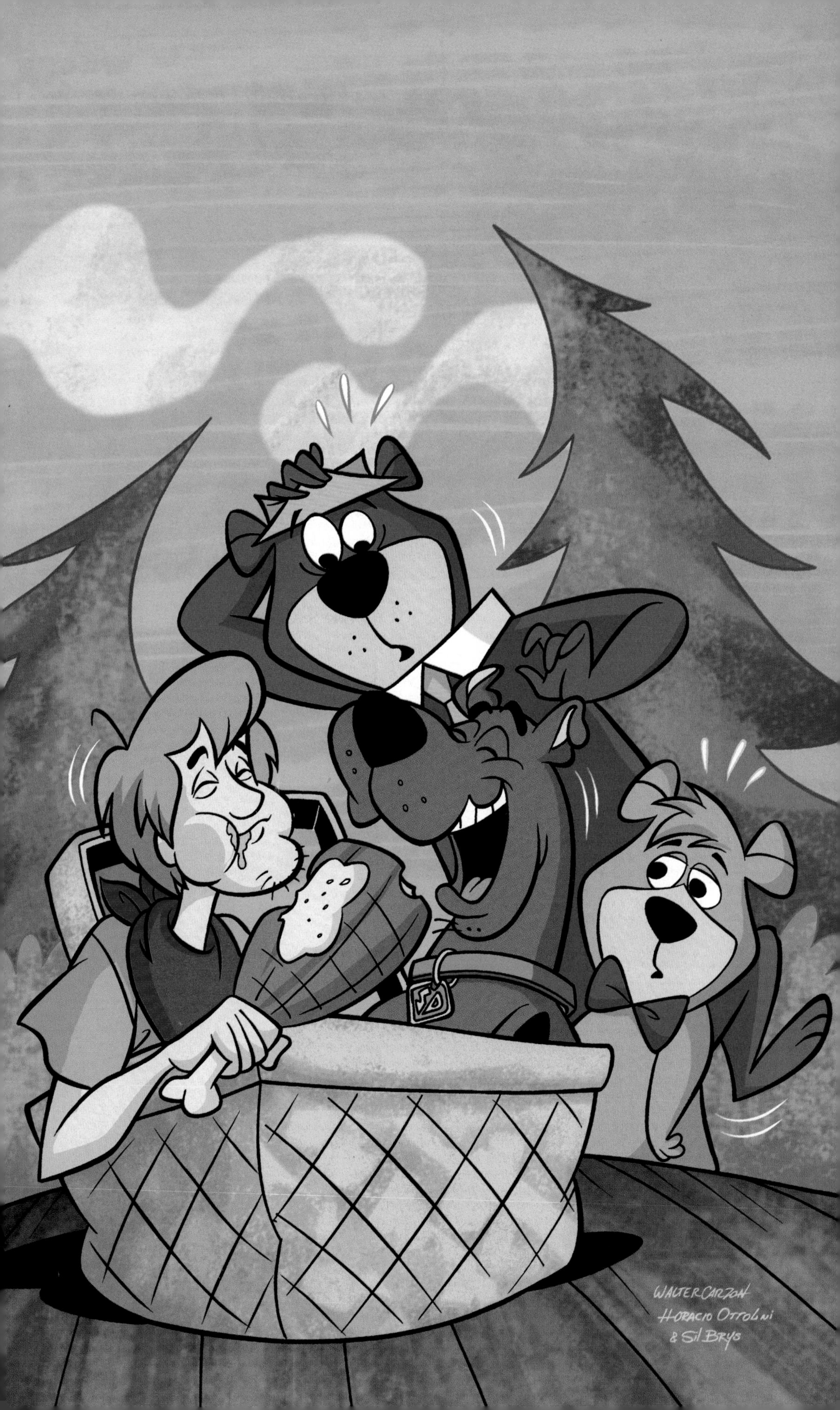
WALTER CARZON
HORACIO OTTOLINI
& SIL BRYS

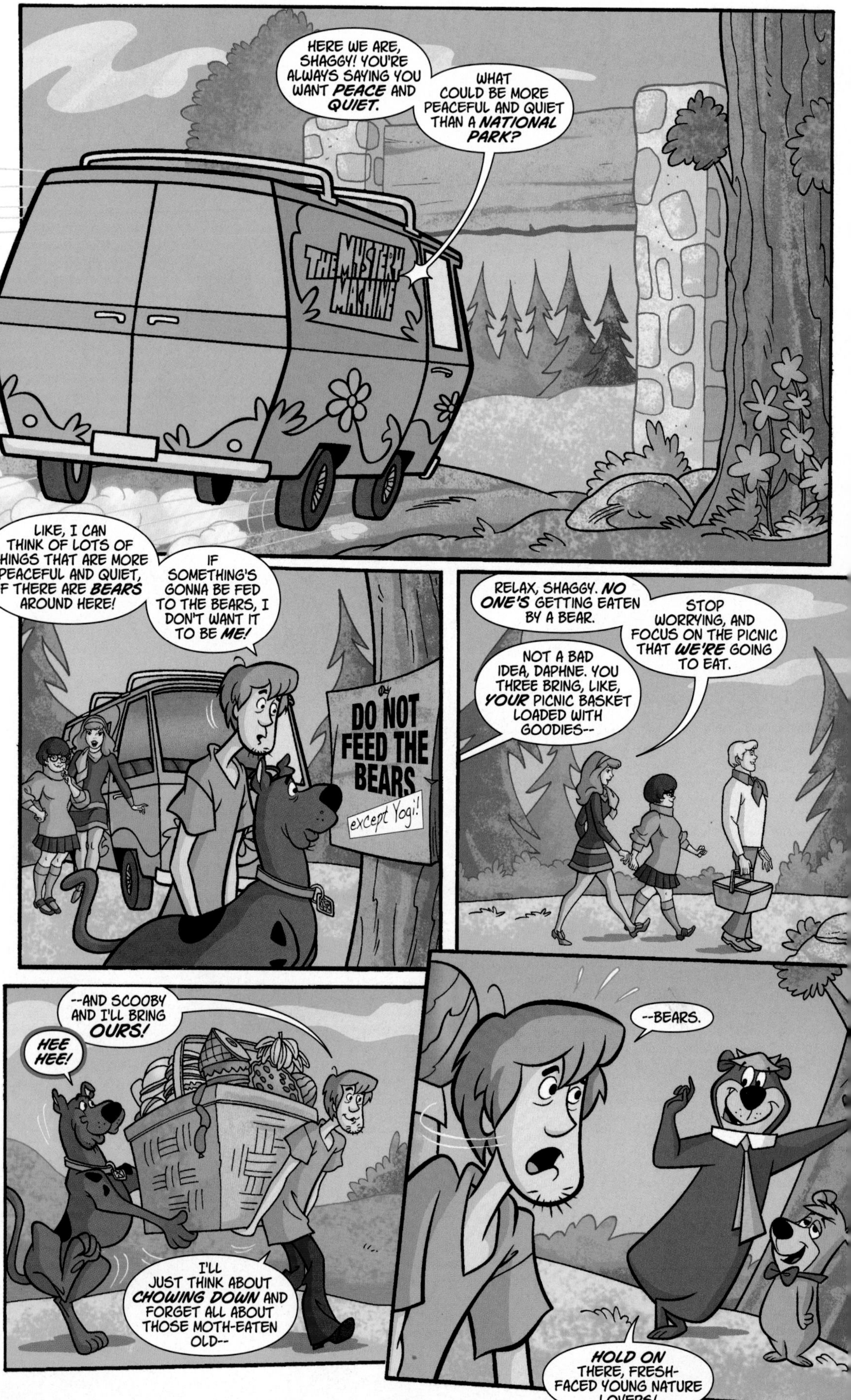

HERE WE ARE, SHAGGY! YOU'RE ALWAYS SAYING YOU WANT PEACE AND QUIET.
WHAT COULD BE MORE PEACEFUL AND QUIET THAN A NATIONAL PARK?
THE MYSTERY MACHINE
LIKE, I CAN THINK OF LOTS OF THINGS THAT ARE MORE PEACEFUL AND QUIET, IF THERE ARE BEARS AROUND HERE!
IF SOMETHING'S GONNA BE FED TO THE BEARS, I DON'T WANT IT TO BE ME!
DO NOT FEED THE BEARS
except Yogi!
RELAX, SHAGGY. NO ONE'S GETTING EATEN BY A BEAR.
STOP WORRYING, AND FOCUS ON THE PICNIC THAT WE'RE GOING TO EAT.
NOT A BAD IDEA, DAPHNE. YOU THREE BRING, LIKE, YOUR PICNIC BASKET LOADED WITH GOODIES--
--AND SCOOBY AND I'LL BRING OURS!
HEE HEE!
I'LL JUST THINK ABOUT CHOWING DOWN AND FORGET ALL ABOUT THOSE MOTH-EATEN OLD--
--BEARS.
HOLD ON THERE, FRESH-FACED YOUNG NATURE LOVERS!

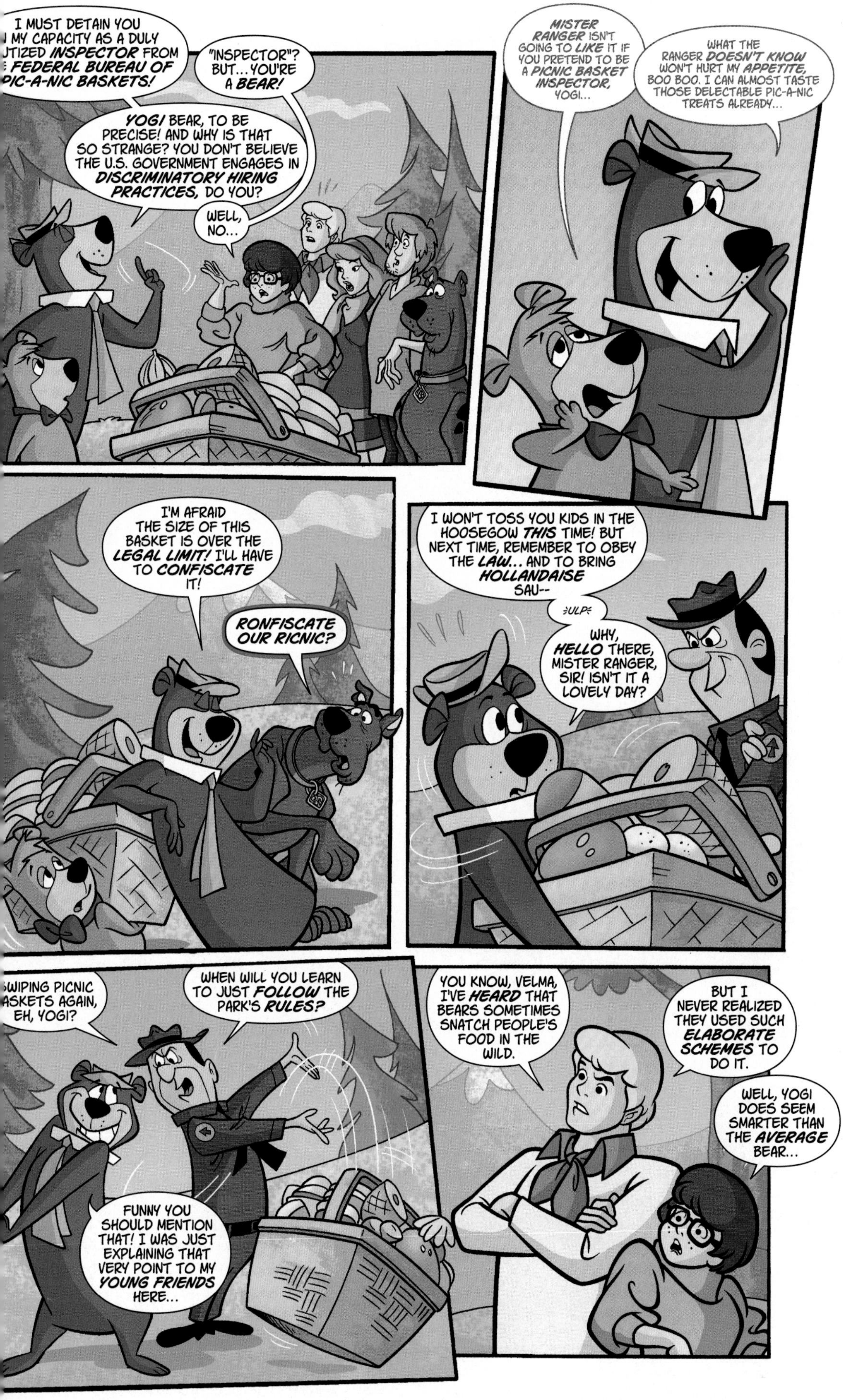
I MUST DETAIN YOU
N MY CAPACITY AS A DULY
UTIZED INSPECTOR FROM
E FEDERAL BUREAU OF
PIC-A-NIC BASKETS!
"INSPECTOR"? BUT... YOU'RE A BEAR!
YOGI BEAR, TO BE PRECISE! AND WHY IS THAT SO STRANGE? YOU DON'T BELIEVE THE U.S. GOVERNMENT ENGAGES IN DISCRIMINATORY HIRING PRACTICES, DO YOU?
WELL, NO...
MISTER RANGER ISN'T GOING TO LIKE IT IF YOU PRETEND TO BE A PICNIC BASKET INSPECTOR, YOGI...
WHAT THE RANGER DOESN'T KNOW WON'T HURT MY APPETITE, BOO BOO. I CAN ALMOST TASTE THOSE DELECTABLE PIC-A-NIC TREATS ALREADY...
I'M AFRAID THE SIZE OF THIS BASKET IS OVER THE LEGAL LIMIT! I'LL HAVE TO CONFISCATE IT!
RONFISCATE OUR RICNIC?
I WON'T TOSS YOU KIDS IN THE HOOSEGOW THIS TIME! BUT NEXT TIME, REMEMBER TO OBEY THE LAW... AND TO BRING HOLLANDAISE SAU--
ULP
WHY, HELLO THERE, MISTER RANGER, SIR! ISN'T IT A LOVELY DAY?
SWIPING PICNIC
ASKETS AGAIN,
EH, YOGI?
WHEN WILL YOU LEARN TO JUST FOLLOW THE PARK'S RULES?
FUNNY YOU SHOULD MENTION THAT! I WAS JUST EXPLAINING THAT VERY POINT TO MY YOUNG FRIENDS HERE...
YOU KNOW, VELMA, I'VE HEARD THAT BEARS SOMETIMES SNATCH PEOPLE'S FOOD IN THE WILD.
BUT I NEVER REALIZED THEY USED SUCH ELABORATE SCHEMES TO DO IT.
WELL, YOGI DOES SEEM SMARTER THAN THE AVERAGE BEAR...

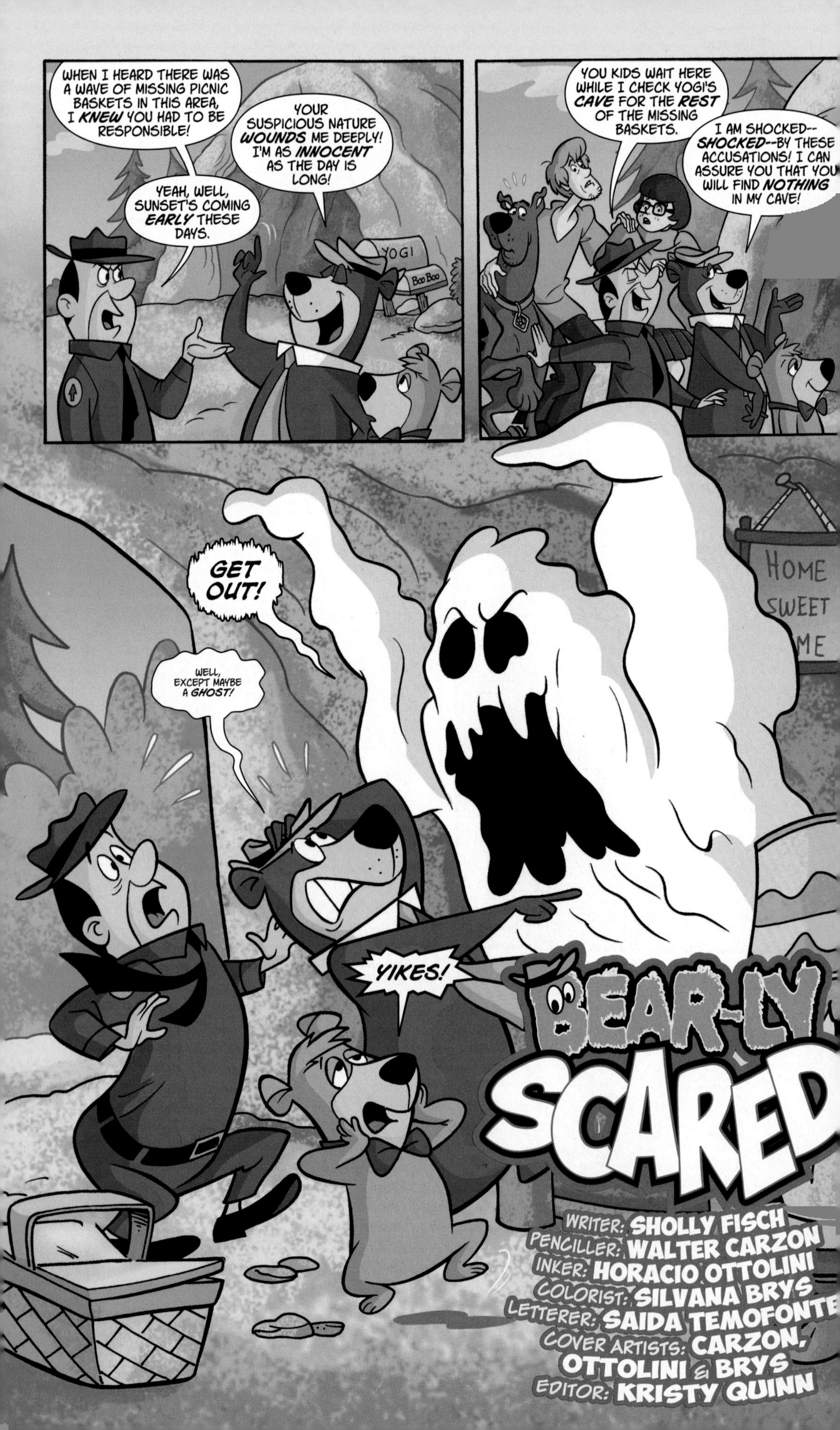
WHEN I HEARD THERE WAS A WAVE OF MISSING PICNIC BASKETS IN THIS AREA, I KNEW YOU HAD TO BE RESPONSIBLE!
YOUR SUSPICIOUS NATURE WOUNDS ME DEEPLY! I'M AS INNOCENT AS THE DAY IS LONG!
YEAH, WELL, SUNSET'S COMING EARLY THESE DAYS.
YOGI
BOO BOO
YOU KIDS WAIT HERE WHILE I CHECK YOGI'S CAVE FOR THE REST OF THE MISSING BASKETS.
I AM SHOCKED-- SHOCKED--BY THESE ACCUSATIONS! I CAN ASSURE YOU THAT YOU WILL FIND NOTHING IN MY CAVE!
GET OUT!
WELL, EXCEPT MAYBE A GHOST!
HOME SWEET
ME
YIKES!
BEAR-LY SCARED
WRITER: SHOLLY FISCH
PENCILLER: WALTER CARZON
INKER: HORACIO OTTOLINI
COLORIST: SILVANA BRYS
LETTERER: SAIDA TEMOFONTE
COVER ARTISTS: CARZON, OTTOLINI & BRYS
EDITOR: KRISTY QUINN

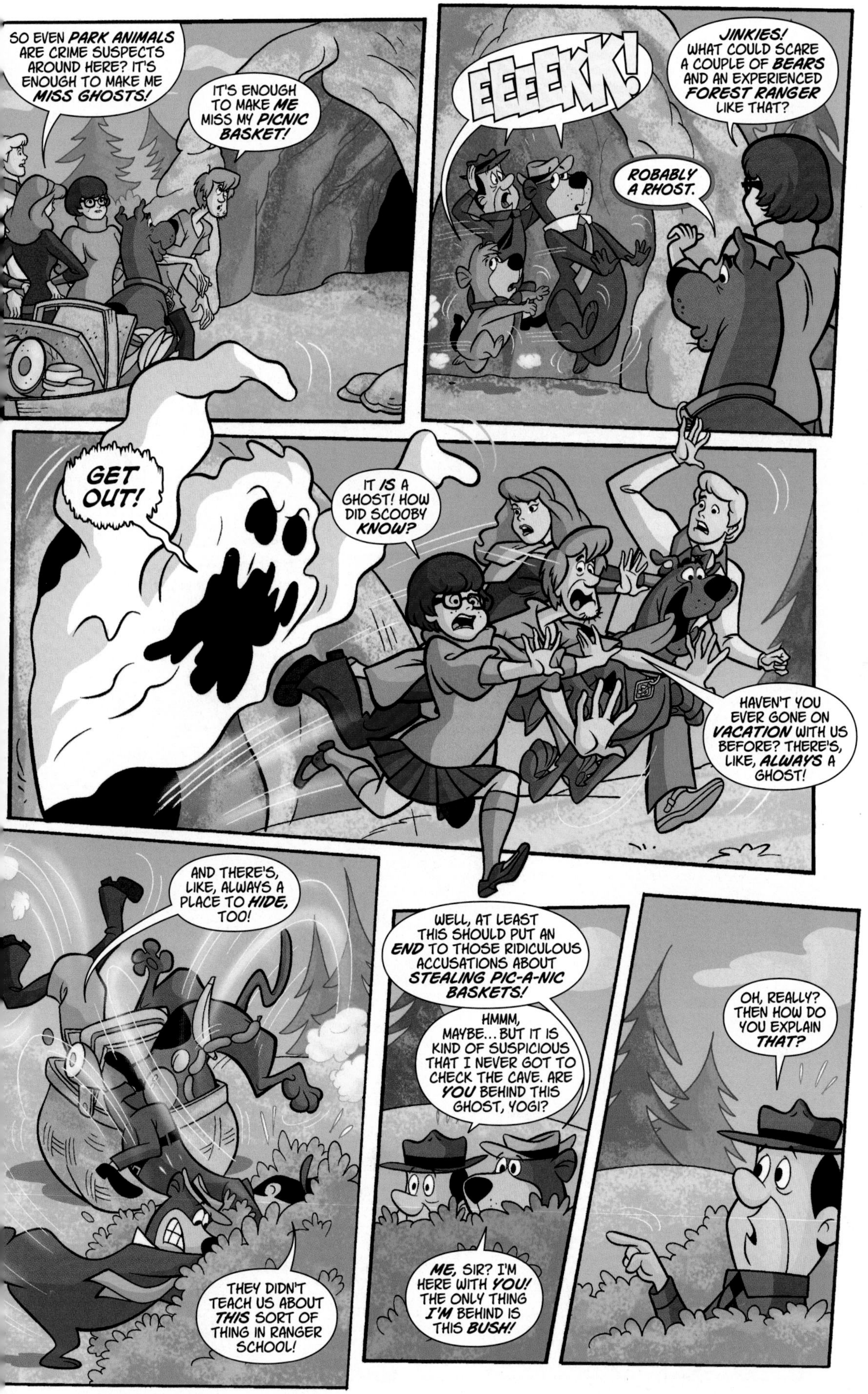
SO EVEN PARK ANIMALS ARE CRIME SUSPECTS AROUND HERE? IT'S ENOUGH TO MAKE ME MISS GHOSTS!
IT'S ENOUGH TO MAKE ME MISS MY PICNIC BASKET!
EEEEKK!
JINKIES! WHAT COULD SCARE A COUPLE OF BEARS AND AN EXPERIENCED FOREST RANGER LIKE THAT?
ROBABLY A RHOST.
GET OUT!
IT IS A GHOST! HOW DID SCOOBY KNOW?
HAVEN'T YOU EVER GONE ON VACATION WITH US BEFORE? THERE'S, LIKE, ALWAYS A GHOST!
AND THERE'S, LIKE, ALWAYS A PLACE TO HIDE, TOO!
THEY DIDN'T TEACH US ABOUT THIS SORT OF THING IN RANGER SCHOOL!
WELL, AT LEAST THIS SHOULD PUT AN END TO THOSE RIDICULOUS ACCUSATIONS ABOUT STEALING PIC-A-NIC BASKETS!
HMMM, MAYBE... BUT IT IS KIND OF SUSPICIOUS THAT I NEVER GOT TO CHECK THE CAVE. ARE YOU BEHIND THIS GHOST, YOGI?
ME, SIR? I'M HERE WITH YOU! THE ONLY THING I'M BEHIND IS THIS BUSH!
OH, REALLY? THEN HOW DO YOU EXPLAIN THAT?

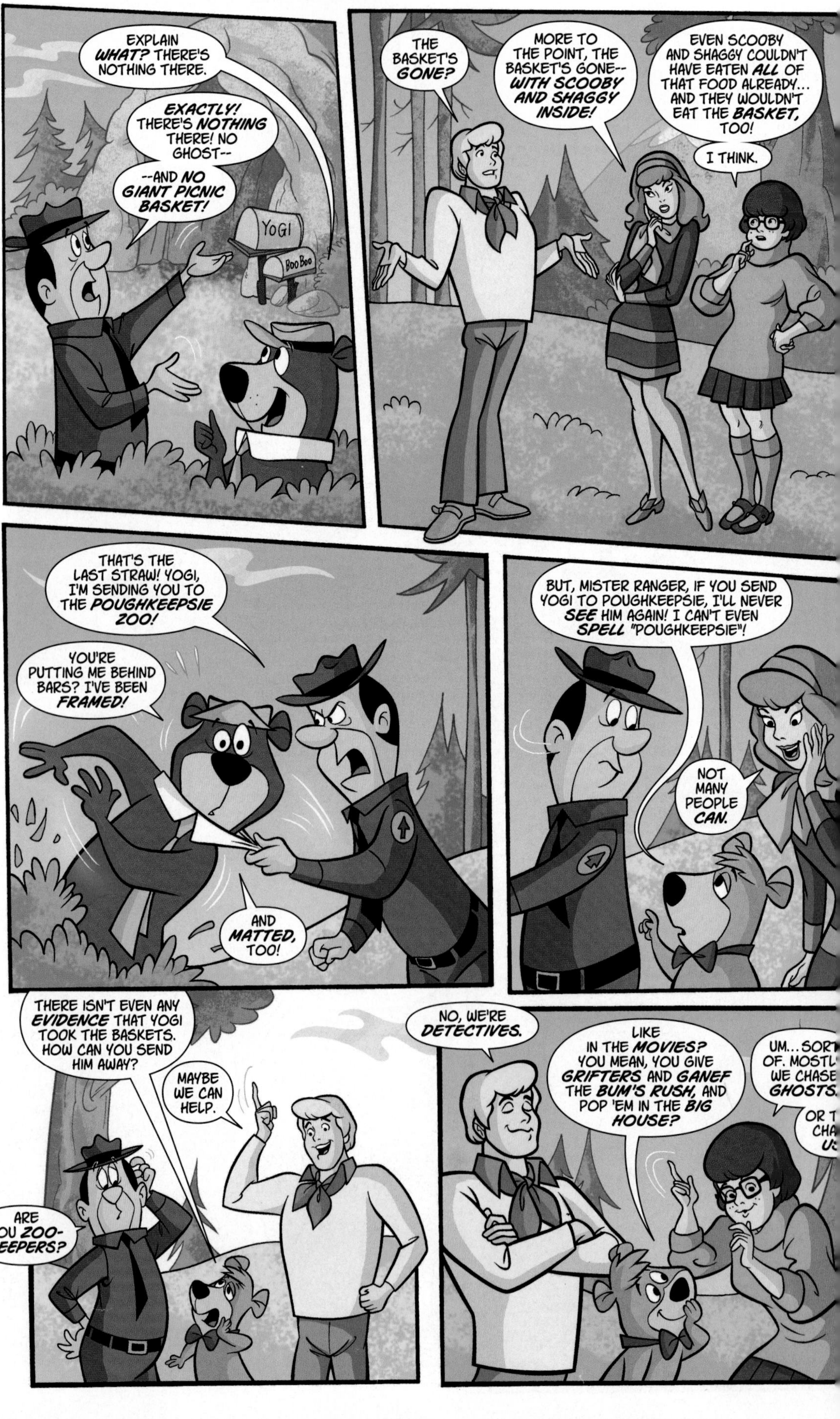
EXPLAIN WHAT? THERE'S NOTHING THERE.
EXACTLY! THERE'S NOTHING THERE! NO GHOST--
--AND NO GIANT PICNIC BASKET!
YOGI
Boo Boo
THE BASKET'S GONE?
MORE TO THE POINT, THE BASKET'S GONE--WITH SCOOBY AND SHAGGY INSIDE!
EVEN SCOOBY AND SHAGGY COULDN'T HAVE EATEN ALL OF THAT FOOD ALREADY... AND THEY WOULDN'T EAT THE BASKET, TOO!
I THINK.
THAT'S THE LAST STRAW! YOGI, I'M SENDING YOU TO THE POUGHKEEPSIE ZOO!
YOU'RE PUTTING ME BEHIND BARS? I'VE BEEN FRAMED!
AND MATTED, TOO!
BUT, MISTER RANGER, IF YOU SEND YOGI TO POUGHKEEPSIE, I'LL NEVER SEE HIM AGAIN! I CAN'T EVEN SPELL "POUGHKEEPSIE"!
NOT MANY PEOPLE CAN.
THERE ISN'T EVEN ANY EVIDENCE THAT YOGI TOOK THE BASKETS. HOW CAN YOU SEND HIM AWAY?
MAYBE WE CAN HELP.
ARE YOU ZOO-KEEPERS?
NO, WE'RE DETECTIVES.
LIKE IN THE MOVIES? YOU MEAN, YOU GIVE GRIFTERS AND GANEF THE BUM'S RUSH, AND POP 'EM IN THE BIG HOUSE?
UM...SORT OF. MOSTL WE CHASE GHOSTS.

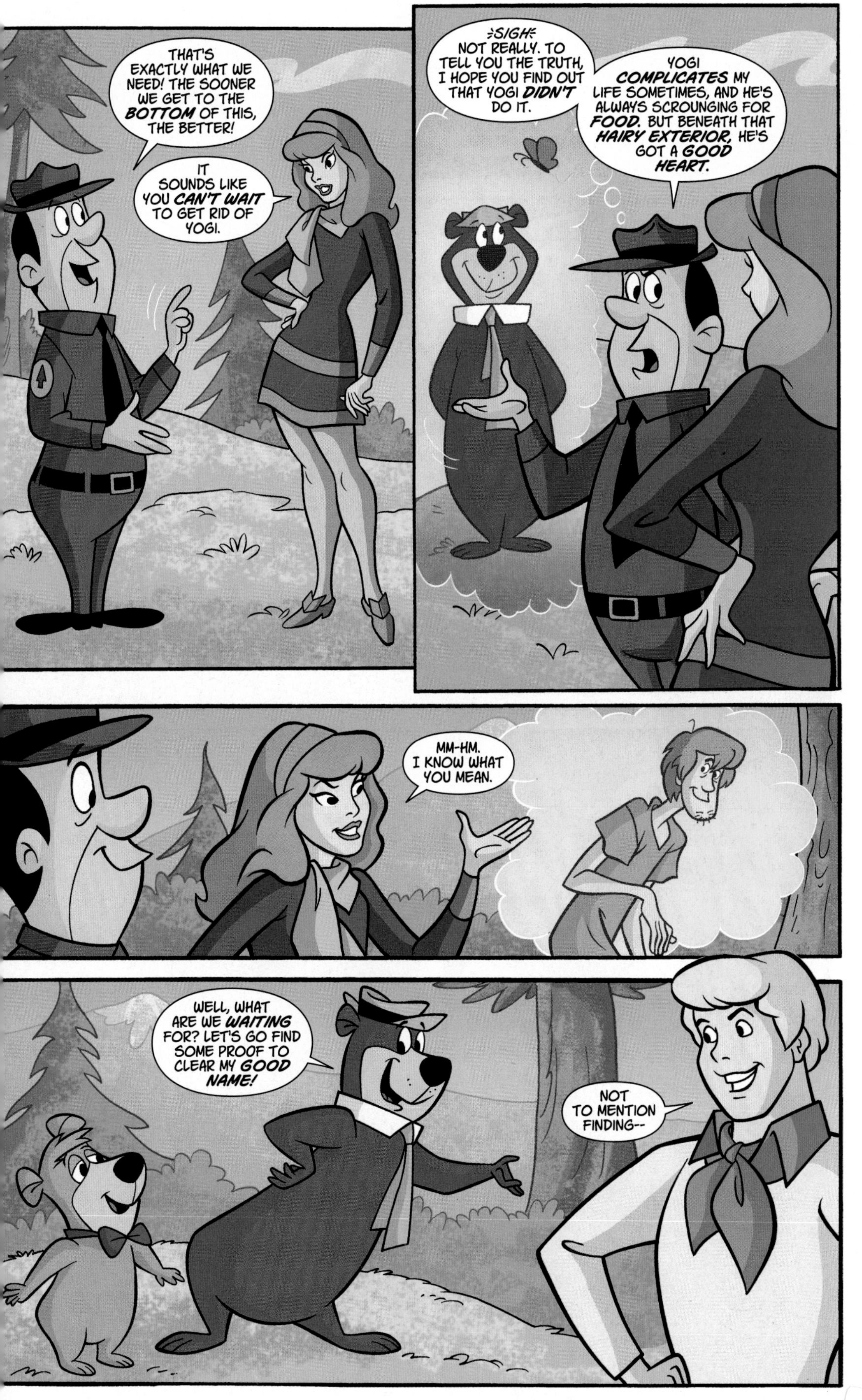
THAT'S EXACTLY WHAT WE NEED! THE SOONER WE GET TO THE BOTTOM OF THIS, THE BETTER!
IT SOUNDS LIKE YOU CAN'T WAIT TO GET RID OF YOGI.
SIGH
NOT REALLY. TO TELL YOU THE TRUTH, I HOPE YOU FIND OUT THAT YOGI DIDN'T DO IT.
YOGI COMPLICATES MY LIFE SOMETIMES, AND HE'S ALWAYS SCROUNGING FOR FOOD. BUT BENEATH THAT HAIRY EXTERIOR, HE'S GOT A GOOD HEART.
MM-HM. I KNOW WHAT YOU MEAN.
WELL, WHAT ARE WE WAITING FOR? LET'S GO FIND SOME PROOF TO CLEAR MY GOOD NAME!
NOT TO MENTION FINDING--

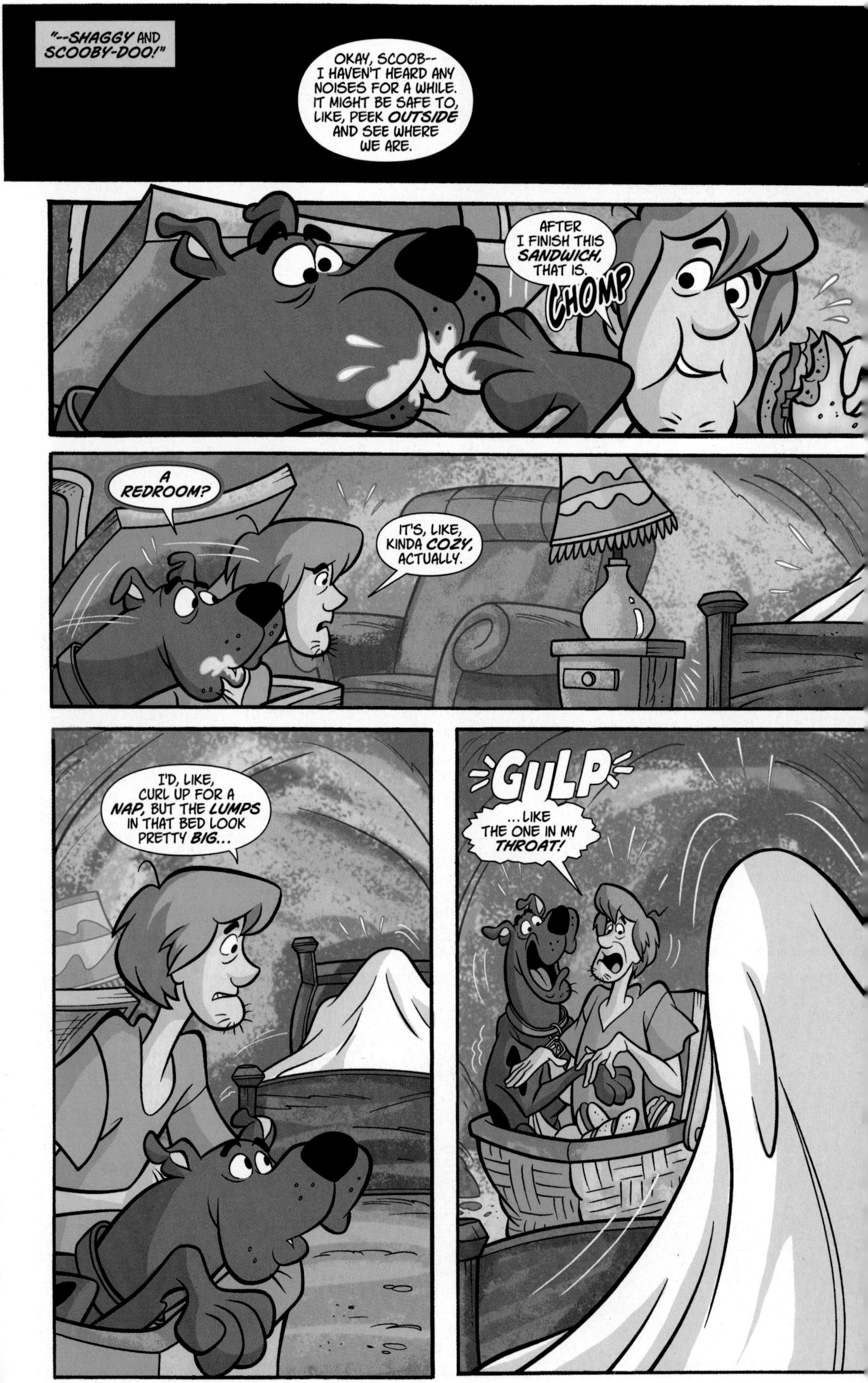
"--SHAGGY AND SCOOBY-DOO!"
OKAY, SCOOB-- I HAVEN'T HEARD ANY NOISES FOR A WHILE. IT MIGHT BE SAFE TO, LIKE, PEEK OUTSIDE AND SEE WHERE WE ARE.
AFTER I FINISH THIS SANDWICH, THAT IS.
CHOMP
A REDROOM?
IT'S, LIKE, KINDA COZY, ACTUALLY.
I'D, LIKE, CURL UP FOR A NAP, BUT THE LUMPS IN THAT BED LOOK PRETTY BIG...
GULP
...LIKE THE ONE IN MY THROAT!

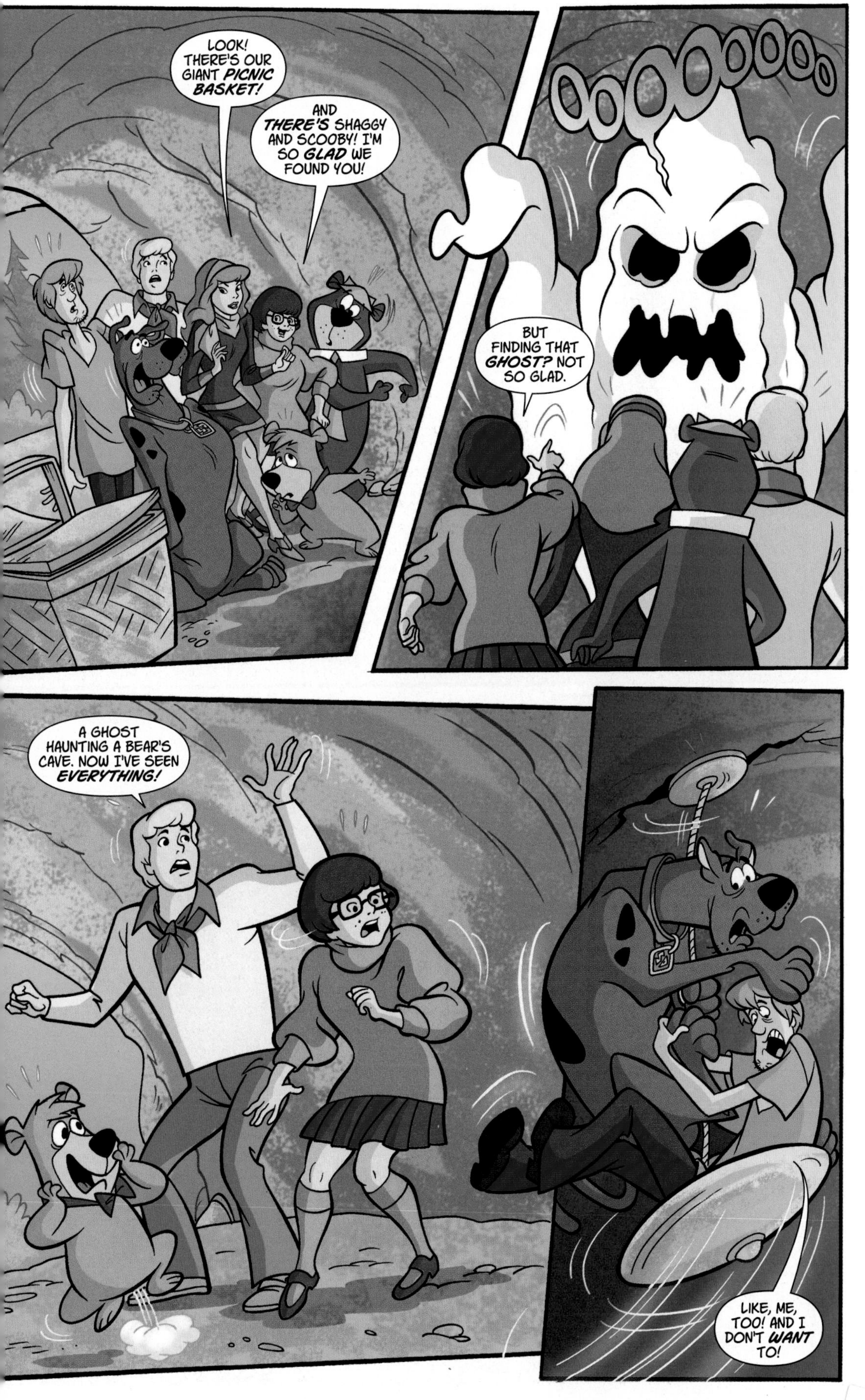
LOOK! THERE'S OUR GIANT PICNIC BASKET!
AND THERE'S SHAGGY AND SCOOBY! I'M SO GLAD WE FOUND YOU!
OOOOOOOOO
BUT FINDING THAT GHOST? NOT SO GLAD.
A GHOST HAUNTING A BEAR'S CAVE. NOW I'VE SEEN EVERYTHING!
LIKE, ME, TOO! AND I DON'T WANT TO!

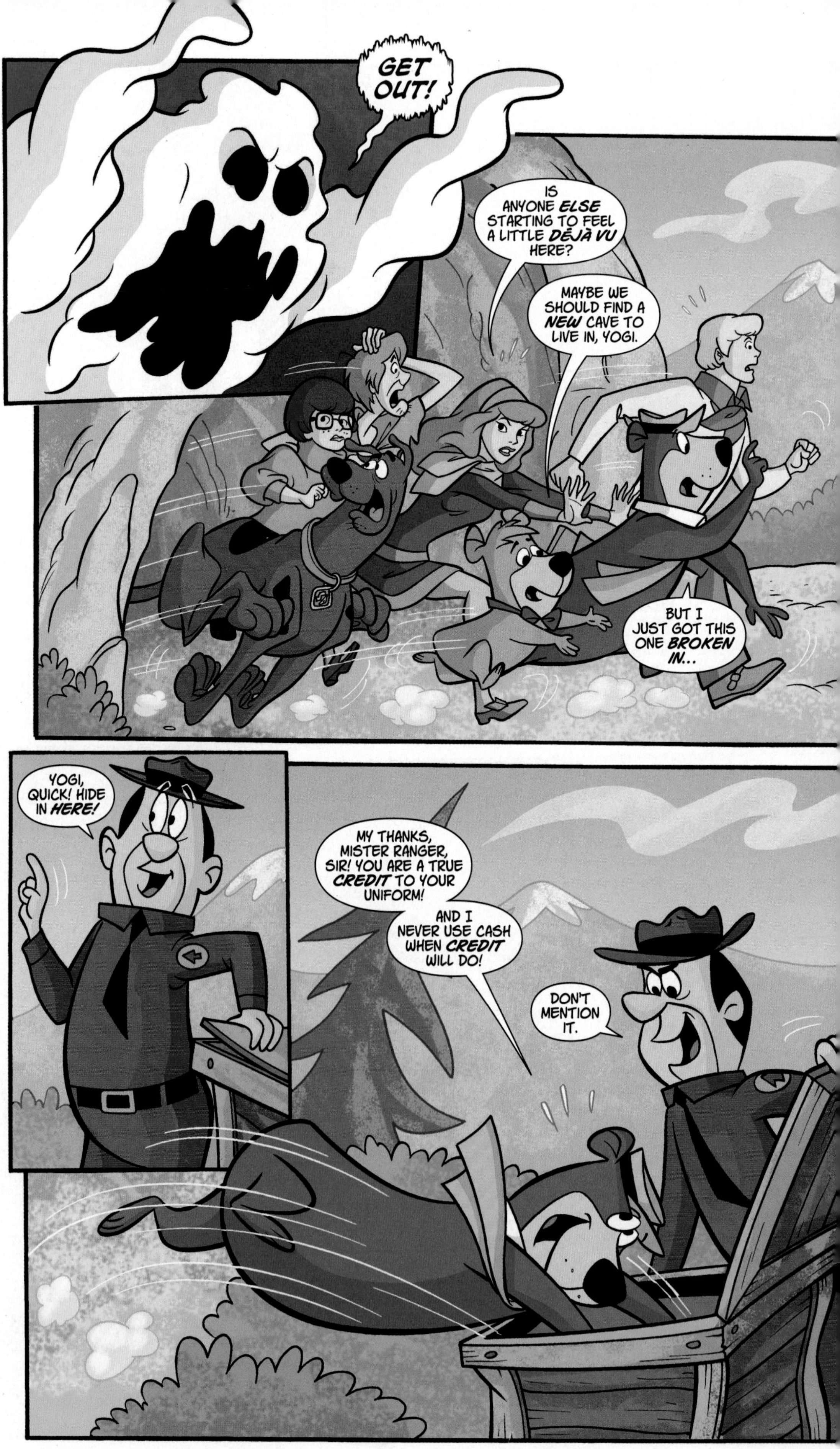
GET OUT!
IS ANYONE ELSE STARTING TO FEEL A LITTLE DÉJÀ VU HERE?
MAYBE WE SHOULD FIND A NEW CAVE TO LIVE IN, YOGI.
BUT I JUST GOT THIS ONE BROKEN IN...
YOGI, QUICK! HIDE IN HERE!
MY THANKS, MISTER RANGER, SIR! YOU ARE A TRUE CREDIT TO YOUR UNIFORM!
AND I NEVER USE CASH WHEN CREDIT WILL DO!
DON'T MENTION IT.

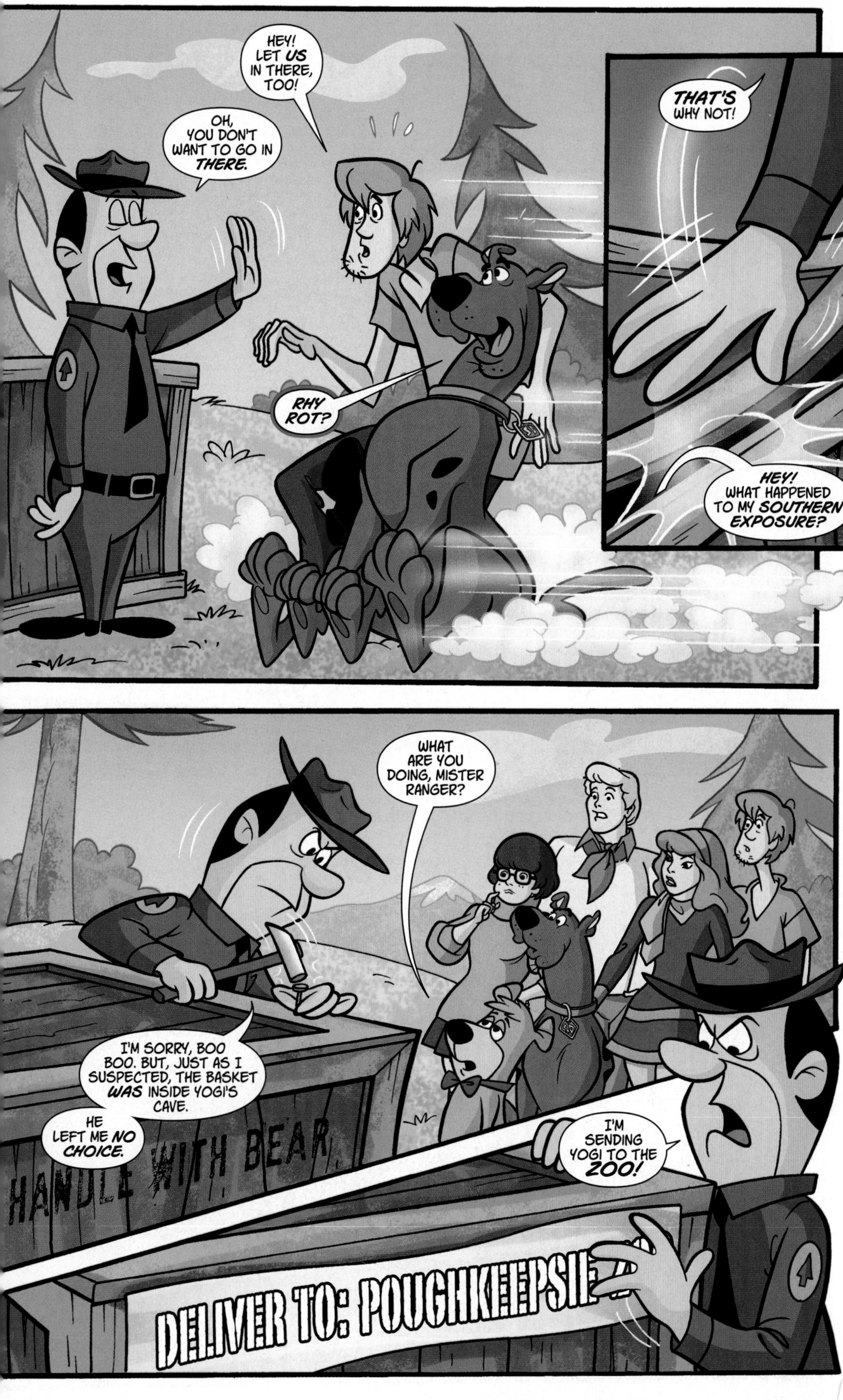
OH, YOU DON'T WANT TO GO IN THERE.
HEY! LET US IN THERE, TOO!
RHY ROT?
THAT'S WHY NOT!
HEY! WHAT HAPPENED TO MY SOUTHERN EXPOSURE?
WHAT ARE YOU DOING, MISTER RANGER?
I'M SORRY, BOO BOO. BUT, JUST AS I SUSPECTED, THE BASKET WAS INSIDE YOGI'S CAVE.
HE LEFT ME NO CHOICE.
HANDLE WITH BEAR
I'M SENDING YOGI TO THE ZOO!
DELIVER TO: POUGHKEEPSIE

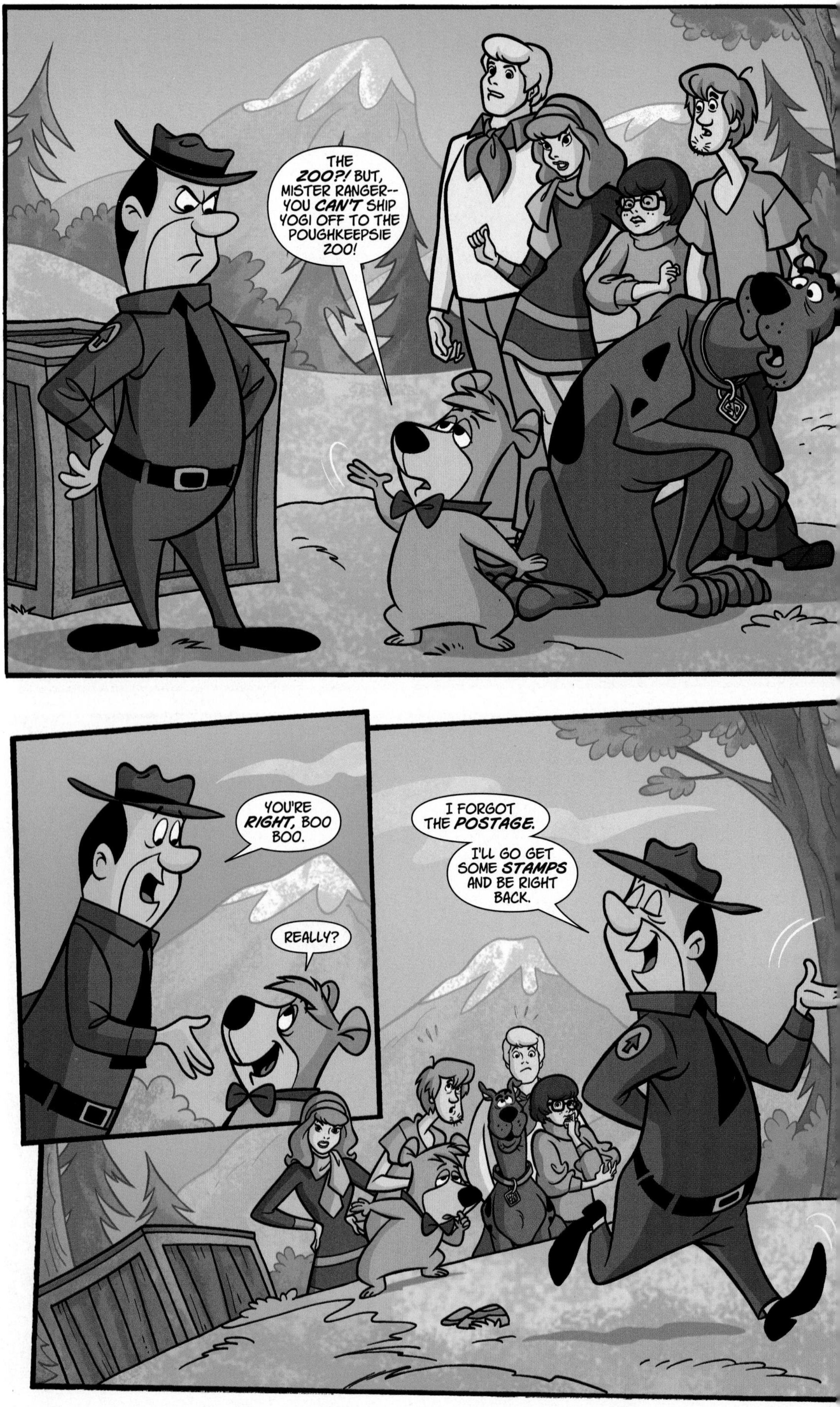
THE ZOO?! BUT, MISTER RANGER-- YOU CAN'T SHIP YOGI OFF TO THE POUGHKEEPSIE ZOO!
YOU'RE RIGHT, BOO BOO.
REALLY?
I FORGOT THE POSTAGE.
I'LL GO GET SOME STAMPS AND BE RIGHT BACK.

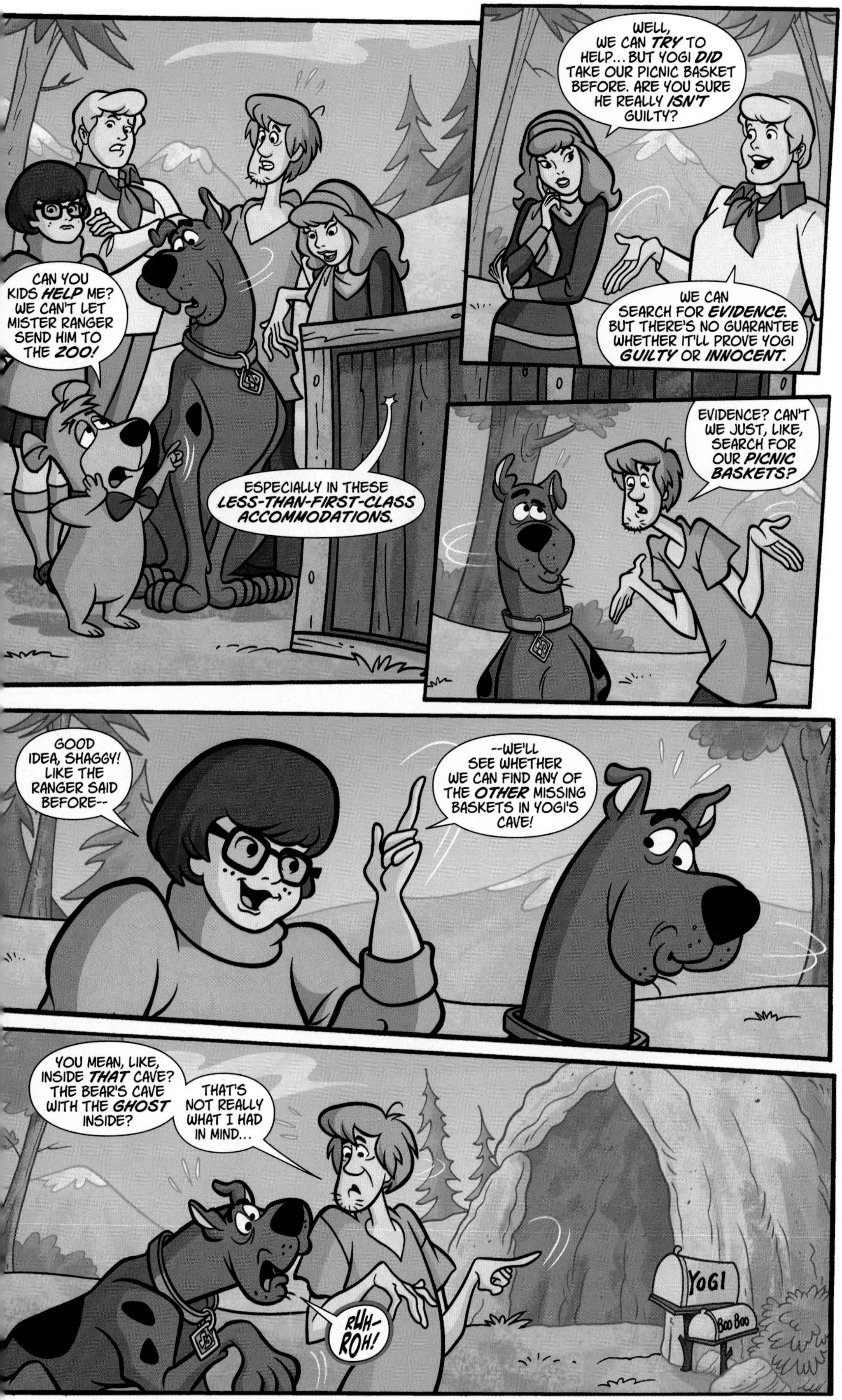
CAN YOU KIDS HELP ME? WE CAN'T LET MISTER RANGER SEND HIM TO THE ZOO!
ESPECIALLY IN THESE LESS-THAN-FIRST-CLASS ACCOMMODATIONS.
WELL, WE CAN TRY TO HELP... BUT YOGI DID TAKE OUR PICNIC BASKET BEFORE. ARE YOU SURE HE REALLY ISN'T GUILTY?
WE CAN SEARCH FOR EVIDENCE. BUT THERE'S NO GUARANTEE WHETHER IT'LL PROVE YOGI GUILTY OR INNOCENT.
EVIDENCE? CAN'T WE JUST, LIKE, SEARCH FOR OUR PICNIC BASKETS?
GOOD IDEA, SHAGGY! LIKE THE RANGER SAID BEFORE--
--WE'LL SEE WHETHER WE CAN FIND ANY OF THE OTHER MISSING BASKETS IN YOGI'S CAVE!
YOU MEAN, LIKE, INSIDE THAT CAVE? THE BEAR'S CAVE WITH THE GHOST INSIDE?
THAT'S NOT REALLY WHAT I HAD IN MIND...
RUH-ROH!
YOGI
BOO BOO

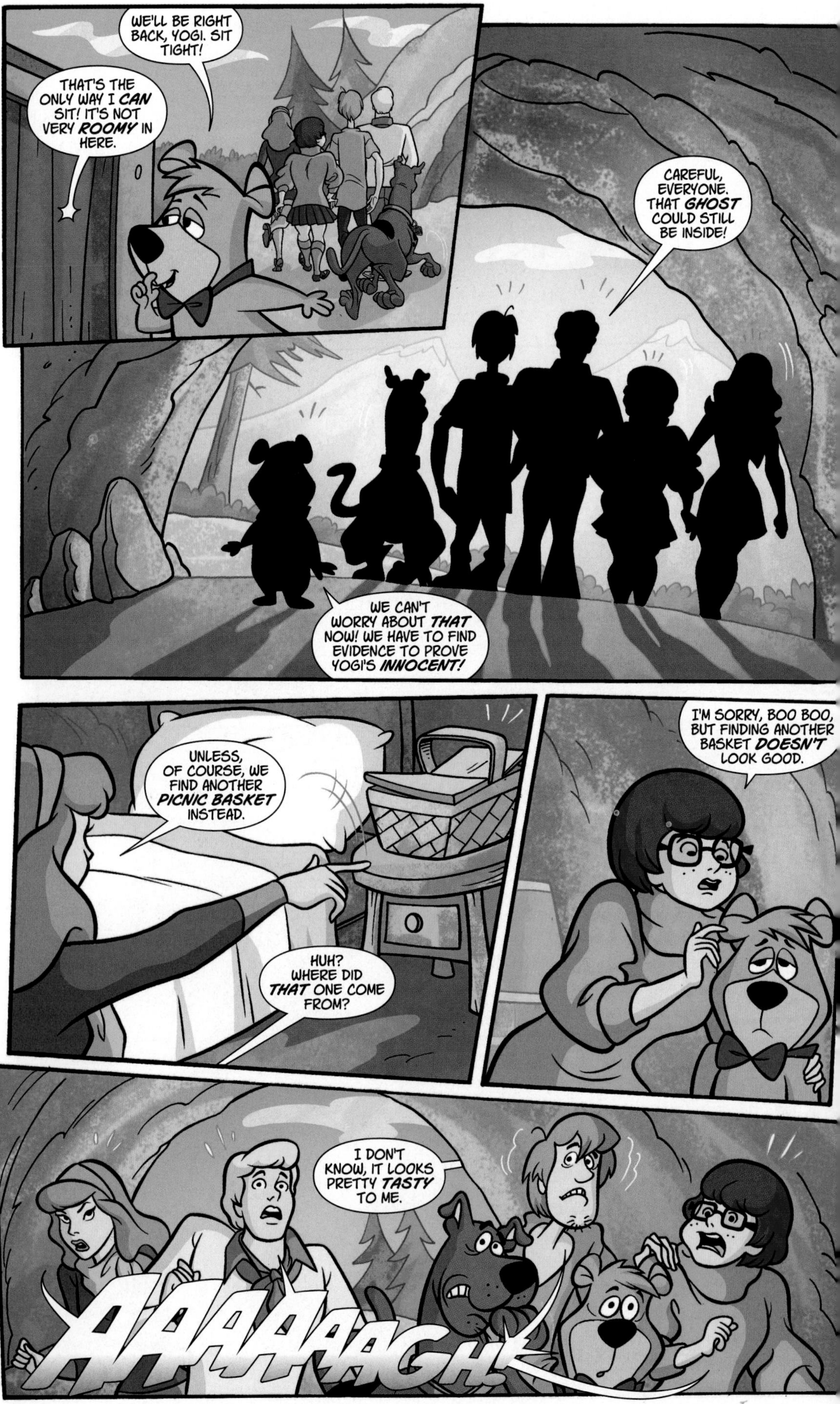
WE'LL BE RIGHT BACK, YOGI. SIT TIGHT!
THAT'S THE ONLY WAY I CAN SIT! IT'S NOT VERY ROOMY IN HERE.
CAREFUL, EVERYONE. THAT GHOST COULD STILL BE INSIDE!
WE CAN'T WORRY ABOUT THAT NOW! WE HAVE TO FIND EVIDENCE TO PROVE YOGI'S INNOCENT!
UNLESS, OF COURSE, WE FIND ANOTHER PICNIC BASKET INSTEAD.
HUH? WHERE DID THAT ONE COME FROM?
I'M SORRY, BOO BOO, BUT FINDING ANOTHER BASKET DOESN'T LOOK GOOD.
I DON'T KNOW, IT LOOKS PRETTY TASTY TO ME.
AAAAAAGH!

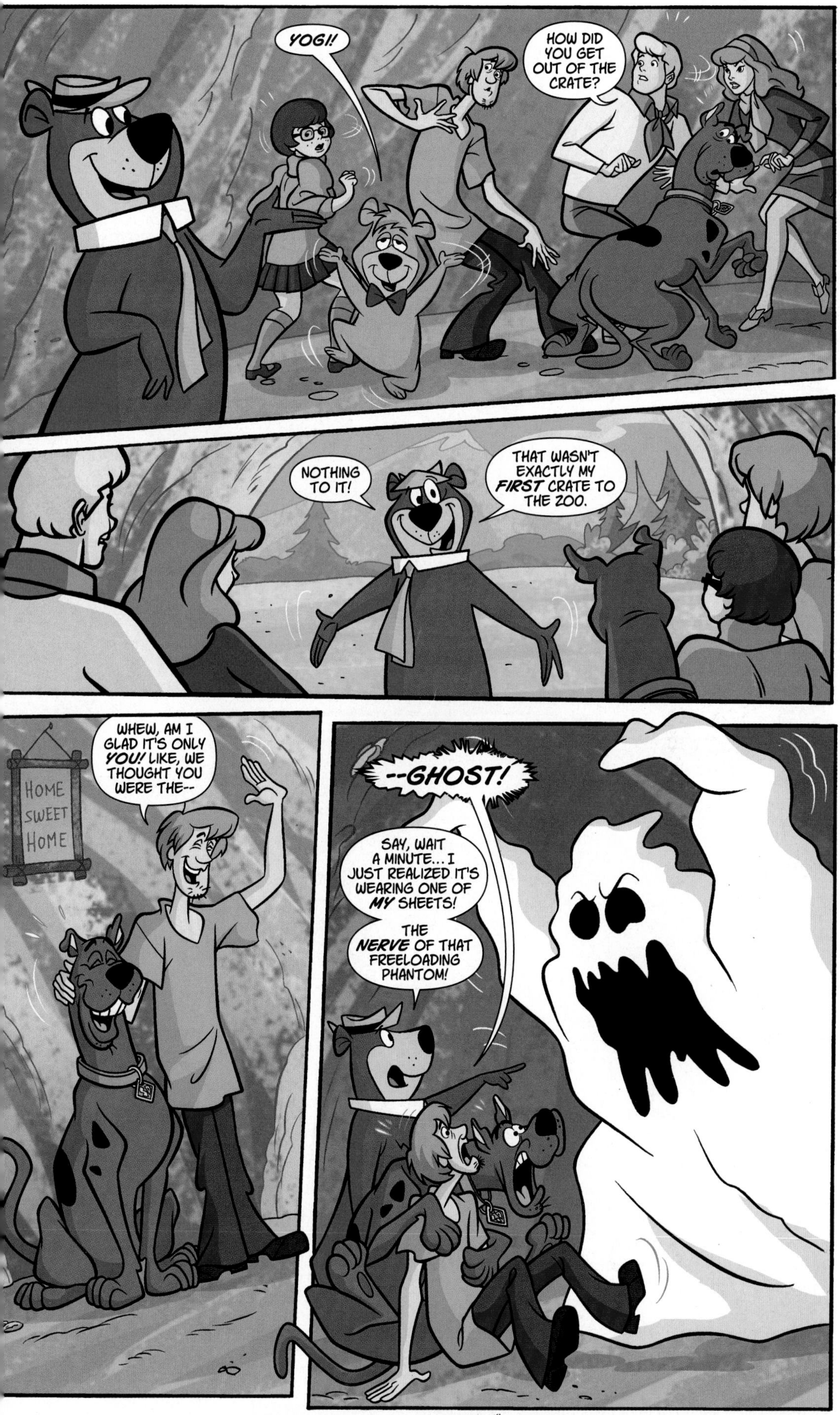
YOGI!
HOW DID YOU GET OUT OF THE CRATE?
NOTHING TO IT!
THAT WASN'T EXACTLY MY *FIRST* CRATE TO THE ZOO.
HOME SWEET HOME
WHEW, AM I GLAD IT'S ONLY *YOU!* LIKE, WE THOUGHT YOU WERE THE--
--GHOST!
SAY, WAIT A MINUTE... I JUST REALIZED IT'S WEARING ONE OF *MY* SHEETS!
THE *NERVE* OF THAT FREELOADING PHANTOM!

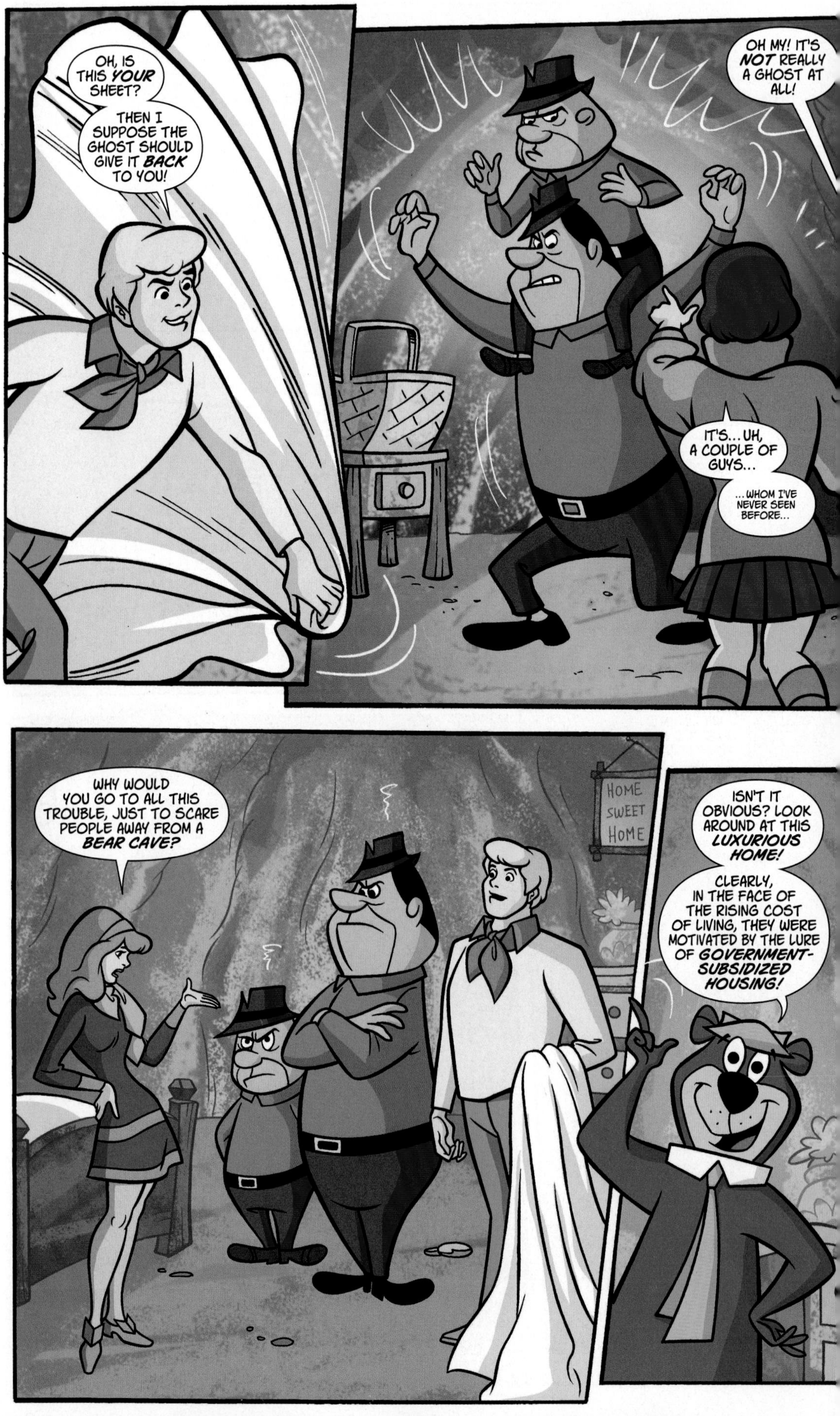
OH, IS THIS YOUR SHEET?
THEN I SUPPOSE THE GHOST SHOULD GIVE IT BACK TO YOU!
OH MY! IT'S NOT REALLY A GHOST AT ALL!
IT'S... UH, A COUPLE OF GUYS...
...WHOM I'VE NEVER SEEN BEFORE...
WHY WOULD YOU GO TO ALL THIS TROUBLE, JUST TO SCARE PEOPLE AWAY FROM A BEAR CAVE?
HOME SWEET HOME
ISN'T IT OBVIOUS? LOOK AROUND AT THIS LUXURIOUS HOME!
CLEARLY, IN THE FACE OF THE RISING COST OF LIVING, THEY WERE MOTIVATED BY THE LURE OF GOVERNMENT-SUBSIDIZED HOUSING!

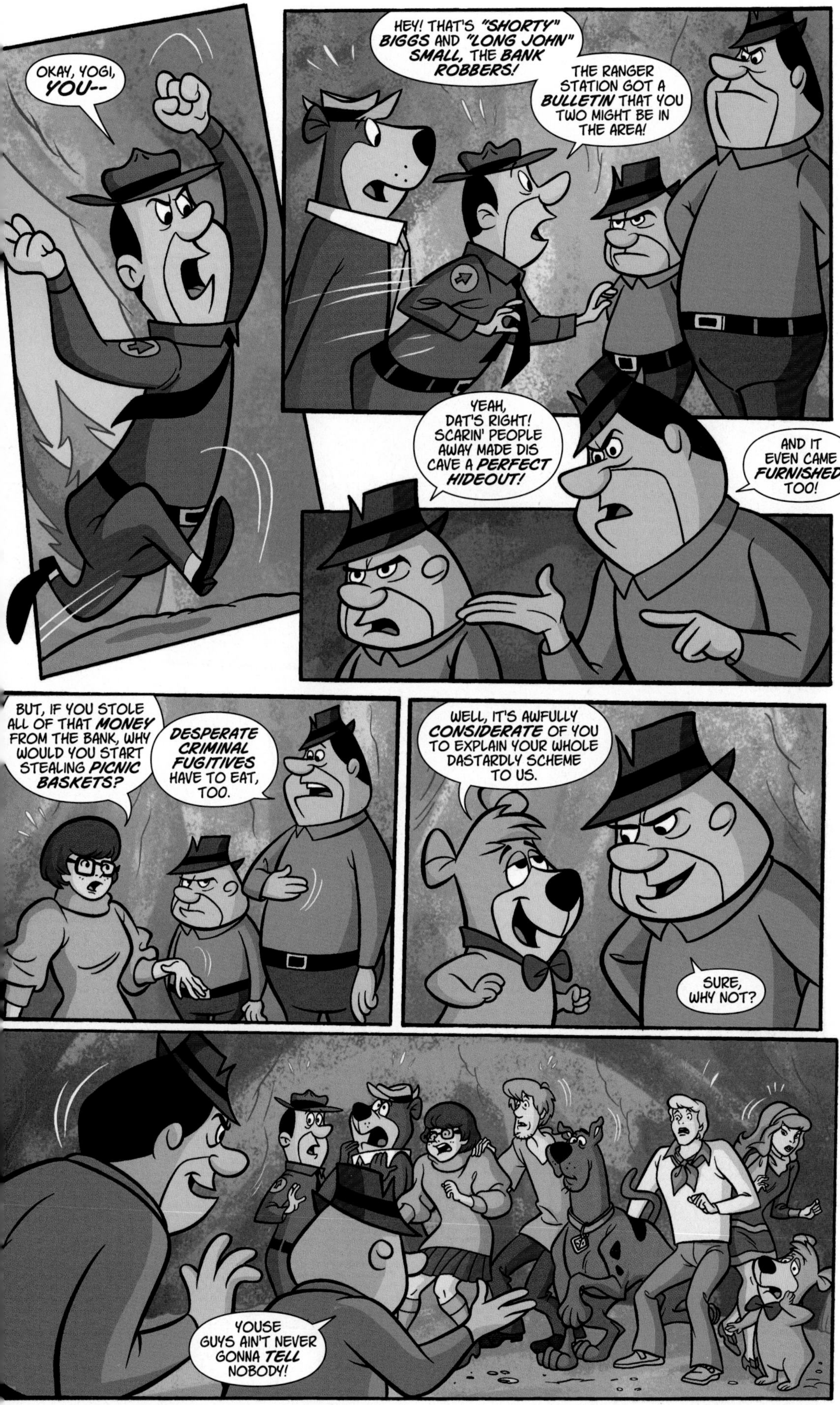
OKAY, YOGI, YOU--
HEY! THAT'S "SHORTY" BIGGS AND "LONG JOHN" SMALL, THE BANK ROBBERS!
THE RANGER STATION GOT A BULLETIN THAT YOU TWO MIGHT BE IN THE AREA!
YEAH, DAT'S RIGHT! SCARIN' PEOPLE AWAY MADE DIS CAVE A PERFECT HIDEOUT!
AND IT EVEN CAME FURNISHED, TOO!
BUT, IF YOU STOLE ALL OF THAT MONEY FROM THE BANK, WHY WOULD YOU START STEALING PICNIC BASKETS?
DESPERATE CRIMINAL FUGITIVES HAVE TO EAT, TOO.
WELL, IT'S AWFULLY CONSIDERATE OF YOU TO EXPLAIN YOUR WHOLE DASTARDLY SCHEME TO US.
SURE, WHY NOT?
YOUSE GUYS AIN'T NEVER GONNA TELL NOBODY!

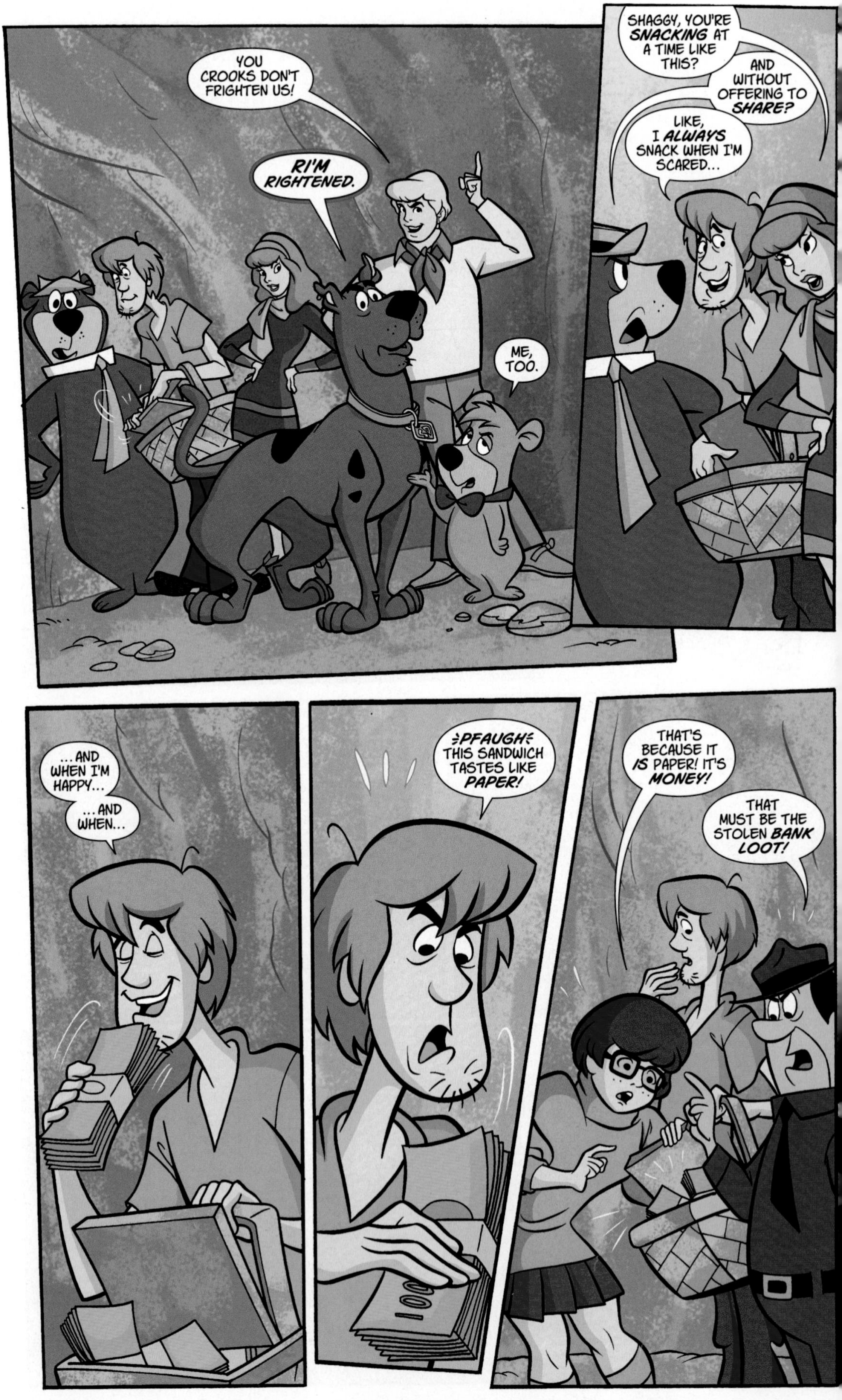
YOU CROOKS DON'T FRIGHTEN US!
RI'M RIGHTENED.
ME, TOO.
SHAGGY, YOU'RE SNACKING AT A TIME LIKE THIS?
AND WITHOUT OFFERING TO SHARE?
LIKE, I ALWAYS SNACK WHEN I'M SCARED...
...AND WHEN I'M HAPPY...
...AND WHEN...
PFAUGH! THIS SANDWICH TASTES LIKE PAPER!
THAT'S BECAUSE IT IS PAPER! IT'S MONEY!
THAT MUST BE THE STOLEN BANK LOOT!

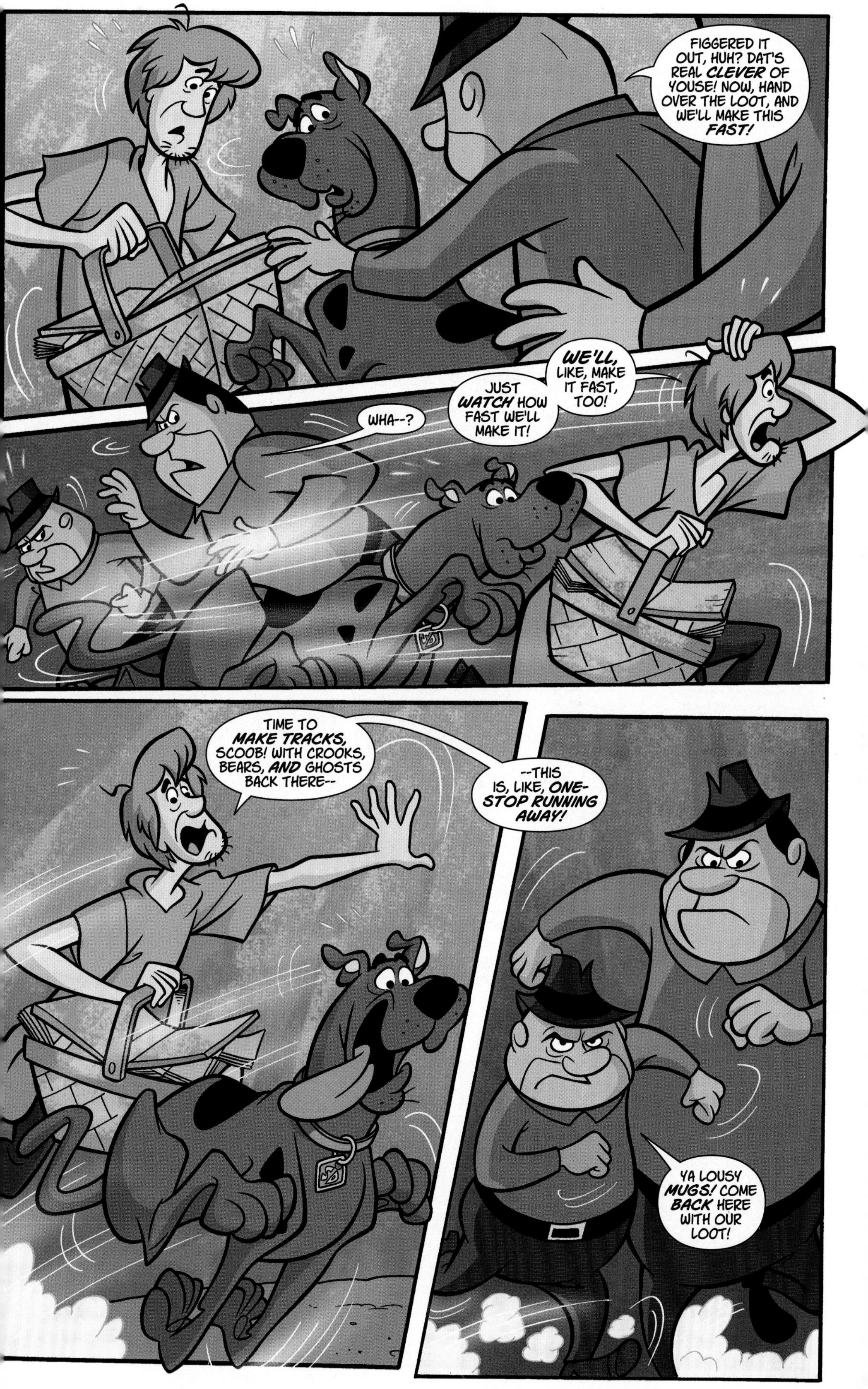
FIGGERED IT OUT, HUH? DAT'S REAL CLEVER OF YOUSE! NOW, HAND OVER THE LOOT, AND WE'LL MAKE THIS FAST!
WE'LL, LIKE, MAKE IT FAST, TOO!
JUST WATCH HOW FAST WE'LL MAKE IT!
WHA--?
TIME TO MAKE TRACKS, SCOOB! WITH CROOKS, BEARS, AND GHOSTS BACK THERE--
--THIS IS, LIKE, ONE-STOP RUNNING AWAY!
YA LOUSY MUGS! COME BACK HERE WITH OUR LOOT!

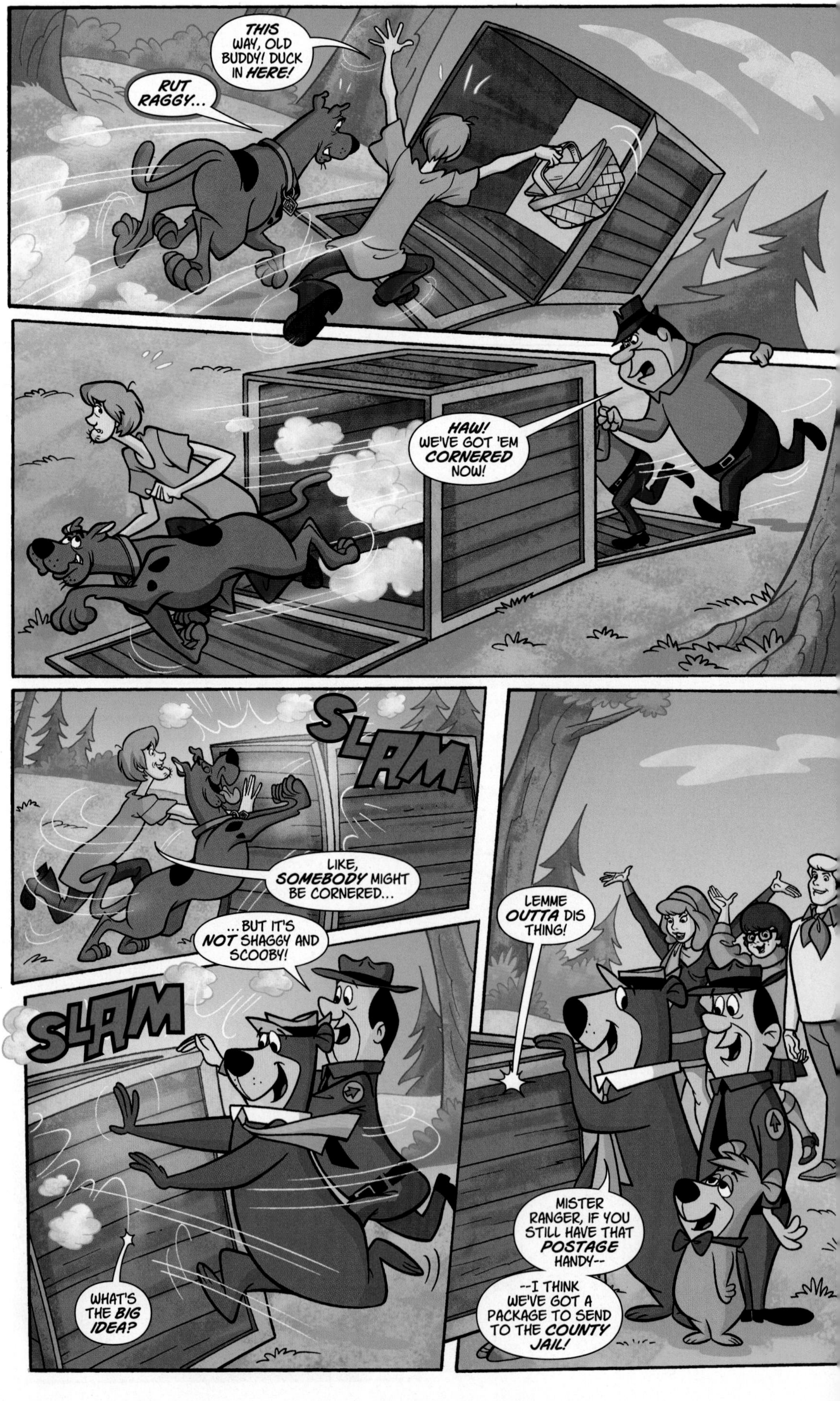
THIS WAY, OLD BUDDY! DUCK IN HERE!
RUT RAGGY...
HAW! WE'VE GOT 'EM CORNERED NOW!
SLAM
LIKE, SOMEBODY MIGHT BE CORNERED...
...BUT IT'S NOT SHAGGY AND SCOOBY!
SLAM
WHAT'S THE BIG IDEA?
LEMME OUTTA DIS THING!
MISTER RANGER, IF YOU STILL HAVE THAT POSTAGE HANDY--
--I THINK WE'VE GOT A PACKAGE TO SEND TO THE COUNTY JAIL!

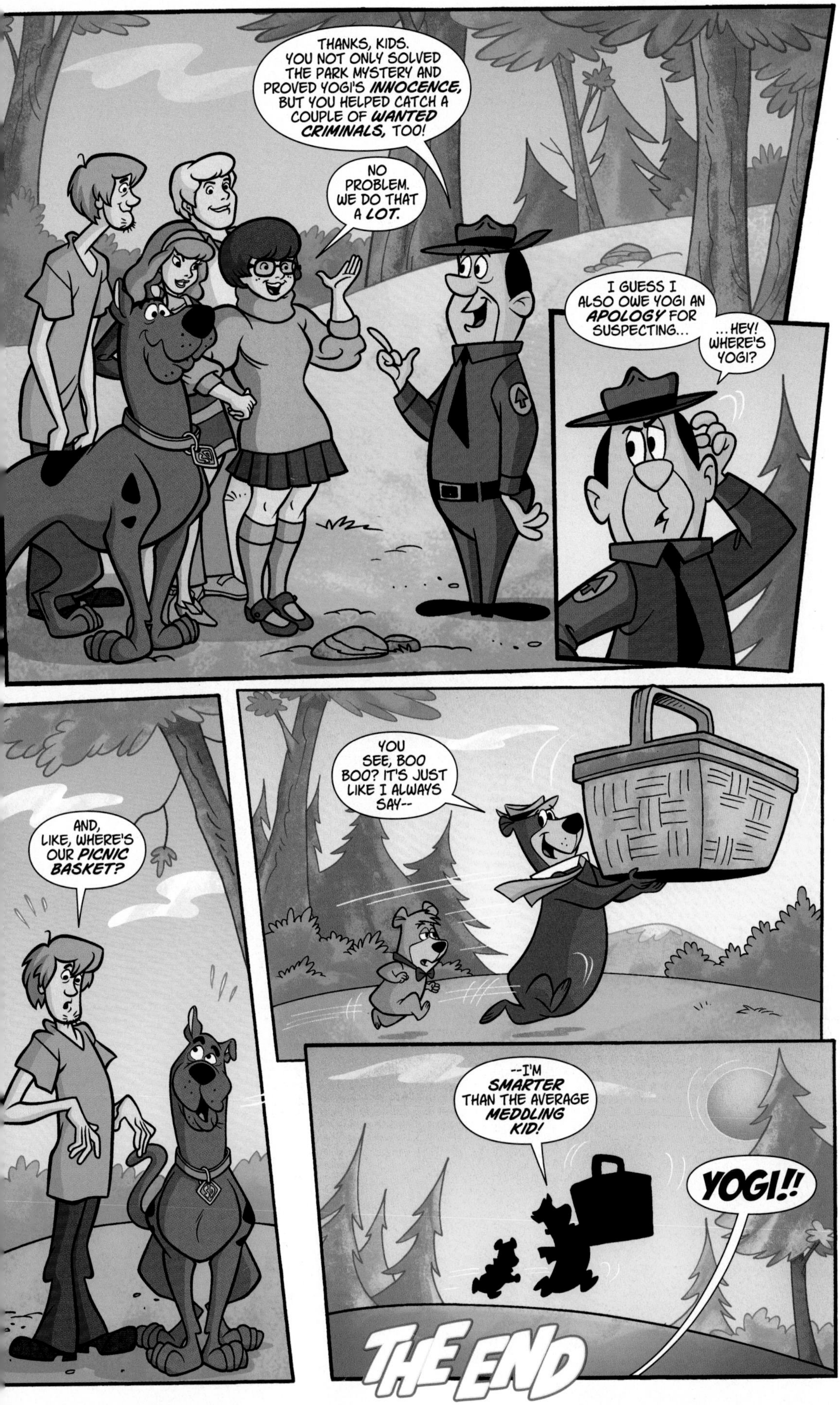
THANKS, KIDS. YOU NOT ONLY SOLVED THE PARK MYSTERY AND PROVED YOGI'S INNOCENCE, BUT YOU HELPED CATCH A COUPLE OF WANTED CRIMINALS, TOO!
NO PROBLEM. WE DO THAT A LOT.
I GUESS I ALSO OWE YOGI AN APOLOGY FOR SUSPECTING...
...HEY! WHERE'S YOGI?
AND, LIKE, WHERE'S OUR PICNIC BASKET?
YOU SEE, BOO BOO? IT'S JUST LIKE I ALWAYS SAY--
--I'M SMARTER THAN THE AVERAGE MEDDLING KID!
YOGI!!
THE END

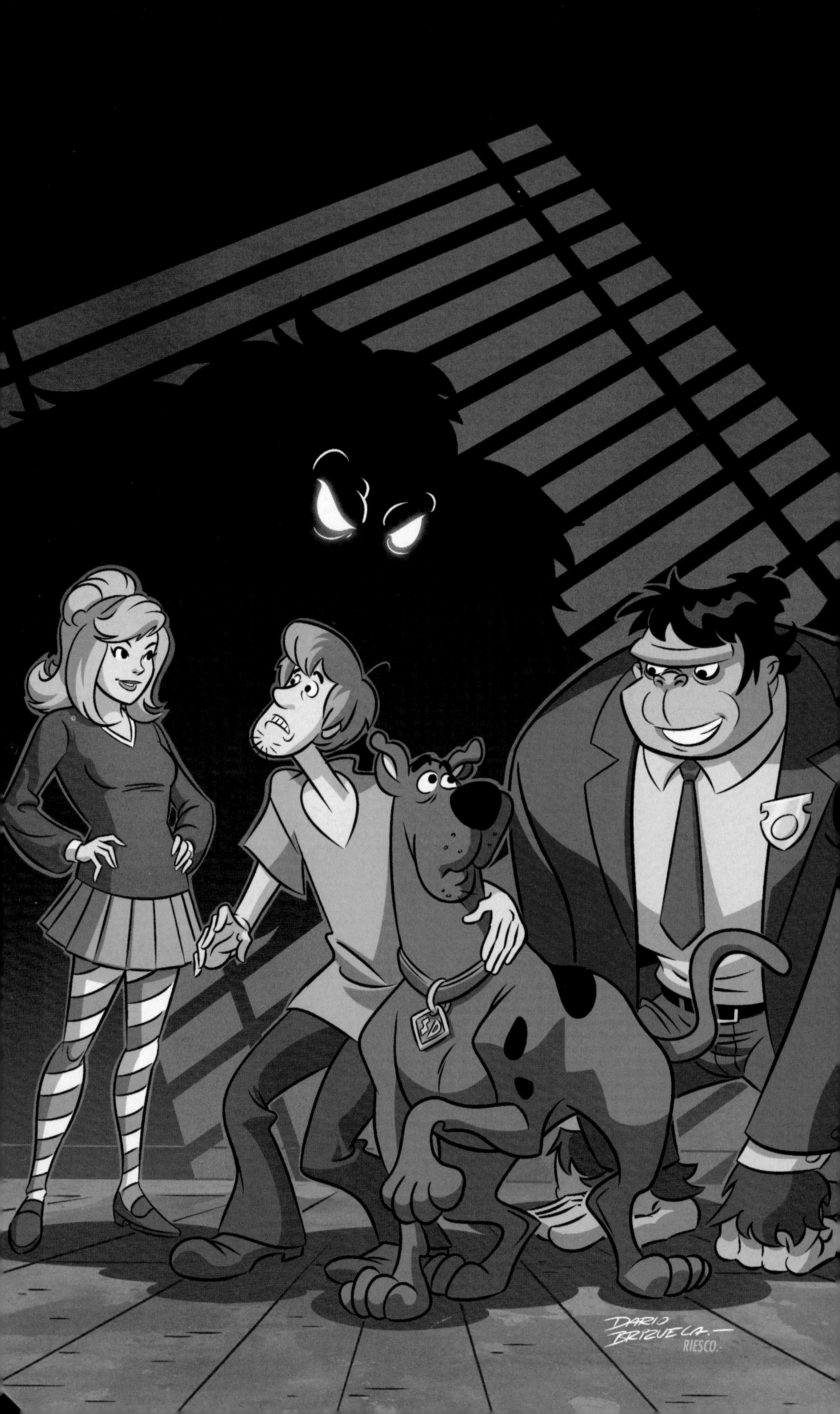
DARIO BRIZUELA
RIESCO.

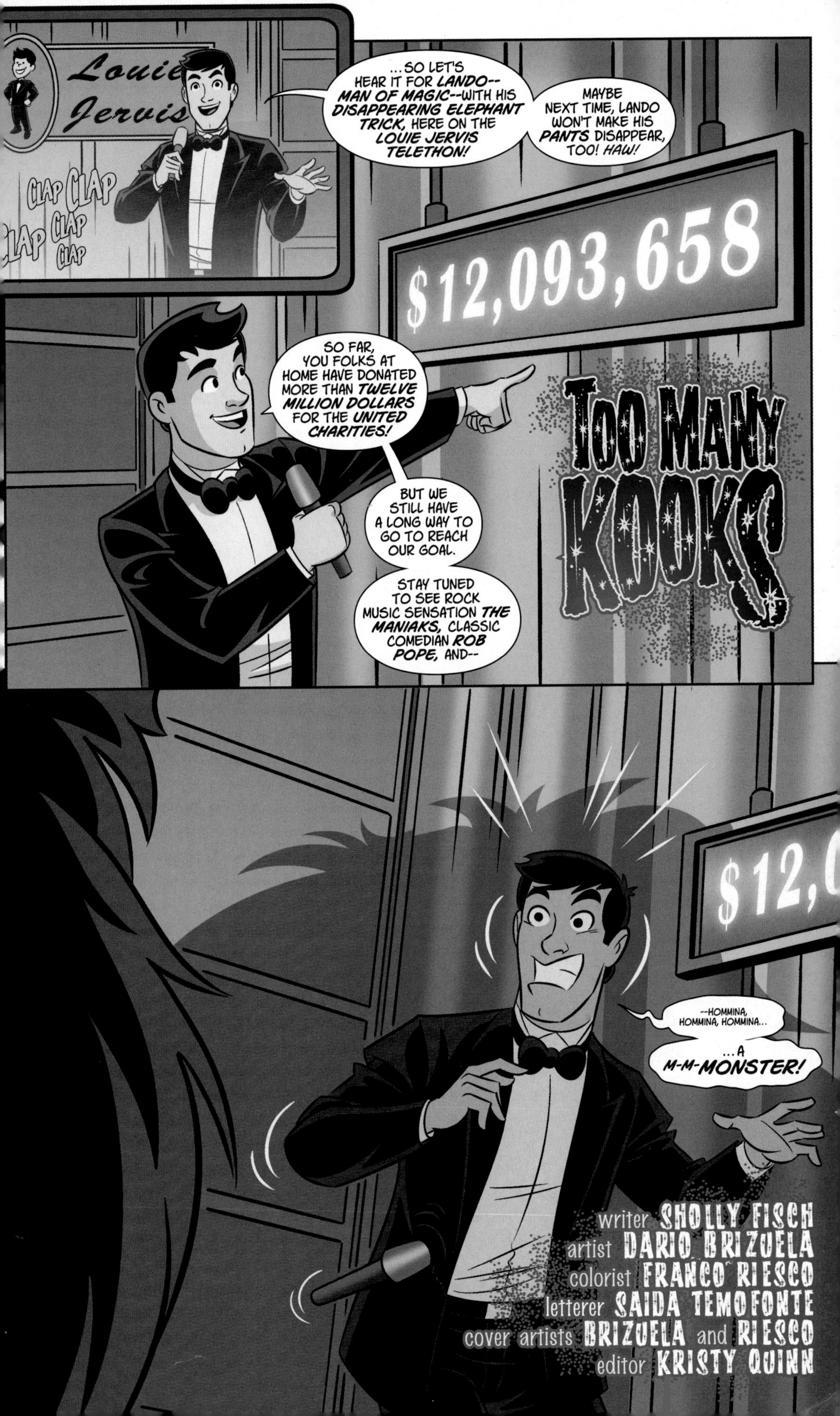
Louie Jervis
...SO LET'S HEAR IT FOR LANDO-- MAN OF MAGIC--WITH HIS DISAPPEARING ELEPHANT TRICK, HERE ON THE LOUIE JERVIS TELETHON!
MAYBE NEXT TIME, LANDO WON'T MAKE HIS PANTS DISAPPEAR, TOO! HAW!
CLAP CLAP CLAP CLAP CLAP
$12,093,658
SO FAR, YOU FOLKS AT HOME HAVE DONATED MORE THAN TWELVE MILLION DOLLARS FOR THE UNITED CHARITIES!
BUT WE STILL HAVE A LONG WAY TO GO TO REACH OUR GOAL.
STAY TUNED TO SEE ROCK MUSIC SENSATION THE MANIAKS, CLASSIC COMEDIAN ROB POPE, AND--
TOO MANY KOOKS
--HOMMINA, HOMMINA, HOMMINA...
...A M-M-MONSTER!
writer SHOLLY FISCH
artist DARIO BRIZUELA
colorist FRANCO RIESCO
letterer SAIDA TEMOFONTE
cover artists BRIZUELA and RIESCO
editor KRISTY QUINN

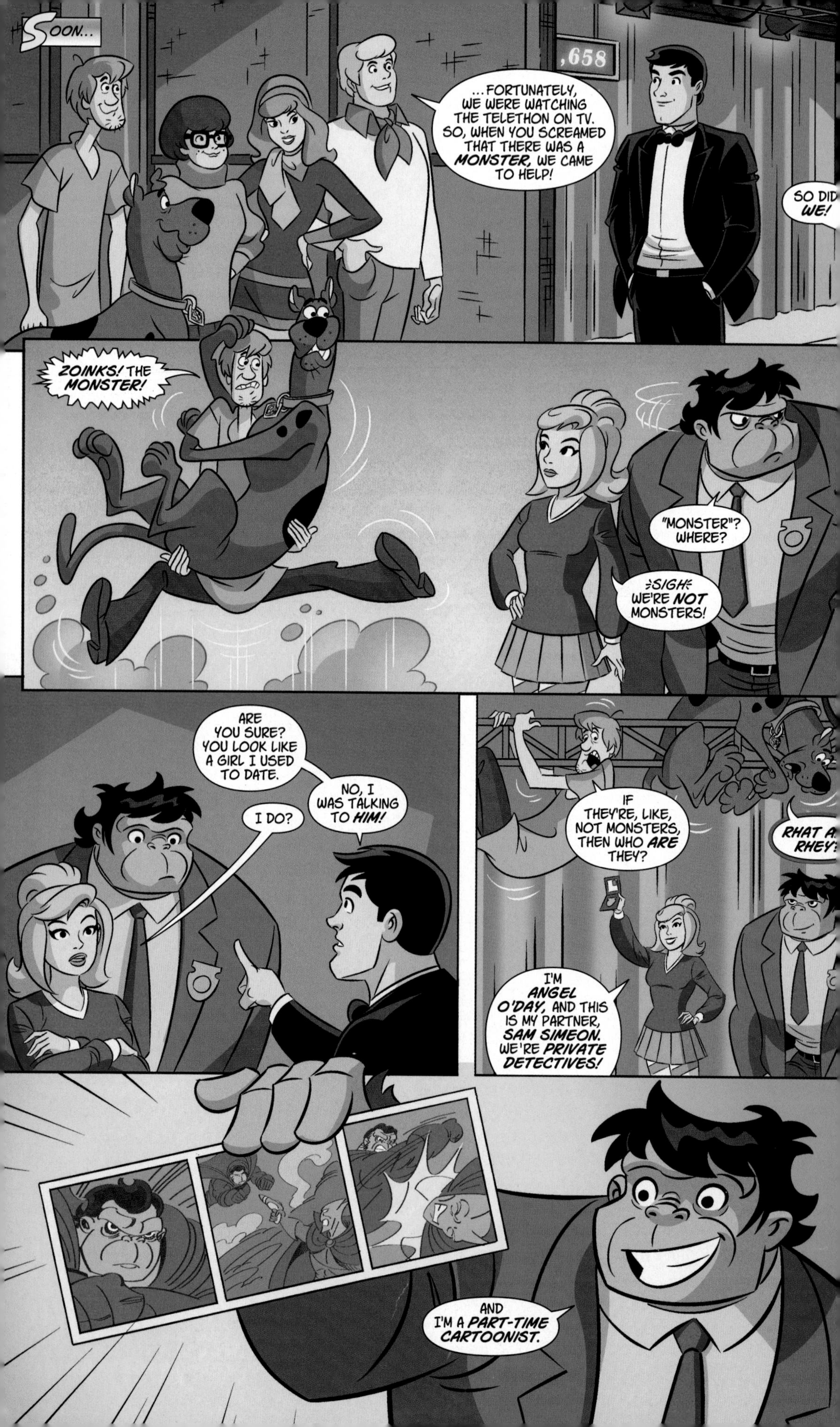
SOON...
...FORTUNATELY, WE WERE WATCHING THE TELETHON ON TV. SO, WHEN YOU SCREAMED THAT THERE WAS A MONSTER, WE CAME TO HELP!
SO DID WE!
ZOINKS! THE MONSTER!
"MONSTER"? WHERE?
SIGH WE'RE NOT MONSTERS!
ARE YOU SURE? YOU LOOK LIKE A GIRL I USED TO DATE.
I DO?
NO, I WAS TALKING TO HIM!
IF THEY'RE, LIKE, NOT MONSTERS, THEN WHO ARE THEY?
I'M ANGEL O'DAY, AND THIS IS MY PARTNER, SAM SIMEON. WE'RE PRIVATE DETECTIVES!
AND I'M A PART-TIME CARTOONIST.
,658

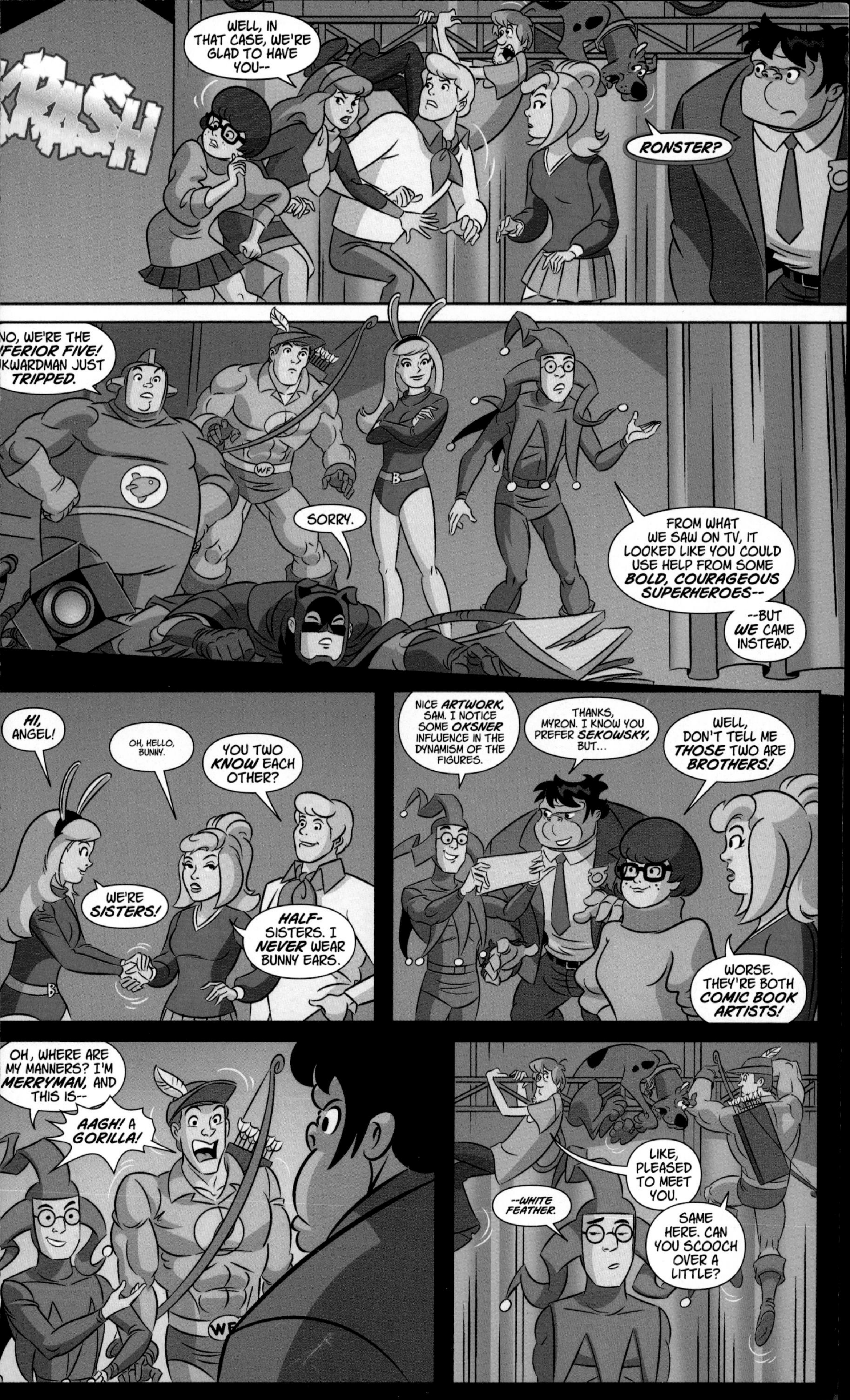
KRASH
WELL, IN THAT CASE, WE'RE GLAD TO HAVE YOU--
RONSTER?
NO, WE'RE THE INFERIOR FIVE! AWKWARDMAN JUST TRIPPED.
SORRY.
FROM WHAT WE SAW ON TV, IT LOOKED LIKE YOU COULD USE HELP FROM SOME BOLD, COURAGEOUS SUPERHEROES--
--BUT WE CAME INSTEAD.
HI, ANGEL!
OH, HELLO, BUNNY.
YOU TWO KNOW EACH OTHER?
WE'RE SISTERS!
HALF-SISTERS. I NEVER WEAR BUNNY EARS.
NICE ARTWORK, SAM. I NOTICE SOME OKSNER INFLUENCE IN THE DYNAMISM OF THE FIGURES.
THANKS, MYRON. I KNOW YOU PREFER SEKOWSKY, BUT...
WELL, DON'T TELL ME THOSE TWO ARE BROTHERS!
WORSE. THEY'RE BOTH COMIC BOOK ARTISTS!
OH, WHERE ARE MY MANNERS? I'M MERRYMAN, AND THIS IS--
AAGH! A GORILLA!
--WHITE FEATHER.
LIKE, PLEASED TO MEET YOU.
SAME HERE. CAN YOU SCOOCH OVER A LITTLE?

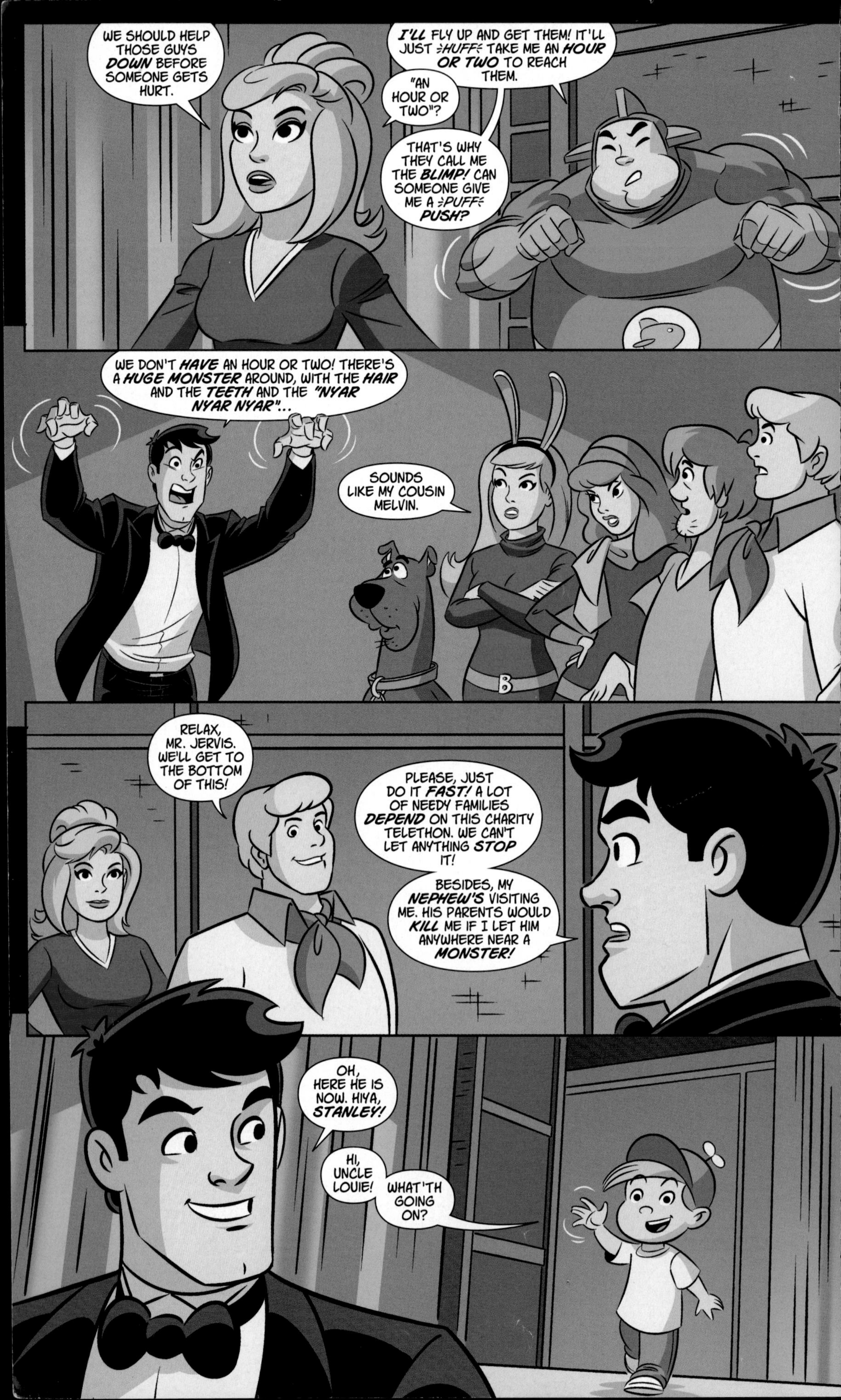
WE SHOULD HELP THOSE GUYS DOWN BEFORE SOMEONE GETS HURT.
I'LL FLY UP AND GET THEM! IT'LL JUST ≶HUFF≷ TAKE ME AN HOUR OR TWO TO REACH THEM.
"AN HOUR OR TWO"?
THAT'S WHY THEY CALL ME THE BLIMP! CAN SOMEONE GIVE ME A ≶PUFF≷ PUSH?
WE DON'T HAVE AN HOUR OR TWO! THERE'S A HUGE MONSTER AROUND, WITH THE HAIR AND THE TEETH AND THE "NYAR NYAR NYAR"...
SOUNDS LIKE MY COUSIN MELVIN.
RELAX, MR. JERVIS. WE'LL GET TO THE BOTTOM OF THIS!
PLEASE, JUST DO IT FAST! A LOT OF NEEDY FAMILIES DEPEND ON THIS CHARITY TELETHON. WE CAN'T LET ANYTHING STOP IT!
BESIDES, MY NEPHEW'S VISITING ME. HIS PARENTS WOULD KILL ME IF I LET HIM ANYWHERE NEAR A MONSTER!
OH, HERE HE IS NOW. HIYA, STANLEY!
HI, UNCLE LOUIE!
WHAT'TH GOING ON?

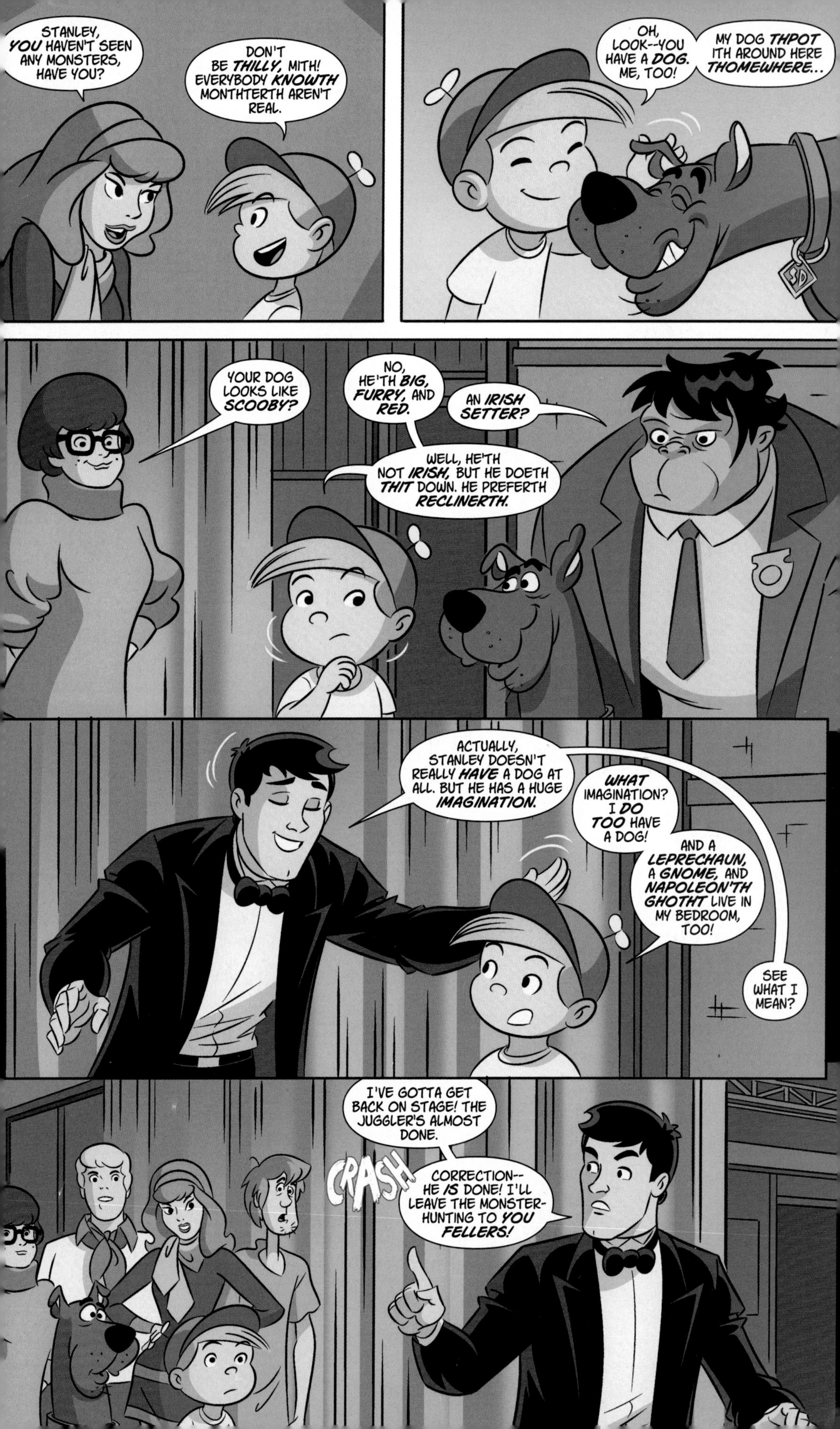
STANLEY, YOU HAVEN'T SEEN ANY MONSTERS, HAVE YOU?
DON'T BE THILLY, MITH! EVERYBODY KNOWTH MONTHTERTH AREN'T REAL.
OH, LOOK--YOU HAVE A DOG. ME, TOO!
MY DOG THPOT ITH AROUND HERE THOMEWHERE...
YOUR DOG LOOKS LIKE SCOOBY?
NO, HE'TH BIG, FURRY, AND RED.
AN IRISH SETTER?
WELL, HE'TH NOT IRISH, BUT HE DOETH THIT DOWN. HE PREFERTH RECLINERTH.
ACTUALLY, STANLEY DOESN'T REALLY HAVE A DOG AT ALL. BUT HE HAS A HUGE IMAGINATION.
WHAT IMAGINATION? I DO TOO HAVE A DOG!
AND A LEPRECHAUN, A GNOME, AND NAPOLEON'TH GHOTHT LIVE IN MY BEDROOM, TOO!
SEE WHAT I MEAN?
I'VE GOTTA GET BACK ON STAGE! THE JUGGLER'S ALMOST DONE.
CRASH
CORRECTION-- HE IS DONE! I'LL LEAVE THE MONSTER-HUNTING TO YOU FELLERS!

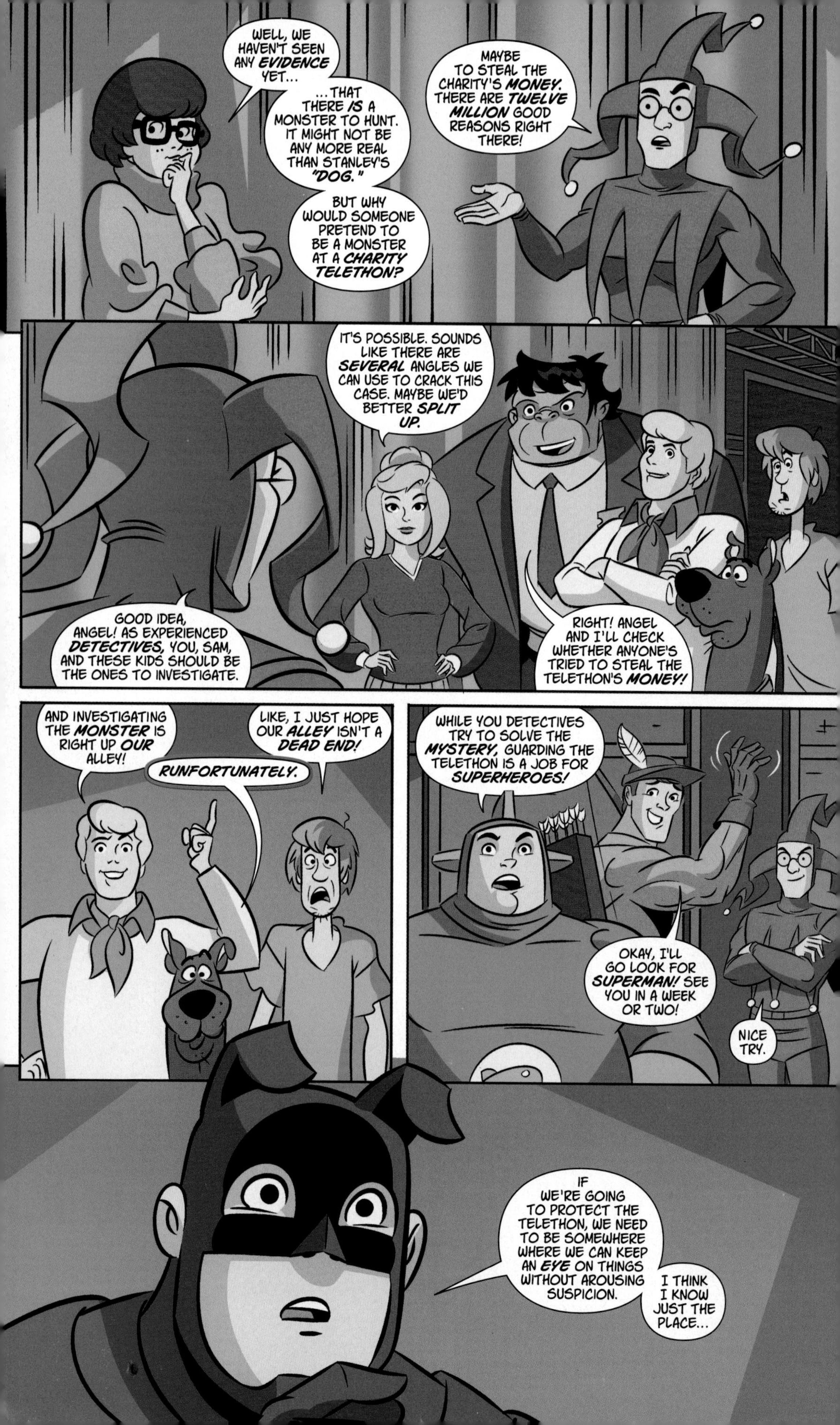

WELL, WE HAVEN'T SEEN ANY EVIDENCE YET...
...THAT THERE IS A MONSTER TO HUNT. IT MIGHT NOT BE ANY MORE REAL THAN STANLEY'S "DOG."
BUT WHY WOULD SOMEONE PRETEND TO BE A MONSTER AT A CHARITY TELETHON?
MAYBE TO STEAL THE CHARITY'S MONEY. THERE ARE TWELVE MILLION GOOD REASONS RIGHT THERE!
IT'S POSSIBLE. SOUNDS LIKE THERE ARE SEVERAL ANGLES WE CAN USE TO CRACK THIS CASE. MAYBE WE'D BETTER SPLIT UP.
GOOD IDEA, ANGEL! AS EXPERIENCED DETECTIVES, YOU, SAM, AND THESE KIDS SHOULD BE THE ONES TO INVESTIGATE.
RIGHT! ANGEL AND I'LL CHECK WHETHER ANYONE'S TRIED TO STEAL THE TELETHON'S MONEY!
AND INVESTIGATING THE MONSTER IS RIGHT UP OUR ALLEY!
LIKE, I JUST HOPE OUR ALLEY ISN'T A DEAD END!
RUNFORTUNATELY.
WHILE YOU DETECTIVES TRY TO SOLVE THE MYSTERY, GUARDING THE TELETHON IS A JOB FOR SUPERHEROES!
OKAY, I'LL GO LOOK FOR SUPERMAN! SEE YOU IN A WEEK OR TWO!
NICE TRY.
IF WE'RE GOING TO PROTECT THE TELETHON, WE NEED TO BE SOMEWHERE WHERE WE CAN KEEP AN EYE ON THINGS WITHOUT AROUSING SUSPICION.
I THINK I KNOW JUST THE PLACE...

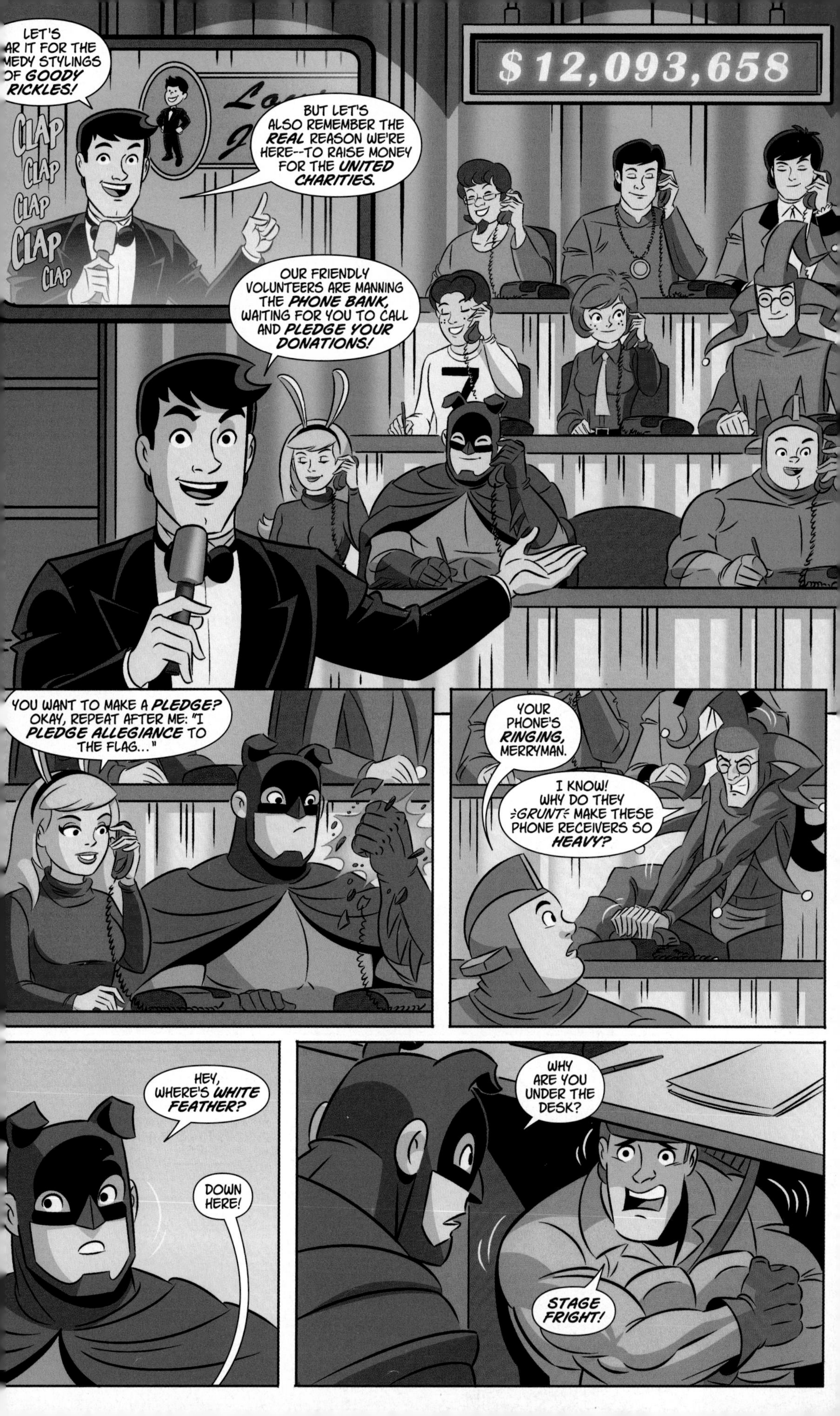
LET'S
AR IT FOR THE
MEDY STYLINGS
OF GOODY
RICKLES!
CLAP CLAP CLAP CLAP CLAP
$12,093,658
BUT LET'S ALSO REMEMBER THE REAL REASON WE'RE HERE--TO RAISE MONEY FOR THE UNITED CHARITIES.
OUR FRIENDLY VOLUNTEERS ARE MANNING THE PHONE BANK, WAITING FOR YOU TO CALL AND PLEDGE YOUR DONATIONS!
YOU WANT TO MAKE A PLEDGE? OKAY, REPEAT AFTER ME: "I PLEDGE ALLEGIANCE TO THE FLAG..."
YOUR PHONE'S RINGING, MERRYMAN.
I KNOW! WHY DO THEY *GRUNT* MAKE THESE PHONE RECEIVERS SO HEAVY?
HEY, WHERE'S WHITE FEATHER?
DOWN HERE!
WHY ARE YOU UNDER THE DESK?
STAGE FRIGHT!

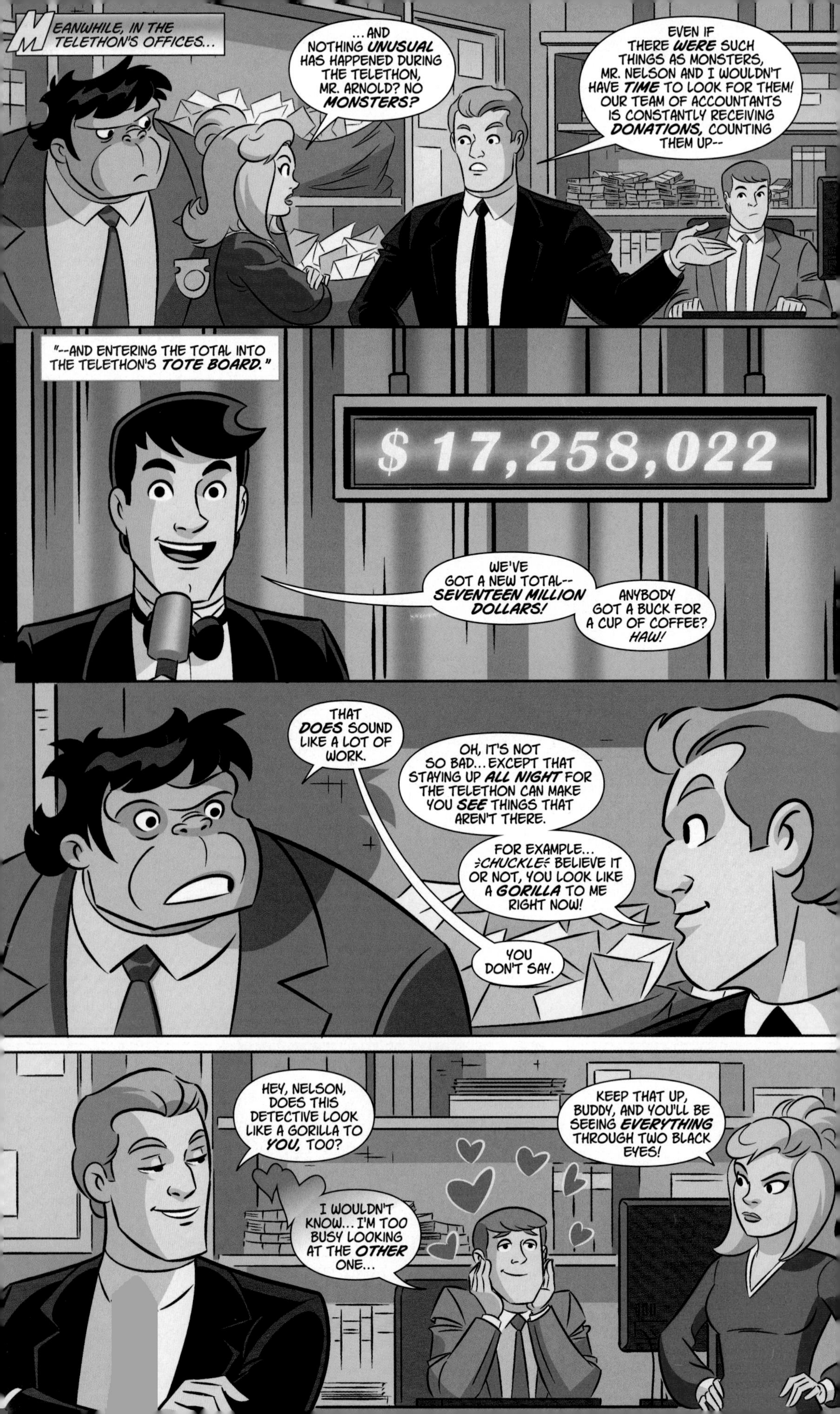
MEANWHILE, IN THE TELETHON'S OFFICES...
...AND NOTHING UNUSUAL HAS HAPPENED DURING THE TELETHON, MR. ARNOLD? NO MONSTERS?
EVEN IF THERE WERE SUCH THINGS AS MONSTERS, MR. NELSON AND I WOULDN'T HAVE TIME TO LOOK FOR THEM! OUR TEAM OF ACCOUNTANTS IS CONSTANTLY RECEIVING DONATIONS, COUNTING THEM UP--
"--AND ENTERING THE TOTAL INTO THE TELETHON'S TOTE BOARD."
$ 17,258,022
WE'VE GOT A NEW TOTAL-- SEVENTEEN MILLION DOLLARS!
ANYBODY GOT A BUCK FOR A CUP OF COFFEE? HAW!
THAT DOES SOUND LIKE A LOT OF WORK.
OH, IT'S NOT SO BAD... EXCEPT THAT STAYING UP ALL NIGHT FOR THE TELETHON CAN MAKE YOU SEE THINGS THAT AREN'T THERE.
FOR EXAMPLE... CHUCKLE BELIEVE IT OR NOT, YOU LOOK LIKE A GORILLA TO ME RIGHT NOW!
YOU DON'T SAY.
HEY, NELSON, DOES THIS DETECTIVE LOOK LIKE A GORILLA TO YOU, TOO?
I WOULDN'T KNOW... I'M TOO BUSY LOOKING AT THE OTHER ONE...
KEEP THAT UP, BUDDY, AND YOU'LL BE SEEING EVERYTHING THROUGH TWO BLACK EYES!

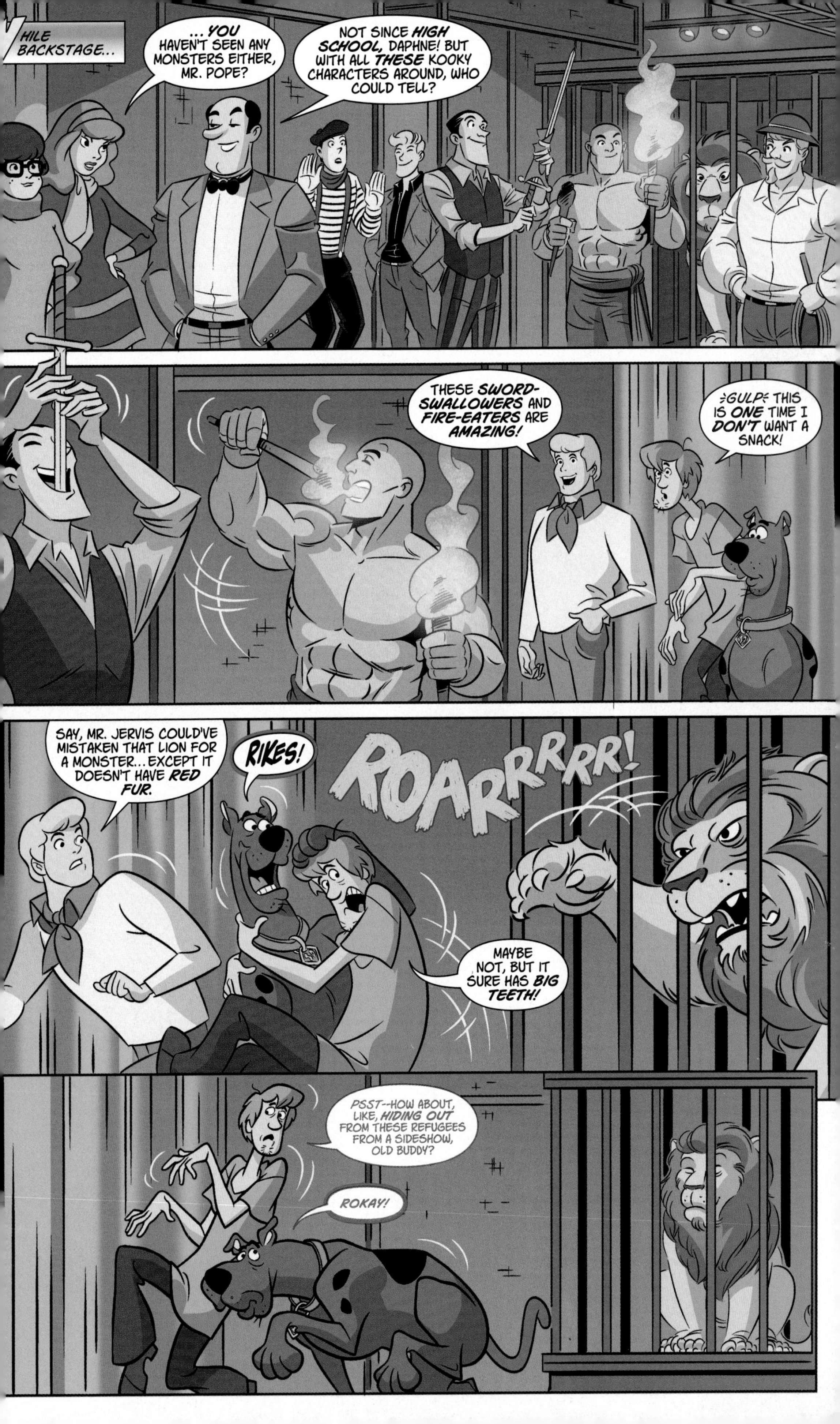
WHILE BACKSTAGE...
...YOU HAVEN'T SEEN ANY MONSTERS EITHER, MR. POPE?
NOT SINCE HIGH SCHOOL, DAPHNE! BUT WITH ALL THESE KOOKY CHARACTERS AROUND, WHO COULD TELL?
THESE SWORD-SWALLOWERS AND FIRE-EATERS ARE AMAZING!
GULP THIS IS ONE TIME I DON'T WANT A SNACK!
SAY, MR. JERVIS COULD'VE MISTAKEN THAT LION FOR A MONSTER...EXCEPT IT DOESN'T HAVE RED FUR.
RIKES!
ROARRRRR!
MAYBE NOT, BUT IT SURE HAS BIG TEETH!
PSST--HOW ABOUT, LIKE, HIDING OUT FROM THESE REFUGEES FROM A SIDESHOW, OLD BUDDY?
ROKAY!

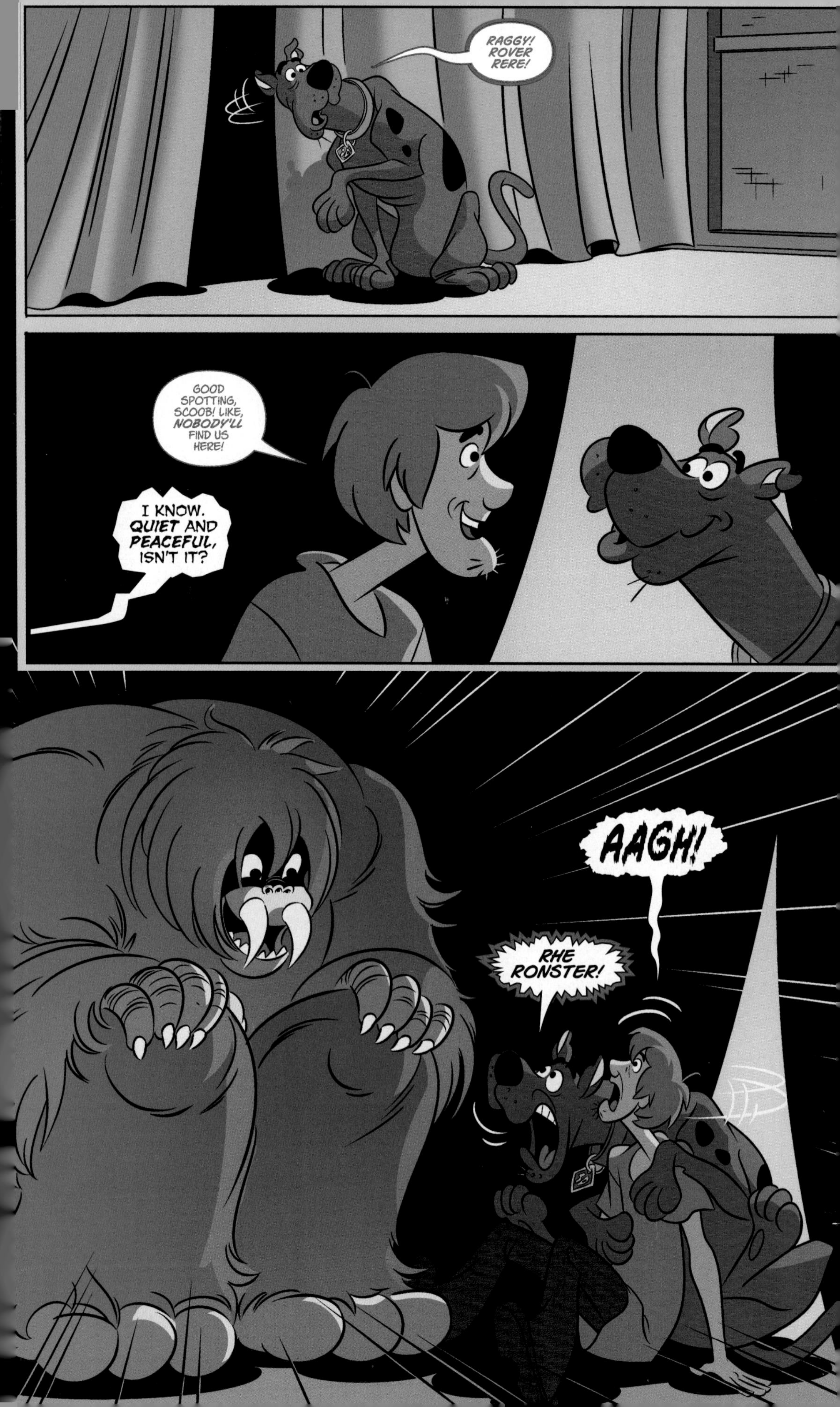
RAGGY! ROVER RERE!
GOOD SPOTTING, SCOOB! LIKE, NOBODY'LL FIND US HERE!
I KNOW. QUIET AND PEACEFUL, ISN'T IT?
AAGH!
RHE RONSTER!

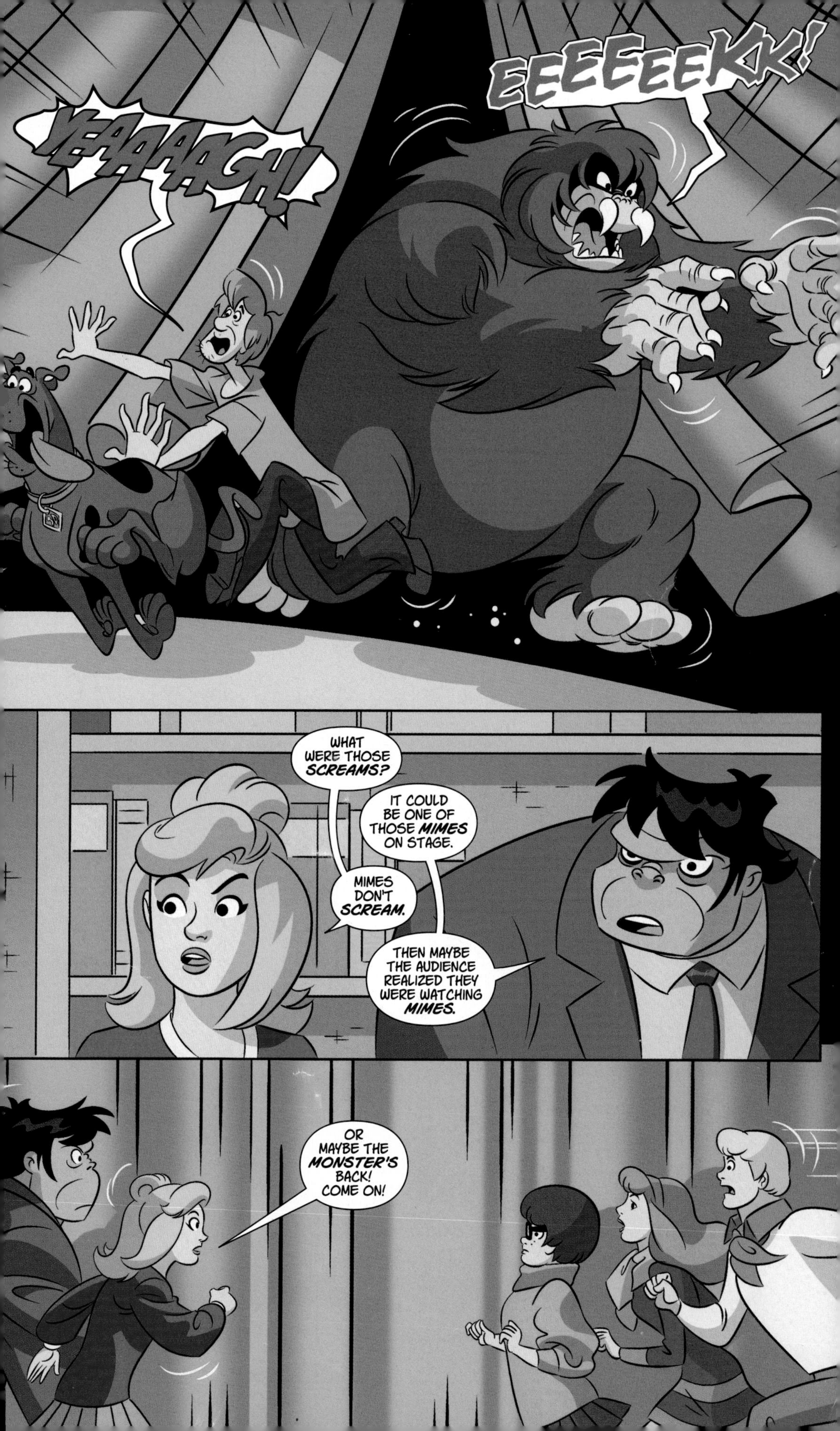
YEAAAAAGH!
EEEEEEEKK!
WHAT WERE THOSE SCREAMS?
IT COULD BE ONE OF THOSE MIMES ON STAGE.
MIMES DON'T SCREAM.
THEN MAYBE THE AUDIENCE REALIZED THEY WERE WATCHING MIMES.
OR MAYBE THE MONSTER'S BACK! COME ON!

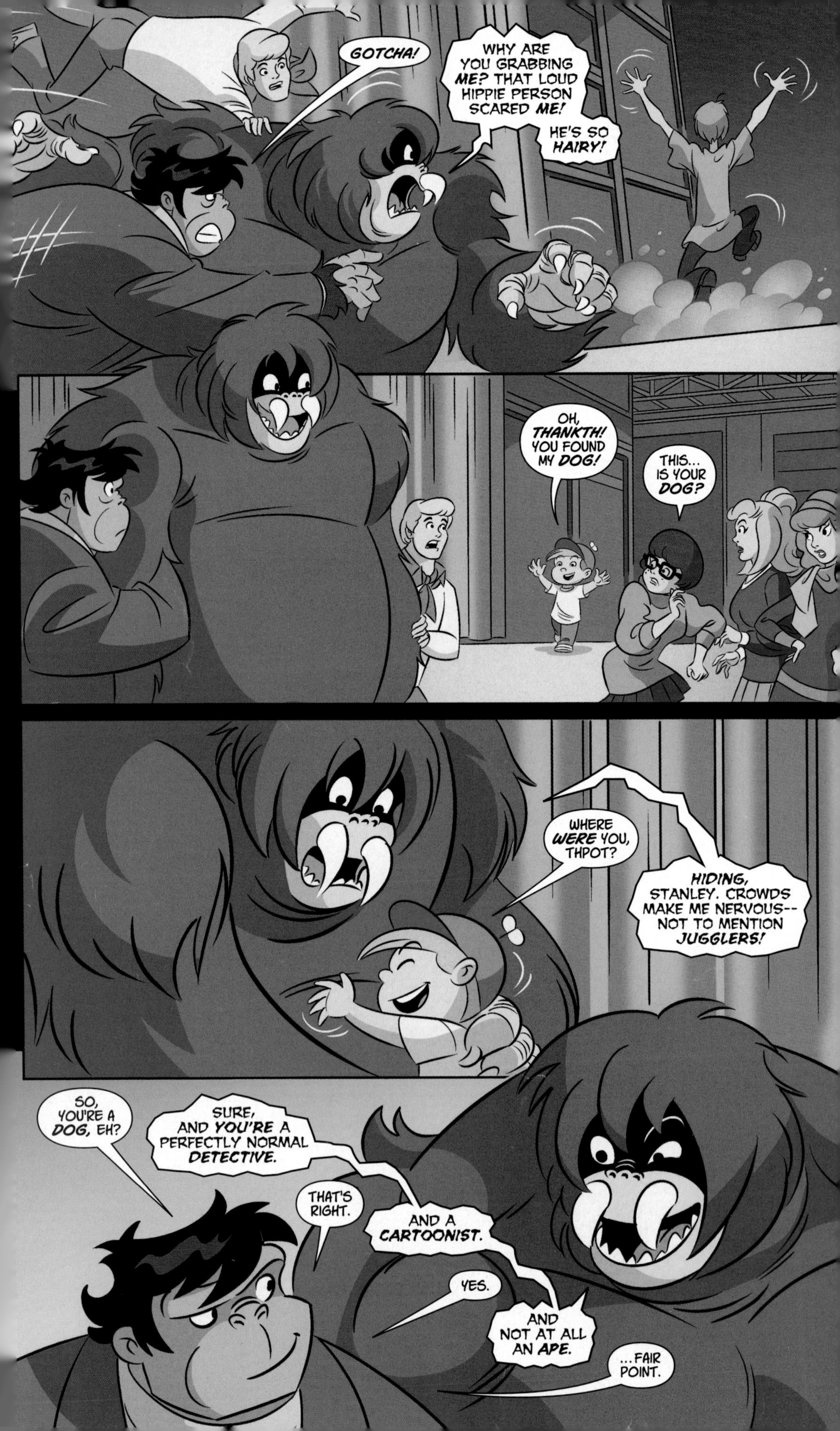
GOTCHA!
WHY ARE YOU GRABBING ME? THAT LOUD HIPPIE PERSON SCARED ME!
HE'S SO HAIRY!
OH, THANKTH! YOU FOUND MY DOG!
THIS... IS YOUR DOG?
WHERE WERE YOU, THPOT?
HIDING, STANLEY. CROWDS MAKE ME NERVOUS-- NOT TO MENTION JUGGLERS!
SO, YOU'RE A DOG, EH?
SURE, AND YOU'RE A PERFECTLY NORMAL DETECTIVE.
THAT'S RIGHT.
AND A CARTOONIST.
YES.
AND NOT AT ALL AN APE.
...FAIR POINT.

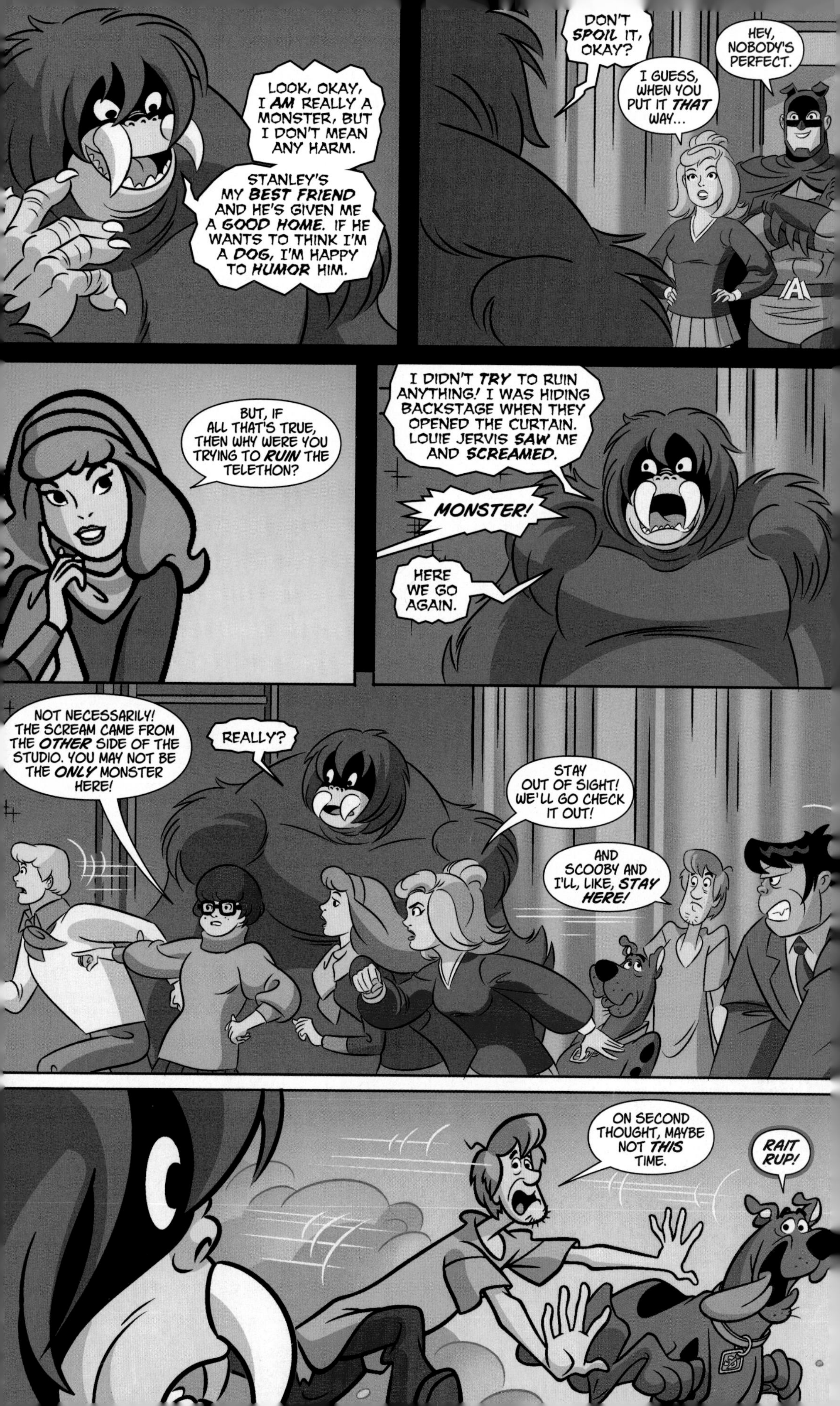
LOOK, OKAY, I AM REALLY A MONSTER, BUT I DON'T MEAN ANY HARM.
STANLEY'S MY BEST FRIEND AND HE'S GIVEN ME A GOOD HOME. IF HE WANTS TO THINK I'M A DOG, I'M HAPPY TO HUMOR HIM.
DON'T SPOIL IT, OKAY?
I GUESS, WHEN YOU PUT IT THAT WAY...
HEY, NOBODY'S PERFECT.
BUT, IF ALL THAT'S TRUE, THEN WHY WERE YOU TRYING TO RUIN THE TELETHON?
I DIDN'T TRY TO RUIN ANYTHING! I WAS HIDING BACKSTAGE WHEN THEY OPENED THE CURTAIN. LOUIE JERVIS SAW ME AND SCREAMED.
MONSTER!
HERE WE GO AGAIN.
NOT NECESSARILY! THE SCREAM CAME FROM THE OTHER SIDE OF THE STUDIO. YOU MAY NOT BE THE ONLY MONSTER HERE!
REALLY?
STAY OUT OF SIGHT! WE'LL GO CHECK IT OUT!
AND SCOOBY AND I'LL, LIKE, STAY HERE!
ON SECOND THOUGHT, MAYBE NOT THIS TIME.
RAIT RUP!

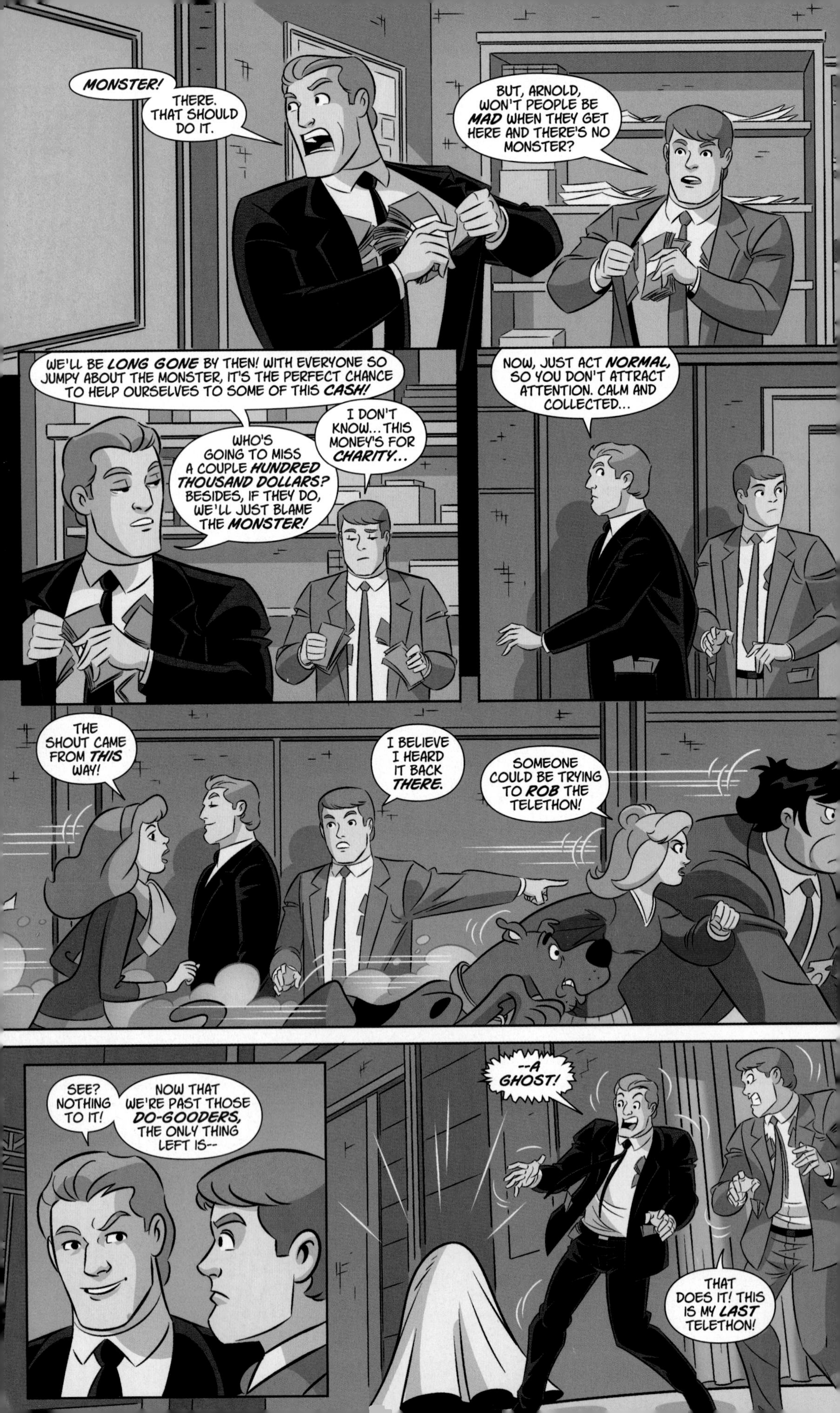
MONSTER!
THERE. THAT SHOULD DO IT.
BUT, ARNOLD, WON'T PEOPLE BE MAD WHEN THEY GET HERE AND THERE'S NO MONSTER?
WE'LL BE LONG GONE BY THEN! WITH EVERYONE SO JUMPY ABOUT THE MONSTER, IT'S THE PERFECT CHANCE TO HELP OURSELVES TO SOME OF THIS CASH!
I DON'T KNOW... THIS MONEY'S FOR CHARITY...
WHO'S GOING TO MISS A COUPLE HUNDRED THOUSAND DOLLARS? BESIDES, IF THEY DO, WE'LL JUST BLAME THE MONSTER!
NOW, JUST ACT NORMAL, SO YOU DON'T ATTRACT ATTENTION. CALM AND COLLECTED...
THE SHOUT CAME FROM THIS WAY!
I BELIEVE I HEARD IT BACK THERE.
SOMEONE COULD BE TRYING TO ROB THE TELETHON!
SEE? NOTHING TO IT!
NOW THAT WE'RE PAST THOSE DO-GOODERS, THE ONLY THING LEFT IS--
--A GHOST!
THAT DOES IT! THIS IS MY LAST TELETHON!

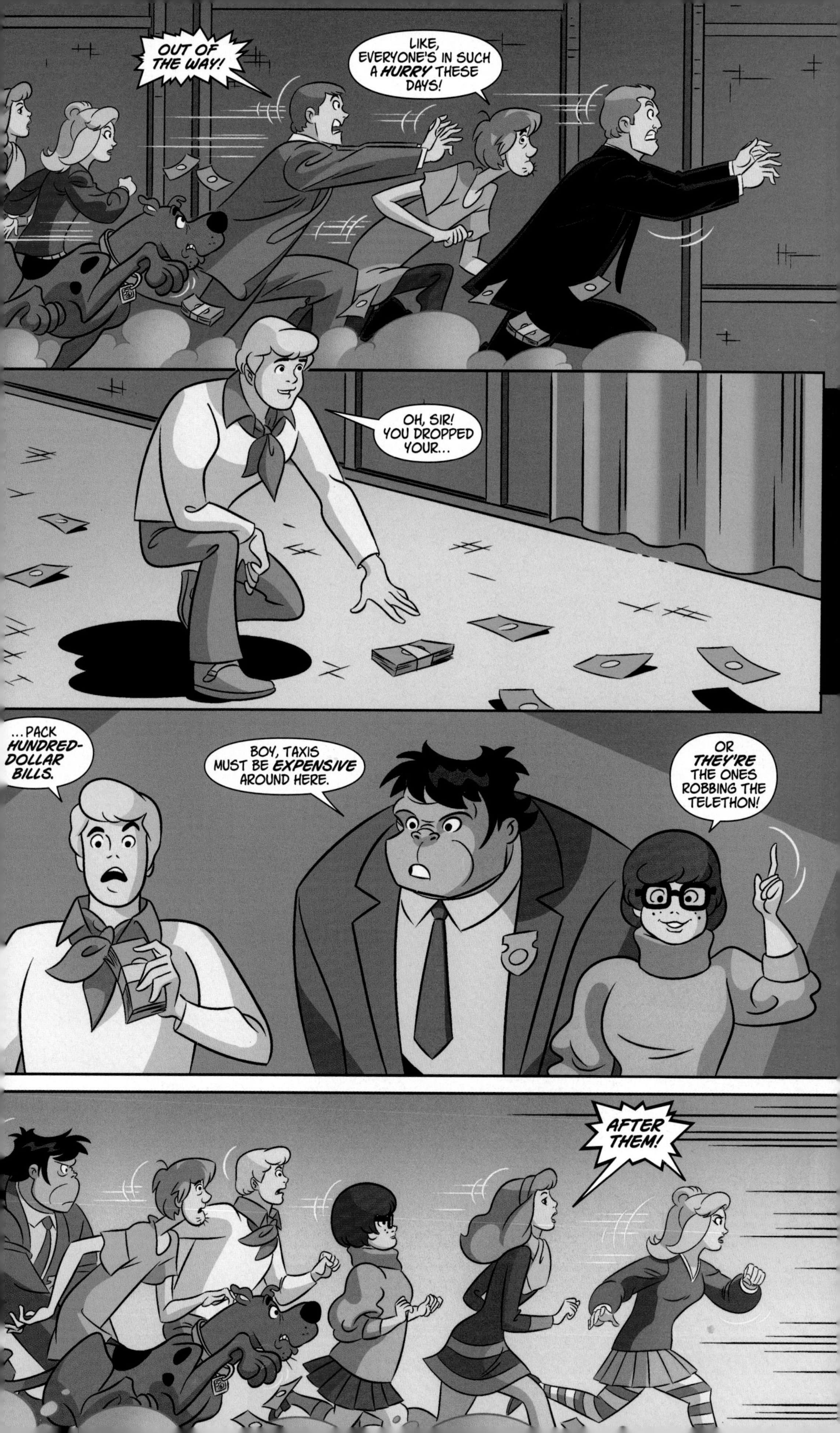
OUT OF THE WAY!
LIKE, EVERYONE'S IN SUCH A HURRY THESE DAYS!
OH, SIR! YOU DROPPED YOUR...
...PACK HUNDRED-DOLLAR BILLS.
BOY, TAXIS MUST BE EXPENSIVE AROUND HERE.
OR THEY'RE THE ONES ROBBING THE TELETHON!
AFTER THEM!

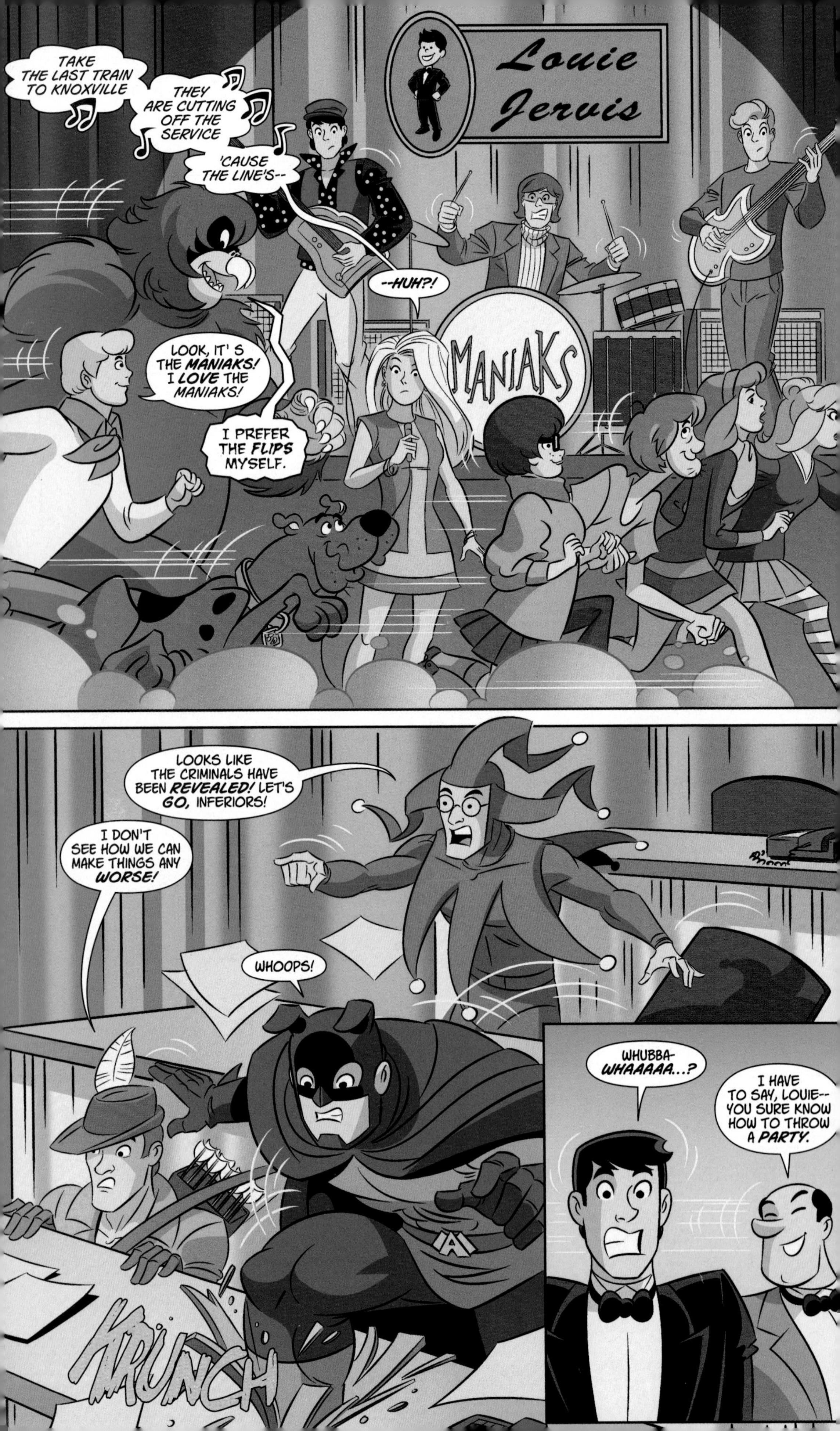
Louie Jervis
TAKE THE LAST TRAIN TO KNOXVILLE
THEY ARE CUTTING OFF THE SERVICE
'CAUSE THE LINE'S--
--HUH?!
MANIAKS
LOOK, IT'S THE MANIAKS! I LOVE THE MANIAKS!
I PREFER THE FLIPS MYSELF.
LOOKS LIKE THE CRIMINALS HAVE BEEN REVEALED! LET'S GO, INFERIORS!
I DON'T SEE HOW WE CAN MAKE THINGS ANY WORSE!
WHOOPS!
KRUNCH
WHUBBA-WHAAAAA...?
I HAVE TO SAY, LOUIE-- YOU SURE KNOW HOW TO THROW A PARTY.

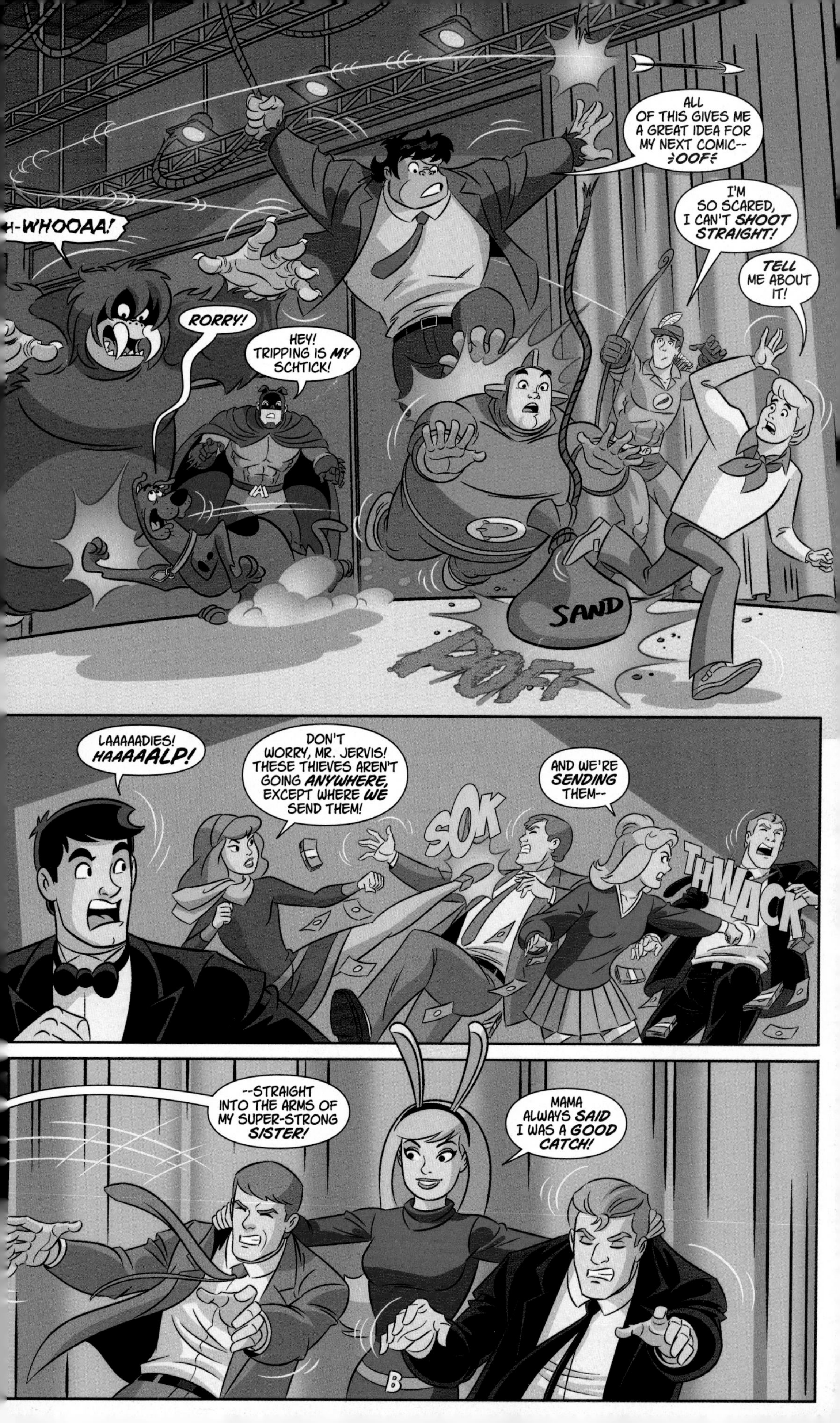

H-WHOOAA!
ALL OF THIS GIVES ME A GREAT IDEA FOR MY NEXT COMIC-- OOF
I'M SO SCARED, I CAN'T SHOOT STRAIGHT!
TELL ME ABOUT IT!
RORRY!
HEY! TRIPPING IS MY SCHTICK!
SAND
POFF
LAAAAADIES! HAAAAALP!
DON'T WORRY, MR. JERVIS! THESE THIEVES AREN'T GOING ANYWHERE, EXCEPT WHERE WE SEND THEM!
AND WE'RE SENDING THEM--
SOK
THWACK
--STRAIGHT INTO THE ARMS OF MY SUPER-STRONG SISTER!
MAMA ALWAYS SAID I WAS A GOOD CATCH!

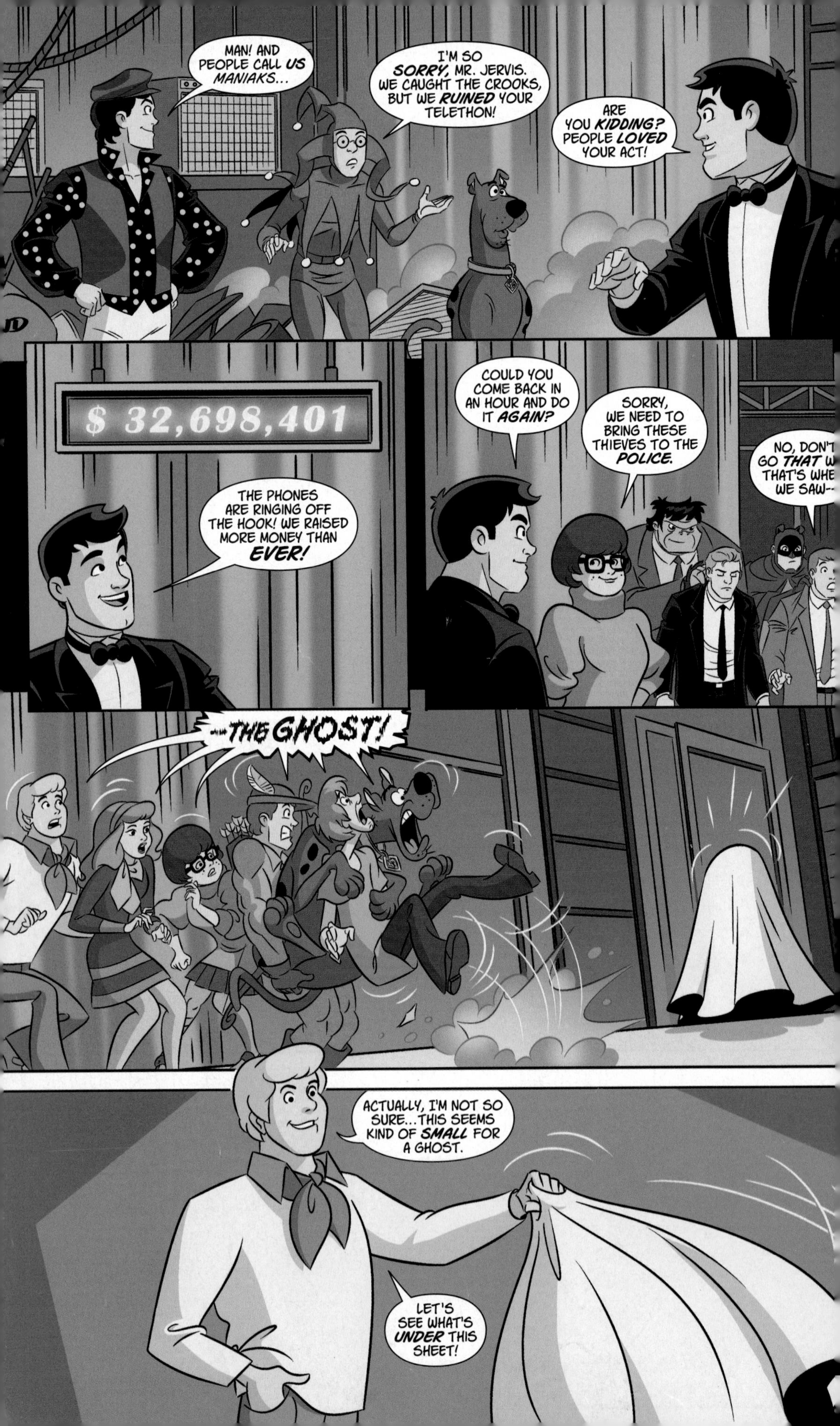
MAN! AND PEOPLE CALL US MANIAKS...
I'M SO SORRY, MR. JERVIS. WE CAUGHT THE CROOKS, BUT WE RUINED YOUR TELETHON!
ARE YOU KIDDING? PEOPLE LOVED YOUR ACT!
$ 32,698,401
THE PHONES ARE RINGING OFF THE HOOK! WE RAISED MORE MONEY THAN EVER!
COULD YOU COME BACK IN AN HOUR AND DO IT AGAIN?
SORRY, WE NEED TO BRING THESE THIEVES TO THE POLICE.
NO, DON'T GO THAT W THAT'S WHE WE SAW--
--THE GHOST!
ACTUALLY, I'M NOT SO SURE...THIS SEEMS KIND OF SMALL FOR A GHOST.
LET'S SEE WHAT'S UNDER THIS SHEET!

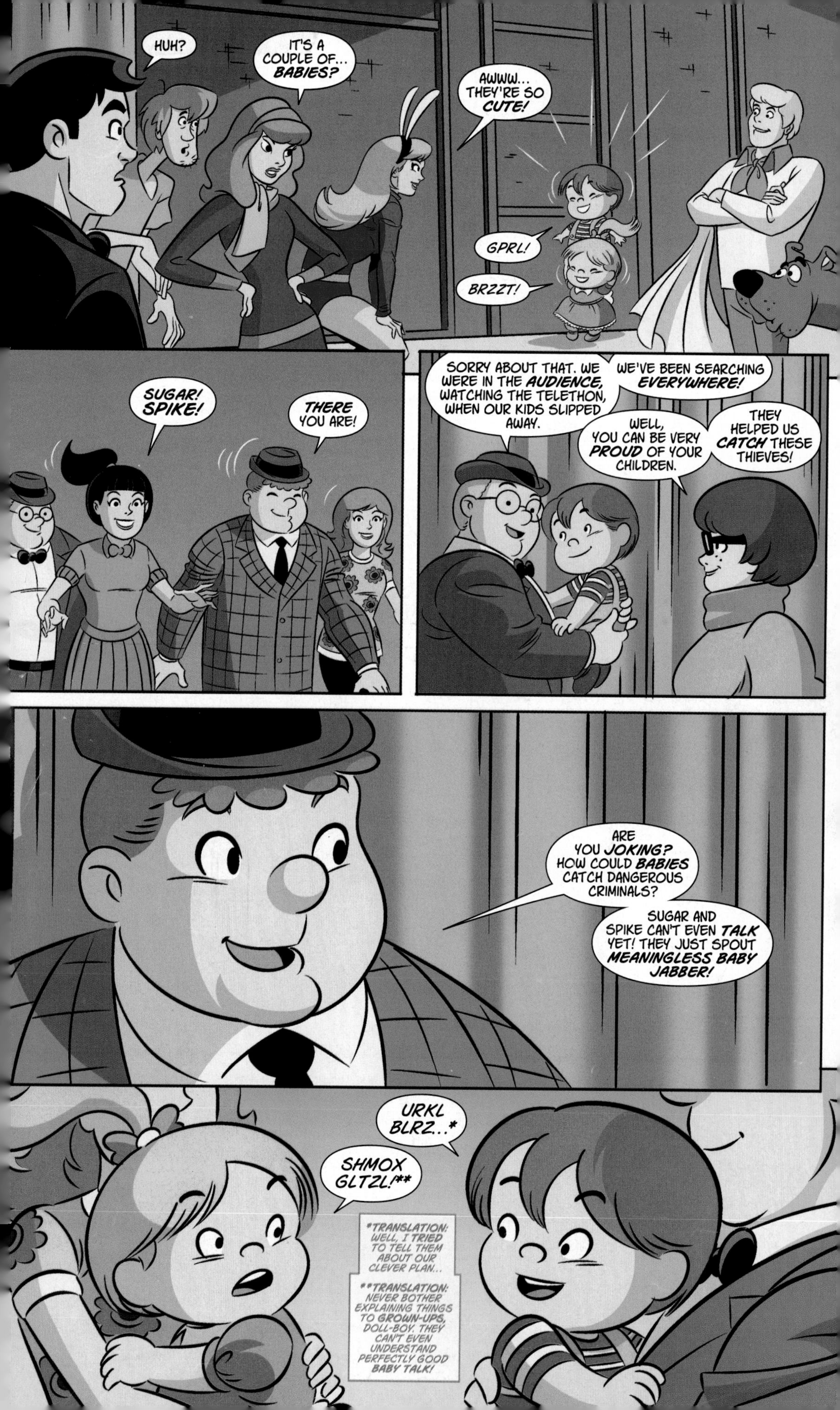
HUH?
IT'S A COUPLE OF... BABIES?
AWWW... THEY'RE SO CUTE!
GPRL!
BRZZT!
SUGAR! SPIKE!
THERE YOU ARE!
SORRY ABOUT THAT. WE WERE IN THE AUDIENCE, WATCHING THE TELETHON, WHEN OUR KIDS SLIPPED AWAY.
WE'VE BEEN SEARCHING EVERYWHERE!
WELL, YOU CAN BE VERY PROUD OF YOUR CHILDREN.
THEY HELPED US CATCH THESE THIEVES!
ARE YOU JOKING? HOW COULD BABIES CATCH DANGEROUS CRIMINALS?
SUGAR AND SPIKE CAN'T EVEN TALK YET! THEY JUST SPOUT MEANINGLESS BABY JABBER!
URKL BLRZ...*
SHMOX GLTZL!**
*TRANSLATION: WELL, I TRIED TO TELL THEM ABOUT OUR CLEVER PLAN...
**TRANSLATION: NEVER BOTHER EXPLAINING THINGS TO GROWN-UPS, DOLL-BOY. THEY CAN'T EVEN UNDERSTAND PERFECTLY GOOD BABY TALK!

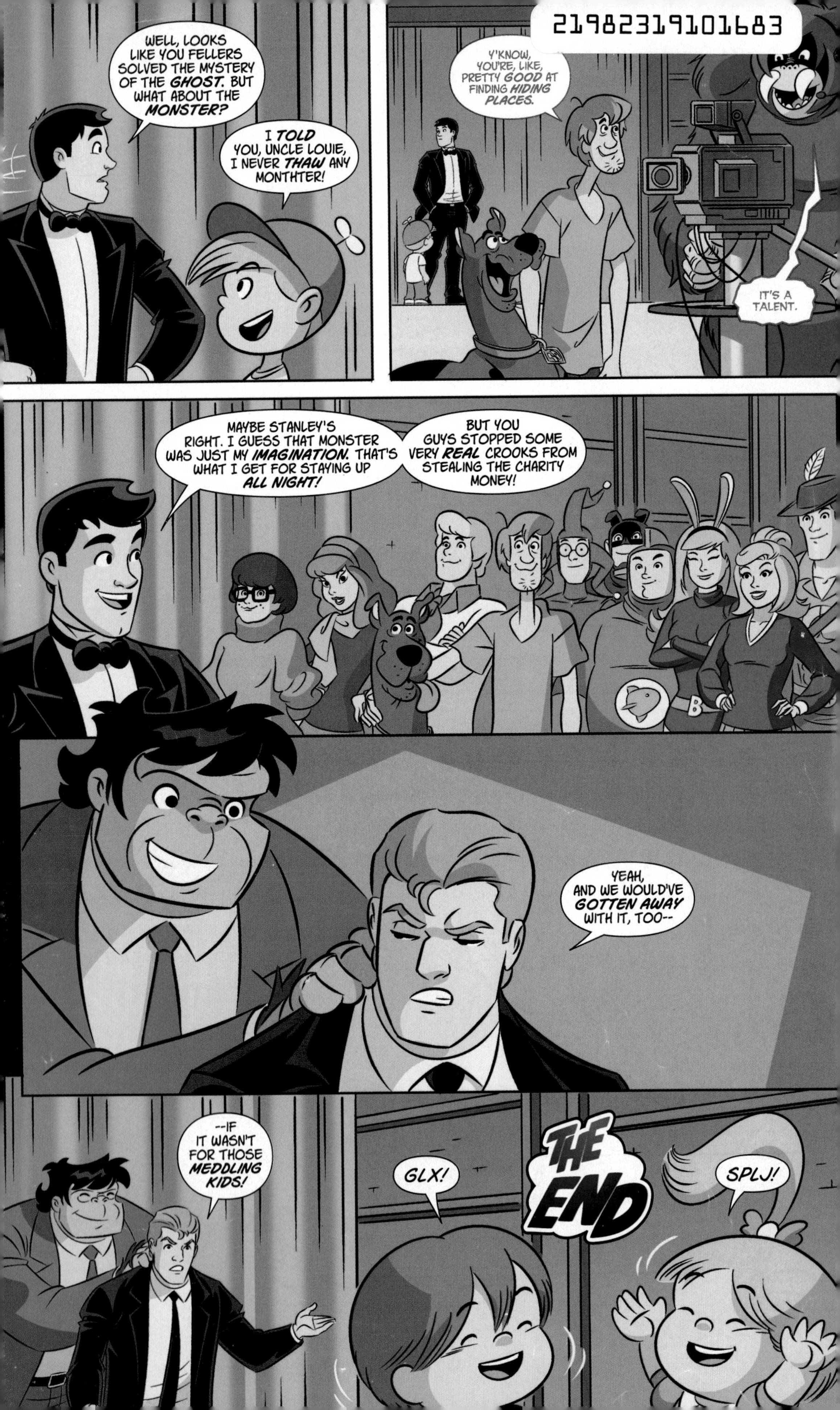
WELL, LOOKS LIKE YOU FELLERS SOLVED THE MYSTERY OF THE GHOST. BUT WHAT ABOUT THE MONSTER?
I TOLD YOU, UNCLE LOUIE, I NEVER THAW ANY MONTHTER!
Y'KNOW, YOU'RE, LIKE, PRETTY GOOD AT FINDING HIDING PLACES.
IT'S A TALENT.
MAYBE STANLEY'S RIGHT. I GUESS THAT MONSTER WAS JUST MY IMAGINATION. THAT'S WHAT I GET FOR STAYING UP ALL NIGHT!
BUT YOU GUYS STOPPED SOME VERY REAL CROOKS FROM STEALING THE CHARITY MONEY!
YEAH, AND WE WOULD'VE GOTTEN AWAY WITH IT, TOO--
--IF IT WASN'T FOR THOSE MEDDLING KIDS!
GLX!
THE END
SPLJ!